THE
DOO...

BY
MARION LENNOX

DARE SHE DREAM
OF FOREVER?

BY
LUCY CLARK

Marion Lennox is a country girl, born on an Australian dairy farm. She moved on—mostly because the cows just weren't interested in her stories! Married to a 'very special doctor', Marion writes Medical Romances™, as well as Mills & Boon® Romances. (She used a different name for each category for a while—if you're looking for her Romances, search for author Trisha David as well.) She's now had well over 90 romance novels accepted for publication.

In her non-writing life Marion cares for kids, cats, dogs, chooks and goldfish. She travels, she fights her rampant garden (she's losing) and her house dust (she's lost). Having spun in circles for the first part of her life, she's now stepped back from her 'other' career, which was teaching statistics at her local university. Finally she's reprioritised her life, figured out what's important, and discovered the joys of deep baths, romance and chocolate. Preferably all at the same time!

Lucy Clark is actually a husband-and-wife writing team. They enjoy taking holidays with their children, during which they discuss and develop new ideas for their books using the fantastic Australian scenery. They use their daily walks to talk over characterisation and fine details of the wonderful stories they produce, and are avid movie buffs. They live on the edge of a popular wine district in South Australia with their two children, and enjoy spending family time together at weekends.

THE SURGEON'S DOORSTEP BABY

BY
MARION LENNOX

MILLS & BOON

First published in Great Britain 2013
by Mills & Boon, an imprint of Harlequin (UK) Limited.
Harlequin (UK) Limited, Eton House, 18-24 Paradise Road,
Richmond, Surrey TW9 1SR

© Marion Lennox 2013

ISBN: 978 0 263 89871 2

Harlequin (UK) policy is to use papers that are natural, renewable and recyclable products and made from wood grown in sustainable forests. The logging and manufacturing process conform to the legal environmental regulations of the country of origin.

Printed and bound in Spain
by Blackprint CPI, Barcelona

Dear Reader

This year our family farm is to be leased out as my brother retires from farming. One of the next generation may well decide farming's the life for them, but it needs to be a decision they make in the future, when the time's right for them. Thus, for now, more than a hundred years of farming history is pausing.

For me this is a sadness. Although I've long left behind the reality of twice-daily milking, our family farm has never lost its power, its warmth, its pull. Happily, though, I can still disappear into a farming community in my books.

As you might have read in my introduction to MARDIE AND THE CITY SURGEON, recently the farm was flooded. At midnight a neighbour rang my brother to say the river had broken its banks, and a paddock full of calves was disappearing under water. My brother and sister-in-law thus spent the night in their kids' ancient canoe, saving every one of their calves.

The story was a fun one, with a happy ending, and the half-grown calves reacted like excited kids when they were finally rescued. The story made me smile—and, as always, it made me think, *What if...?* What if I threw my city surgeon hero into such a scene? What if my heroine had to depend on him? What if...what if I even threw a wounded baby into the mix?

I love my writing, where reality and fantasy can mingle to become pure fun. As you read this, however, know that the calves are real, the happy ending is true and each rescued calf is now a safe and cared-for member of a magnificent herd. Our farm—our heritage—stays alive in the hearts of every one of our family members, and hopefully in the warmth and fun my writing enables me to share.

Warm wishes from a bit of an emotional

Marion

Dedication:

To Cobrico. To Mayfield. To my beloved family who
form the bedrock of who I am.

CHAPTER ONE

As CHIEF orthopaedic surgeon for one of Sydney's most prestigious teaching hospitals, Blake Samford was used to being woken in the middle of the night for emergencies.

Right now, however, he was recuperating at his father's farm, two hundred miles from Sydney.

He wasn't expecting an emergency.

He wasn't expecting a baby.

Maggie Tilden loved lying in the dark, listening to rain on the corrugated-iron roof. She especially liked lying alone to listen.

She had a whole king-sized bed to herself. Hers, all hers. She'd been renting this apartment—a section of the grandest homestead in Corella Valley—for six months now, and she was savouring every silent moment of it.

Oh, she loved being free. She loved being here. The elements could throw what they liked at her; she was gloriously happy. She wriggled her toes luxuriously against her cotton sheets and thought, Bring it on, let it rain.

She wasn't even worried about the floods.

This afternoon the bridge had been deemed unsafe.

Debris from the flooded country to the north was being slammed against the ancient timbers, and the authorities were worried the whole thing would go. As of that afternoon, the bridge was roped off and the entire valley was isolated.

Residents had been advised to evacuate and many had, but a lot of the old-time farmers wouldn't move if you put a bulldozer under them. They'd seen floods before. They'd stocked up with provisions, they'd made sure their stock was on high ground and they were sitting it out.

Maggie was doing the same.

A clap of thunder split the night and Tip, the younger Border collie, whined and edged closer to the bed.

'It's okay, guys,' she told them, as the ancient Blackie moved in for comfort as well. 'We're safe and dry, and we have a whole month's supply of dog food. What else could we want?'

And then she paused.

Over the sound of the driving rain she could hear a car. Gunned, fast. Driving over the bridge?

It must have gone right around the roadblock.

Were they crazy? The volume of water powering down the valley was a risk all by itself. There were huge warning signs saying the bridge was unsafe.

But the bridge was still intact, and the car made it without mishap. She heard the change in noise as it reached the bitumen on this side, and she relaxed, expecting the car's noise to fade as it headed inland.

But it didn't. She heard it turn into her driveway—okay, not hers, but the driveway of the Corella View Homestead.

If the car had come from this side of the river she'd

be out of bed straight away, expecting drama. As district nurse, she was the only person with medical training on this side of the river—but the car had come from the other side, where there was a hospital and decent medical help.

She'd also be worrying about her brother. Pete was in the middle of teenage rebellion, and lately he'd been hanging out with some dubious mates. The way that car was being driven…danger didn't begin to describe it.

But this was someone from the other side. Not Pete. Not a medical emergency. Regardless, she swung her feet out of bed and reached for her robe.

And then she paused.

Maybe this was a visitor for her landlord.

A visitor at midnight?

Who knew? She hardly knew her landlord.

Blake Samford was the only son of the local squattocracy—squattocracies being the slang term for families who'd been granted huge tracts of land when Australia had first been opened to settlers and had steadily increased their fortunes since. The Corella Valley holding was impressive, but deserted. Blake had lived here as a baby but his mother had taken him away when he was six. The district had hardly seen him since.

This, however, was his longest visit for years. He'd arrived three days ago. He was getting over appendicitis, he'd told her, taking the opportunity to get the farm ready for sale. His father had been dead for six months. It was time to sell.

She'd warned him the river was rising. He'd shrugged.

'If I'm trapped, I might as well be truly trapped.'

If he was having visitors at midnight, they'd be trapped with him.

Maybe it's a woman, she thought, sinking back into bed as the car stopped and footsteps headed for Blake's side of the house—the grand entrance. Maybe he'd decided if he was to be trapped he needed company. Was this a woman ready to risk all to reach her lover?

Who knew? Who knew anything about Blake Samford?

Blake was a local yet not a local. She'd seen him sporadically as a kid—making compulsory access visits to his bully of a father, the locals thought—but as far as she knew he hadn't come near when his father had been ill. Given his father's reputation, no one blamed him. Finally she'd met him at the funeral.

She'd gone to the funeral because she'd been making daily medical checks on the old man for the last few months of his life. His reputation had been appalling, but he'd loved his dogs so she'd tried to convince herself he hadn't been all bad. Also, she'd needed to talk to his son about the dogs. And her idea.

She hadn't even been certain Blake would come but he'd been there— Blake Samford, all grown up. And stunning. The old ladies whispered that he'd inherited his mother's looks. Maggie had never known his mother, but she was definitely impressed by the guy's appearance—strong, dark, riveting. But not friendly. He'd stood aloof from the few locals present, expressionless, looking as if he was there simply to get things over with.

She could understand that. With Bob Samford as a father, it had been a wonder he'd been there at all.

But Maggie had an idea that needed his agreement.

It had taken courage to approach him when the service had ended, to hand over her references and ask him about the housekeeper's apartment at the back of the homestead. To offer to keep an eye on the place as well as continuing caring for the dogs his dad had loved. Harold Stubbs, the next-door landowner, had been looking after Bob's cattle. The cattle still needed to be there to keep the grass down, but Harold was getting too old to take care of two herds plus the house and the dogs. Until Blake sold, would he like a caretaker?

Three days later a rental contract had arrived. She'd moved in but she hadn't heard from him since.

Until now. He was home to put the place on the market.

She'd expected nothing less. She knew it'd be sold eventually and she was trying to come up with alternative accommodation. She did *not* want to go home.

But right now her attention was all on the stupidity of his visitors driving over the bridge. Were they out of their minds?

She was tempted to pull back the drapes and look.

She heard heavy footsteps running across the veranda, and the knocker sounded so loudly it reverberated right through the house. The dogs went crazy. She hauled them back from the door, but as she did she heard the footsteps recede back across the veranda, back down the steps.

The car's motor hadn't been cut. A car door slammed, the engine was gunned—and it headed off the way it had come.

She held her breath as it rumbled back across the bridge. Reaching the other side. Safe.

Gone.

What on earth…?

Kids, playing the fool?

It was not her business. It was Blake's business, she told herself. He was home now and she was only caring for her little bit of the house.

Hers. Until Blake sold the house.

It didn't matter. For now it was hers, and she was soaking up every minute of it.

She snuggled back down under the covers—alone.

If there was one thing Maggie Tilden craved above everything else, it was being alone.

Bliss.

On the other side of the wall, Blake was listening, too. He heard the car roar over the bridge. He heard the thumps on his front door, the running footsteps of someone leaving in a hurry, and the car retreating back over the bridge.

He also thought whoever it was must be crazy.

He and his tenant—Maggie Tilden—had inspected the bridge yesterday. The storm water had been pounding the aged timbers; things were being swept fast downstream—logs, debris, some of it big. It was battering the piles.

'If you want to get out, you should go now,' Maggie had said. 'The authorities are about to close it.'

Did it matter? He'd been ordered to take three weeks off work to recuperate from appendicitis. He needed to sort his father's possessions, so what difference did it make if he was stranded while he did it?

'It's up to you,' Maggie had said, as if she didn't mind either way, and she'd headed back to her part of the house with his father's dogs.

She kept to herself, for which he was profoundly grateful, but now... A knock at midnight. A car going back and forth over the bridge.

Was this some friend of hers, playing the fool? Leaving something for her at the wrong door?

Whoever they were, they'd gone.

On Maggie's side of the house he'd heard the dogs go crazy. He imagined her settling them. Part of him expected her to come across to check what had just happened.

She didn't.

Forget it, he told himself. Go back to bed.

Or open the door and make sure nothing had been left?

The knock still resonated. It had been loud, urgent, demanding attention.

Okay, check.

He headed for the front door, stepped outside and came close to falling over a bundle. Pink, soft...

He stooped and tugged back a fold of pink blanket.

A thick thatch of black hair. A tiny, rosebud mouth. Snub nose. Huge dark eyes that stared upwards, struggling to focus.

A tiny baby. Three weeks at most, he thought, stunned.

Lying on his doorstep.

He scooped the infant up without thinking, staring out into the night rather than down at the baby, willing the car to be still there, willing there to be some sort of answer.

The bundle was warm—and moist. And alive.

A baby...

He had nothing to do with babies. Yeah, okay, he'd

treated babies during medical training. He'd done the basic paediatric stuff, but he'd been an orthopaedic surgeon for years now, and babies hardly came into his orbit.

A baby was in his orbit now. In his arms.

He stared down at the baby, and wide eyes stared back.

A memory stabbed back. A long time ago. Thirty or more years? Here, in this hall.

A woman with a baby, placing the baby by the door in its carry basket, pointing at Blake and saying, 'I've brought the kid his baby sister.'

After that, his memory blurred. He remembered his father yelling, and his mother screaming invective at his father and at the woman. He remembered the strange woman being almost hysterical.

He'd been six years old. While the grown-ups had yelled, he'd sidled over and looked at the baby it seemed everyone was yelling about. She'd been crying, but none of the grown-ups had noticed.

A baby sister?

He shook himself. That had been the night his mother had found out about his father's lover. He'd never seen either the woman or her baby again.

This baby was nothing to do with his history. Why was he thinking of it now?

He should call the police. He should report an abandoned baby.

Who looked like a baby he'd seen a long time ago?

And then he thought of Maggie, his tenant, and he remembered the references she'd given him.

She was the district nurse and she was also a midwife.

The relief that surged over him was almost over-whelming. This was nothing to do with him. Of course it wasn't. The whole valley knew Maggie's job. If a woman wanted to abandon an unwanted child, what better way than dump it on a woman you knew could look after it? Maybe Maggie had even cared for the mother during her pregnancy.

'Hey,' he said, relaxing, even holding the baby a little tighter now he knew what he was dealing with. The child seemed to be staring straight up at him now, dark eyes wondering. 'You've come to the wrong door. Okay, I know you're in trouble but you *have* come to the right place—just one door down. Hold on a minute and we'll take you to someone who knows babies. To someone who hopefully will take responsibility for getting you out of this mess.'

Maggie was snuggling back down under the duvet when someone knocked on *her* door and the dogs went nuts again.

What? What now?

She'd worked hard today. She'd set up the entire clinic, moving emergency gear from the hospital over the river, trying to get everything organised before the bridge closed. As well as that, she'd made prenatal checks of women on farms that were so wet right now that every able body was moving stock and if Maggie wanted her pregnant ladies to be checked then she went to them.

She was really tired.

Was this another evacuation warning? Leave now before the bridge is cut?

She'd gone to the community meeting. This house

was high above the river. Short of a tsunami travelling two hundred miles inland, nothing worse was going to happen than the bridge would give way, the power would go and she'd have to rely on the old kerosene fridge for a few days.

What?

Another knock—and suddenly her irritation turned to fear. She had eight brothers and sisters. A couple of the boys were still young enough to be stupid. Pete… What if…?

What if the car had come with news?

Just open the door and get it over with.

Take a deep breath first.

She tucked her feet into fluffy slippers, wrapped her ancient bathrobe around her favourite pyjamas and padded out to the back porch.

She swung open the door—and Blake Samford was standing in the doorway, holding a baby.

'I think this one's for you,' he said, and handed it over.

She didn't drop it.

To her eternal credit—and thinking back later she was very, very proud of herself—she took the baby, just like the professional she was. Nurse receiving a baby at handover. She gathered the baby as she'd gather any infant she didn't know; any child when she didn't know its history. Taking care to handle it lightly with no pressure, anywhere that might hurt. Cradling it and holding it instinctively against her body, giving warmth as she'd give warmth to any tiny creature.

But for the moment her eyes were on Blake.

He looked almost forbidding. He was looming in her

doorway, six feet two or three, wide shoulders, dark, dark eyes made even darker by the faint glow of moonlight, deep black hair, a shadowy figure.

Tall, dark and dangerous.

Heathcliff, she thought, suddenly feeling vaguely hysterical. Very hysterical. Here she was presented with a baby at midnight and she was thinking romance novels?

The dogs were growling behind her. They'd met this guy—he'd been here for three days and she'd seen him outside, talking to them—but he was still a stranger, it was midnight and they didn't know what to make of this bundle in their mistress's arms.

Neither did she, but a baby was more important than the dark, looming stranger on her doorstep.

'What do you mean, you think it's for me?' she managed, trying not to sound incredulous. Trying to sound like he'd just dropped by with a cup of sugar she'd asked to borrow earlier in the day. She didn't want to startle the dogs. She didn't want to startle the baby.

She didn't want to startle herself.

'Someone's obviously made a mistake,' he told her. 'You're the local midwife. I assume they've dumped the baby here to leave it with you.'

'Who dumped it?' She folded back the blanket and looked down into the baby's face. Wide eyes gazed back at her. Gorgeous.

She loved babies. She shouldn't—heaven knew, she'd had enough babies to last her a lifetime—but she had the perfect job now. She could love babies and hand them back.

'I don't know who dumped it,' he said, with exaggerated patience. 'Didn't you hear the car? It came, the baby was dumped, it left.'

She stared up at him, incredulous. He met her gaze, and didn't flinch.

An abandoned baby.

The stuff of fairy-tales. Or nightmares.

She switched her gaze to the little one in her arms.

'Who are you?' she whispered, but of course there was no answer. Instead it wrinkled its small nose, and opened its mouth—and wailed.

Only it wasn't a wail a baby this age should make. It was totally despairing, as if this baby had wailed before and nothing had been forthcoming. It was a wail that was desperation all by itself—a wail that went straight to the heart and stayed there. Maggie had heard hungry babies before, but none like this. Unbearable. Unimaginable that a little one could be so needful.

She looked down at the sunken fontanel, the dry, slightly wrinkled skin. These were classic signs of dehydration. IV? Fast?

But if the little one could still cry…

It could indeed still cry. It could scream.

'Can you grab the bag from the back of my car?' she snapped, and whirled and grabbed her car keys and tossed them to him. 'This little one's in trouble.'

'Trouble?'

She wheeled away, back to the settee. The fire was still glowing in the hearth. She could unwrap the baby without fear of losing warmth. 'Basket,' she snapped at the dogs, and they headed obediently for their baskets at each side of the fire. Then, as Blake hesitated, she fixed him with a look that had made lesser men quail. 'Bag. Now. Go.'

* * *

He headed for the car, feeling a bit...stunned. And also awed.

The only times he'd seen Maggie Tilden she'd seemed brisk, efficient and...plain? She dressed simply for work and she'd been working the whole time he'd been here. Plain black pants. White blouse with 'Corella Valley Medical Services' emblazoned on the pocket. She wore minimal make-up, and her soft brown curls were tied back in a bouncy ponytail. She was about five feet four or five, she had freckles, brown eyes and a snub nose, and until tonight he would have described her as nondescript.

What he'd just seen wasn't nondescript. It was something far from it.

What?

Cute, he thought, but then he thought no. It was something...deeper.

She'd been wearing faded pink pyjamas, fluffy slippers and an ancient powder-blue bathrobe. Her brown hair, once let loose, showed an auburn burnish. Her curls tumbled about her shoulders and she looked like she'd just woken from sleep. Standing with her dogs by her sides, the fire crackling in the background, she looked...

Adorable?

She looked everything the women in his life weren't. Cosy. Domestic. Welcoming.

And also strong. That glare said he'd better move his butt and get her bag back inside, stat.

She wouldn't know he was a doctor, he thought. When the baby had wailed he'd recognised, as she had, that the little creature was in trouble. The light-bulb over his door had blown long since, but once he'd been under the light of her porch he'd seen the tell-tale signs of dehydration, a baby who looked underweight; malnourished. He'd reached to find a pulse but her movement to defend the child was right. Until she knew what was wrong, the less handling the better.

She was reacting like a midwife at her best, he thought with something of relief. Even if she needed his help right now, this baby wasn't his problem. She was more than capable of taking responsibility.

She was a professional. She could get on with her job and he could move away.

Get the lady her bag. Now.

The bag was a huge case-cum-portable bureau, wedged into the back of an ancient family wagon. He grabbed it and grunted as he pulled it free—it weighed a ton. What was it—medical supplies for the entire valley? How on earth did a diminutive parcel like Maggie handle such a thing?

He was a week out from an appendectomy. He felt internal stitches pull and thought of consequences—and headed for the back door and grabbed the wheelbarrow.

Medical priorities.

If he broke his stitches he'd be no use to anyone. Worse, he'd need help himself.

One bag coming up. By barrow.

He pushed his way back into the living room and Maggie's eyes widened.

She'd expected landlord with a bag.

What she got was landlord, looking a bit sheepish, with her firewood-carting wheelbarrow, plus bag.

'Appendectomy,' he said before she could say a word. 'Stitches. You don't want two patients.'

Oh, heck. She hadn't thought. He'd told her he was here recovering from an appendectomy. She should have…

'It's fine,' he said, quickly, obviously seeing her remorse. 'As long as you don't mind tyre tracks on your rugs.'

'With my family I'm not used to house-proud. Thanks for getting it. Are you okay?'

'Yes.'

She cast him a sharp, assessing look, and he thought she was working out the truth for herself, and she figured he was telling it.

'If I tell you how, can you make up some formula? This little one's badly dehydrated.'

'Can I see?' he said, over the baby's cries.

The baby was still wailing, desperation personified.

He stooped beside her. He didn't try and touch the baby, just pushed back the coverings further from its face.

Maggie had obviously done a fast check and then re-wrapped the infant, leaving the nappy on, tugging open the stained grow suit to the nappy but leaving it on, re-wrapping the baby in the same blanket but adding her own, a cashmere throw he'd seen at the end of the sofa.

With the blankets pulled aside and the grow suit unfastened, he could see signs of neglect. This was no rosy, bouncing baby. He could see the tell-tale signs of severe nappy rash, even above the nappy. He could see signs of malnourishment.

She was right about dehydration. They needed to get the little one clean and dry—but first they needed to get fluids in and if it was possible, the best way was by mouth.

'Tell me where, tell me how,' he said, and she shot him a grateful glance and proceeded to do just that. Five minutes later he had a sterilised bottle filled with formula, he offered it to Maggie, she offered it to one tiny baby—who latched on like a leech and proceeded to suck like there was no tomorrow.

The sudden silence was deafening. Even the dogs seemed to sigh in relief.

Maggie's wide, expressive mouth curved into a smile. 'Hey,' she said softly. 'You've just saved yourself from evacuation, hospital and IV drips. Now, let's see what we have here.' She glanced up at Blake. 'Are you man enough to cope with the nappy? I'd normally not try and change a baby in mid-feed but this one's practically walking on its own and I hate to imagine what it's doing to the skin. It needs to be off but I don't want to disturb the baby more than necessary. While the bottle's doing the comforting we might see what we're dealing with.'

He understood. Sort of. There was a medical imperative.

What he'd really like to do was offer to take over the holding and feeding while she coped with the other end, but he'd missed his opportunity. There was no way they should interrupt established feeding when it was so important. This baby needed fluids fast, and Maggie was the one providing them.

So...the other end.

He was a surgeon. He was used to stomach-churning sights.

He'd never actually changed a baby's nappy.

'You'll need a big bowl of warm, soapy water,' she told him. 'The bowl's in the left-hand cupboard by the stove. Get a couple of clean towels from the bathroom and fetch the blue bottle on the top of my bag with the picture of a baby's bottom on the front.'

'Right,' he said faintly, and went to get what he needed, with not nearly the enthusiasm he'd used to make the formula.

Baby changing. He had to learn some time, he supposed. At some stage in the far distant future he and Miriam might have babies. He thought about it as he filled the bucket with skin-temperature water. He and Miriam were professional colleagues having a somewhat tepid relationship on the side. Miriam was dubious about attachment. He was even more dubious.

He suspected what he was facing tonight might make him more so.

'Oi,' Maggie called from the living room. 'Water. Nappy. Stat.'

'Yes, Nurse,' he called back, and went to do her bidding.

CHAPTER TWO

BLAKE removed the nappy and under all that mess…
'She doesn't look like she's been changed for days,'
Maggie said, horrified…they found a little girl.

They also found something else. As he tugged her
growsuit free from her legs and unwrapped her fully,
he drew in a deep breath.

Talipes equinovarus. Club feet. The little girl's feet
were pointed inwards, almost at right angles to where
they should be.

Severe.

He didn't comment but he felt ill, and it wasn't the
contents of the nappy that was doing it. That someone
could desert such a child… To neglect her and then just
toss her on his doorstep…

How did they know Maggie would be home? Maggie had dogs. How did they know the dogs wouldn't be
free to hurt her?

Seeing the extent of the nappy rash, the dehydration—and the dreadful angle of her feet—he had his
answer.

Whoever had done this didn't care. This was an imperfect baby, something to be tossed aside, brought to
the local midwife, but whether she was home or not
didn't matter.

Returning damaged goods, like it or not.

He glanced up at Maggie and saw her face and saw what he was thinking reflected straight back at him. Anger, disgust, horror—and not at the tiny twisted feet. At the moron who'd gunned the car across the bridge, so desperate to dump the baby that he'd take risks. Or *she'd* take risks.

'Surely it was a guy driving that car?' Maggie whispered.

Sexist statement or not? He let it drift as he cleaned the tiny body. The little girl was relaxed now, almost soporific, sucking gently and close to sleep. She wasn't responding to his touch—he could do anything he liked and it was a good opportunity to do a gentle, careful examination.

Maggie was letting him touch now. She was watching as he carefully manipulated the tiny feet, gently testing. As he felt her pulse. As he checked every inch of her and then suggested they lower her into the warm water.

She'd had enough of the bottle on board now to be safe. He doubted she'd respond—as some babies did—to immersion—and it was the easiest and fastest way to get her skin clean.

'You're a medic,' Maggie said, because from the way he was examining her he knew it was obvious. And he knew, instinctively, that this was one smart woman.

'Orthopaedic surgeon.'

She nodded as if he was confirming what she'd suspected. 'Not a lot of babies, then?'

'Um...no.'

'But a lot of feet?'

'I guess,' he agreed, and she smiled at him, an odd little smile that he kind of...liked.

Restful, he thought. She was a restful woman. And then he thought suddenly, strongly, that she was the kind of woman he'd want around in a crisis.

He was very glad she was there.

But the priority wasn't this woman's smile. The priority was one abandoned baby. While Maggie held the bottle—the little girl was still peacefully sucking—he scooped her gently from her arms and lowered her into the warm water.

She hardly reacted, or if she did it was simply to relax even more. This little one had been fighting for survival, he thought. Fighting and losing. Now she was fed and the filth removed. She was in a warm bath in front of Maggie's fire and she was safe. He glanced at Maggie and saw that faint smile again, and he thought that if he was in trouble, he might think of this woman as safety.

If this baby was to be dumped, there was no better place to dump her. Maggie would take care of her. He knew it. This was not a woman who walked away from responsibility.

He glanced around at the dogs on either side of the fire. His father's dogs. When his father had gone into hospital for the last time he'd come down and seen them. They were cattle dogs, Border collies, born and raised on the farm. The last time he'd seen them—six months before his father had died—they'd been scrawny and neglected and he'd thought of the impossibility of taking them back to the city, of giving them any sort of life there.

His father hadn't wanted him here—he'd practically yelled at him to get out. And he'd told him the dogs were none of his business.

Despite the old man's opposition, he'd contacted the

local hospital and asked for home visits by a district nurse.

Maggie had taken his father on, and the dogs, and when his father had died she'd suggested she take this place on as well. It had solved two problems—the dogs and an empty farmhouse.

This woman was a problem-solver. She'd solve this little one's problems, too.

The baby had fallen asleep. Maggie removed the bottle, then took over from him, expertly bathing, carefully checking every inch of the baby's skin, wincing at the extent of the nappy rash, checking arm and leg movement, frowning at a bruise on the baby's shoulder. A bruise at this age... Put down hard? Dropped? Hit?

'There are basic baby clothes at the bottom of my bag,' she said absently, all her attention on the baby. 'And nappies. Will you fetch them?'

He did, thinking again that no matter who the lowlife was that had cared for the baby until now, at least they'd had the sense to bring her to the right place.

He brought the clothes back as Maggie scooped the baby out of the water, towelled her dry and anointed the sores. Looked again at her feet.

'They should be being realigned now,' he growled, watching as Maggie fingered the tiny toes. 'Three weeks after birth... We're missing the opportunity when the tissue is soft and malleable. The longer we leave it, the longer the treatment period.'

'I've only seen this once before,' Maggie said. 'And not as severe as this.'

'It's severe,' he said. 'But fixable.'

'We have basic X-ray facilities set up at my clinic—

at the church hall,' she said tentatively. 'We've brought them in so I can see the difference between greenstick fractures and fractures where I need evacuation.'

'We don't need X-rays tonight. This is long-haul medical treatment.'

'I don't want to call out emergency services unless I have to.' Maggie was still looking worried. 'They have their hands full evacuating people who are being inundated, and in this rain there's no safe place for the chopper to land.'

'There's no urgency.'

'Then we'll worry about tomorrow tomorrow,' she said, her face clearing, and she dressed the little one so gently he thought the dressing was almost a caress in itself. The baby hardly stirred. It was like she'd fought every inch of the way to survive and now she knew she was safe. She knew she was with Maggie.

Maggie wrapped her in her soft cashmere rug—the one she'd tugged from her settee—and handed her over to Blake. He took her without thinking, then sat by the fire with the sleeping baby in his arms as Maggie cleared up the mess.

She was a restful woman, he thought again. Methodical. Calm. How many women would take a child like this and simply sort what was needed? Taking her from peril to safe in an hour?

She was a midwife, he told himself. This was what she did.

This baby was her job.

She was gathering bottles, formula, nappies. Placing them in a basket.

A basket. He'd been drifting off in the warmth but suddenly he was wide awake. What the…?

'Are you thinking we should take her to hospital?' he asked. 'I'm not driving over that bridge.'

'Neither am I,' she said, and brought the basket back to him. 'She looks fine—okay, not fine, neglected, underweight, but nothing so urgent to warrant the risks of crossing the river again. I think she'll be fine with you. I'm just packing what you need.'

'Me?'

'You,' she said, gently but firmly. 'Your baby tonight.'

'I don't want a baby,' he said, stunned.

'You think I do?'

'She was brought to you.'

'No,' she said, still with that same gentleness, a gentleness with a rod of inflexibility straight through the centre. 'She was brought to you. If I didn't think you were capable of caring then I'd step in—of course I would—and I'm here for consulting at any time. But this little one is yours.'

'What are you talking about? You're the midwife.'

'It's got nothing to do about me being a midwife,' she said, and searched the settee until she found what she was looking for. 'I found this when you were making the formula. It was tucked under her blanket.'

It was a note, hastily scribbled on the back of a torn envelope. She handed it to him wordlessly, and then stayed silent as he read.

Dear Big Brother
The old man's dead. He never did anything for me in my life—nothing! You're the legitimate kid, the one that gets everything. You get the farm. You get the kid.
This kid's your father's grandkid. My father's

grandkid. I don't want it—just take a look at its feet—they make Sam and me sick. I called it Ruby after my Mum's mum—my grandma—she was the only one ever did anything for me—but that was before I figured how awful the feet were. So it's deformed and we don't want it. Change the name if you like. Get it adopted. Do what you want. Sam and me are heading for Perth so if you need anything signed for adoption or anything stick an ad in the Margaret River paper. If I see it I'll get in touch. Maybe.
Wendy

Silence. A long, long silence.

'Wendy?' Maggie said gently at last.

'My…my half-sister.' He was struggling to take it in. 'Result of one of my father's affairs.'

'Surname?'

'I don't even know that.'

'Whew.' She looked at him, still with that calmness, sympathetic but implacable. 'That's a shock.'

'I… Yes.'

'I think she'll sleep,' Maggie said. 'I suspect she'll sleep for hours. She's not too heavy for you to carry. If you need help, I'm right through the door.'

'This baby isn't mine.' It was said with such vehemence that the little girl—Ruby?—opened her eyes and gazed up at him. And then she closed them again, settling. She was dry, warm and fed. She was in Blake's arms. All was right with her world.

'She's not mine,' Blake repeated, but even he heard the uselessness of his words. Someone had to take responsibility for this baby.

'I'm a nurse, Blake,' Maggie said, inexorably. 'I'm not a parent. Neither are you but you're an uncle. Your sister's left her baby with you. You're family. Let me know if you're in trouble.' She walked across to the porch and opened the door. 'But for now… You have everything you need for the night. I'll pop in in the morning and see how you're going.'

'But I know nothing about babies.'

'You're a doctor,' she said cordially. 'Of course you do.'

'Looking after them?'

'If fifteen-year-old girls can manage it, you can. It's not brain surgery.'

'I'm not a fifteen-year-old.' He was grasping at straws here. 'And I've just had my appendix out.'

'Fifteen-year-olds who've just had Caesareans manage it. How big are babies compared to an appendix? Toughen up.'

He stared at her and she stared right back. She smiled. He thought he sensed sympathy behind her smile, but her smile was still…implacable.

She'd given him his marching orders.

He was holding his niece. *His.*

Maggie was holding the door open; she was still smiling but was giving him no choice.

With one more despairing glance at this hard-hearted nurse, at the crackling fire, at the sleeping dogs, at a domesticity he hardly recognised, he accepted he had no choice.

He walked out into the night.

With…his baby?

She shouldn't have done it.

The door closed behind him and Maggie stared at it like it was a prosecutor in a criminal court.

Maggie stands accused of abandoning one defence-less baby...

To her uncle. To a doctor. To her landlord.

To a guy recovering from an appendectomy.

To a guy who was capable of driving from Sydney to the valley, to someone who was well on the way to recovery, to someone who was more than capable of looking after his baby.

His baby. Not hers.

This was not her problem. She was a professional. She cared for babies when they needed her medical intervention, and she handed them right back.

She'd done enough of the personal caring to last a lifetime.

She gazed down into the glowing embers of the fire and thought, *My fire*.

It had taken so much courage, so much resolution, so much desperation to find a house of her own. Corella Valley had practically no rental properties. She had so little money. It had taken all the courage and hope she possessed to gird her loins, approach Blake at the funeral and say, 'I'm looking after your dad's dogs; why don't you let me take care of your house until you put it on the market? I'll live in the housekeeper's residence and I'll keep the place tidy so if you need to use it it'll be ready for you.'

The feeling she'd had when he'd said yes...

Her family still lived less than a mile away, on this side of the river. She was still here for them when they needed her—but she wasn't here for everyone when they needed her. She was not 'good old Maggie' for Blake. This baby was Blake's problem. Blake's niece. Blake's baby, to love or to organise another future for.

If she'd responded to the desperation in his eyes, she'd have a baby here, right now. A baby to twist her heart as it had been twisted all her life.

Eight brothers and sisters. Parents who couldn't give a toss. Maggie, who spent her life having her heart twisted.

'Of course you'll stay home today and look after your brother. Yes, he's ill, but your father and I are heading for Nimbin for a couple of days for the festival... You're a good girl, Maggie.'

Two guitar-toting layabouts with nine kids between them, and Maggie, the oldest, the one who had cared for them all.

She did not need any more responsibility, not in a million years. She had two dogs. She had her own apartment, even if it was only until Blake sold the property.

She was not taking Blake's baby.

And on the other side of the wall, Blake settled the sleeping baby into a cocoon of bedding he'd made in a tugged-out bureau drawer, then stood and stared down at her for a very long time.

Even in two hours she'd changed. Her face had filled out a little, and the signs of dehydration were fading. She'd been stressed since birth, he thought. She was sleeping as if she was intent on staying asleep, because being awake was frightening and lonely and hard.

He was reading too much into the expression of one sleeping baby. How did he know what she'd been through? How could he possibly guess?

This little one was nothing to do with him. As soon as the river went down he'd hand her over to the appropriate authorities and let them deal with her. But until then…

Maggie should take her, he thought. That was the reasonable plan. A trained midwife, accustomed to dealing with babies every day of her working life, was a far more suitable person to take care of a little one as young as this.

But there was something about Maggie that was implacable. *Not My Problem.* The sign was right up there, hanging over her head like a speech bubble. Said or not, it was what she meant and it was how she'd acted.

She'd sent him home with his niece.

His niece.

He watched her sleep for a while longer. Ruby, he thought.

His niece?

He didn't feel like he had a niece. He didn't feel like he had a sister. He'd only seen his sister that one appalling time, when she'd been little older than Ruby. The moment had been filled with sounds enough to terrify a six-year-old, two women screeching at each other, his father threatening, the baby crying and crying and crying.

He remembered thinking, *Why don't they stop yelling and cuddle her?* He'd even thought of doing it himself, but six was too young to be brave. He'd wanted a cuddle himself. He'd been scared by the yelling and far too young to cope with a baby.

Was he old enough now?

He didn't feel old enough.

He looked down at the tightly wrapped bundle and thought of the tiny feet, facing inwards, needing work to be aligned. He could do that. He was an orthopaedic surgeon. Fixing twisted limbs was what he did.

Not the rest.

Maggie was just through the door. A trained mid-wife.

The phone rang and he picked it up with relief. It'd be Maggie, he thought, changing her mind, worrying about a baby who should rightly be in her charge.

It wasn't. It was Miriam, doing what she'd promised. 'I'll ring you when I've finished for the day,' she'd told him. 'You don't mind if it's late? You know I'd like to be with you but the board meets next week to appoint the head of ophthalmology and I need to be present to be in the running.'

Of course he'd agreed. They were two ambitious professionals, and a little thing like an appendectomy shouldn't be allowed to get in the way of what was needed for their careers.

A little thing like a baby?

Miriam didn't notice that he was preoccupied. She asked about the floods. He told her briefly that the bridge was blocked, that he was fine, that she needn't worry. Not that she'd have worried anyway. She knew he could take care of himself.

There was little she didn't know about him. They'd been colleagues for years now, in a casual relationship, maybe drifting toward marriage.

And now...

Now he was about to shock her.

'I have a baby,' he told her, and was met with stunned silence. He heard her think it through, regroup, decide he was joking.

'That was fast. You only left town on Friday. You've

met a girl, got her pregnant, had a baby...' She chuckled—and then the chuckle died as she heard his continued silence. 'You're not serious?'

He outlined the night's events, the letter, Maggie, their decision not to call for medical evacuation and Maggie's insistence that he do the caring. He heard her incredulity—and her anger towards a nurse she'd never met.

'She's dumped it on you?'

'I guess.' But it was hardly that.

'Then dump it right back,' she snapped. 'Fast. She has to take care of it. She's the local nurse. It's her job. This is like someone turning up in your office with a fractured leg and you refusing to help.'

'She did help. She bathed and fed her.'

'Her?'

'She's a little girl. Ruby.'

'Don't even think about getting attached.' Miriam's voice was almost a hiss. 'That's what she'll be counting on. You being soft.'

'I'm not soft.'

'I know that, but does she? The nurse? And this sister you've never told me about... Who is she?'

'I know nothing about her other than she's called Wendy. I can't be soft to someone I don't know.'

'So call in the authorities, now. If the bridge is properly cut...'

'It is.'

'How did they get over?'

'They went round the road block and risked their lives.'

'Okay,' she conceded. 'I don't want you risking your

life. You'll probably have to wait till morning but then call for a medical evacuation.'

'She's not sick, Mim.'

'She's not your problem,' Miriam snapped. 'And don't call me Mim. You know I hate it. Call the police, say you have a baby you know nothing about on your doorstep and let them deal with it.'

'This is my father's grandchild. My...niece.'

There was a hiss of indrawn breath. 'So what are you saying? You want to keep it?'

'No!' He was watching the baby while he talked. She'd managed to wriggle a fist free from the bundle Maggie had wrapped her in, and her tiny knuckles were in her mouth. They were giving her comfort, he thought, and wondered how much she'd needed those knuckles in her few short weeks of life.

This was not his problem. Nothing to do with him.

She was his niece. His father's grandchild.

He'd loathed his father. He'd left this place when he'd been six years old and had had two short access visits since. Both had been misery from first to last.

His father had been a bully and a thug.

Maggie had known him better, he thought. Had there been anything under that brutish exterior?

He could ask.

'Just take the baby back to the midwife and insist,' Miriam was saying. 'It's her professional responsibility. You could...I don't know...threaten to have her struck off if she doesn't?'

'For handing a baby back to her family?'

'You're not her family.'

'I'm all she has.'

'Her parents are all she has. The police can find them

tomorrow. Meanwhile, lean on the nurse. You're recovering, Blake. You do not need this hassle. Okay, misconduct mightn't fly but there are other ways. You're her landlord. Threaten to evict her.'

'Mim—'

'Just do whatever you need to do,' she snapped. 'Look, love, I rang to tell you about the paper I presented this afternoon. It went really well. Can I finally tell you about it?'

'Of course,' he said, and he thought that would settle him. He could stand here and listen to Miriam talk medicine and he could forget all about his little stranger who'd be gone tomorrow.

And he could also forget about the woman who'd refused to take her.

Maggie.

Why was he thinking about Maggie?

He was remembering her at the funeral. It had been pouring. She'd been dressed in a vast overcoat and gumboots, sensible garments in the tiny, country graveyard. She'd stomped across to him, half-hidden by her enormous umbrella, and she'd put it over him, enclosing him for the first time, giving him his only sense of inclusion in this bleak little ceremony.

'I took on your father's dogs because I couldn't bear them to be put down,' she'd said. 'But I'm sharing a too-small house with my too-big family. The dogs make the situation unworkable. I assume your dad's farm will be empty for a while. It has a housekeeper's residence at the back. If I pay a reasonable rent, how about you let me live there until you decide what to do with it?'

'Yes,' he'd said without any hesitation, and he'd watched something akin to joy flash across her face.

'Really?'

'Really.'

'You won't regret it,' she'd said gruffly. 'The dogs and I will love it.' Then she'd hesitated and looked across at the men filling in the open grave. 'He was a hard man, your father,' she'd said softly. 'I'm sorry.'

And he'd thought, uncomfortably, that she understood.

Did this whole district understand? That he and his father had had no relationship at all?

They weren't a family.

Family...

His mother had gone on to three or four more relationships, all disastrous. He'd never worked out the concept of family. Now...

He listened on to Miriam and he watched the sleeping baby. Would he and Miriam ever have babies? Family?

Now wasn't the time to ask, he thought, and he grimaced as he realised he hadn't heard a word she'd said for the last few minutes.

Focus, he told himself. Do what the lady says. Concentrate on medicine and not baby. Tomorrow give the baby back to Maggie or get rid of it some other way. Do whatever it takes. This was an aberration from the past.

One baby, with twisted feet and no one to care for her. An aberration?

He carried on listening to Miriam and he thought, Maggie's just through the wall. She might even be listening to half this conversation.

The thought was unnerving.

Forget it, he thought. Forget Maggie. And the baby? Do whatever it takes.

If only she wasn't sucking her knuckles. If only she wasn't twisting his heart in a way that made him realise a pain he'd felt when he'd been six years old had never been resolved.

She was his father's grandchild. She was the child of his half-sister.

Family?

It was his health that was making him think like this, he told himself. He'd had his appendix out barely a week before, and it had been messy. He was tired and weaker than he cared to admit, and he was staying in a house that held nothing but bad memories.

He had a sudden, overwhelming urge to thump a hole in the wall in the sitting room. Let his father's dogs through.

See Maggie.

Heaven knew what Miriam was saying. He'd given up trying to listen. It had been an important paper she'd presented. Normally he'd listen and be impressed. Tonight, though, he looked at one tiny baby, sleeping cocooned in Maggie's cashmere blanket, and suddenly he felt tired and weak—and faintly jealous of the deep sleep, the total oblivion.

And he also felt…alone.

If the bridge was safe, maybe he'd suggest Miriam come down.

Don't be nuts, he told himself. She'd never come, and even if she did there'd be nothing for her to do.

She wouldn't care for a baby.

He had to.

Baby. Floods. Maggie. The images were drifting around his head in a swirl of exhausted confusion.

Baby. Floods. Maggie.

'I need to go,' he told Miriam, cutting her off in mid-sentence. 'Sorry, love, but I'll ring you back tomorrow. The baby needs me.'

'The midwife—'

'She's gone to sleep,' he said. 'That's where I'm heading, too. Hours and hours of sleep. I just have to get one baby called Ruby to agree.'

CHAPTER THREE

MAGGIE fed the hens at six the next morning and she heard Ruby crying.

She sorted feed, cut and chopped a bit of green stuff and threw it into the chookpen—there'd been a fox sniffing around and she wasn't game to let them out. She collected the eggs.

Ruby was still crying.

It wasn't her business, she told herself. Not yet. What district nurse dropped in at this hour? She'd make a professional visit a little later. Meanwhile, she should make breakfast and head to the makeshift clinic she'd set up in the back of the local hall, to do last-minute preparations and sort equipment.

That could wait, though, she conceded. The authorities had only put the roadblock up yesterday. Everyone who'd needed anything medical had had two days' warning. The weather forecast had been implacable. The water's coming. Get your stock to high ground. Evacuate or get in any supplies you need because it may be a week or more before the river goes down.

The pharmacy over the river and the doctors at the Valley Hospital had worked tirelessly over the last few days, checking every small complaint, filling prescriptions to last a month. The Valley people had seen floods before. There'd be no last-minute panic.

There would, however, be no doctor on this side of the river for a while.

Except Blake. The thought was strangely comforting.

Floods often meant trauma as people did stupid things trying to save stock, trying to fix roof leaks, heaving sandbags. Knowing she had a doctor on this side of the river, even one recovering from an appendectomy, was a blessing. If he'd help.

And if she expected him to help…maybe she could help him with his baby?

She'd made it clear she wasn't taking responsibility. That was what he wanted her to do, but even if she agreed, she couldn't care for a newborn as well as for the medical needs of everyone on this side of the river.

So she'd been firm, which wasn't actually like her. But firmness was her new resolve.

Right now, though, she was figuring that firm didn't mean cruel. The guy really didn't know anything about babies. If she had a teenage mum floundering, she'd move in to help.

Hold that thought, she decided, and she almost grinned at the thought of one hunky Blake Samford in the role of teen mum.

She'd help—even at six a.m.

So she knocked on his back door and waited. No answer. The wailing got louder.

She pushed the door tentatively inwards and went to investigate.

Blake was standing in the living room, in front of the vast, stone fireplace that was the centre of this huge, old homestead. The room was as it always was when she did her weekly check on the whole house, huge and faded and comfortable. A vast Persian rug lay on the worn, timber floor. The room was furnished with squishy leather settees, faded cushions and once opulent drapes, now badly in need of repair. The fire in the vast fireplace made it warm and homelike. The house was a grand old lady, past her prime but still graciously decorous.

Not so the guy in front of the fire. He was wearing boxer shorts and nothing else. He looked big, tanned, ripped—and not decorous at all.

Maggie was a nurse. She was used to seeing human bodies in all shapes and sizes.

She wasn't used to seeing this one.

Tall, dark and dangerous. Where had that phrase come from? She wasn't sure, but she knew where it was now. It was flashing in her head. Danger, danger, danger. A girl should turn round and walk right out of there.

Except he was holding a baby—all the wrong way—and his look spoke of desperation.

She put down her bucket of eggs, headed wordlessly to the kitchen to wash her hands, then came back and took the little one into her arms.

Blake practically sagged with relief.

'You need to wrap her,' she said, brisk and efficient because brisk and efficient seemed the way to go. 'She's exhausted.'

She cradled the little one tightly against her and felt an almost imperceptible relaxation. Babies seemed to respond instinctively to those who knew the ropes. To their mothers, who learned from birth how to handle them. To midwives, who'd delivered too many babies to count.

'She's been safely in utero for nine months,' she told him. 'She's been totally confined, and now her legs and arms are all over the place. It feels weird and frightening. She can handle it if she's relaxed, but not if she's tired and hungry.'

'But she won't feed,' he said helplessly, motioning to the bottle on the table. 'I can't—'

'She's gone past it. She needs to be settled first.' She sat on the settee and almost disappeared. These settees must be older than Blake, she thought. Old and faded and stuffed loosely with goosedown. She'd never seen such huge settees.

In truth she was finding it hard to thinking about settees. Not with that body...

Get a grip. Settees. Baby.

Not Blake.

She set about rewrapping Ruby, bundling her tightly so those flailing little legs and arms could relax, and the baby attached to them would feel secure. But she was a midwife. Bundling babies was second nature. She had more than enough time to think about settees and baby—and Blake Samford's body.

Which was truly awesome. Which was enough to make a girl...make a girl...

Think unwisely. Think stupid, in fact. This was her landlord—a guy who wanted to get rid of a baby.

You show one hint of weakness and you'll have a baby on your hands, she told herself. And if you fall for this baby...

She'd fallen for two dogs. That was more than enough.

She lived in this man's house as a tenant, and that

was all. If babies came with the territory then she moved out.

This was dumb. She was thinking dramatic when the situation simply needed practical. This guy had a problem and she could help him, the same way she'd help any new parent. She'd help and then she'd leave.

Ruby was still wailing, not with the desperation of a moment ago but with an I-want-something-and-I-want-it-now wail.

She lifted the bottle and flicked a little milk on her wrist. Perfect temperature. She offered it, one little mouth opened and accepted—and suddenly the noise stopped.

The silence was magical.

She smiled. Despite very real qualms in this case, Maggie Tilden did love babies. They sucked you in.

Her mother had used that to her advantage. Maggie's mother loved having babies, she just didn't like caring for them.

Over to Maggie.

And that was what Blake wanted. Over to Maggie.

Do not get sucked in, she told herself desperately. Do not become emotionally involved.

Anything but that. Even looking at Blake.

At his chest. At the angry red line she could see emerging from the top of his shorts.

Appendix. Stitches. Even if the external ones had been removed, it'd take weeks for the internal ones to dissolve.

'So no keyhole surgery for you?' she asked, trying to make her voice casual, like this was a normal neighbourly chat. 'You didn't choose the right surgeon?'

'I chose the wrong appendix,' he said, glancing down at his bare abs. 'Sorry. I'll cover up.'

'I'm not squeamish about an appendix scar,' she told him. 'I'm a nurse. So things were messy, huh?

'Yes.'

'No peritonitis?'

'I'm on decent antibiotics.'

Her frown deepened. 'Are you sure you're okay to stay on this side of the river?'

'Of course.'

But she was looking at problems she hadn't foreseen. Problems she hadn't thought about. 'If there's the least chance of infection... I assumed you'd had keyhole surgery. If I'd known...'

'You would have ordered me to leave?'

'I'd have advised you to leave.'

'You're in charge?'

'That's just the problem,' she said ruefully. 'I am. Until the water goes down there's no way I can get anyone to medical help. There's just me.'

'And me.'

She nodded, grateful that he was acknowledging he could help in a crisis—having a doctor on this side was wonderful but one who'd so recently had surgery? 'That's fine,' she told him. 'Unless you're the patient.'

'I don't intend to be the patient.' He was looking down at the blissfully sucking baby with bemusement. 'Why couldn't I do that?'

'You could. You can.' She rose and handed the bundle over, bottle and all, and Blake was left standing with an armload of baby. 'Sit,' she told him. 'Settle. Bond.'

'Bond?'

'You're her uncle. I suspect this little one needs all the family she can get.'

'It's she who needs medical help,' he said, almost savagely, and Ruby startled in his arms.

'Sit,' Maggie said again. 'Settle.'

He sat. He settled, as far as a man with an armload of baby could settle.

He looked…stunning, Maggie thought. Bare chested, wearing only boxer shorts, his dark hair raked and rumpled, his five o'clock shadow a few hours past five o'clock. Yep, stunning was the word for it.

It'd be wise if she failed to be stunned. She needed to remember she was here for a postnatal visit. Maternal health nurse visiting brand-new parent…

Who happened to be her landlord.

Who happened to be a surgeon—who was telling her the baby had medical needs.

She needed to pay attention to something other than how sexy he looked, one big man, almost naked, cradling a tiny baby.

With medical needs. Get serious.

'If you think her legs are bad enough to require immediate medical intervention I can organise helicopter evacuation,' she said. She knelt and unwrapped the blanket from around the tiny feet and winced.

'I can't believe her mother rejected her because of her feet,' she whispered, and Blake shook his head.

'No mother rejects her baby because of crooked feet.'

'Some fathers might. Some do. A daughter and an imperfect one at that. If the mother's weak…'

'Or if the mother's on drugs…'

'There doesn't seem any sign of withdrawal,' Maggie said, touching the tiny cheek, feeling the way the baby's face was filling out already. 'If her mother's a drug addict, this little one will be suffering withdrawal herself.'

'She's three weeks old,' Blake said. 'She may well be over it. But if she was addicted, those first couple of weeks will have been hell. That and the talipes may well have been enough for her to be rejected.'

'That and the knowledge that you've come home,' Maggie said thoughtfully. 'If your sister knows you're here, and thinks you're in a position to care for her, then she might see you as a way out.'

'She's not my sister.'

'Your father is her father.'

'I don't even know her surname.'

'No, but I do,' she said smoothly. 'She's Wendy Runtland, twenty-nine years old, and she lives on a farmlet six miles on the far side of the base hospital. Ruby was born on the twenty-first of last month. Wendy only stayed overnight and refused further assistance. The staff were worried. They'd organised a paediatrician to see the baby to assess her feet but Wendy discharged herself—and Ruby—before he got there.'

'How the—?'

'I'm a midwife employed by the Valley Health Service,' she told him. 'If I'm worried about babies, I can access files. I rang the hospital last night and asked for a search for a local baby born with talipes. Ruby's the only fit. The file's scanty. No antenatal care. First baby. Fast, hard labour with a partner present for some of the time. They were both visibly upset by the baby's feet and there's a note in the file that the guy was angry and abusive.

'The next morning Wendy discharged herself and the baby against medical advice. There were no grounds to involve the police but staff did notify Social Services. The maternal health nurse has tried to make home visits but each time she's found gates locked and dogs that didn't allow her to go further. There's a phone number but the phone's been slammed down each time she's rung. You might have more luck. You want to try while I check the bridge?'

'What's to check?'

He looked almost dumbfounded, she thought. Man left with abandoned baby. Surgeon way out of his comfort zone.

'I've been listening to the radio and it's still raining up north,' she said evenly. 'There's a vast mass of water coming down. If the water keeps rising it might be a while before you can get her to Social Services.'

'Social Services?'

'Unless we can get her back to her mother—or unless you want her—I assume that's where she'll be placed. Either way, the decision has to be made soon. Those feet need attention now, although I assume you know that.'

'I know it,' he growled, and then he fell silent.

He stared down at the baby in his arms and she thought…there was something there, some link.

Family.

He'd said he didn't have a sister. He'd said he didn't even know her full name.

This was a guy who was an intelligent, skilled surgeon, she thought, a guy who'd know how to keep his emotions under control. But his recent surgery would have weakened him, and a sleepless night would have weakened him still more.

She had a feeling this guy didn't let his defences down often, but they were down now. He was gazing at the child in his arms and his face said he didn't know where to go with this.

Evacuate her? Hand her over to Social Welfare? Keep her until the river went down?

Risk attachment?

She couldn't help him. It was his decision.

'I'll try and phone Wendy,' he said at last, and she nodded and got to her feet and collected her eggs.

'Excellent. I'll leave some of these in your kitchen. Tell me how you go.'

'Maggie?'

She paused. Met his gaze. Saw desperation.

'Stay here while I ring,' he said, and she thought maybe she could at least do that.

But as he handed back the now fed, sleeping Ruby, and she gathered her into her arms and watched Blake head for the phone, she thought…she thought…

She thought this was as far as she should go.

Babies did things to her. Her mother had used that, played on it, trapped her with it. And now…

The sight of Blake was doing things to her as well.

He was all male, one gorgeous hunk of testosterone, but it wasn't that that was messing with her head.

It was the way he'd looked at Ruby—and the way he'd looked at her when he'd asked her to stay.

Under that strength was pure vulnerability.

Maggie had lived most of her life in this valley and she'd heard stories about this family; this man. His mother had been glamorous and aloof and cold, and she'd walked out—justifiably—when Blake had been six. His father had been a womanising brute.

Blake may come from the richest family in the district but the locals had felt sorry for him when he'd been six, and that sympathy hadn't been lessened by anything anyone had heard since.

What sort of man was he now? Like his mother? Like his father?

She couldn't tell. She was seeing him at his most vulnerable. He was wounded, shocked, tired and burdened by a baby he didn't know.

Don't judge now, she told herself. Don't get any more involved than you already are.

Except…she could stay while he rang his sister.

She sank down on the settee and put her feet towards the fire. This was a great room. A family room.

She lived on the other side of the wall. Remember it, she told herself.

Meanwhile, she cuddled one sleeping baby and she listened.

Blake had switched to speakerphone. He wanted to share.

She could share, she decided, at least this much.

Blake punched in the numbers Maggie had given him and a woman answered on the second ring. Sounding defensive. Sounding like she'd expected the call.

'Wendy?'

There was a long silence and Maggie wondered if she'd slam down the receiver as she'd slammed it down on the district nurse.

'Blake,' she said at last. She sounded exhausted. Drained. Defeated.

The baby was three weeks old, Maggie thought, and wondered about postnatal depression.

'You know my name,' Blake was saying, tentatively, feeling his way. 'I didn't even know yours.'

'That would be because our father acknowledged you.'

'I'm sorry.'

'Bit late to be sorry now,' she hissed. 'Thirty years.'

'Wendy, what my father did or didn't do to you isn't anything to do with me.'

'You got the farm.'

'We can talk about that,' he said evenly. 'But right now we need to talk about your daughter.'

'She's not my daughter,' she snapped. 'I didn't even want her in the first place. Now Sam says he won't even look at her.'

'Too right, I won't,' a man's voice growled, and Maggie realised it wasn't only Blake who was on speakerphone. 'We never wanted kids, neither of us. We're going to Western Australia, but there's no way we're taking a deformed rat with us. By the time Wendy realised she was pregnant it was too late to get rid of it but neither of us want it. We should have left it at the hospital, but all them forms... Anyway, she's getting her tubes tied the minute we get settled, and that's it. If you want the kid adopted, we'll sign the papers, but we don't have time for any of that now. Meanwhile, the kid's yours. Do what you like with it. We're leaving.'

'Let me talk to Wendy,' again, he said. 'Wendy?'

Wendy came on the line again, just as defensive. 'Yeah?'

'Is this really what you want?' he asked urgently. 'This shouldn't be about our past. It's now. It's Ruby. Do you really want to abandon your daughter?'

'Yeah,' Wendy said, and defence gave way to bitterness. 'Yeah, I do, but I'm not abandoning her. I'm giving her to you. My family's done nothing for me, ever, so now it's time. I don't want this kid, so you deal with it, big brother. Your problem.'

And the phone was slammed down with a force that must have just about cracked the receiver at the other end.

Silence.

Deathly silence.

Blake put the phone back in its charger like it might shatter. Like the air around him might shatter.

Maggie looked at his face and looked away.

She looked down at the little girl in her arms.

Deformed rat.

Thank God she was only three weeks old. Thank God she couldn't understand.

Suddenly the way her mother had looked at Maggie's brothers and sisters flooded back to her. Over and over she remembered her mother, exhausted from childbirth, arriving home from hospital, sinking onto her mound of pillows in the bed that was her centre, handing over the newest arrival to her eldest daughter.

'You look after it, Maggie.'

Her mother wasn't close to as bad as this, but there were similarities. Her parents did what they had to do, but no more. Life was fun and frivolous, and responsibility was something to be handed over to whoever was closest.

Her mother liked being pregnant. Her parents liked the weird prestige of having a big family, but they wanted none of the responsibility that went with it.

Deformed rat.

She found herself hugging the little one closer, as if she could protect her from the words. From the label.

Abandoned baby.

Deformed rat.

And then the baby was lifted from her arms. Blake had her, was cradling her, holding her as a man might hold his own newborn. The way he held her was pure protection. It was anger and frustration and grief. It was an acknowledgement that his world had changed.

'She won't change her mind,' he said grimly, and it was hardly a question.

'I suspect not,' Maggie whispered. 'Not after three weeks. Mothers often reject straight after birth if there's something seriously wrong—or if depression or psychosis kicks in—but she's cared for her—after a fashion—for three weeks now. And the anger… I'm thinking this is a thought-out decision, as much as either of them sound like they can think anything out. After three weeks with this one, there should be an unbreakable bond. If there's not, it won't form now. All we can hope for is to maintain contact.'

'You'd want Ruby to maintain contact with a family who think of her as…?' He broke off, sounding appalled. 'We'll have to organise adoption. Surely there's a family who'll want her.'

'There will be,' Maggie said. 'Of course. But without the papers…she'll need to go into foster-care first.'

'And let me guess, there's no foster-carers over this side of the river.'

'I'm organising evacuation,' she said, and he stared at her. As well he might. This decision had been made a whole two seconds ago.

'Sorry?'

'For both of you,' she said briskly. 'I read up on talipes last night. I haven't seen a baby with it before but I know what needs to be done. She needs careful manipulation and casts, starting now. The Ponseti technique talks about long casts on both legs, changed weekly. I can't do that. Then there's the fact that you had appendicitis with complications a week ago.'

'I didn't have complications.'

'So why didn't you have keyhole surgery?' She fixed him with a look she'd used often on recalcitrant patients. 'Right. Complications. So in summary, I have a man who may end up needing urgent help from previous surgery. I have a baby who needs urgent medical attention. The rain has eased this morning but the forecast is that more storms will hit tonight. I can get you out of here right now. You can have Ruby back in Sydney in the best of medical care, organising foster-care, organising anything you need, by this afternoon. I'll make the call now.'

'You're kicking me out?'

'You have medical training, too,' she said. 'You know it's for the best.'

She was right.

Of course she was right. If she made the call, all problems would be solved. Evacuation was justified. If he didn't accept the offer—the order?—he could well end up stuck here with a baby for a couple of weeks.

He could take Ruby back to Sydney, right now.

He could be home in his own, clean, clinical apartment tonight, with Ruby handed over to carers, and all this behind him.

Maggie was waiting. She stood calmly, her bucket of eggs in her hand, ready to take action.

He thought, stupidly, Who'll eat the eggs if I go?

It was sensible to go.

The phone rang again. He picked it up without thinking. It was still on speakerphone—his father's landline. He half expected it to be Wendy, but it was a child's voice, shrill and urgent.

'Maggie?'

The eggs were back on the floor so fast some must have broken, and Maggie had the phone in an instant.

'Susie, what's wrong?'

'Christopher's bleeding...' On the other end of the line, the child hiccupped on a sob and choked.

'No crying, Susie,' Maggie said, and it was a curt order that had Blake's eyes widen. It sounded like sergeant major stuff. 'You know it doesn't help. What's happened?'

'He slid on the wet roof and he cut himself,' Susie whimpered. 'His blood is oozing out from the top of his leg, and Mum's screaming and Pete said to ring and say come.'

'I'm coming,' Maggie said, still in the sergeant major voice. 'But first you listen, Susie, and listen hard. Get a sheet out of the linen cupboard and roll it up so it's a tight, tight ball. Then you go out to Christopher, you tell Mum to shut up and keep away—can you do that, Susie? Imagine you're me and just do it—and tell Pete to put the ball of sheet on his leg and press as hard as he's ever pressed in his life. Tell him to sit on it if he must. He has to stop the bleeding. Can you do that, love?'

'I... Yes.'

'I'll be there before Mum even stops yelling,' Maggie said. 'You just make Pete keep pressing, and tell everyone I'm on my way.'

CHAPTER FOUR

ONE minute she was readying Blake for medical evacuation. The next she was heading a mile down the road to the ramshackle farmhouse where her parents and four of their nine children lived.

With Blake and baby.

How had it happened?

She hardly had time to wonder. Her entire concentration was on the road—apart from a little bit that was aware of the man beside her.

She'd headed for the door, out to the wagon, but by the time she'd reversed and turned, Blake had been in pants and shirt, standing in front of the car, carrying Ruby.

'If he's bleeding out, you'll need me,' he'd snapped, and she hadn't argued. She'd fastened a seemingly bemused Ruby into the baby carrier she always carried—as district nurse her car was always equipped for carting kids—and now she was heading home and Blake was hauling his shoes on while she drove.

Christopher was twelve years old. He'd had more accidents than she could remember.

'I should never have left them,' she muttered, out loud but addressed to herself.

'You should never have left home?' Blake had tied

his shoes and was now buttoning his shirt. He was almost respectable. Behind them, Ruby had settled into the baby carrier, like this was totally satisfactory—baby being taken for an after-breakfast drive by Mum and Dad.

Mum and Dad? Ha!

'My parents aren't responsible people,' Maggie said through gritted teeth. 'They should have been neutered at birth.'

'Um…there's a big statement.' Blake looked thoughtful. 'That'd mean there'd have been no Maggie.'

'And none of the other eight they won't look after,' she snapped. 'But Nickie, Louise, Raymond and Donny are out of the valley now, studying. Susie's ten—she's the youngest. I thought they were getting independent. With me only a mile away I thought they'd be safe.'

'They're as safe as if you were living there and gone to the shops for milk,' Blake said, and she let the thought drift—and the tight knot of fear and guilt unravelled a bit so that only fear remained.

And the fear was less because this man was sitting beside her.

But she still didn't know what she was dealing with. If Chris had cut his femoral artery…

'She said oozing,' Blake said, as if his thoughts were running concurrent with hers. 'If it was the artery she'd have used a more dramatic word.'

The fear backed off a little, too. She allowed a glimmer of hope to enter the equation, but she didn't ease her foot from the accelerator.

'No hairpin bends between here and your place?' Blake asked, seemingly mildly.

'No.'

'Good,' Blake said. 'Excellent. No aspersions on your driving, but Ruby and I are very pleased to hear it.'

They pulled up outside a place that looked like a cross between a house and a junkyard. The house looked almost derelict, a ramshackle, weatherboard cottage with two or three shonky additions tacked onto the back. The veranda at the front was sagging, kids' toys and bikes were everywhere and Blake could count at least five car bodies—or bits of car bodies. An old white pony was loosely tethered to the veranda, and a skinny, teenage girl came flying down from the veranda to meet them.

'Maggie, round the back, quick…'

Maggie was out of the car almost before it had stopped, and gone.

Blake was left with the girl.

Maggie had left her bag. The girl was about to dart off, too, but Blake grabbed her by the shoulder and held on.

'I'm a friend of Maggie's,' he said curtly. 'I'm a doctor. Will you stay with the baby? Take care of her while I help Maggie?'

The girl stared at him—and then stared into the car at the baby.

'Yes,' she whispered. 'Blood makes me wobble.'

As long as babies didn't, Blake thought, but it was cool and overcast, Ruby was asleep and in no danger of overheating, and Maggie might well need him more.

He thrust the girl into the passenger seat and she sat as if relieved to be there. Then he hauled open Maggie's bag. Maggie was methodical, he thought. Equipment was where he expected it to be. He couldn't handle the whole bag but he grabbed worst-case scenario stuff and headed behind the house at a run.

His stitches pulled, but for the first time since the operation, he hardly noticed.

Behind the house was drama. Maggie was already there, stooped over a prostrate child. Around them was a cluster of kids of assorted ages, and a woman was down on her knees, wailing. 'Maggie, it's making me sick. Maggie...'

The kids were ignoring the woman. They were totally intent on Maggie—who was totally intent on the child she was caring for.

Christopher was a miniature version of Maggie, he thought as he knelt beside her to see what they were dealing with. Same chestnut hair. Same freckles.

No colour at all.

Maggie was making a pad out of a pile of sheets lying beside her. An older boy—Peter?—his face as white as death—was pressing hard on a bloodied pad on his brother's thigh. As Blake knelt beside her, Maggie put her own pad in position.

'Okay, Pete, lift.'

The boy lifted the pad away, and in the moment before Maggie applied her tighter pad, Blake saw a gash, eight to ten inches long. Pumping. Not the major artery—he'd be dead by now if he'd hit that, but bad enough.

Leg higher than heart.

Maggie had replaced the pad and was pressing down again. Blood was oozing out the sides.

Whoever had grabbed the sheets had grabbed what looked like the contents of the linen cupboard. He grabbed the whole pile and wedged them under the boy's thighs, elevating the leg. Maggie moved with him and they moved effortlessly into medical-team mode.

The oozing blood was slowing under her hands, but not enough. Pressure could only do so much.

Maggie was looking desperate. She knew what was happening.

Blake was already checking and rechecking the equipment in his hands. Hoping to hell her sterilisation procedures were thorough. Knowing he had no choice.

He'd wrapped the stuff in a sterile sheet he'd pulled from plastic. He laid it on the grass, set it out as he'd need it, then hauled on sterile gloves.

'On the count of three, take your hands away,' he said to Maggie, and she glanced up at him, terror everywhere, saw his face, steadied, and somehow moved more solidly into medical mode.

'You're assisting, Nurse,' he said flatly, calmly. 'Don't let me down. Pete, hold your brother's shoulders, tight. Christopher, I'm about to stop the bleeding. It'll hurt but only for a moment. Grit your teeth and bear it.'

He'd swabbed and slid in pain relief while he talked but he didn't have time for it to take effect.

'Ready?' he snapped to his makeshift theatre team.

'R-ready,' Maggie faltered.

'You stay calm on me,' he snapped. 'Pete, have you got those shoulders? Not one movement. Use all your strength to hold your brother still. Chris, are you ready to bite the bullet, like they say in the movies? We need you to be a hero.'

'I… Yes.'

'Good kid,' Blake said. 'You don't need to pretend— you are a hero. I need to hurt you to stop the bleeding but I'll be fast. This is superhero country. Pretend you're armed with kryptonite and hold on.'

Maggie was terrified.

She was a nurse assisting a surgeon in Theatre, and somehow the second took priority over the first. Blake's calm authority, his snapped, incisive instructions, the movements of his fingers…it was all that mattered. It had to be all that mattered.

Instead of being a terrified sister, she was a theatre assistant and only that. She was focussed entirely on anticipating Blake's needs, swabbing away blood so she could see what he was doing, handing him what he needed as he needed it.

A torn artery…

Worse, it had retracted into the wound. She could see the blood seeping from the top of the rip in the skin. This was no exposed artery to be simply tied off.

If there was time for anaesthetic…

There wasn't, and she held her breath as Blake produced a scalpel and fast, neatly, precisely, extended the tear just enough…just enough…

Chris jerked and cried out, but magically Pete held him still.

She swabbed and could see.

He was before her. The scalpel was back in her hand—not dropped when they might need it again—and forceps taken instead. Somehow she'd had them ready.

Blake was working inside the wound, manoeuvring, while she tried desperately to keep the wound clear, let him see what he was dealing with.

'Got it,' he said, amazingly calmly, as if the issue

had never been in doubt, and almost as he said it, the bleeding slowed.

He was using the forceps to clamp.

'Suture,' he said.

She prepared sutures faster than she'd thought possible. She watched as his skilled fingers moved in and out, in and out.

She swabbed and cut and cleaned and she thought, Thank you, God.

Thank you, Blake.

He'd done it. The bleeding had slowed to almost nothing. He sat back and felt the same sense of overwhelming dizziness he always felt after such drama.

Cope first, faint second? It was an old edict instilled in him by a long-ago surgery professor when he'd caught his knees buckling.

'There's no shame in a good faint,' the professor had said. 'We all suffer from reaction. Just learn to delay it.'

He'd delayed it—and so had Maggie. In no other circumstances would he have permitted a relative to assist in a procedure on a family member. For her to hold it together...

She'd done more than that. She'd been calm, thorough, brilliant.

They weren't out of the woods yet. What was needed now was replacement volume. He felt Chris's pulse and flinched. With this blood pressure he was at risk of cardiac arrest.

They needed fluids, now.

But Maggie's capacious bag had provided all he needed. Thank God for Maggie's bag. Thank God for district nurses.

While Maggie worked under orders, applying a rough dressing that kept the pressure up—he'd need to remove it later when the pain relief kicked in fully to do a neater job—he lifted the boy's arm, swabbed it fast and slid in the IV. A moment later he taped it safely, grabbed a bag of saline and started it running.

He checked the pulse and checked again that he had adrenalin close.

He checked the pulse again and decided not yet.

'Do we have plasma?' he asked.

'At the clinic,' Maggie said. 'Ten minutes' drive away.'

It wasn't worth risking driving for yet. He'd run the saline and wait.

The lad seemed close to unconscious, dazed, hazy, hardly responding, but as the saline dripped in and the drugs took effect, they saw a tiny amount of colour return.

The pulse under Blake's fingers regained some strength.

Around them the family watched, horrified to stillness, willing a happy ending. As did Blake. As, he thought, did Maggie. Her face was almost as white as the child's.

This child was her brother.

Brothers and sisters.

He thought suddenly of the baby he'd seen thirty years before when he'd been six years old. His sister. He'd never had this connection, he thought, and then he thought of Ruby and wondered if this was a second chance.

It was a crazy time to think of one tiny baby.

Think of Christopher.

The saline dripped in. He kept his fingers on the little boy's pulse, willing the pressure to rise, and finally it did. Christopher seemed to stir from semi-consciousness and he whimpered.

'Christopher, love, keep still,' Maggie said urgently, but he heard the beginnings of relief in her voice. 'It's okay. You've cut your leg badly, so you need to keep it still, but Dr Samford's fixed it. It'll be fine. What a duffer you were to try and climb on the wet roof.'

'You slide faster when it's wet,' he whispered. 'But it hurts. I won't do it again.'

Blake let out his breath. He hadn't actually been aware that he hadn't been breathing but now…

He remembered another rule instilled into him a long time ago by the professor who'd taken him for his paediatric term. 'Rule of thumb for quick triage. If a child is screaming, put it at the end of the queue. If it's quiet but whinging, middle. If it's silent, front, urgent, *now*.'

Christopher had suddenly moved from front of the line to the middle.

He glanced at Maggie and she seemed to sag. There was relief but also weariness. Desperation.

He glanced around and he thought, How many times had this scene played out? Maggie, totally responsible.

The mother—a crazy, hippy-dressed mass of sodden hysteria, was incoherent in the background, slumped on the grass crying, holding onto yet another kid, a little girl who looked about ten. As Blake watched, the little girl tried to pull away to come across to Maggie, but her mother held her harder.

'Hold me, Susie,' she whimpered. 'I'll faint if you don't. Oh, my God, you kids will be the death of me.'

Let her faint, he thought grimly, and glanced again at Maggie and saw a look…

Like a deer trapped in headlights.

How much responsibility did this woman carry for this family?

'Swap places and I'll bind it,' he told her. He needed to take the pressure off Maggie so she could react to the needs of these kids—to Chris but also to brave Pete, who'd held his brother all this time, and to Susie, who'd held her mother. 'Do we have somewhere we can stitch it properly?' He glanced at the house—and Maggie's mother—and thought, I just bet it's not clean inside.

'Maggie's not stitching me,' Christopher whimpered. 'She hurts.'

'You've stitched your brother before?' he demanded, astounded.

Maggie gave a rueful smile. 'Not unless I've have no choice,' she told him. 'But Christopher doesn't give his family many choices.'

'You have a choice now,' he said, still seeing that trapped look. 'I can do this. You said you've set up a clinic. With a surgery?'

'A small one.'

'Excellent.' He smiled down at Christopher. 'If you'll accept me as a substitute for your sister, we'll bind your leg so you don't make a mess of her car, then we'll take you to the clinic she's set up. I'll fix your leg properly where I have equipment and decent light. I need to check for nerve damage.' But already he was checking toes and leg for response, and he was thinking Christopher had been lucky.

'But what about Ruby?' Maggie demanded

And he thought...*Ruby.*

Uh-oh. Ruby.

His baby?

She was not his baby, he told himself harshly. She

was merely his responsibility until she could be evacuated or her mother reclaimed her. No more.

'Your sister's caring for her,' he told Maggie. 'In the car,' he added, and hoped she was.

'If she's with Liselle, she'll be fine,' Maggie assured him. 'Liselle loves babies. She makes money babysitting.' But she was frowning, obviously thinking ahead.

'Blake, Chris obviously needs careful stitching.' She glanced at the leg Blake had now bound so tightly the bleeding had completely stopped. 'I think…even if Christopher's okay with it, it might be too big a job to do here. I can cope with simple suturing, but this might need more. On top of that, Ruby's legs need attention. The sooner the pair of them get professional care, the better. Added to that, I don't want the responsibility for your appendix. The sensible plan is to organise evacuation for the three of you. I'll get the chopper in now—they'll fly you all over to the hospital.'

'I don't want to go to hospital,' Christopher whimpered, sounding panicked, and suddenly Blake was right there, concurring.

'I don't either,' he said. 'I can fix this.' He put a hand on Christopher's shoulder, settling him. 'I'm a surgeon and I do a neat job of stitching,' he said. 'No criticism of your sister but she's a girl. What do girls know abut needlework?'

That produced a faint smile on the boy's wan face. 'Yeah, right.'

'So it's okay if I put your leg back together instead of your sister? Without sending you to hospital?'

'Okay,' Christopher whispered, and Maggie hugged him.

Blake wondered why Maggie was doing the hugging instead of the wimp of a woman that was their mother.

'I'm going to make myself a nice cup of tea,' the woman was saying, staggering to her feet. 'I'm Barbie, by the way. Barbara, but my friends call me Barbie. Maggie, you might have introduced me.'

Right, Blake thought. Introductions before saving her son's life?

Christopher was slipping towards sleep. The saline was pushing his blood pressure up. The painkillers were taking effect. They had time to think this through but what he was suggesting—staying here—still seemed sensible.

Even to him.

'What about Ruby?' Maggie asked as her mother disappeared, jerking him back to his baby, his responsibility.

But responsibilities weren't only his. His thoughts were flying tangentially, from a wounded child to a baby—and to one lone nurse.

One look at this family and he'd seen what Maggie was facing. The mother was feeble and hysterical, the father was nowhere to be seen, and these kids were too young to be alone. Maggie seemed to be caring for everyone. More than that, she was taking on the medical needs for the entire population of this side of the valley. Until the water receded, she was on her own.

Christopher would live. If Maggie had been on her own, he might well not have. They both knew that. Maggie's white face told him she'd seen it and was still seeing it. But together they'd worked well. They'd worked as a team.

He was on leave. He needed to sort the house. How hard would it be to provide back-up for this woman?

And care for a baby while he did?

She'd help him with Ruby, he thought. Maggie was that sort of woman.

'No,' she said.

'No?'

Her eyes narrowed, and she made her voice resolute. 'I know what you're thinking and no. I'm *not* helping look after your baby and you *are* being evacuated.'

'I wasn't asking you to look after my…my sister's baby,' he said, and thought, Okay, he might have been going to suggest it but he wasn't now. 'And you don't need to look after my appendix. In case you hadn't realised it, most appendectomies result in removal of same, and I've left mine safely in Sydney.' Then, as she opened her mouth to protest some more, he held up his hand to pre-empt her.

'Plus,' he said, 'I was looked after by colleagues, medical mates who know they'll get joshed for ever if I'm hit by complications, so I have enough antibiotics on board to protect a horse. I'm healing nicely. Plus…' she'd opened her mouth again… 'if you send Ruby to hospital the first thing they'll do is to organise an orthopaedic surgeon opinion. I'm suspecting Corella Valley doesn't run to an orthopaedic surgeon. The nearest orthopaedic surgeon would therefore be me, and I'm on this side of the river. Maggie, not only can I assess Ruby, I can manipulate and cast her legs. I can do everything she needs until the water comes down.'

'And look after her?'

'I… Yes,' he said, and he met her gaze full on. 'And Wendy knows where she is right now,' he said. 'She might change her mind. That option's not available if Ruby's sent to the city.'

'I doubt—'

'So do I doubt,' he said softly. 'But Wendy's my sister so maybe I should care for this little one for a week or two and give her that chance.'

'Would you want her to go back to…that?' she demanded, appalled.

'No,' he said truthfully. 'But I do want to talk to Wendy. I do want to figure this mess out. I don't want to walk away…'

'From your family,' she said, her voice softening.

'I've figured it,' he told her, glancing up at the roof. 'Risks are everywhere. If I turn my back, the next thing I know Ruby will be roof-sliding.'

'You'll take responsibility for her?'

'For a week or so,' he said, wondering what on earth he'd let himself in for. But there was something about this moment…something about the way this woman was shouldering so much responsibility—that made him think, One baby for a week. Was that a lot to ask?

Family for a week.

He could do this, he thought, and somehow…maybe it'd be his only chance to make reparation for a sister who'd never had a Maggie.

Why?

Because he'd thought of Wendy. For whatever reason, he'd thought of that baby, glimpsed only that once.

He hadn't had a great childhood, but many had it worse. His mother had had enough strength to walk away from her abusive husband. She hadn't been a particularly affectionate mother but the man she'd married next had been distantly kind. Money had never been an issue. He'd gone to a great school, to an excellent university.

Wendy, though…

He knew enough of his father to know there'd have been no support for an illegitimate child. He didn't know who her mother was, but he remembered hysteria, threats, floods of tears, and he thought… He thought Wendy must have had the worst side of the deal by far.

You've got the farm… She'd thrown that at him as an accusation.

Did he have the right to accept it? For the first time he was questioning it.

Maggie was watching him. Waiting for him to realise what he was letting himself in for. Waiting for him to realise that evacuation was the easiest way to go.

But then he thought back to that moment all those years ago. Seeing a child… Thinking for one amazing moment that he had a little sister.

Family.

He didn't do family. He was a loner. Miriam was all he needed—a woman as caught up in her career as he was in his.

Miriam would think he was nuts.

'Hey, mister, I think your baby's filled her nappy. You want me to change it? I can but I charge babysitting rates.' It was a yell from the far side of the house and it jerked him out of introspection as nothing else could have. It even made him smile.

'He's coming, Liselle,' Maggie said. She was cradling Christopher, hugging him close, surveying Blake like he was an interesting insect species. She was watching to see what he'd do. 'There's no need for him to waste money employing nappy-changers, and there are no nappy-changers available for hire anyway. There are nappies in my bag,' she told him. 'Or there's still the choice of evacuation. What's it to be?'

And he looked down at Christopher—who'd need to be evacuated with him—that wound needed careful stitching and it was too much to expect Maggie to do it. He looked at Maggie, who'd taken on responsibility for the valley.

He thought about Ruby, whose need had just graphically been described.

'I guess I'm staying,' he said, and Maggie smiled up at him. It wasn't a confident smile, though. Maybe she still thought he'd be more trouble than he was worth.

'You're a brave man,' she told him. 'Changing nappies isn't for sissies.'

'Then I guess I can't be a sissy,' he told her, grinning back at her. Thinking this could be a very interesting week. Thinking Here Be Dragons but he could just possibly tackle them and do this woman a favour in the process. 'I can't be a sissy until the floods subside.'

'Or until after you've coped with one nappy,' Maggie said. 'Nappy or floods…take your pick.'

'I have a feeling I'm facing both.'

They tucked Christopher into the back seat of Maggie's wagon. It was a tight fit around the baby seat but they stuffed the leg space with cushions so he could lie down, they wrapped him in blankets and he settled. It wasn't only the drugs that made him relax, Maggie thought. Whenever one of the kids was ill it was 'We want Maggie.' More, it was 'We *need* Maggie.' And they did.

She slid behind the steering-wheel, checked on her

now sleeping little brother, an awake but changed and clean Ruby—and one recovering appendectomy patient beside her.

Mother hen with all her chicks.

Blake wasn't quite a chick.

He was staying.

She should be relieved. She was relieved. He'd been brilliant with Christopher. She might have got the bleeding checked in time, but she might not have. The odds said not. She glanced again at Christopher and her heart twisted.

She glanced at Blake—and something inside twisted in a different direction.

Weird?

Yes, it was weird. This guy was a doctor, a surgeon. He was here to help and she should be overjoyed, in a purely professional capacity. But there was a little bit of her that wasn't professional, which was reacting to the sense of this guy sitting beside her, which was saying that Blake deciding to stay might cause problems...

What problems? She was being ridiculous. It was the shock of what had just happened, she told herself firmly. It was the shock of almost losing one of her family.

She loved the lot of them. All eight. They held her heartstrings and she was tied for life.

So put the weird way she was feeling about Blake right away—forget it.

'Why did you decide to leave them?' Blake asked and she concentrated on the road for a while, concentrated on getting her thoughts in order, concentrated on suppressing anger and confusion and whatever else was whirling in her traitorous mind.

'You think I should still be living with them?'

'I don't think,' Blake said mildly. 'But I'm wondering if your father's a bit more capable than your mother.'

'He's not,' she said shortly. 'And he doesn't live there any more.'

'I'm sorry.'

'I'm not,' she said. 'It's one less responsibility.' Then she caught herself. 'Sorry. That sounds like they're all hard work. They're great kids. Nickie, Louise and Raymond have scholarships and are at university. Donny's in his last year as an apprentice motor mechanic. They're all safe.'

'How did you train?' he asked, mildly, thinking if she had been responsible for them all...had she left and come back?

'Luck,' she said briefly. 'Dad was restless and moved us all to Cairns. It was dumb—we knew no one there and ended up reliant on Social Services but it took four years to get enough money together to come back, so I was able to do my basic nursing training while I lived with them. Otherwise I'd be stuck with nothing.'

'Stuck with your family?'

'That's it,' she said quietly. 'And it's a quandary. The kids love me and need me, but they're growing up. Gradually they're making their way into the world, so I need to work out my own independence as well. I know I have eventual escape, but Liselle, Peter, Christopher and Susie are seventeen, fifteen, twelve and ten and too young to be left with the cot case that's my mother. But I didn't have a choice—until your father's farm became available.'

'You're saying you left your family to take care of my father's farm?'

'I left my family for me,' she said grimly, and there

was a moment's silence while she obviously decided whether to reveal more of herself. And came down on the yes side.

'My dad left two years ago,' she told him. 'He's as bad as my mum. Totally irresponsible. Six months ago, just as your dad was dying, he turned up with a new young partner in tow. Sashabelle. What sort of name is that? Anyway they giggled and mooned over each other and Sashabelle kept saying how cute Susie was and how she'd love to have a daughter—all in my mother's hearing—and then Dad looked at me and grinned and said to her, "Yeah, sweetheart, you know I love travelling but if you really want a kid…if worst comes to worst we can always bring her home to Maggie."'

'And I thought that's exactly what would happen. Just like Wendy's dumped Ruby on you—only I've already cared for eight and I'm d— I'm darned if I'll look after more. So I told him no more, ever, I was moving out. Then I had to find somewhere where I could reach the kids in a hurry when they need me, but my useless parents know that I've drawn a line and any more kids—no way. Once Susie's left home, I'm out of it. Good ole Maggie… I love my brothers and sisters to bits but the end's in sight.'

'So that's why you won't take on Ruby?'

Her face froze. 'No,' she said through gritted teeth. 'It's not why I won't take on Ruby. I'm not taking on Ruby because she's not my family, and it's totally, crassly, cruelly irresponsible for you to ask it of me. I'm your tenant, Blake, but if babies are involved you won't see me for dust. Put that in your pipe and smoke it—and don't forget it. And here we are.'

They'd pulled into the grounds of the local hall. A

dumpy little lady in her forties was tacking a banner to the fence.

'*Medical Clinic, Temporary, Corella Valley East.*'

A sign hung on a nail in front of it.

'*Maggie's Not Here.*'

As Maggie swung into the gate the lady at the fence beamed, waved and swapped the sign over.

'*Maggie's Here.*'

'Very professional,' Blake said dryly, and Maggie cast him a wry look.

'So how would you organise it, city boy?'

'Regular hours?'

'And when another kid falls off a roof I still stay here because I need to be regular? I'll be here when I can.' She climbed out of the car and hugged the lady doing the signs. 'Ronnie, this looks great. Fantastic. And we have our first patient. Christopher.'

Ronnie sighed and tugged away to look into the back seat. 'Oh, Christopher, what have you done now?' And then she paused as Blake emerged from the passenger seat. 'Oh…'

'This is Blake Samford,' Maggie said briefly. 'He's Bob's son—and a doctor. He's offered to help. Blake, this is Veronica Mayes. Ronnie. She's a schoolteacher, but the school's on the other side of the river.'

'You're a doctor.' Ronnie's eyes grew huge. 'A medical doctor—here? On this side. Oh, Maggie, that's wonderful.' She peered again into the back seat. 'But Christopher…?'

'Sliding on roof ended badly,' Maggie said curtly. 'Badly cut thigh. It needs stitching and Blake's offered to help.'

'And…the baby?' She was still staring into the car.

'Ruby,' Maggie said. 'Blake's baby. If he asks nicely, he might be persuade you to take care of her while he stitches.'

'You've brought your family here?' Ronnie demanded of Blake, beaming her excitement.

'Just his baby,' Maggie said. 'I suspect Blake thinks that's enough.'

The wound on Christopher's leg was jagged and bone deep. He was incredibly lucky to have escaped nerve damage, Blake thought as he cleaned, debrided and inserted internal stitches as well as external to hold everything together. They'd sedated the boy heavily, so he wasn't out of it completely but he was wafting in a drug-induced haze. Maggie was doing the reassurance, prattling on about some weird video game Christopher loved, but at the same time she was giving him every inch of assistance he needed.

She was an excellent nurse, Blake thought. The valley was lucky to have her.

As he started the final suturing and dressing, Ronnie poked her head round the door and said apologetically, 'Maggie, love, Joan Kittle's here with Angus with asthma.'

'I can handle Angus's asthma,' Maggie told Blake. 'Mild asthmatic, hysterical mum.'

'There seems to be an abundance of hysterical mothers in this valley,' he noted, keeping on working. 'Christopher, is it okay if your sister goes out to take care of a child with asthma?'

'Yeah,' Christopher said sleepily. 'You'll look after me, and everyone always needs Maggie.'

They did. He had that pretty much figured by now.

He finished stitching and dressing and tucked the little boy under blankets. Ronnie appeared again with a sleepy Ruby in her arms. He asked her to stay with Christopher and went to find out what was happening.

Angus was obviously sorted. Maggie was now examining a toe, attached to a very large, very elderly guy who looked like he'd just come in from the cowshed. He sat slumped in a rather rickety chair in the makeshift waiting room, his boot off and his foot stuck straight out in front of him.

Maggie turned as he entered and he was hit by a smile of sheer, anticipatory gratitude.

'Mr Bowen has a splinter,' she said.

'Went out to chop the wood in me slippers,' the old man said. 'Dumb. Coulda chopped me foot off with an axe. Didn't. Hit the wood with the splitter, though, and a bit of wood went right in. I've been digging round all morning with a needle and can't get it. Maggie says you're a doc.'

He was an orthopaedic surgeon, Blake thought faintly. Was he supposed to go digging for splinters?

But that's what he did. He inserted local anaesthetic. He did a part resection of the nail of the big toe and managed the careful removal of a shattered splinter.

He administered a decent shot of antibiotics—the guy had indeed been digging into the wound and Blake hated to imagine what he'd used to do it. He added a tetanus booster and a dressing and the man was ready to heave himself up and leave—but not before commenting on what had happened and on who Blake was.

'Bob's son, eh?' he said jovially. 'You sure don't take after your old man. I can't see Bob Samford pulling splinters out of anyone's toes—he'd be more likely driving them in. And Ronnie tells me you're here with your daughter. How about that? A whole new generation for Corella Valley Homestead. I'll tell the wife to bake a cake.'

And before Blake had a chance to rebut or even answer, he was hit by a slap on the back that made him stagger and the guy was gone.

Leaving him...speechless.

Blake Samford returns to the family property with daughter...

Not so much.

Maggie was cleaning up. She had her back to him. She didn't say a word.

He wanted to see her expression. He badly wanted to see her expression.

She'd better not be laughing.

'All finished,' Ronnie asked, opening the door so they could see through to Christopher. 'Chris wants to go home. Is he going back to your mum, Maggie, or will you take him back with you?'

'He'll need to come with me,' Maggie said doubtfully. 'Mum won't keep him quiet.'

'Then you'll need Liselle,' Ronnie decreed. She eyed Blake thoughtfully while she spoke, obviously planning ahead. 'At seventeen Liselle's more than competent to do some babysitting,' she told Blake. 'And she'll love getting away from her mother's weird music so she can do some serious study. Unless *you're* happy to stay home all the time.' She arched her eyebrows at Blake, and grinned.

'That's exactly what Blake should be doing,' Maggie retorted. 'He's recovering from appendicitis.'

'Really?' Ronnie was bug-eyed. 'You've come home to recover? Isn't that nice.'

'I've come home... I've come *back* to put the farm on the market,' he growled, and she grinned.

'That sounds more like your dad. But you're going to be useful while you do it, which isn't like your dad at all. So... Christopher and Liselle...they won't fit in that tiny apartment of yours, Maggie.'

'Christopher can share my bed. You know we do that when any of them are ill. Liselle can sleep on the sofa.'

'I've seen your sofa,' Ronnie said darkly. 'Charity-shop reject if ever I saw one. Poor Liselle.' Then she looked—archly—at Blake. 'Your house, though, has more bedrooms—and more beds—than you can poke a stick at. If you're going to be useful, why not be properly useful? Let Liselle and Christopher stay in your part of the house. Maggie won't even go through your door except to dust, and it's always seemed such a waste.'

'Ronnie,' Maggie snapped. 'You know—'

'I know you've made a huge effort to get away from your family and I know why,' Ronnie said. 'But this wouldn't be you taking them in. It'd be Dr Blake taking them in, in exchange for Liselle occasionally looking after his baby. She can't get to school but she needs to study. I suspect she'll get more study done at your place than at your mother's.' Then, as Maggie looked doubtful, she said, more gently, 'Surely your mum can cope with just Peter and Susie?'

'I guess...' Maggie said slowly. 'I worry about Pete—those mates of his are wild but he has two new computer games he's obsessed with, and he's promised... And Susie'll be fine. She spends her time with the little girl next door. But—'

'Then there you are,' Ronnie said, beaming, refusing to listen to buts. 'Problem solved. Corella Homestead will have two adults and three kids. It's built for more but it's a start.'

'Ronnie, it's Blake's house.'

'But he's helping,' Ronnie said, pseudo innocent. 'It's a flood. Everyone helps in a flood. Isn't that right, Dr Samford?'

Open his house up, Blake thought, floundering. To three kids and one nurse? This hadn't been in the contract when he'd taken Maggie in as a tenant.

The house was built for more.

He thought of the house as he remembered it, exquisitely furnished by his mother. It still was, even though the furnishings were long faded. She'd set up all the bedrooms for guests who'd never come—one hint of his father's temper had been enough to drive them away.

He had five bedrooms, plus the tiny apartment that was Maggie's.

What harm in letting them be used?

Letting a family into his life…

Don't be dramatic, he told himself harshly, and another voice in his head said it would diffuse the situation. He wouldn't be stuck with one baby. He didn't need to bond. With a house full of people Ruby would be just one more.

'She's starting to fret,' Ronnie told him, and before he could demur she'd handed Ruby over, an armful of needy baby. 'Get out of here. Go home and feed your baby. Maggie, your wagon's full. You want me to go and fetch Liselle and bring the kids' gear over?'

'Blake hasn't even said yes yet,' Maggie said, a trifle desperately, and Ronnie put her hands on her hips and fixed him with a schoolmarm look.

'He hasn't either,' she said. 'So what's it to be, Dr Samford? Do you want me to fetch Liselle, or can you look after your baby all by yourself? She does baby-sitting for pocket money. She's studying for her university entrance exams. She has Maggie for a sister. She's good.'

'But Maggie herself...' he said, feeling helpless.

'Maggie's busy,' Ronnie snapped, glancing at Maggie. 'It's Liselle or nothing. And you might be generous. You don't have to be like your father, you know.'

'That's blackmail,' Maggie retorted, and Ronnie grinned.

'I know but it's working. Look at his face.'

And of course it was. *You don't have to be like your father...*

It was a powerful statement.

The valley was flooded. These were emergency conditions. A man had to pull his weight.

By letting a family into his life?

He didn't do family.

He was holding family in his arms.

'Fine,' he said, and Ronnie's grin widened.

'That's very gracious. You might say fine and mean it. Liselle's lovely and almost as competent as her sister. Christopher's fun. Maggie's magnificent. You're getting a very good deal, Dr Samford.'

'Fine,' he repeated, but this time he managed a weak smile. 'Let's do it.' He met Maggie's gaze and for the first time he realised she was looking almost as trapped as he was.

She was Maggie the magnificent, he thought—who also didn't do family. Or who didn't want to. She was Maggie who was more trapped than he was.

'Fine,' he said for the third time. 'We can do this, can't we, Maggie? For a week or so... For a week or so we can put up with anything.'

CHAPTER FIVE

BEFORE they left the clinic Blake took basic X-rays of Ruby's legs—enough to confirm what he needed to know. Then they went back to the homestead, with Blake taking what he needed with him.

Ruby's feet needed urgent attention. The X-rays showed there was no underlying complication, but at birth the tissues were soft and pliable and every day that passed meant manipulation would be harder and the treatment longer. By six months she'd be facing surgery, but at three weeks of age there was still time for the feet to be manoeuvred into the right position.

Maggie settled Christopher and Liselle into the bedrooms closest to her part of the house. He listened to their amazement at the opulence of his parents' former life while he did what he'd needed to since last night.

He did a careful, thorough examination of Ruby's feet.

A full CT scan of her feet would be good, but that meant evacuation. He could scarcely justify using emergency services when he felt sure the X-rays had shown enough. But there were other factors at play. If he accepted evacuation with Ruby and he went with her, it seemed a statement that he wasn't ready to make. That she somehow belonged to him. But if he didn't leave with her, if he sent her away on her own, that meant welfare. Foster-parents. Losing control.

No. Not yet. For some strange reason he was starting to feel that, whatever this little girl's future was, he wanted a say in it.

Since last night he'd been holding her, feeding her, cradling her, and somehow she was starting to change him. She was starting to make him feel as he'd never expected to feel.

He and Miriam had never talked about having children. Children weren't on their horizon. Now, though, as he held Ruby, as he felt her tiny head nuzzle into the crook of his neck, searching for the security of his warmth and his strength, he felt his world shift a little.

The thought kept coming back…the memory of the tiny girl he'd seen once when he'd been six years old.

She'd been wailing and he'd wanted to do something. He'd wanted to shout at the adults to stop fighting and make the baby better.

He hadn't realised it had had such an impact, but now, all these years later, this baby was in his hands, and maybe he could help this time.

To make her better?

Maggie had thrust this baby at him. She expected him to help.

She wasn't with him now. She was caught up settling Christopher, but it felt like she was right here, watching.

Judging?

Do no harm. That was the first principle of medicine. He examined the X-rays and was satisfied. He carefully manipulated Ruby's tiny, twisted feet and he grew more and more certain that this was straight congenital talipes equinovarus, with no other factors coming into play.

There was no major deformity—it had just been the way she'd lain in utero, her feet twisted and gradually setting in a position that, if left untreated, would cause lifelong problems.

He'd set her on Maggie's cashmere rug in the middle of his bed. She'd just been fed but she wasn't asleep. It almost seemed like she was enjoying him playing with her feet, gently massaging, gently manipulating.

Her eyes were huge. She was up to focussing, but not smiling. He thought, though, that she was almost there.

He was examining her feet but he was also trying to make her smile.

'Five weeks,' Maggie said from the door, and he started like he'd been caught stealing. Trying to steal a smile?

'What…?'

'Babies are generally five weeks old until you can reliably say the smile's not wind. But not your baby, of course.' She grinned. 'Every parent thinks their baby's far, far smarter and it's not wind at all. So what's the prognosis?'

Every parent…

The words hung. He should refute them. He did, in his head, but he didn't say it out loud.

It was something to do with the way Ruby was looking up at him. The contact was fleetingly—her focus was short lived—but he had established eye contact.

Part of him wanted to say, *I am not this child's parent*, but to do that when he'd been trying to make her smile…

'They twist your heartstrings, don't they?' Maggie said gently. 'Family. I have Christopher next door. He's settling to sleep and my heart's only just beginning to beat again.'

And Christopher was twelve, Blake thought. Twelve years of heartstrings. And for Maggie that was multiplied by eight.

He couldn't begin to comprehend that sort of commitment.

'Will the other two be okay with their mother? Pete and Susie?'

'You mean should I bring them here, too?' she asked wryly. 'Um, no. Mum'd come then, too, and Dad and his girlfriend might well decide why not come as well, and where would you be then?'

He stopped looking at Ruby. He looked...stunned. How many Tildens?

'Don't worry,' she told him, and grinned. 'Your dad did you a favour. The whole district knows the Samfords are mean and grumpy. I doubt Mum'll dare to come close—she doesn't care enough about Christopher to try. But she's not a terrible mother, if that's what you're worrying about. She doesn't drink or belt the kids. She just goes about making dandelion tea or goat's-milk balm or practising her latest yoga moves while the kids do what they like. I think they'll be safe enough—and I'm here as back-up.'

'So I don't get your whole family under my roof?'

'Heaven forbid,' she said, quite lightly but he could hear a whole depth of emotion behind those words. 'So you're tackling Ruby's feet. Do you want help?'

And here she was again, practical Maggie, moving in to do what was necessary—and then moving out again.

He was starting to see, very clearly, exactly how and why those boundaries had been put in place.

'I brought back the things I need,' he told her.

'I saw you collecting them from the clinic. Like what?'

'The makings for casts,' he told her, going back to massaging the little girl's feet. 'I'm sure this is straight-forward congenital talipes. See how I can move them? It's not causing her pain when I manipulate—the tis-sue's still incredibly pliable. The trick is to get the feet into the right position before we lose that pliability. Which is now.

'What we do is manipulate the feet back as far as we can, then apply casts. We leave the casts on for a week, then remove them and do the same thing again. We're inching her feet into correct position. The majority of cases can be corrected in six to eight weeks. Before we apply the last plaster cast we'll probably need to cut the Achilles tendons—an Achilles tenotomy—but that's a small procedure, nothing like the drama of a torn Achil-les tendon in an adult. But that's weeks away.'

'You mean…she'll be cured within a few weeks?'

'They'll be back in position then, but if left they'll re-vert. She'll need to wear a brace for twenty-three hours a day for three months and then at night-time for three to four years. She may end up with slightly smaller feet than she otherwise would, and her feet might not be ex-actly the same size, but by the time she goes to school she'll be essentially normal.'

'Wow,' Maggie breathed. 'That's awesome. I learned about talipes in training but I've never seen it. I was imagining disability for life.'

'I imagine that's what Wendy thought, too,' Blake said grimly.

'Are you going to tell her?' She hesitated. 'You know,

if Wendy thought she had a normal baby girl she might not have abandoned her.'

'I've thought of that.'

He'd also thought… He could phone her. Come and get your daughter because she's normal.

He raked his hair and thought about it some more. He looked down at his niece and he thought…

Deformed rat. The vindictiveness of what had been said. The bruise on her shoulder. And Wendy hadn't stood up for her.

'Not yet,' he said, and it came out harshly. 'Let's see if she misses her first.'

She'd have to make some effort, he thought. Make some contact. For him to hand this little one back to a pair who'd tossed her aside…

'You're falling in love with her,' Maggie said on a note of discovery and he thought…he thought…

Actually, he thought nothing. The statement left him stunned, like all the air had been sucked from the room.

Love.

What sort of statement was that?

He gazed down at the baby and while he he was looking at her thought he saw a tiny flicker of a smile.

'Wind,' Maggie said.

'It was a smile.'

'See,' Maggie said, and grinned. 'Parents.'

The air disappeared again. Parents. Family.

'So what do we do?' Maggie said, and there was another word.

We.

It made what was happening less terrifying, he thought.

'If you're happy to help…'

'Of course I am.'

'Unless I ask for babysitting.'

'That's not my job and you know it's not—Doctor,' she said primly. 'Let's keep this professional. So what's the plan?'

If she was to be professional, so could he. He looked down at those tiny feet and thought of what had to be done.

'The first manipulation aims to raise the first metatarsal, decreasing the cavus,' he told her, thinking it through as he spoke. 'We'll apply long leg casts to hold everything in position after the manipulation. You had everything we needed back in the clinic. Are you treating greenstick fractures yourself?'

'Hopefully not, but if I have to I will. We can't depend on evacuation. That's why the X-ray machine.'

'It's great for us that it's there. It makes me confident of what we're dealing with, and I can feel pretty much what I need to feel now. We'll get the feet into position and in casts. In a week we take them off. The next manipulations involve abduction of the forefoot with counter-pressure on the neck of the talus. Carefully. You don't pronate—and you never put counterpressure on the calcaneus or the cuboid.'

'I promise I won't,' she said—and she grinned. 'Doctor. Whatever calcaneus or cuboids are. Wow, isn't Ruby lucky to have an orthopod as an uncle?'

'I wouldn't call Ruby lucky,' he said grimly.

'I don't know,' Maggie said, suddenly thoughtful. 'If you'd told me a week ago that being born into the Samford family was lucky I'd have said you had rocks in your head—for all this place is worth a fortune. But now…I'm seeing a seriously different Samford and I'm impressed.'

'Don't be,' he growled. 'I'm out of here in a week.'

'So you're being nice for a week?'

'Until the bridge is safe.'

'Well, then,' Maggie said briskly, 'tell me what you need to do and we'll start doing it. If Ruby and I only have a week of niceness, we'd best make the most of it.'

The procedure to manipulate and cast Ruby's legs was straightforward enough, but it was also enough to show Maggie that in Blake she had a seriously skilled operator.

This was one tiny baby. His fingers were as gentle as a mother's, fingering the tiny toes, carefully, gently massaging, moving, wiggling, taking all the time in the world so Ruby felt no pain. Instead she seemed to be enjoying it, lying back on pillows, wide awake, seemingly savouring the sensation of this big man caressing her twisted legs, playing with her—and smiling at her while he did it.

He'd be a good surgeon, Maggie thought with sudden perception. If she were an old lady with a broken hip, she'd like it to be this man treating her. She thought suddenly, Samford or not, this smile was not just for this baby.

He'd used it on Christopher who, terrifyingly reckless at the best of times, was usually a total wimp when it came to doctors and needles. Christopher was tucked up in bed, happy and safe, because of this man.

Ruby was having her legs encased in casts and she looked not the least bit perturbed. She looked as if she had total trust in Blake as well.

In a Samford.

In a man no one knew anything about.

Maggie reminded herself of that, over and over, as she handed Blake what he needed, as she held the little legs in position as Blake wound the dressings, as she watched as he took the first steps to make this little girl perfect.

And she thought… Uh-oh.

This was one sexy male, and there weren't a lot of sexy males in Maggie's orbit. She needed to keep a clear head and remember—this guy was a Samford. Son of the local squattocracy. She was a Tilden. Daughter of the local welfare bludgers.

As well as that, he was here for a week. She was here for life.

So she'd better stop what she was thinking right now, she told herself. Just because the man had the sexiest, most skilful hands and was smiling at Ruby with a smile to make a girl's toes curl…

Maggie couldn't understand why Ruby wasn't beaming back—but a girl had to keep her feet firmly on the ground and remember relative positions in the world. This guy was her landlord and she needed to stay professional and get back to her side of the wall, *now*.

But Liselle and Christopher were on this side of the wall and Blake would need her advice with Ruby so she'd be on his side of the wall at other times, and boundaries were blurring.

It was up to her to keep them in place—and stop looking at this guy's smile!

By the time they were finished, Ruby was fast asleep. So much for a traumatic medical procedure. She was snuggled on her pillows, dead to the world, sucking her fist and totally, absolutely contented with her lot.

As Maggie cleared the remains of the dressings, Blake looked down at his niece as if he didn't quite know what to do next.

'How about sleep?' Maggie suggested, and he looked at her like he'd forgotten she was there.

'She's already asleep.'

'You,' she said gently. 'Appendicitis. Recovery. I just bet your surgeon said get lots of rest.'

'He might have.' It was a grudging admission.

'Then sleep.'

'I need to move her,' he said, sounding helpless, and she grinned.

Ruby was on the left side of the bed. She took two pillows and tucked them against the edge so even if Ruby managed a roll—pretty much impossible at three weeks—she'd go nowhere.

'That leaves you the whole right-hand side of the bed,' she said. 'She'll sleep better knowing you're close. Babies sense these things.'

'Nonsense.'

It might be nonsense, Maggie thought, but she wasn't telling this guy that. What she was aiming for—what Ruby needed more than anything in the world—was for someone—anyone—to bond with her. To bond so tightly that they'd fight for her for life.

'There's lots of room for both of you,' she said briskly. 'Bed. Now! Would you like me to bring you a cup of tea? Toast?'

'No,' he said, sounding revolted. 'I'm not a patient.'

'But you're not fully healed,' she told him. 'And I'm treating you like the goose that lays the golden eggs. In you I have a qualified surgeon on my side of the river and there's no way I'm planning on letting you have a relapse. Bed. Now. Egg on toast, coming up.

'Maggie?'

'Yes' she said, and raised an enquiring brow—like an old-fashioned matron faced with an impertinent patient who should know better than to question her medical edicts.

'Never mind,' he said, and she grinned.

'Good boy. You just hop into bed with your baby and let Nurse Maggie judge what's best.'

And how was a man to respond to that?

Everyone seemed headed for a nap. Even Liselle had been shaken enough by the morning's events to want to snooze. She'd brought books to study but she was ensconced in one of Corella View's gorgeous, if faded, guest rooms, she had an entire double bed to herself and she couldn't resist.

'This place is fabulous, Mags,' she whispered as she snuggled into an ancient feather eiderdown and a pile of goosedown pillows. 'I could stay here for ever.'

'Blake's selling the house and he'll be gone in a week,' Maggie said, a bit too waspishly, and Liselle looked up at her in concern.

'Does that upset you?'

'I… No.'

'It means you'll come home to us,' Liselle said sleepily. 'That's good. I like sharing my bedroom with you.'

Maggie smiled at her—but she didn't mean that smile. Going home to her family…

But where else could she live in this valley that wasn't home? Blake had been charging her peppercorn rent in return for caring for the house and dogs. She was a mile away from her family, and that was about the extent of safe range. Today had proved that.

She left her sister to sleep, made herself tea and toast and went out to sit on the veranda.

It was starting to rain again.

She was sick to death of rain.

She was sick to death of this valley.

Actually, it wasn't true. She loved the valley. Her parents' time in the city had been a nightmare and she'd returned home with them feeling nothing but relief.

But she wanted to be free.

What would it be like, she wondered, to spend a couple of weeks lying on a beach somewhere it wasn't raining? Somewhere all by herself?

It couldn't happen. The kids needed all her spare income for their schoolbooks and extra expenses. The welfare payments her mother received could only go so far. They depended on her.

So no holidays for Maggie.

So you might as well quit whinging, she told herself, and glanced back at Blake's bedroom window as though he might have heard the thought.

She hoped he was asleep.

Her cellphone beeped. She checked it and winced. Old Ron Macy from up on the ridge had fallen and his ulcerated leg was bleeding. She needed to go.

But at least she had support. Blake was here, with Liselle as back-up.

She didn't even need to tell him she was leaving, she thought, and she thought back to last night, to Blake calmly handing over the baby to her. *Here you are, your problem.*

She couldn't help grinning. She could go now, and the whole household would be *his* problem.

Blackie was restless. The dogs had learned by now that the phone usually meant she had to go. He was whining and she knew why. She rubbed his ears and then she tiptoed through the house to Blake's bedroom and stealthily unlatched the door to Blake's bedroom. Thunderstorms were due. The forecast was horrendous, and Blackie was probably already hearing thunder in the distance.

If storms hit in earnest Blake would find himself with two dogs on his bed—or under his bed—but it'd be better than them turning themselves inside out with fear.

She was leaving Blake with baby and dogs and her siblings.

He was recovering from an appendectomy.

'He's a big boy,' she said, hardening her heart, but she didn't have to harden it too much. Blake was snuggled in bed while she had to brave the elements.

And then she thought she didn't mind this. A house full of people where she didn't have responsibility.

It was sort of like a holiday, she told herself—only different.

Blake woke up and Ruby was wailing, two dogs had their noses in his face and two wan kids were huddled in the doorway.

And the sky was falling.

Okay, it wasn't quite, but that's what it sounded like. It was either dusk or the storm was so bad the light had disappeared—the natural light, that was, because the lightning was almost one continuous sheet. There was no gap between the lightning and thunder. The rain was pounding so hard on the roof it almost felt as if the house itself was vibrating.

He must have been tired to have slept until now, but suddenly he was wide awake. Wet dog noses would do that to you. Both the dogs were shivering wrecks. The next bout of thunder boomed, and Ruby's cry turned to a yell—and the kids from the door saw he was awake and suddenly they were right in bed with him.

Dogs, too. Why not? This was a huddle of quivering terror and he was in the middle.

'Um…it's just a thunderstorm, guys,' he managed, trying to wake up, and in response they cringed closer. He moved over and lifted Chris nearer so his bandaged leg wasn't squashed. With Ruby on the other side of him he was practically a Blake sandwich. 'You should be in your own beds.'

'We don't like thunderstorms,' Liselle said. 'And Maggie's gone.'

Gone. For one appalling moment he had visions of Maggie doing what Ruby's parents had done—cutting and running. Heading over the threatened bridge, taking off for Queensland, leaving him with Ruby and Christopher and Liselle and Blackie and Tip.

'There….there's a note on the kitchen table,' Liselle quavered. 'Mr Macy on the ridge has fallen over and she had to go up and put a dressing on his leg. She says she'll be back by teatime but if I'm worried about Christopher then talk to you.'

'You shouldn't be worried,' Christopher said, not very stoutly. 'I'm okay.'

Except he was scared and he was hurting, Blake

thought wryly. He shouldn't have tried bearing weight on that leg.

'The dogs are scared, too,' Liselle whispered, and the dogs whimpered in response. Blackie edged closer, edging around Christopher, her ancient nose pushing his chest—and suddenly she got what she wanted. The bedclothes were pushed back a bit and she was right down the foot of the bed so she was a mound of dog, like a wombat in a burrow, nestled hard against his feet.

Christopher giggled.

Ruby's wails grew louder.

Way back in Sydney, a really long time ago, Blake had wondered what he should do during his enforced convalescence. He had an excellent apartment with views over the harbour. Miriam was there in the evenings. He had a housekeeper to keep the place in order—everything he wanted. More. There were other medics—colleagues—in his apartment block and he wasn't left alone. His mates dropped in at all hours— *just to keep you company.* The decision to come here had been made partly for practical reasons but also because for some reason he was craving privacy.

Privacy had always been an issue for him. He'd learned early, in his parents' conflicted household, to disappear into his own world, and as an only child, even when his mother had remarried someone more reasonable, he'd known he'd been expected to fade into the background.

Isolation kept him out of emotional drama. It was a defence. Maybe that's why he and Miriam got on so well together—they instinctively respected personal space.

But he'd been at the same hospital for eight years now

and lots of his colleagues no longer respected that space. Hence he'd decided that coming here was an option.

'I...I'll make Ruby's bottle, shall I?' Liselle quavered, and he looked at the slight seventeen-year-old who was obviously just as nervous as her brother.

'I'll get it,' he said, and swung back the covers, dislodging Tip in the process, who cast him a look of reproach. Then the next thunderclap boomed and the dog was down under the covers with Blackie.

'Maggie said you had to rest,' Liselle said.

'I'll rest. I'll get the bottle first.'

'And then you'll come back to us?'

To us. To a bed that was big but was now decidedly crowded. Two kids, two dogs, one baby.

'Yes,' he said, goaded.

'Maggie should be here,' Christopher whispered.

'Maggie wouldn't fit,' he retorted. 'You lie still and don't move that leg.' And then he went to fill his niece's very vocally broadcast requirements.

Maggie was heading home, feeling guilty.

So what was new? She'd felt guilty all her life. From the time her mother had made it very clear she needed her, anything Maggie had ever wanted to do for herself had been wasted time.

Now...she'd sort of wanted to stay in the big house and play with one baby and watch one guy bond with that baby, but she'd had no choice but to head up the valley to see Roy Macy. His leg was a mess but there was no way he'd come to her. His neighbour would have driven him but she knew exactly how he'd respond. 'No, don't fuss, leave it be.'

Left alone it'd turn into a septic mess, so good old Maggie had headed out into the storm and fixed it.

And left Blake with her responsibilities.

No. Ruby was his responsibility.

Why did it feel like she was hers?

Because she was used to feeling guilty. She'd sort of wanted to stay—but she'd felt guilty about leaving.

'I should have loaded Christopher into the car with me,' she said out loud. 'Just so I wouldn't feel like this.'

But she still would have. Guilt was unavoidable. Baby Ruby had crept round her heart like a small, need-ful worm and no matter how much she told herself she was nothing to do with her, she knew it wasn't true.

'It's only until the river level drops,' she told herself, looking bleakly out into the driving rain. 'Then they're out of here. I don't know what he'll do with Ruby, but it's not my problem. Not My Problem. Blake Samford is on his own. Just let the rain stop. Just let the river drop before I fall any deeper for one baby...'

And for the man who went with her?

'I'm not attached to Blake,' she said, astonished at the places her thoughts were taking her. 'As if. Yes, he's gorgeous, but as if I have time...'

Time to notice how gorgeous he was?

She'd noticed.

She did not have time. She did not have the incli-nation.

Liar. Of course she had the inclination, only what chance was there ever for a love life for her when there were still four kids almost totally dependent on her?

'You'll start singing sad love songs next,' she told herself dryly. 'It's just the way things are. Get over it. And stop thinking of Blake Samford's body. Blake

Samford's smile. Blake Samford's hands as he cradles his tiny niece...'

Whoa.

'The sooner the river drops the better for all concerned,' she muttered, and then she paused.

The thunder had been booming almost continuously since she'd left home and it was still booming, but over the noise she could hear...something else.

It was a roar, building from maybe imagined to real, growing more real by the moment.

Instinctively she swung the car away from the river road, up the slope of the valley.

To a place where she could see the massive force of water bursting down the valley as the dam upstream gave way.

To a place where she could see the bridge disappear in a maelstrom of rushing water, and the shallow slopes of the valley disappear within it.

CHAPTER SIX

'The heifers…'

Blake was still in bed. He'd heard the bridge go. One part of him thought he should go and investigate the noise. The other part thought this farm was high and safe, he'd just got Ruby to sleep, the kids were settled, and there wasn't a lot he could do about a collapsing bridge.

Until Maggie burst in.

'The dam's burst upstream,' she said. She sounded exhausted, as though she'd run. She was soaking, her shirt was almost transparent, her curls were dripping round her shoulders, and the drips were making a puddle around her. 'Your heifers are trapped.'

'*My* heifers?' He didn't get it.

'Your calves,' she snapped. 'Your dad's yearlings. The water's come up too fast. I thought the bridge might go but not the dam. They're in the paddock on the far side of the road from the river, but the road's now under water. So's most of their paddock. There's a rise in the middle but it only holds half a dozen and the rest are already being forced to swim. If I can get them away from the rise, I can drive them to higher ground, but all they can see is the stupid island that's only going to let six or so survive. Liselle can't swim. She's scared of deep water and no one else is close enough to help. I know you're recovering but I don't have a choice. We can't let them drown. I need your help and I need it now.'

With Liselle left in charge of Christopher and Ruby— there was no choice but to depend on her—they drove the tractor to the calves' paddock.

Actually, Maggie drove the tractor. Blake stood on the footplate and hung on, feeling like a city kid, totally out of his depth.

He hadn't been on a tractor since he'd been six. He was riding as sidekick to save his cattle. He was Maggie's sidekick. He felt ludicrous.

Then he saw the calves and any temptation he had to laugh died right there.

They were in deathly trouble.

'The water's still rising,' Maggie whispered as she cut the engine. 'Oh, dear God, they'll drown.'

He stared out at the mass of water, at the terrified calves, at the impossibility of what lay before them. The calves could swim—most of them were swimming now—but they were all focussed on one thing and one thing only—the tiny island that was growing smaller while they watched.

'It's too late,' Maggie moaned. 'I thought I might be able to wade out there and drive them off. We could hack a hole in the fence higher up and you could guide them through. Once they see any of their mates on dry land they'll follow. But neither of us can swim out there and herd cows at the same time.'

They couldn't. Even if they were incredible swimmers, to swim and make cows follow directions would be impossible. Blackie was with them but a dog was useless as well.

There was a deathly silence while man, woman and dog watched the heifers struggle.

Then…

'The canoe,' Blake said, almost as an extension of his thoughts. All his focus was on the heifers. These calves were strong but how long until the first slipped under?

'Canoe?' Maggie's voice was a desolate whisper, but Blake's thoughts were firming.

'There's a two-man canoe under the house, or there was last time I was here. It's ancient. I've done some kayaking. I can handle it. But, Maggie, I can't do this alone. My stitches need protecting, plus I know zip about herding cows. But I don't think I'll pull my stitches paddling. Not if I don't push myself.'

'What are you talking about?'

'I need to get the canoe up on the tractor. That'll require both of us lifting, but Liselle can help. We need to get it here and launched. Then…if we stick Blackie in the front, do you reckon you could persuade him to bark?'

'He'll bark on command.' And Maggie was with him.

'So we could get the canoe amongst them with a barking dog. If you told me what to do herding-wise…'

'Yes!' she said, and the desolation was gone. It was practically a shout. Maggie was suddenly a woman of action—a woman with a plan where there'd been no hope. She was already swinging herself back onto the tractor. 'What are we waiting for?'

It took them ten minutes to get back to the calves. Liselle had come out when they'd yelled and had helped heave the decrepit canoe out from under the house and get it up on top of the tractor in the driving rain. Somehow Maggie managed to drive with Blake holding the canoe steady—or as steady as possible, which wasn't very steady at all.

He had internal stitches, he thought ruefully. If he had been his patient, he'd tell him he was out of his mind.

Eighty drowning calves didn't give him that option.

Maggie was gunning the tractor, not worrying about bumps, cutting corners, just going for it.

'Your other career's as a racing-car driver?' he demanded faintly, and she grinned.

'Eat your heart out. Oh, Blake, they're still there.'

She'd rounded the bend, the road disappeared under water and they could see them again, swimming in panicked circles around that tiny rise, fighting for a foothold.

In seconds the tractor was stopped. They shoved the canoe off—much easier getting it off than getting it on—then pushed it through the submerged road gate and into the water.

Maggie had brought bolt-cutters. As he climbed aboard and organised the paddle, she heaved the bolt-cutters in, lifted Blackie in as well, and slid in herself after that.

'Can you take me round the back?'

To the far side of the paddock? He could see why she needed to go there. The fence there was also under water but beyond the fence the land rose sharply. The dry land beyond was obvious, as it wasn't obvious where they were now. For the last couple of hundred yards they'd driven over a road a foot deep in water.

'I'll cut the fence there,' she said. 'I'll get them out if you and Blackie can scare them into swimming in my direction. They're terrified, but they'll follow a leader and they're not dumb like sheep. If you get the canoe near the island and shoo the calves there into the water they'll look for the next best option. Which will be me and a cut fence and dry land behind me. We can do this. Go.'

He went.

He'd had his appendix out a week ago.

She was under no illusions that this man should not be pushing a canoe through floodwater. He should be lying around in bed, convalescing.

She should never have asked him to help.

But the alternative had been to let eighty calves drown. She hadn't been able to do it, and neither could he.

Like he couldn't send away a baby?

He was soft in the middle, Maggie thought, but outside he looked as tough as the heavy-duty bolt-cutters she was holding.

He was wearing fawn chinos and a soft cotton shirt, with the top buttons undone and the sleeves rolled up to the elbows. He'd kicked off his shoes. The water was plastering his shirt to his body, delineating every muscle. His dark hair was soaked from the rain. Rivulets of water were running down his face but he wasn't brushing them away. He was totally focussed on what he was doing.

He looked like a warrior, she thought, suddenly and inappropriately. He looked lean and hard and dangerous.

She had a sudden flash of what this man would be like as a surgeon. She'd done a theatre stint in training;

she'd watched men like this at work. They took lives into their hands…

She'd never been able to figure how they found the courage to take that first cut, but she could see it now. Surroundings were forgotten. Pain was forgotten—and he must be in pain—a week after an appendectomy it'd hurt even to laugh, and here he was, slicing the old-fashioned paddle through the water with total rhythm, total focus—as if he was paddling for the Olympics and not for cows.

'Blake…'

'Yes?' His response was clipped, hard, sharp, a surgeon in Theatre, wanting to know why a nurse was interrupting. He was focussed totally on what he was doing, but not so focussed that he forgot outside complications were possible.

She wanted to help. The stupid canoe only had one paddle. She could only sit like a princess, in the bow of the boat, holding Blackie.

'Steer well around the island,' she managed. 'I don't want them panicked further before I've cut the fence.'

'Fair enough.' The canoe's course altered slightly, and she thought that was no mean feat either. This canoe was ancient and high and wobbly. There were all sorts of obstacles in the water and the water itself was a mass of whirls and eddies. She was sitting as still as she could, as centred as she could, holding Blackie tightly as if by sheer concentration she could help this man.

He must work out. He must…she didn't know…run? He must do something to keep that lean body whip-sharp. His face was a study in concentration as he sliced across the current, and she could only guess how hard it must be.

She glanced across at the calves and saw one slip

from the island, then get pushed under by another struggling to find purchase.

She held her breath but it surfaced again.

Eighty young cows, depending on one ailing surgeon.

Maggie, depending on one ailing surgeon.

Finally they reached the far fence. The water here was only eighteen inches deep. As soon as she could grab the fence wires, she was out of the boat, steadying her bolt-cutters.

'Stay,' she snapped at Blackie. 'Sit. Stay.'

He was a great dog. He whined but he stayed in the bow as Blake turned the canoe and headed back out to the middle.

She hacked into the wires with a strength born of desperation then, as the last wire fell away, she headed out of the water, up the rise, so hopefully the calves could see the gap in the fencing, and see her standing on dry land beyond.

'Oi,' she yelled, trying to make the panicked calves look at her. 'Oi, Oi, Oi, Oi, Oi.'

Blake was behind the island now, cutting his way through the calves in the water, heading for the few on dry land.

'Speak,' she yelled to Blackie, and Blackie did just that.

He barked and barked, while Maggie yelled, and Blake manoeuvred his shaky little craft behind the herd, beached himself on the island, stood on the tiny piece of dry land and proceeded to remove the calves' last place of refuge.

He knew nothing about calves. They knew nothing about him, and maybe that was a good thing because they reacted to him and to the barking dog as if they were worse threats than the water.

The calves headed away from him, away from their target island. He was waving his arms like an idiot and Blackie was barking, so they launched themselves in the opposite direction—and suddenly they were swimming towards Maggie.

Maybe they knew her voice, or maybe she'd herded more cows than he had in his lifetime, but the calves seemed to be instinctively turning toward her.

If he was a calf, he'd turn toward Maggie.

There was a stupid thought.

He was hurting. He was standing on the only piece of dry land for fifty yards. He was waving and shouting like a fool—and he still had time to think... Think that Maggie was gorgeous?

She was wearing faded jeans and a shirt that had become almost transparent. She was soaked to the skin. Her chestnut curls were dripping around her shoulders, plastered to her face. Her feet were bare, she was yelling louder than he was...and the calves were heading toward her. And he knew why.

What was beautiful about her?

Bone structure? Facial features? Sense of fashion?

Um...none of those things, though the freckles and the gorgeous curves surely helped.

But it was the sheer courage of her. The way she tackled life head on.

The way she'd refused to care for his baby?

But she would care. He knew instinctively that she would. If he hadn't been here, if she hadn't figured he was more than capable of caring for his niece, then he knew she'd have taken her on, as she'd taken in Christopher last night, and Liselle, and he knew there only had to be a drama and she'd have more people sharing her tiny living space. That he'd offered to share his side of the house had seemed a blessing and a surprise to her. He wondered how many dramas she'd had since she'd moved into his tiny housekeeper's residence—but he knew without being told that without his urging, she'd never have let her life edge through the dividing door into his home.

Only it wasn't his home. It was a mausoleum of a homestead, redecorated in the fashion of the time by his mother and not touched since.

This morning, in bed, it had felt more like a home than it ever had in his childhood.

Because of Maggie?

'Oi!'

Her yelling had grown more insistent, riveting his attention totally on what was happening. The calves were shoving together in the water, seeking safety in numbers, swimming as a herd, but they weren't heading totally in the right direction.

They hadn't seen the gap in the fence.

Okay, boy, he thought grimly. Back in your boat.

'Are you okay?' Maggie called, and he thought all this and she was remembering his stitches.

'Blackie and I are fine,' he called. 'I'm bosun, he's cox. If I can just persuade these calves to join us, we'll be a crew.'

His side was hurting. Badly. What had his surgeon said? No stretching for six weeks. Ha. Block it out, he told himself, and he headed for the calves, paddling hard, cutting through the water, focussing doggedly on what he was doing rather than the pain in his side.

He was cutting the calves off from heading back to the island, herding them forward but sideways. He had to turn and turn again as the calves took fright and tried to scatter, but between them, yelling, barking, shoving the canoe at them, he and Blackie made them swerve and kept going.

They were exhausted, he thought, and he was expecting at any minute that one would slip under. They had to see…

The fence was about four feet high, so the gap was obvious. If they could see it they'd be safe.

'Oi,' Maggie yelled again, and Blackie barked, and he veered the canoe behind them—and the calf in the lead lifted its head as if casting round for one last desperate chance…

And saw.

And then the entire herd was surging through the gap. Maggie was stepping aside, the calves were through, rising out of the floodwater, finding their feet, scrambling onto dry land.

The calves bolted upwards as if the water was chasing them. As they realised they were safe they turned into calves again. They looked like kids after a scary adventure, one they could boast about to their mates. A few kicked their heels like this was fun, yay, dry land, safe.

He was still paddling. He reached the gap and Maggie started pulling the canoe out of the water almost before he was out of it.

'I can…' he said, reaching down, but she slapped his hands away.

'You shouldn't.' And he saw she was weeping. 'I should never have let you. You'll have burst all sorts of internal stitches. I didn't realise until I saw you… how hard it was…that paddling was awful… I should never have let you do it and you'll have killed yourself and it's my fault.'

Okay, let's get rid of the drama, he decided. She'd been frightened enough for one day. He'd take himself out of the equation.

'I suspect I've killed my phone,' he admitted, hauling it out of his soaking back pocket and looking at it with apprehension. 'But otherwise I'm alive. And pretty damned pleased with myself.' Then, despite her objections, he helped her haul the canoe to dry land. What harm would another pull be when there'd been so many?

But she still looked terrified. She still looked…like the sky was about to fall.

He tried not to notice. He looked at the calves, turning into kids again. Then, because he couldn't help himself, he looked again at this bedraggled slip of a woman, standing with the rain mingling with her tears, and he felt something change inside him…

Something he'd never felt before.

She was gorgeous, he thought. She was simply, unutterably, indescribably gorgeous.

She'd put everything she knew into saving these calves, and now she was feeling guilty. Guilty for saving calves that weren't even hers. Guilty for risking hurting him. Guilty even for his damaged phone?

She was unbelievable.

And before he knew what he intended, before he even realised what he was doing, he'd tugged her into his arms and held her close.

She'd been terrified, and in truth he'd been the same.

Out of his comfort zone. Hurting. Worried the dratted calves would drown.

It wouldn't hurt to hold her, to comfort her—and to take comfort in return.

But…was this about comfort?

He held her close, closer, and he felt the thump of her heartbeat against his, and thought maybe it wasn't.

'Yay for us,' she whispered, and her voice was muffled by his chest. 'You were great. Are you sure you're not hurt?

'I'm not hurt,' he said, and then as her heart kept on thumping, he thought it had been terror for him as well as terror for the calves that was making her heart race.

He cupped her chin with his hand and tilted her face so he could force her to look at him. Her eyes were huge. Her eyes still held remorse and fear.

'I'm fine,' he said. 'I'm great and you're terrific.'

And then, as she kept gazing up at him, he couldn't resist.

He kissed her.

One minute she was feeling like she was losing eighty calves and ripping Blake's stitches to bits and there wasn't a thing she could do about it.

The next she was being kissed so thoroughly, so amazingly that there wasn't a thing she could do about that either.

Not that she wanted to.

If she wished, she could pull away. He wasn't holding her so tightly, so strongly that she couldn't tug back and get him to release her.

But how could she tug back when she was being kissed…like this.

Fire meeting fire.

Fire?

How could she be feeling heat, when she was cold and dripping and shaking from reaction to what had just happened? There was no answer and even as she asked the question, she forgot it.

She forgot everything.

There was only the feel of this man's mouth. The fire, the heat, the strength and warmth and...the maleness of him.

There'd been too few men in Maggie's life. Too little opportunity. Too little time.

This was hardly an opportunity, hardly the time, but there was no way she was pulling back.

Her lips opened, seemingly of their own accord, welcoming him, wanting him.

Wanting him?

Yes. She did want him. Her body seemed to mould itself to him all by itself. Her breasts crushed against him, their wet shirts disappeared almost to nothing, so nothing seemed between them but white-hot want.

His mouth was exploring hers. His hands were in the small of her back, tugging her closer, and hers did the same to him. She was melting into him, dissolving, aching to be closer, closer, closer...

She'd never felt like this. She'd never dreamed she could feel like this. Her entire body was on fire, every sense screaming that here was her man, she was part of him, she belonged.

Maybe it was supposed to be a kiss of relief and of comfort. It was surely a kiss of need—both of them needed the assurance of human contact, that they were safe and life went on and they'd succeeded—but it was more than that.

It was a kiss that changed her. It was a kiss that made her feel as she'd never felt—as if every sense was suddenly alive.

Sleeping Beauty, wakened by a kiss?

Well, that was ridiculous.

There was a tiny part of her mind that was still analysing. It was like she was falling off a cliff and thinking as she fell, How am I feeling right now?

She was feeling pretty good, actually. No matter about the ground rushing up, she was feeling pretty amazing.

Where had this heat come from? What was making her feel like her entire body was sizzling, waking from slumber and turning into something she didn't know it was possible to be?

She was falling and she didn't care.

So far it was so wonderful.

How high was the cliff? How long could she stay in freefall, savouring this moment, the feel of him, the strength, the way his hands held her, the way she seemed totally enfolded, protected, frail even...

Strong Maggie, melting at a man's touch.

Strong Maggie, melting and loving it.

And then Blackie barked.

He'd done his bit. He was expecting praise. Expecting attention. Or maybe it was that his mistress was being mauled by a strange man and the dog was confused and wondering what he should do about it.

He barked again, and finally, achingly, Maggie tugged away.

Freefall over, she'd reached her destination. She almost expected to feel shattered. That was crazy but she did feel… Bruised? Dazed? Exposed?

Confused was the least of it.

'Well, that was unexpected,' Blake murmured, and something in his deep, growly voice said he was almost as confused as she was. 'Adrenalin, do you think?'

'Either that or it's something in the water,' she managed, and carefully turned away and looked up the hill.

The calves were settling. They were high up on the hill, and as they watched, a couple put their heads down and started to graze.

Back to life as they knew it.

Right, she told herself, trying not to feel breathless. Trying to make this strange, needy…*kissed*?…sensation go away. Trying to go back to life as she knew it. 'That's that fixed. Well done, us. And thanks, Blake, I could never have done it without you.'

'They're my cattle.'

'They haven't been your responsibility for a very long time.'

'Maggie?' He hadn't turned to watch the cows. He'd stayed watching her the whole time—which wasn't doing anything for the state of her discombobulation.

'Mmm?'

'They're my responsibility, and thank you,' he said. 'And thank you for the kiss. It was…'

'Nice,' she said hurriedly, before he could say anything more. 'It was very nice indeed, but there's no need for you to be worrying that I expect to take it further. We might be staying in the same house but there's a door with a lock between us.'

'And two kids and a baby.'

'That, too.' She hesitated. 'I don't know what came over me.'

'Over *us*.'

'Over us,' she repeated, though she wasn't sure where me and us separated in the kissing stakes. 'But…' She tried hard to get her feet on firm ground—a bit hard when she was standing in six inches of water. 'I…I have work to do. Are you sure you're okay? Can I check your scar?'

'No!'

'I didn't think so,' she said, and she managed a chuckle. 'But you would tell me if there was something wrong, wouldn't you?'

'Probably not.'

'That's reassuring.'

'I hurt,' he told her. 'But there's no piercing pain. I think I've pulled but not torn. Bruised but not broken. Should we take this canoe back over the far side and see if we can get it back up on the car?'

'Let's not,' she said faintly. 'For eighty calves I was prepared to let you risk it. Now I'm thinking of your stitches again. We'll secure it here in case it's needed again but that's it. I'll walk the long way round and bring the tractor home. You head over the rise and reach the house without getting even more wet.'

'Maggie…'

'Mmm?'

He stared down at her. She was adjusting the canoe, tying the rope to a fencepost.

She was suggesting—no, decreeing—they go their separate ways.

That was surely sensible. That's what this woman was. Sensible.

She was also vulnerable—and beautiful.

She was also saddled with kids and family and responsibility, chained to a life that was alien to everything he knew.

Maggie waded back to the tractor, skirting the worst of the high water.

The road was only a few inches underwater. They could never have headed the calves this way—to push them forward when all they could see was water would have been impossible—but the road was still safe enough to drive on.

She'd still be able to get back and forth to her clinic, she thought, which was just as well.

She'd be needed.

The locals had never thought the dam could burst. She made a fast mental list of the houses close to the river and thought none would be so close to water level that they'd be flooded. The early settlers had been wary of floods and had built accordingly. There'd have been more than just Maggie and Blake desperately trying to move stock in a hurry, though. People would be doing stupid things, putting themselves at risk.

As Blake had put himself at risk.

She should never have asked it of him. The man was a week out from an appendectomy, and for him to manoeuvre the canoe as he had…

He could sue her, she thought grimly, but then she thought, They were his calves. He could have said let them drown.

He couldn't—as he couldn't evacuate Ruby and hand her over to others.

Her thoughts were running off at crazy tangents. She

was thinking of the way he held Ruby—of the way he looked at her. There were things going on in Blake's background she had no idea of. He looked at Ruby and he almost looked…hungry.

She grinned at that, thinking, Nope, big bad wolf wasn't the image she was going for.

So, hungry for what?

What sort of childhood had this man had? His mother had been glamorous and flighty—the local gossip was that she'd married for money. His father had been an oaf. Where had that left him?

And why had he kissed her?

She put her fingers to her lips as she walked, thinking they felt…different.

Why had he kissed her?

'Well, who wants to know?' She said it out loud and kicked a spray of water up in front of her. 'You? You know already. We thought the calves would drown, we got them out, and in moments of triumph, people kiss.'

Only it hadn't been like that. At least, it hadn't been like that for her.

'And that's because you're close to a thirty-year-old spinster without a life of your own,' she snapped, and kicked up more water. 'That's because every minute of every day is taken up with your work or your family, and your hormones are telling you it's not enough.

'So what are you intending to do about it?'

She laughed at that, morosely, because some questions already had answers. Some questions weren't even worth asking.

What was she intending?

One big fat nothing.

She had a job. Almost half her pay went towards

helping the kids out with what they needed so they'd get the qualifications she had, tickets out of the valley, escape paths from the cloying demands of her mother. Apart from one tiny, tiny nest egg, the rest of her money went on living. Putting one foot in front of another. Doing her job and keeping the kids safe.

In a couple of weeks the water would be down and Blake would be gone. End of story.

But maybe, while he's here…

'Don't even think about it,' she told the silence, and she kicked so hard the water went up and over her, making her wetter than ever. 'He's my landlord and if he hasn't burst anything today he's a doctor who can help if I need him. Nothing more. Put yourself back in your box, Maggie, and stay there. Now.'

CHAPTER SEVEN

HE got back to the homestead—and there were more kids.

Plus Maggie's mother.

Liselle was on the veranda, clutching a sleeping Ruby, and looking almost as if she was holding her mother at bay.

'Dr Samford,' Liselle breathed when she saw him, and there was real relief in her voice. 'I...I didn't invite her.'

Then Maggie arrived. She pulled in through the gate, climbed from the tractor, squelched across and joined him—and looked at her mother.

'Mum,' she said blankly, and Barbie beamed. She was standing by an ancient family wagon. She hauled up the tailgate and lifted out a suitcase.

'This is lovely,' she said. 'I was so pleased Dr Samford's decided to share. Did you remember our living-room roof is leaking? I told you last week, Maggie, and you've done nothing about it. And now the dam's burst and the kids are scared.'

She was dressed as a hippy. Fiftyish, long, flowing skirt, beads everywhere, vivid dyed-blonde hair hanging past her shoulders.

Shudder territory.

And obviously Maggie thought so, too.

'You're not staying here,' she said, in a cold, dead voice that had Blake glancing at her sharply. She sounded like she was in pain.

'Well, I'm not staying in that house by myself.' Her mother's voice became shrill and accusing. 'You can't expect me to. I had to sleep in Susie's bed last night because there was a drip right by mine, and both the kids are whining for you.'

Susie verified the statement by sidling across to Maggie and tucking her hand in her big sister's.

Blake saw Maggie's shoulders slump.

She looked like a deer caught in headlights, he thought. She'd escaped her family, but her family had tracked her down.

'Can you carry my suitcase inside, Dr Samford?' Barbie said—and simpered.

It was her right to be looked after.

Blake looked at her and looked at Maggie. Barbie was a world away from the woman who'd been his own mother but there were similarities. He was sure she'd married his father for money and she'd gone on to marry three other men who were expected to look after her every whim. Right now she was in the States with yet another besotted lover.

Maggie's mother had never had the beauty or the style to attract lovers to obey her commands but the way she was looking at Maggie now, he knew the story. Maggie had been the servant. Maggie still was the servant.

No more. A line had to be drawn, and Maggie's face had him drawing it.

'Maggie's brothers and sisters are welcome to stay

until the waters recede,' he said. 'But no one else. The evacuation notice says that if anyone's worried, they can camp in the local hall. If the kids want to join you there, that's fine.'

'You're not separating me from my kids!'

'Of course I'm not.' Blake strode up the veranda steps and lifted Ruby from a stunned Liselle's arms. 'I'm not fussed if your kids stay here or not,' he said, in a bored voice that told her to take it or leave it. 'If Maggie wants them to, then that's fine. If you don't permit it, then that's fine, too. All I'm saying is that the invitation is for kids only. Sort it out between you. I need to feed Ruby.'

And he walked in the front door—on his side of the house—and closed the door behind him, leaving all the Tildens on the other side.

Maggie came to find him ten minutes later. He was in his kitchen, fixing formula. He had Ruby nestled in her drawer-cum-bed by the fire stove. He was feeling incredibly domestic.

He was also feeling like he'd been sucked into another world. Babies and kids and dogs and cows and mothers.

And Maggie.

She opened the kitchen door and it was all he could do not to drop the bottle he was holding and take her into his arms. He'd never seen a woman look so…caged.

'I'm so sorry,' she managed. 'But they all want to stay. I can't make them go with her.'

'She's not staying.' He made his voice flat, definite, sure. He spooned formula into the bottles and when he glanced at her again a little of the tension had eased.

'She thinks you mean it. She's not game to call your bluff.'

'It's no bluff. She walks in, I'll pick her up and throw her out.'

'Can…can I ask why?'

'Because she makes you cringe,' he said. 'That's good enough for me. I don't know what's gone on in your past, Maggie, but I know appalling parenting when I see it. I avoided my father and I continue to avoid my mother. You should be allowed to do the same. Has she gone?'

'Yes, but all the kids are here.'

'The whole eight?'

She managed a smile at that. 'No. Just four.'

'Then it's five, counting Ruby. We have ourselves a houseful.'

'Blake, I didn't mean to impose—'

'If you had meant to impose—like your mother certainly meant to impose—I would have sent you packing as well,' he told her, still concentrating on his bottles. Surgical precision was required. Ruby wasn't going to get anything but perfect milk on his watch. 'I extended the invitation, Maggie, not you,' he added. 'I can see the kids are scared and they need you. They're welcome to stay here, but only until the road is open again. This isn't open-ended.'

'You're fantastic.'

'I'm not,' he said shortly.

'Yes, you are,' she said, and her eyes misted. 'Heroic. Like you told Chris he was. But you've done more. You've saved him, you've saved your cows and now… you've taken in my whole family.'

'But you don't want them here.' It was a question, a guess—and it found its mark.

She stilled. She watched him, then watched her feet and took her time answering.

'I have this dumb dream,' she said at last. 'From the time I first remember, it's always been: "Maggie, watch your brother. Take Liselle for a walk. Stay home from school today because your father and I have a gig…" It's just…how it is. Mostly I accept it, only every now and then I dream that I'm backpacking round Europe, sipping kir in a café on the Left Bank in Paris, or watching the sunset over the Nile and having no one talk to me for hours on end.

'It's a dumb dream but it stays. When the kids are older, that's what I decided I'll do. Then recently— when Mum and Dad split—I realised they're getting dependent as well. I'm starting to be scared that after looking after their kids all my life I might end up looking after them.'

'It's not going to happen.'

'No,' she said softly. 'That's why I moved out. Blind terror, if you like. But the kids still need me. I'll probably end up going home.' She took a deep breath. 'But not tonight. Tonight you solved my problem for now. You let me care for the kids and you've forced Mum to be independent—and it didn't even have to be me who was nasty to do it. Plus you saved all those heifers. To watch them drown would have killed me. I should never have asked you but I couldn't bear not to. But now…'

She glanced down at Ruby, who was wide awake but not complaining yet. There was time. 'Now I'm checking your tummy,' she decreed. She motioned to the leather-covered bench at the side of the huge kitchen. 'Sit. Lie. I want to see.'

'There's no need.' To say he was astonished was an understatement. She'd been grateful and emotional, but suddenly she was brisk again, efficient—and bossy. 'I'm fine.'

'For me,' she said, still implacable. 'If you think I can calmly sleep tonight knowing you might have done yourself damage…'

'Maggie…'

'You're a hero,' she said, and she grinned at him. 'Heroes are brave enough to bare a little skin.'

'I'll check myself.'

'Doctor, heal thyself?' she quoted. 'I don't think so. Humour me. Lie down.'

'Maggie…'

'Just do it.'

He gazed down at her and she gazed back—implacable, immoveable, strong as iron. This woman had raised eight children, he thought, and right now he felt like a ninth.

'Now,' she said, and lifted the bottle from his hand and set it on the bench. 'Do it.'

Why not?

Because he felt vaguely foolish? Because he felt exposed; vulnerable? Because he didn't want this woman thinking of him as a patient?

All of which were dumb reasons.

He was sore. He had pulled his stitches.

Sensible was the way to go—surely.

He sighed—and went and lay on the bench and tugged his shirt up and undid his belt.

If this was Miriam he wouldn't mind, he thought.

Their relationship could be professional—it usually was. So what was different about Maggie?

He had no answer. He could only lie and wait and submit.

He had hurt himself. She'd seen him wince as he'd climbed from the boat. She'd also seen a tell-tale spattering of blood on his pants and she'd known she'd have to check. He also knew it was sensible, she thought. The guy in him didn't want her near him. The doctor in him said submit.

He submitted. He hauled his shirt up, undid his belt, and she unzipped his pants before he could protest.

His abdomen was rock hard, muscled, ripped. As his shirt fell open she was hit once more with the sight of a male body that was pure muscle. She felt the strength of him as her fingers touched his skin while undoing his zip.

She glanced up at him and saw his face set hard. She wasn't hurting him. She was barely touching him.

This man didn't like being exposed, she thought. This was a guy who walked alone.

But not tonight, she thought ruefully. Five children, two dogs, and her. She was taking over this guy's life.

She wouldn't mind…

Um, no. For the sensation of that kiss had flooded back, and suddenly Maggie Tilden wasn't feeling professional at all. She was bending over a near-naked man—which she'd done before,she was a nurse, for heaven's sake—but she wasn't feeling like a nurse. She wanted…

She could want all she liked. She couldn't have—*and this man was a patient.*

Focus.

She focussed.

He had torn the wound open, just a little, right at the top. The internal stitches must still be holding, she thought, examining the wound with care, as there was no sign of swelling, no sign of internal bleeding. And Blake might look uncomfortable but he wasn't writhing in pain.

There was only an inch or so that had pulled apart a little and bled, and even that wasn't terrible.

'It's okay,' she told him, glancing up at him and seeing him with his hands behind his head, staring straight at the ceiling with a look so grim he might as well be expecting her to attack with a scalpel. 'Hey, I'm not about to dive in and have a fish around,' she joked. 'I thought I might settle for a wash, some disinfectant, some steri-strips and orders for a good sleep.'

His face lost a little of its severity but, she thought, he was forcing himself to relax. He was well out of his comfort zone.

'Want to tell me what's going through that head of yours?' she asked, expecting him not to answer, or to deflect the question, but to her surprise he did answer.

'The last time I lay on this couch, it was because my father hit me,' he said. 'I must have been about five. He spilt my face above the eye. Minor stuff. My mother put a plaster on and screeched at him the whole time. Funny thing, though. No matter how much he hit me— and he did—it took the knowledge that he'd been sleeping around before she took me away.'

'Then I guess you have Ruby—or Ruby's grandmother—to thank that she finally did take you,' she said, forcing her voice to be light. She was carefully cleaning, focussing on the wound, not the man—but part of her was thinking this man had been incredibly isolated. She was so surrounded. Which was worse?

Blake's childhood, she thought. Her parents were dodgy as parents went, but they'd never hit, and the tribe of nine kids had provided their own love and support to each other.

She dared another glance at his grim face and thought, Absolutely, crowds every time.

She'd crammed his house with kids and dogs. She was doing him a favour, she decided—and she grinned.

'What's funny?'

'I'm just thinking of the great protective screen I've erected round you,' she said. 'Five kids and me and the dogs... No one can hit you now, Blake Samford.' She dried his skin with care and thought that no one could hit him anyway. Not with those muscles. But she wasn't telling him that. There was no way she was admitting— even to herself—how awesome she found his body. She started adjusting steri-strips, gently tugging together the slight gaps where the wound had parted. Her concentration was absolute.

He didn't speak, just lay and stared at the ceiling, but the rigidity had gone. She'd defused the moment, she thought. Kids had to be good for something.

'I'll dress it...'

'I don't need a...'

'Remind me to ask next time I need medical advice,' she said severely. 'You'll be dressed whether you want it or not.'

'Very civilised,' he said, and she chuckled, and dressed her carefully applied steri-strips and then went to tug up his zip.

His hand closed over hers.

'I can do that, at least,' he said, and his hand held... for just a moment too long.

He needed to sit up. Instead of tugging her hand away, she gripped his and tugged—and he rose a little too fast.

She was a little too close.

A lot too close.

They'd been here before. She'd kissed this man. This man had kissed her.

He was so close. He was so...so...

Compelling? For he'd placed his fingers under her chin and was tilting...

'No.' Somehow she managed to say it. Somehow she hauled some vestige of common sense from the back of her addled brain and made herself step back.

Her foot hit the bowl of water on the floor, it spilled and she was almost glad.

'Look what you made me do,' she said, a trifle too breathlessly. A lot too breathlessly.

'If you'd let me kiss you, you wouldn't have tripped.'

'You don't want to kiss me.'

'And you know that because...?'

'Because I come with encumbrances.' She stalked over to the pantry—she'd spent six months nursing Blake's father so she knew her way around this place—and grabbed a wad of old dishcloths. She tossed them onto the floor, then went down on her knees and started drying. 'I'm a workhorse,' she said, scrubbing with more ferocity than she needed to. 'Not a show pony. You're only kissing me because I'm the only female available.' She sat back on her haunches and glared. 'But you're wrong. You have Ruby who has need of all the kisses you can give her. Concentrate on what's important, Blake Samford.'

'I'm thinking you're important, Maggie Tilden.'

'Then think again,' she snapped. 'You're trapped, you're wounded, you're exhausted, and I have the right chromosomes. Nothing more. Get a grip.' She pushed herself to her feet, which was hard when she realised he'd stepped toward her to help and she had no intention of letting him help. She gathered the bowl, the dressing wrappers, the dishcloths and turned away.

'This is the main house,' she muttered. 'I live in the servants' quarters. My brothers and sisters might have infiltrated their way over here but me...me, I'm scared stupid. Leave it, Blake. I have a flood, a dependent community and a dependent family, and I need no other complications. None. Your wound is fixed. You need to feed Ruby and put yourself to bed. By yourself,' she added, as she saw what looked suspiciously like laughter in his dark eyes.

'You're overreacting.'

'That's the story of my life,' she muttered, stalking to the door. 'Setting boundaries and hoping people respect them. And being told I'm overreacting when they don't.'

'Maggie...'

'I have to check I'm not needed at the clinic. Liselle will look after my kids.' She glanced down at Ruby. 'You look after yours. Goodnight, Blake.'

And she walked out and closed the door behind her.

What had just happened?

Blake stared at the closed door and thought he'd just been hit over the head with a sledgehammer. That's what it felt like.

He'd really, really wanted to kiss her. The need had felt extraordinary, but it hadn't been a simple sexual urge. It had been all about the smattering of freckles on her nose. The shadows under her eyes. The way she'd stood in the top paddock and yelled, 'Oi, oi, oi.'

It had been about the way her fingers had felt, gently touching his skin. She was a nurse. She'd been doing her job but it hadn't felt like that. It had felt…electric. It was as if everywhere she'd touched there had been this frisson, this connection, two halves desperate to come together.

But it wasn't true. His half was all for it. Her half was backing away like a startled rabbit.

Did she think he was about to seduce her? Local landowner taking advantage?

His father's reputation had gone before him.

She didn't know him.

And he didn't know her, he told himself. She was like no one he'd ever met. There was no artifice about her—what you saw was what you got. She was taking care of this valley, taking care of her siblings, taking care of…him?

At his feet Ruby finally tired of waiting. She'd been perfectly patient while her uncle had been treated, but enough was enough.

She opened her mouth and she wailed.

Maggie wasn't taking care of Ruby. Fair enough, he thought ruefully. He could hardly expect it of her.

As if in rebuttal, her head appeared around the door.

'You should be in bed,' she said, and she sounded reluctant, like this was her conscience talking. 'If you like, I'll feed her and we'll take care of her on our side for the night. Only for tonight, mind.'

'You're going back to the clinic.'

'There are five of us. One thing the Tilden kids learned early is to take care of each other. For tonight only, we can do it.'

She would, too, he thought. She was looking at him and seeing a guy who was recovering from appendicitis, who'd pushed himself too far.

He did not want to be this woman's patient.

'Ruby and I will be fine,' he said, a bit too shortly.

'You're sure?'

'I'm sure.'

'Knock if you change your mind,' she told him, sounding relieved. 'And I'll check when I get home. Sleep tight, Blake. Sleep tight, Ruby.'

She closed the door again—and he felt even more...

Like he wanted the door to stay open.

He fed Ruby.

He wandered out to see what the kids were doing.

Ruby had gone to the clinic. The rest of the kids were in his big sitting room.

Liselle was hunched over a side table with a bunch of books in front of her that looked truly impressive.

'Calculus?' he asked, checking over her shoulder.

'Yes,' she said tersely.

'Trouble?'

'This,' she said, and pointed hopelessly. He sat and helped her integrate a complex equation, with techniques he thought he'd long forgotten, and felt absurdly pleased with himself when it worked.

If Maggie was out saving the world, he could at least do maths.

Susie was under the table with her dolls.

Christopher was propped up on cushions, his leg high in front of him. The painkillers would be making him feel sleepy but he'd obviously decided he wanted to be with his siblings. He was watching something violent on television. Was it suitable for a twelve-year-old? But then he thought these kids must be pretty much independent by now.

'It's okay,' Liselle said briefly, seeing him watching the TV and reading his doubt. 'Maggie and Chris go through the guide once a week, Chris reads out the reviews of what he wants to watch and they negotiate.'

Fair enough, he thought, feeling awed.

He looked down at Ruby, who was still in his arms, and wondered who'd negotiate for her.

What was this baby doing to his head? He'd had one image of his baby sister, embedded in his memory thirty years ago. He'd hardly thought of her since, and yet this little one, a baby of that baby, was calling to something he hadn't been aware he had.

A need for family?

He gazed round the living room, at the kids sprawled over the furniture. Sleepy Christopher with his bandaged leg, who'd come so close to death but was recovering fast. Susie, spilling out from under the table with her dolls. Pete with his video games and Liselle keeping vague watch as she studied. Maggie must have lit the fire before she'd left—or maybe Liselle had. They were independent kids, but he just knew...

Threaten one and you threatened them all.

Family.

Ruby was dozing in his arms. He should put her to bed. He should put himself to bed, he thought. He didn't understand the way he was feeling...

It was all about weakness, he decided. It was the af-
ter-effects of appendicitis, the shock of Ruby's arrival,
working with Christopher and the physical demands of
rescuing the calves.

And the way he was feeling about Maggie?

Um…no. Family. Maggie. That was emotional stuff,
feelings he'd long suppressed because they ought to be
suppressed. He had a very practical, very satisfactory
life and the sooner he could go back to it, the better.

'You look tired,' Liselle said. 'You want me to cuddle
Ruby until Maggie comes home?'

So Maggie could come home and see that he hadn't
managed one baby?

'Thank you,' he said gravely. 'But I'm fine.'

'Call us if you need us,' Pete said, emerging from
his computer game for a moment. 'I've buried nappies
before,' he offered nobly. 'One spade, one hole and the
job's done.'

The kids chuckled and so did he, and then he escaped.

They were great kids, he thought, and then he
thought of Maggie.

They weren't great kids because of their parents, he
thought. They were great kids because they had a great
big sister. An awesome big sister.

A really cute, really sexy, big sister.

That was exactly what he didn't want to think. He
needed to think of practicalities. Ruby. Bed.

Not Maggie.

She had two patients to see at the clinic. Both minor
complaints. Aida Batton had cricked her neck lifting
piglets out of a sty that was becoming waterlogged.

Anyone else would have figured that driving the sow out first and leaving the piglets to follow was the best option, but Aida considered herself an earth mother, and thought the sow might slip in the mud and squash one of her babies—and now she was paying the price.

Maggie gave her a gentle massage, sent her home with anti-inflammatories and a heat pack, and was promised a side of bacon in exchange.

Robbie Neal—a mate of Christopher's—had decided to use the run-off from the hill beside his house as a water slide. He'd used a tyre tube, there hadn't been a lot of control from the beginning and he'd hit a tree. He had grazes and bruises everywhere but as far as Maggie could see, the damage was superficial.

No hint of loss of consciousness. No sign of head injury. She cleaned him up and sent him home with his long-suffering parents.

She cleaned the clinic, walked through into the hall where the locals had set up a temporary evacuation centre, noted that her mother wasn't there—she'd be sponging on any of half a dozen neighbours, she thought grimly, no communal evacuation centre for Barbie—and then she thought she shouldn't care.

How did you turn off caring?

She drove home thinking just that. And also…how did you stop yourself starting to care?

For a guy who'd kissed her?

It was nothing, she told herself fiercely, but unbidden her fingers wandered to her lips as if she could still feel…

'I can feel nothing,' she said harshly into the silence. 'I can't afford to feel anything. Honestly, how many complications do you want in your life? A womanising Samford is exactly what you don't need.'

A womanising Samford...

She was tarring him with the same brush as his father, she thought. Was that fair?

Of course it wasn't. Up until now he'd been awesome. He'd helped her care for her little brother. He'd saved his life. He'd saved his cows. He'd dispatched her mother.

He'd kissed her.

'Which has turned you into a simpering schoolgirl,' she snapped. 'Grow up, Maggie. It was only a kiss.'

Only it didn't feel like just a kiss. It felt...so much more.

The house was silent. It was eleven o'clock and she was dead tired.

She checked the fire, checked each of the kids, made sure Christopher was okay.

Christopher and Liselle both stirred and hugged her as she leaned over them—something they'd done since they'd been babies.

Part of her loved it.

How could she ever walk away?

She couldn't, she thought, as she tucked them in and kissed them goodnight. When Blake sold the farm she'd move back home. Of course she would. The events of the day had shown her just how dangerous it was to leave the kids with her mother.

Tonight she didn't even have the luxury of her own bed. Susie had demurred at sleeping in a big, strange bedroom by herself. She was very definitely sharing with Maggie.

It's fine, Maggie told herself. You've had six months' luxury of having your own place. That's it.

She was so tired…

But she did need to check on Blake. Just in case, she told herself. He'd pushed himself past the limit this afternoon. If he was bleeding internally, if he was in pain, would he call her?

Maybe he wouldn't and the nurse in her wouldn't let herself go to bed without checking.

She slipped through the darkened house. His bedroom door was open, just a crack.

She had no wish to wake him—or Ruby—if he was asleep. She pushed the door just enough for her to slip inside.

He had the curtains wide open. The clouds had cleared for once, and the almost full moon was lighting the bed, the man sleeping in it, and the baby tucked in her bed beside him.

They were both soundly asleep.

Blake was bare to the waist. He was sleeping right on the edge of the bed, and his arm was trailing down so his fingers were resting beside Ruby's face.

It was as if he'd gone to sleep touching her. Giving her human contact. Letting her know he cared?

Something was twisting…

This man…

Don't, she told herself fiercely. No. Put your hormones right back where they belong.

He stirred and she backed out of there so fast she almost tripped over her feet. He was fine. She didn't need to check again.

She didn't need to go near this man when he was half-dressed, or in his bedroom, or when he was smiling, or when he was feeding Ruby, or when he was doing any of the stupid, dumb things that were mounting up that made her feel…

Like she had no business feeling. When the river went down he'd head back to his city hospital, to his independent life, and she'd just…

Just…

She needed to get a grip. Any minute now she'd be putting something violinish and maudlin on the sound system and start weeping into her beer.

The phone rang and she grabbed it with real relief. Work. That way lay sanity—not looking at half-naked men in the moonlight.

But the phone call wasn't for her.

One problem with sharing Blake's house was that she shared his phone.

Bob Samford's existing line had never been disconnected. An extension of that same line rang in her apartment. She'd been covering the costs since she moved in.

Maggie had a cellphone. The locals knew it, but they disliked using the longer phone number and contacting her cellphone was a more costly call.

When she'd lived with her mother, no matter how much she'd discouraged it, they'd rung her there. As soon as she'd moved, they'd simply phoned here. So when the phone rang as she reached the hall, she answered it fast, to stop it waking the house.

'Maggie Tilden,' she said, polite and professional.

'Who is this?' a female voice demanded.

Uh-oh. She didn't recognise this voice. It was cool, slightly arrogant and startled. Like she was expecting someone else.

She guessed this was Blake's call.

'I'm the district nurse,' she said, a tad too quickly. 'Maggie Tilden.'

'The woman living at the back of Blake's house?'

How could you dislike a woman after two sentences? Not possible. She got a grip and managed a bright smile. Someone had said smile on the phone and the person at the other end could hear it. She tried—hard.

'That's right,' she said, determinedly chirpy. 'Did you wish to speak to Blake?'

'Yes.'

'I'm sorry, but he's asleep.'

'It's only eleven.'

'Yes, but he's had a very big day. He had to save his calves from drowning and Ruby needs feeding in the night.' She paused. 'I'd rather not wake him.'

'He's not answering his cellphone.'

'He dropped it in the water. I don't believe it's working.'

There was a deathly silence. Then, 'He's been in floodwater?'

'I… Yes.'

'To save calves?' It was practically a screech.

'Yes.' She was trying to be polite—but this was hurting her ear.

'You won't look after the baby—*and you expect him to save cows?*'

'They're his cows,' she said mildly. 'And it's his baby.'

'It's not his baby.'

'He's taking responsibility for her.'

'He has no right—'

'It's his sister's baby,' she said gently. 'He has more right than most.'

'You're the midwife. He says you won't—'

'Be professional? I'm being exceedingly professional. I don't take patients home.' She glanced behind her and winced at the mess the kids had made of Blake's fabulous, faded living room—and thought actually she'd brought everything else home.

'Blake needs help,' she snapped. 'He's ill. If you're a nurse, help him.'

'I'm doing what I can.' She'd coped with belligerent patients before—and their relatives. She was deliberately keeping her voice calm, unruffled—but implacable. 'I don't believe there's any need to worry. I'd prefer not to wake him, though. If you give me your name, I'll tell him you called.'

'Miriam Donnington,' she snapped. 'Dr Donnington. Blake's fiancée.'

Why did her stomach lurch? No reason at all.

Or lots of reasons. How stupid did she feel? How had her hormones led her down a path she didn't know she was treading until right now?

Blake belonged in another life. He was a city doctor with a city fiancée. He was trapped here. The kiss they'd shared had been the result of adrenalin, from shared danger and from victory and nothing more. She'd known it. She just…knew it better now.

So why was she standing silent, she demanded of herself, as if she was in shock? Get over it, she told herself harshly—and sensible Maggie emerged, as sensible Maggie always did.

'I didn't know he was engaged,' she managed, and somehow she kept her smile firmly in place. 'Congratulations. I can see why you're concerned. I'll let him know you've called. I suspect his phone might still be out of action even when it's dried, but you can usually raise him on this number. Unless he's asleep. I'm trying my best to keep him in bed.' She listened to how that sounded and decided maybe she'd better lighten it. Make it even more professional. 'He's not a very co-operative patient,' she confessed, nurse to doctor.

'Blake knows what's good for him,' Miriam snapped. 'He doesn't need a nurse telling him what to do. What he needs is peace, not a nurse and a baby complicating his life.'

'Plus my four kids,' she said, letting her temper emerge just a little, deciding why not tell it like it is? Even wind it up a little.

He'd kissed her. He had a fiancée. Toe rag!

'Four kids?'

'Blake doesn't mind,' she said cheerfully. 'All my kids are here. Pete says Blake's even been playing his computer games with him. Now, was there anything else you wanted?'

'I… No.' She sounded stunned.

'Goodnight, then,' Maggie chirped, still managing to smile, and she put the phone down—and turned to find Blake watching.

He was leaning against the wall, arms crossed, bare chested, bare legged, ruffled from sleep—simply watching.

He destroyed her professional detachment, just like that.

Nurse, midwife…woman? With Blake around she was all woman, and her body reacted accordingly.

Fiancée. Fiancée.

Keep your head. Get off that dratted path.

'Miriam?' he asked, and she nodded.

'Your fiancée.'

'That's what she told you?'

'She wanted me to wake you. I refused. I'm sorry. You can ring her back.'

'I will.' His eyes searched her face. 'She gave you a hard time?'

'For not looking after you—which might be justified. If you were being flown out right now with internal bleeding, I'd be to blame.' She was sounding so calm she was proud of herself.

'As you said,' he said mildly, 'they're my cows. My choice. And, yes, Maggie, Ruby's my niece.'

'Will Miriam help you take care of her?' It was none of her business, she thought. She shouldn't ask, but the question was out there now, like it or not.

'Someone has to,' he said. 'Unless I take Pete's way out and bury the nappies.'

She managed a half-hearted smile back at him. 'Pete'd bury dishes, too, if it was up to him. But good luck. You should ring her back. She sounds genuinely worried.'

'I will. And, Maggie...'

'Mmm?' He was too close, she thought. Too close, too big, too bare.

'I'm sorry she upset you.'

'She didn't.' How was that for a lie? 'I'm accustomed to my patients' worried relatives.'

'I'm not a patient,' he said, so softly that she shivered.

'You ought to be,' she managed. 'It'd be a whole lot easier if you were.'

And before he could retort she'd turned and headed into her own small apartment, closing the door very firmly behind her.

* * *

He should ring Miriam right back. Instead, Blake stood and watched the closed door for a very long time.

Maggie was behind that door.

She'd be in bed with her ten-year-old sister. His father's two dogs would be under her bed. She was surrounded.

Miriam would be at her desk in their cool, grey and white apartment with a view of the harbour.

His fiancée?

She wasn't. Why had she said it?

To protect him, maybe? To stop Maggie thinking she could take advantage?

Was she taking advantage?

No. Ruby would be here even if Maggie wasn't—and he'd invited her siblings to stay. As well as that, he'd talked to the doctors who'd cared for his father. Without Maggie the old man would have been hospitalised far earlier. Bob had been no one's idea of an easy man but Maggie had worked to make his last months as good as they could be.

She was not a woman to take advantage...

Fiancée...

He rang and Miriam answered on the first ring. 'Blake...I knew you'd be awake. That woman wouldn't fetch you.'

That woman. It sounded...wrong.

That woman was Maggie.

'She's doing a hell of a job,' he said mildly. 'She's taking care of the whole valley.'

'Not you. Were you really dumb enough to stand in floodwater?'

'If I hadn't, eighty calves would have drowned.'

'For heaven's sake, Blake, what's worth more? All that skill, all that training...'

'Not to mention me,' he said mildly. 'Even without the medical degree I'd still have missed me.'

'For heaven's sake,' she snapped.

And he thought...he thought...

Fiancée?

They'd drifted into this relationship. They'd competed against each other at university, studied together, pushed each other. They were both driven.

He wondered suddenly whether, if he didn't have his medicine, would he have Miriam?

Would she want him?

Would he want her?

It was a crazy thing to think at midnight, when his feet were cold on the floorboards and he could hear Ruby starting to stir in the background, but think it he did.

'When the water comes down,' he said, speaking slowly, thinking it through as he spoke, 'I'd like you to visit here before I come back. I'd like you to get to know Ruby. Help me make a decision about her.'

There was a sharp intake of breath.

'What sort of decision?'

'She's my family, Mim.'

'I'm not Mim.' Suddenly her voice was almost shrill. 'I'm not taking on anyone else's baby. I don't even know if I want one of my own yet.'

'Of our own?' he queried.

'I... Yes.'

'Fiancée?'

There was a moment's pause. It turned out longer. It ended up stretching a very long time indeed.

'I said it for your benefit,' she said at last. 'I thought you might need it. If you're staying in the same house…'

'We have five kids staying here now,' he said gently. 'They're chaperons enough. But…are you thinking I'd need them?'

'I don't care what you do,' she said fretfully.

There was another silence at that. 'Really?' he said at last, and he looked at the closed door and thought of Maggie in bed with Susie and the dogs underneath and he thought…Maggie was a woman who cared.

'Look, this is a dumb conversation,' Miriam snapped at last, regrouping. 'What we have is sensible, Blake. Do you want to mess it up?'

'Would it mess it up if I was unfaithful?'

'If I were to know about it, yes.'

'And if you didn't?'

'Look, I don't care,' she snapped. 'I'm tired and I have a long day tomorrow and if you want to have a torrid little affair with your tenant/nurse—*who has how many children*?—then it's fine by me. But there's no way I'm coming down there.'

'No,' he said bleakly, and he glanced behind him, to his open bedroom door, where he could see Ruby's bedclothes wriggling. Any minute now she'd open her mouth and yell.

And then, suddenly, he was thinking of Maggie again, and Christopher, and his television rules. Boundaries. And he thought…if ever he had an affair with Maggie she'd give him boundaries—and they wouldn't be do what you like but don't tell me about it.

'I'll be moving apartments when I get back to Sydney,' he said, and he heard Miriam's breath draw in with shock and with anger.

'So it's true. Your stupid little nurse…'

'It has nothing to do with Maggie,' he told her, though maybe it did, and it was simply too soon to acknowledge it. 'But it has to do with family. You and me, Mim…we're friends. Colleagues. But we've never been family and it's too late to start now. Our relationship needs to stop. It's going nowhere and it's time we acknowledged it. I'm sorry, Mim…Miriam, but it's over.'

'So you're starting…what, a family? Down there?' The viciousness in her voice was appalling.

'I have no idea where or what I'm starting,' he told her. 'All I know is that we're wrong. Thank you for trying to protect me, Miriam, but I don't need a fiancée. I'm not sure what I need. Oh, actually, yes, I am. I need to make one bottle for one baby and then go back to bed. Right now, I'm not capable of thinking further.'

CHAPTER EIGHT

THE river stayed impassable. The rain was interminable. There was nothing for it but for the valley to hunker down and wait.

If anyone had told Blake he could spend a week trapped in a farmhouse with five children and be…almost content, he'd have labelled them crazy, but that's exactly what he did.

Maggie was frantically busy. That rush of water through the valley had caught everyone unprepared. There'd been stock loss—nothing dire, but farmers had been caught by surprise and there were sprains and bruises from rushing to save stock, grazes that had turned septic from floodwater, leg abscesses that had got wet and stayed wet too long, back problems as people heaved belongings higher than the water.

Blake helped when he could, relishing the times he could go out with her to the outlying farms, helping to debride ulcers, double-checking her diagnoses, or just plain giving reassurance that Maggie was right, they didn't need evacuation to the hospital over the river.

To his surprise, he was enjoying it. He'd never thought of country medicine, but its variation was almost…fun.

But frustrating for Maggie.

'What is it about having doctor in front of your name?' she demanded. She'd spent an hour telling Maisie Goodall her leg was starting to heal and the antibiotics were taking effect, but Maisie was still frightened. Blake had walked in, examined the ulcerated leg for a whole two minutes and smiled his reassurance.

'This is healing beautifully, Miss Goodall. See the faint film over the edges? That's slowly working its way in to form a seal. Try and keep it elevated and dry, watch lots of telly, cuddle your cats—' the woman was surrounded by them '—and I reckon by the time the water's down you'll be good as new.'

Maisie almost purred as loudly as her cats, and Maggie climbed back into her car beside Blake and glowered.

'I can speak until I'm blue in the face,' she muttered. 'But you walk in with your doctor-ish bedside manner and you don't do a single thing and suddenly Maisie doesn't want a helicopter, she just wants another visit from you tomorrow.'

'Basic Bedside Manner,' Blake said smugly. 'Taught in med school. Kept secret from nurses for generations.'

'You mean you're good looking, you're male and you smile at her,' she snapped.

'There is that.' He looked smug and she had to chuckle.

'Okay, it's useful,' she conceded. 'If I could just bottle you and keep you in my medical kit...'

'I won't be put.'

'No.' She sighed. 'You shouldn't even be out here.' She'd brought him out of desperation because Maisie had been so scared, but she kept reminding herself that he, too, was a patient. But he was recovering. He was moving with ease, the stiffness and the grimacing had gone and he was well on the way to recovery.

They had Ruby in the baby seat. Bringing her with them for the minor stuff meant Liselle could keep studying and, besides, patients liked it. Maggie had no doubt there'd be a pair of bootees from Maisie's knitting needles by the end of the week. That was okay as well because it meant Maisie would sit with her leg up while she knitted. That'd help her healing—but healing was what Maggie should be organising for Blake, rather than letting him accompany her on her rounds.

But he seemed to enjoy it, she conceded, and he was very skilled, very efficient, very friendly—and very useful. Also accepted. Because of his links to the valley the locals treated him as one of them. Local boy made good.

Also local boy made interesting—and there was the complication. Interest meant speculation. The locals looked at Blake, they looked at Maggie, they looked at Ruby—and Maggie could see exactly what the valley was thinking. That made her think…and thinking was exactly what she was trying not to do. It was bad enough having Blake sitting beside her, but a girl didn't need to think about it.

She glowered at the steering-wheel—and the ignition light lit up.

Excellent—a diversion.

Or maybe not excellent. Ignition light…trouble?

She should be driving a Health Services car on her rounds. Normally she would, but the bridge closure had happened earlier than expected, catching them all by surprise. Her dependable hospital car was on the other side of the river and she was left with her own.

Which wasn't so dependable. She used it in emergencies, but patients had been known to groan when she pulled up in her battered wagon.

Ignition light...

'What's wrong?' Blake asked as she pulled over to the verge.

'Sister, farmer, nurse, mechanic,' she said. 'You've met three. Welcome to the fourth.'

She climbed out and hauled up the bonnet, and he climbed out after her.

Cars weren't his thing. Yeah, he could drive them, but his garage was right by the hospital and apart from the odd tyre change he'd never concerned himself with them.

Underneath the bonnet looked as decrepit as the outside of the car, and a lot more mysterious, but Maggie was sighing and heading for the rear.

'Panty hose,' she said.

'Panty hose?'

'A girl's best friend. Never go anywhere without them.' She hauled out a pair of black tights that looked like they'd seen better days. 'Can you find some scissors in my bag and chop the legs off?' she asked. He did, while Maggie did...other stuff.

'Fanbelt?' he guessed, thinking he ought to try and sound intelligent. They were in the middle of nowhere. Where was the nearest tow truck?

But Maggie wasn't thinking about tow trucks. 'You've got it.' She was head down in the engine, tossing out a very decrepit belt. 'I did a course a while back to learn what to do. The fanbelt transmits drive from the engine to the alternator and water pump. Without it, the battery doesn't charge and the engine overheats.

It's okay. I have a spare at home and the panty hose will get us there. I just need to make a smooth knot so it'll spin. I'll loosen the alternator mounting bolts and push the alternator towards the other pulleys. Then I'll slip on my pantyhose, lever the alternator until the loop's tight and do up the bolts. I'll only use the crank and pump pulleys. It's hard to make the panty hose tight when it's fitted over more.'

'Right,' he said faintly, and she glanced back up at him and grinned.

'So mechanic doesn't fit in your job description.'

'No.'

'Lucky you.' She straightened and took the chopped panty-hose leg from him. She had a smudge of grease on her nose. He thought she looked…she looked…

'Hop back in the car,' she said gently. 'I can cope on my own. Miriam would have my hide if she could see me dragging you with me on my medical rounds—and I don't need you to hold my spanner.'

'Miriam's not my fiancée,' he said, and she paused and stared at him—and then bit her lip and dived under the bonnet again.

'Not?'

'She's a colleague.'

'She said—'

'She's been my partner. Sort of. We studied together at university. When we got jobs at the same hospital, we figured we could afford an amazing apartment if we got it together.' He hesitated. 'That doesn't totally sum up our relationship,' he said honestly. It's drifted past friendship but the other night…I realised it needs to stop drifting.'

'Because I was sharing a house with you?' she said,

not looking at him, concentrating fiercely on whatever it was she was concentrating on. 'Because you kissed me? If you think I'm taking responsibility for breaking up your relationship...'

'I didn't say that.'

'You want me to phone her and tell her there's an oak door and five kids between us?'

'I already have.'

'Then it's ridiculous.'

'Is it?'

'Of course it's ridiculous.' She thumped something with a spanner. 'You've lost a potential fiancée. Why aren't you sounding heartbroken?'

'Because I'm not in love with Miriam. Neither of us has ever pretended to be in love with the other. Because, even though I've known you for less than two weeks, even though it makes no sense at all, the kiss we shared was electric and I've never felt that with Miriam. Ever. So moving on from Miriam...it had to be done. It's not fair on anyone to continue.'

There was a moment's silence. Deathly silence. Actually, it was more than a moment. It lasted for a very long time.

Then the spanner thumped again. She went back to work. He waited—and he thought...

Why had he said that? Confessed all?

Because her backside under the bonnet was really, really sexy? Because the smudge of grease on her nose made him want to wipe it away for her and then kiss it? Because the whole package of Maggie, woman, sister, farmer, nurse, mechanic was doing something to him he couldn't understand and he couldn't fight?

She was the most desirable woman he'd ever met.

*He'd suggested what they had together was unique.
One kiss?*

He'd done this all wrong. He'd confessed he'd been
blown away by a kiss, while the woman in question was
covered in grease and doing something a guy would tra-
ditionally do but which he had no hope of doing.

Had he scared her?

He *had* scared her. He saw it in her body language.
He saw it in the way she concentrated fiercely on doing
what she had to do.

He'd been really, really stupid.

Why?

He thought up a barrage of excuses. Appendix.
Floods. Baby. Maggie herself.

The kiss.

Together they were a package designed to knock any
man off kilter, he decided—and maybe Maggie realised
it. When she finally hauled herself back from under the
bonnet she had her face under control.

She dropped the bonnet into position with a bang,
wiped her hands on the remains of the panty hose, slid
into the driver's seat and waited until Blake had climbed
back into the car beside her.

She started the car, watched the ignition go out with
satisfaction, pulled back onto the road and finally, eventually she spoke.

'I hope what you said back there was an aberration,'
she said.

'It was…a fairly awesome kiss,' he said, thinking
caution was the way to go here.

'Fairly?'

'Okay, very,' he conceded. 'And just now… There
was grease on your nose. You looked sexy as hell. I love
a girl with a spanner.'

She managed a smile at that, but it was a wobbly smile.

'Just as well I've put my spanner away, then,' she said. 'Blake...' Her voice turned serious. 'Don't read anything into what happened between us, and for heaven's sake don't call things off with Miriam because of me. I come with a lot more encumbrances than a spanner, and I'm not in the market for a relationship. One kiss does not a relationship make.'

Where could he fit caution into this reply? He tried, but failed. When in doubt, opt for honesty. 'One kiss makes me feel like I've never felt before,' he said, and it felt okay. It felt right.

'It was a good kiss,' she conceded. 'But don't even think of taking it further. I'm heading for Africa.'

'Africa?' he said, startled.

'And possibly Siberia. Not to mention Sardinia, Istanbul and Paris. All by myself. I have a bank account...' She took a deep breath, glanced at him—quickly—and obviously decided to go on. 'When I was a kid I used to collect drink cans,' she told him. 'Outside footy matches, from the richer kids at school, wherever I could find them. I squashed them and sold them by weight. They made me a pittance but it was *my* pittance. When things got bad at home I used to escape and search for cans. Even today I think of escape in the form of drink cans.'

She hesitated then, and he wondered why she was telling him this—why she was turning what must surely be a joking conversation—a mistake?—into a conversation about saving. But something in her expression told him this was important. And maybe it was something she'd told no one else.

'Mum and Dad were always broke,' she told him. 'Desperately broke. If they'd known I had even a tiny fund they'd have used it in an instant and it'd be gone, so I kept hiding it and they never knew. All my life I hid it. As a teenager I babysat, like Liselle does. Some of the money I earned went into my secret fund. When I started nursing I kept doing it, squirrelling away my pittances. Ninety-nine per cent of all I've ever earned has gone to keeping me or helping the kids, but one per cent is mine. My tiny fund is almost enough to get me to Africa—but not back.'

'But you will come back?' he asked, startled, and she shrugged and grinned.

'Of course I will. I suspect the family will always need me—Good Old Maggie. But I will go.' It was a declaration, almost a vow. 'The moment Susie leaves home, I'm off.'

'Susie's ten,' he said faintly. 'That's seven years.'

'I'll have the return fare by then,' she said resolutely. 'More. The less they need me the more I'll be able to save. I'm aiming to travel for at least six months. All by myself… Remember that backpacking dream I told you about? Sitting on the Left Bank in Paris drinking kir, with not one single person to answer to. Lying in the sun on a Greek island. Seeing a rhinoceros in the wild. I really do hope to turn that into a reality one of these days.' She glanced across at him and bit her lip and turned her attention deliberately to the road again. 'So don't you—and Ruby—dare mess with my dream!'

'I wouldn't dare.'

'Good,' she said. 'Just so we understand each other.'

* * *

They drove on and he kept right on kicking himself. Of all the morons… Why had he frightened her? Why had he made a big deal out of one kiss? Why had he forced her to tell him her life dreams?

He'd known this woman for little more than a week. He'd kissed her once. To suggest it could be the foundation of a relationship…to tell her it was the reason he'd broken up with Miriam…

The whole thing was dumb.

He was a city surgeon, ambitious, career focussed, totally centred on getting as good at his job as it was possible to get. Maggie lived in Hicksville, surrounded by kids and cows and not even the scent of decent coffee.

And never the twain should meet.

It was cabin fever, he told himself. He'd been trapped with Maggie for a week now. Any more time in this place and anyone with an X chromosome would start looking good. Even a woman with grease spots on her nose.

Only it was more than that, he conceded as they drove on. Maybe Maggie represented something he'd never thought about—or maybe something he'd repressed. A need for home?

He'd lived in this place until the age of six. After that, his mother had moved from place to place, from man to man. This valley must have some sort of long-term emotional hold over him.

And then there was Ruby. He glanced behind at his tiny niece, sleeping deeply in her baby cocoon.

What to do with Ruby?

She needed family, and right now she had it. She had him, and Maggie as back-up, and she had four siblings,

Liselle, Pete, Chris and Susie, who all regarded her as their personal plaything.

She was starting to smile and everyone in the house was working for those smiles.

'Hey, I got one. I'm in front by two.' That had been Chris that morning, crowing with delight, and the memory made him smile.

The way Maggie handled Ruby made him smile, too. While he was unwieldy when Ruby was distressed, Maggie stepped in, calm and sure, and made things right.

But even put together, those things weren't enough to define as love. To start thinking long-term relationship...

Nostalgia. Need. Isolation.

A girl with a grease spot on her nose.

Weakness and need was all it was, he told himself harshly, but now he had Maggie looking at him like he had a kangaroo loose in the top paddock. She'd even felt the need to explain her long-term life plans, spelling out that they didn't include him.

Which was all fine—only why was he sitting here thinking he'd made a huge mistake? It was because something within him was telling him Maggie was important for far more than practical or nostalgic reasons. Maggie was someone the likes of whom he'd never met before and might never meet again.

Maggie. Grease spots. Maggie. Love and laughter.

Yes, she came with terrifying baggage—but to have the right to hold her...

He'd known her a little more than a week and he'd scared her.

'Cabin fever must be getting to me,' he said into

the loaded silence, and she cast him a glance that contained…gratitude? He was letting her off the hook. Setting things back to normal?

'It must be,' she said, sounding relieved. 'You should ring Miriam and tell her isolation's playing with your head.'

'Can isolation happen in a house with five kids, two dogs and how many cows?'

'It comes in all forms,' she said, and her voice changed a little, and suddenly he heard a note of desolation. 'I've been surrounded all my life and I've longed for isolation, yet in a sense I already have it. Define isolation?' She took a deep breath. 'Sorry. It's getting to me, too. You're right, cabin fever. We need to avoid kissing—we're likely to jump each other through sheer frustration. But the authorities are saying the water level's starting to drop, and the forecast is for the weather to finally clear. Within a week they'll set up a barge. The kids can go back to school. You can go back to Sydney. Life can get back to normal.'

'Is that what you want?'

'Of course it is,' she said tightly. 'I have a seven-year plan, remember? I've been working on it since I was ten years old and I have no intention of deviating from it now.'

But she was deviating.

Only in her mind, she thought savagely. Only when she let herself turn from practical Maggie into someone who let her mind wander all along sorts of crazy, impractical paths.

Paths that ended with Blake.

She should avoid him. She couldn't.

They went home and it was time to redo Ruby's legs. She'd been wearing casts for a week now. They needed to be removed, the tiny feet manipulated some more, inched closer to normal, and new casts applied.

So Maggie watched and helped as Blake tended his tiny niece with all the care in the world.

At least she could focus on Ruby rather than her uncle.

Left unattended, these feet would cripple this little girl—they'd make her life a torturous nightmare, with a wheelchair a real, long-term option.

But once the casts came off she could see improvement. The feet had been twisted far back at birth. They were still twisted, and left now they'd revert, but at rest, the little feet lay at an angle that was slightly closer to normal.

'Can you run her a bath?' Blake asked, as he started playing with the tiny feet, and she did. Well, okay, not a baby bath—this place didn't run to it—but the kitchen sink was big, porcelain, perfect. She did a quick scrub, filled it with warm water and lined it with towels so Ruby wouldn't be lowered against the hard surface.

She half expected Blake to hand Ruby to her, but it was he who lowered her into the water. It was Blake who looked down as Ruby's eyes widened with surprise at this strange, new sensation.

They'd bathed her the night she'd come, before the first cast had gone on, but she'd been a very different baby then—malnourished, abandoned, unloved.

This was a Ruby who'd had a full week of regular feeds, regular cuddles—a regular family?

It wasn't exactly regular, Maggie thought, thinking of her weird assortment of brothers and sisters handing her around—but now Ruby had the thing she most needed in the world. A constant.

Blake.

He was holding her as if she was the most precious thing in the world. She hardly needed to have put the towels down—his hands held her with warmth, security and love.

Love?

She looked into his face and saw emotions she didn't understand.

This man was falling for this baby, she thought, and he was falling hard.

Blake Samford was a city doctor, aloof, a stranger. He was nothing to do with this valley or her. He'd sell this farm and be gone from her life.

But today he'd said…

Forget what he'd said. Concentrate on Ruby, not Blake.

But some things were just plain impossible. The way he was looking at this baby was twisting her heartstrings. This was no doctor looking at a patient. Neither was it a man who planned on handing Ruby to foster-parents as soon as he could.

He was an enigma, and even though she'd sworn to stay distant, she couldn't help herself. She wanted to know more.

'Tell me about your sister,' she said, as Ruby discovered she could wiggle her arms and her cast-free feet and feel even more amazing sensations in the warm water. 'About Wendy.'

'I never knew her.'

'I think you must have,' she said gently. 'The way you're looking at Ruby.'

And then, amazingly, he told her. He cradled Ruby and played with her while he talked of a baby he'd seen only once—a baby who'd destroyed his parents' marriage.

He told of being six years old and crouching by the baby while everyone around them yelled. He told her of placing his hand in the baby's carrycot and feeling her finger tightening around his. He told of being six years old and terrified and thinking this baby was his little sister and she must be terrified, too.

And then he talked of the strange woman taking her away, of his parents never speaking of her again, and of his family no longer existing.

'A psychologist would have a field day,' he said, half mocking.

And she looked up at him and thought…and thought… if he hadn't been holding his baby she'd touch him. She'd run her fingers down that strong cheekbone and caress the lines of pain and self-mockery.

The image of tall, dark, dangerous was receding.

There were worse things than being one of nine neglected kids, she decided. This man had been alone all his life.

But now he'd found Ruby.

Focus back on Ruby, she thought desperately. That was the plan. She had to have a plan around this man because she did not want to feel like she was feeling. It seemed like a vortex, a whirlpool, dark, sweet, infinitely enticing, but who knew what lay inside?

'Don't you need to manipulate?' she managed, and he glanced at her and caught himself and she saw him swap—with difficulty—back to professional as well.

'Of course I do,' he said. 'And it might be easier if we do the first part while she's happy in the water.'

So he handed her over, and as their hands touched as they inevitably had to during handover, and she held his baby while his big, skilled hands manipulated those tiny legs with all the tenderness in the world, as she stood close to him and watched his face and watched his hands, she realised she was in so much trouble.

He'd broken off a relationship with Miriam because of one kiss. That was crazy.

But maybe the condition was catching.

Warm, dry, fed—and confined in her new cast—Ruby was fretful. She'd had a lovely time when her whole body had been free to move, and now she was back to being constricted. It'd be a long haul, Blake thought. Six weeks of casts, an operation to cut the Achilles tendon to let it heal in the new correct position, months of twenty-three hours a day in a brace, then more in a brace at night.

'It's the price you'll pay for being able to dance at your wedding,' he told her, but she wasn't taking any comfort from that.

She was tired after her bath, and so was he. His mate back in Sydney had been right—the operation had knocked the stuffing out of him. Maggie didn't need him right now. He could settle on his bed with Ruby beside him, and try and settle her.

Tell her stories of what their life would be like together?

For he was keeping her—as simple as that. Some time during the last week she'd twisted her way around his heart and she was staying.

He'd be joining the ranks of single dads.

How did they cope?

How would he cope?

How would he cope without Maggie?

'Is that what the conversation in the car was all about?' he demanded of Ruby. 'Or is it my subconscious knowing it'd be easy if she fell for me—if she took you on as well as her brood. After all, she's stuck here for the next seven years anyway.'

There's a romantic way of looking at a relationship, he thought wryly. Red roses didn't even begin to cut it in comparison.

But it had to be more than that. The way he was feeling...

'How can I know what I'm feeling' he asked Ruby, and watched her eyelids grow heavier and heavier until she drifted off to sleep. 'Yeah, I'm smitten with you, and that's cracking open places I don't want to go. I want my independence.'

How could he be independent and keep Ruby?

Make Maggie fall in love with him? Work out how to bend his career so he could fit in family? Live happily ever after.

Was that independence? There was a part of him that was saying it was a solution to all their problems—but another part of him was telling him he'd be giving up way too much. Even if Maggie agreed.

But Ruby was so needy, and that kiss... The possibilities were there. As he watched his tiny niece sleep and thought of Maggie next door, with the weight of the world on her shoulders, he decided a man had to try.

The forecast was saying it would be another week

before the river would be safe to cross. He wasn't due back at work for another two weeks.

Anything was possible in two weeks, he thought.

Including making a family?

He'd never thought about a family. Why was he thinking about one now?

She had enough of a family without including him. She told herself that over and over during the next few days, and she meant it.

As much as possible Maggie kept her brood on her side of the oak door. They had to use Blake's large sitting room—there wasn't enough room for them anywhere else—but the kids were under threat of death not to disturb him. She cooked for her siblings and fed them in her own small kitchen. The kids thought they should invite Blake, too, but it seemed...dangerous? Inviting him into her tiny kitchen or letting her brood loose in his seemed equally fraught.

She needed to stay apart. That kiss...telling her he'd split with Miriam... It was a sweet seduction, she told herself fiercely. He'd get her over to his side of the house, she'd fall for Ruby and she'd be trapped again. Man gets landed with abandoned baby, man makes moves on motherly nurse... Coincidence? Ha.

So she needed to be firm. Doing his own cooking was part of caring for Ruby, living with her, making a life for her. It was part of Blake's bonding process that was proceeding beautifully. She wanted no part in it, and she wasn't interfering with it for the world.

Occasionally she needed him medically. Occasionally he needed her for advice on Ruby. That's all the contact they needed, she told herself, and anything else was scary.

But the kids kept on telling her she was nuts. Even cruel.

'When you're not here he comes in and plays computer games with us, and helps me with maths, and he even helped Susie tie hair ribbons on her doll,' Liselle told her. 'We love playing with Ruby. Only when you come in and he's here, you back out again so he doesn't come in when you're home. That seems mean.'

It did, Maggie conceded. But it also seemed safe. She was being defensive, and somehow she had need of all the defences she could muster.

'And he makes life less boring,' Pete muttered from the couch. 'I'm so-o-o bored. The guys are making mud slides on the far side of the valley. Tom's taking them over in his dad's car. If Tom's dad says it's okay, why won't you?'

Because Tom's father was a moron and Tom behind the wheel was a danger to everyone, Maggie thought, but she didn't say so.

'You know Mum's forbidden it,' she said, more mildly, because she'd worked on this one. Barbie didn't particularly care what her kids did, but Maggie had learned that if she put her under enough pressure—like threatening to withdraw financial help—Barbie could be persuaded to utter edicts. '*You won't drive with Tom.*'

Pete couldn't tell his mates Maggie said no. 'Mum says no' hurt his pride less.

'Mum doesn't care,' Pete said sullenly. 'Tom says she's staying at Archie Harm's place. She hasn't even phoned to find out how Chris is.'

'She does care,' Maggie said, without conviction. 'And you're not to go with Tom.'

'Then let me ask Blake to play this video game with me. It's too hard for Chris, and Liselle won't.'

'Don't disturb Blake.'

'Why not?'

'Because he's not part of our family,' Maggie snapped. 'He's our landlord. Nothing else.'

The week dragged.

The longer the river remained impassable the busier Maggie became. Medical niggles became major. The authorities organised helicopter drops of essentials and evacuation of a few people who'd just got sick of staying.

Maggie's mother was one of them.

'Archie and I are fed up,' she told Maggie on her first phone contact since Chris had hurt his leg. 'You have the kids. Why should I stay? We're visiting Archie's daughter in Sydney.'

'Can you take Pete?' Maggie asked, knowing already what the answer would be but she had to try. 'He's so bored I'm scared he'll do something dumb.'

'You think Archie's daughter wants kids?' Barbie asked incredulously. 'Of course she doesn't. Pete's a good boy. You worry too much, Maggie.'

And she was gone.

Maggie had been using the phone in the hall. She turned and found Blake watching.

Sharing the phone had to stop, she thought. Why wouldn't her mother use the cellphone? Why was Blake watching? And why was her mother's voice so shrill that she knew Blake must have heard?

'Archie?' he asked.

'He's a no-good dropkick from the other side of the valley,' she told him, trying to keep her tone unemotional. 'His wife keeps leaving and then he hangs round Mum. It doesn't last. They'll have a fight, his wife'll take him back and things will get back to normal. As normal as they ever do in our family.'

'So you're totally trapped.'

'The river's trapping me.'

'Even if it goes down…'

'I'm fine,' she said. 'I just need to stay close.'

'When I sell this house, where will you go?'

He saw the colour fade from her face. How many places were available for cheap rent in the farming district close enough to be on call for her siblings? None.

She'd go back home.

'Maggie…'

'It's my business,' she said. 'You have enough on your plate worrying about Ruby.'

'Maybe we could—'

'Maybe we couldn't,' she snapped. 'Maybe there's no we.'

She walked back into side of the house and carefully closed the door behind her. That was rude, she thought. Uncivil. She didn't even know what he'd been about to say.

But there was something about the way he'd looked at her.

There's no *we*.

It was true, she thought. No matter how he looked at her, it was simply another tug at her heartstrings. She had too many already. A guy with his needy baby…

A guy as drop-dead gorgeous as Blake?

A guy who'd hand her yet another responsibility?

'Maggie…' It was Chris, yelling from the other side of the door, Blake's side. 'Pete's got the remote and won't give it to me. Tell him he has to.'

'Pete,' Blake's voice boomed. 'Give your brother the remote or I'll switch the channel to the National Bowling Championships and burn the remote. I mean it.'

There was a loaded silence and then a chuckle and then silence reigned from the living room.

She smiled.

She told herself not to smile.

Because that smile was all about thinking *we*.

There was only manipulation and responsibility and she'd had enough of that to last a lifetime.

CHAPTER NINE

THE household grew more and more tense. Maggie was doing her best to keep the kids happy and not bother Blake, but the valley needed her. She was out a lot.

The weather stayed appalling. Half the problems she was called out for were as the result of people having too much time on their hands—and too much imagination.

'Maggie, I've found a lump on my back. I think it's cancer.'

'Maggie, I've got this funny rash on my neck and I've been reading on the internet about Scabies…'

'Maggie, you know that scary cow disease? Jacob something? My mum used to make me eat brains when I was a kid, and how do I know I don't have it?'

If the river's staying up, the valley should be cut off from the internet, she thought bitterly. The internet was the greatest hypochondria feeder of all time, and she was stuck with it.

Luckily she had Blake. He was great at hosing down panic. By the end of the second week they'd worked out a system. She'd take the initial call. If it was minor and practical she'd go. If it was hysterical and sounding like it could be solved by talking, Blake would go—usually with Ruby, as Ruby herself distracted and defused fear.

If it was major they'd both go, but so far there'd been

only a couple of real dramas. A local farmer had rolled his tractor onto his leg. Blake had been calm, steady and impressive, and she'd been truly grateful for his presence. Amy Southwell had had a major heart attack. There had been nothing either of them could do there, but Maggie had watched Blake comfort Amy's husband of sixty years, grip his shoulders, simply hold him.

She'd thought again—quite desperately—there was no *we*. How could it ever work? A city surgeon with baby and a country nurse with eight siblings.

So stay separate, she told herself, and she did, mostly, until Pete got too bored to continue to obey, climbed into a car with a kid who shouldn't have a licence—and nearly got himself killed.

Maggie was dressing an ulcer on Rose Chibnell's leg when her phone went. It was Tom's mother. Cindy Blayne was a fluffy piece of silliness, and she and her husband let their son do exactly what he wanted. Tom was eighteen going on twelve, and Maggie hated Pete being friends with him.

'Maggie?'

Cindy's first word had Maggie's catching her breath. She could hear terror.

'What's wrong?' She stepped back into Rose's hall, knowing whatever was coming was bad.

'Maggie, Tom's rolled the car.'

A car accident. It was the worst of nightmares in such an isolated place. Her mind was switching straight into triage. She'd need Blake, she thought, and then she remembered he wasn't home. He'd headed over the ridge to see the Misses Ford, who'd decided they both had jaundice, going on for liver cancer. Thanks to the internet.

His cellphone was still out of action.

She'd ring the Ford house. She had to find him.

'Where's the crash?' she asked. 'Where's Tom?'

'Maggie, it's not Tom who's hurt.' Cindy sounded like a trembling mess.

'What do you mean, it's not Tom?' But her heart did this strange, cold clench. Already she sensed what was coming.

'He picked up Pete from your house,' Cindy quavered. 'I know your mum said no, but she's been away and Tom and Pete thought… Anyway, they were in the car together and Tom's okay but Pete was thrown out and he's down the river bank and Tom can't reach him.'

'Dr Blake?'

Miss Harriet Ford answered the phone and handed it to Blake with all the solemnity of a well-paid secretary. Blake took it and another elderly lady was on the other end.

'Dr Blake, this is Rose Chibnell,' the lady said, primly but urgently. 'Maggie's asked me to try and contact you. There's been a motorcar accident at the junction where the river turns north and the road twists away from it. It's Tom Blayne's car.'

He already knew who Tom Blayne was. It was amazing how many of the valley people he was getting to know.

'Is he hurt?'

'That's why Maggie needs you,' Rose said. 'She doesn't know. At least, she knows Tom's okay, but it seems her brother, Pete, was in the car with him. He was thrown out and Tom can't reach him. Tom thought he heard him groaning but he's too far down the river bank for him to see. Do you want me to call the medivac helicopter? I can ask for it to be put on standby.'

'Yes,' he snapped. 'Please. Now.'

And then he turned and looked at two astonished spinsters who didn't have jaundice, much less liver cancer.

'How are you at babysitting?' he demanded, and handed over Ruby before they could reply. 'Thank you,' he said, and went.

Tom was slumped on the roadside, by the steepest incline down to the river in the valley, and Maggie could see at a glance what had happened.

The edge of the road was sodden. Tom had come round the bend too fast and hit the verge. The verge had started to crumble, he'd swerved, overcorrected, hit the bank with the far side of the car, flipped it and rolled.

He was very lucky the car hadn't gone right over.

Maggie wasn't thinking luck, though. She was thinking…Pete.

She was out of the car, bending over Tom, shaking his shoulder. His eyes looked glazed. Shocked. He wasn't a bad kid. Just stupid.

He was bleeding from a cut above his eye but it was shallow, bleeding sluggishly. It was enough to look dramatic but not enough to distract her from her urgent questioning.

'Tom, are you hurt? Apart from your eye?'

'N-no.' He was staring downwards with horror. She glanced down and her heart lurched.

This was no small landslip. The road had given a

little, but a little had become a lot as it had slipped downwards. She saw a swathe of fresh, tumbled mud.

'Pete…'

'There's no seat belt on the passenger side,' he muttered. 'It broke last month. Dad was s'posed to fix it. Pete fell out.'

'Pete's down there?' She'd forgotten to breathe. She'd forgotten everything.

'I can't get down. I tried and the mud moves. I heard him groan at the start but not any more. I can't… You reckon he's dead?'

Dear God.

She stared again at the mud. She cupped her hands and yelled, louder than she'd ever yelled before.

'Pete!'

No answer—but the river was roaring beneath them.

Oh, God, how far had he slipped? How much mud was there? Where…?

Tom was weeping, wringing his hands. She grabbed his shoulders and forced him to look at her.

'I need your help,' she said. 'You know the local numbers. Ring Mrs Mayes, or if you can't get her ring Ted Barnes or Fred Halliday. Tell them I want the emergency chopper with paramedics, and I want tractors and I want as many men as you can get, as fast as they can possibly get them here. And I want them to find Dr Samford. Do you have that, Tom?'

'I… Yes.'

'Ring, fast. Ring everybody. I'm going down.'

'You can't.'

'I'll go down at the edge of the slide,' she snapped. 'I don't have a choice. Phone, now.'

* * *

Clambering down a sodden cliff face beside a mass of tumbled mud and debris was easier said than done. It was appallingly difficult.

She had no choice.

She called as she climbed but she felt…hopeless.

There was too much mud. If Pete had been thrown as the mud had slid he could be buried. He could have been pushed into the river.

She was weeping and climbing and yelling—and the bank was too steep. The rocks were giving under her feet.

Slow down, she told herself. You're no use to anyone if you kill yourself—but her feet wouldn't obey.

Dear God, where was he?

The cliff was getting steeper. She pushed herself harder, clambering, clinging, calling.

She paused on a tiny ledge, forcing herself to take a second to work out the best way to proceed, to look down, search…

And she saw him—well, his blue hoodie… He was a kid, sprawled among the rocks and mud by the river bank.

Not buried.

'Pete,' she screamed, and he raised his arm in a feeble wave.

Not dead. Not dead.

She choked back a sob and stepped off her ledge, heading straight for him.

The ground gave way under her.

She lurched and flailed for something to hold onto.

Everything was moving. She was sliding…the whole world was sliding.

'Pete,' she yelled again, uselessly, and then even more uselessly, 'Blake…'

And then a rock rose up to meet her and there was nothing.

Blake hadn't known he could drive so fast. He hadn't known he could be so afraid.

He hauled his car to a halt beside Maggie's, beside Tom's upturned wreck, and he was beside the shaking Tom almost before the car stopped.

'Maggie?'

'Pete's down there somewhere,' Tom said, pointing uselessly downward. Sobbing. 'An' Maggie went after him. Only then the rocks fell and I heard Maggie scream and there's been nothing since.'

CHAPTER TEN

MAGGIE woke up to whiteness—and to the worst headache she'd ever known.

It was blowing her head away. It was making her feel…

A bowl was right where she needed it, strong hands were holding her steady, and there was a voice…

'It's okay, love. It'll pass soon. We've got you safe. We're getting you stronger pain relief.'

Blake.

She was too weak to ask questions. She was too busy concentrating on the dictates of her stomach, but between spasms…

Blake?

White. Blake. Alive.

The spasms eased. The bowl was removed and Blake's hands, strong and gentle at the same time, guided her back to the pillows. Someone in green… someone at the periphery of her vision…was giving her an injection.

She got that. One arm was having an injection. Blake had the other. It was Blake's hand.

What…? What…?

'Pete…' Somehow she managed to whisper it, but inside the word was a scream.

'Pete's copped a broken leg and a dislocated shoulder,' Blake told her. 'He's had surgery and he's in the next ward. He's fine.'

In the next ward. It was so hard thinking through the fuzz. Ward. Hospital.

Blake.

Kids.

Panic.

'I have to go home.'

'You don't have to go anywhere,' he said gently. 'Ronnie's at home with the kids. They're ringing in every hour to see how you are. They all send their love. They're fine, my love. Close your eyes until the pain eases.'

It was good advice, she decided. It was advice she needed to take. The pain in her head…

She lay back and let the pain take her. She gave in to it, rode it, figured she could live with it if only she stayed absolutely still and didn't let the light in.

'Her pulse is settling,' someone said from a long way away. 'Are you sure about transfer?'

'We can do without it.' That was Blake again. 'Ross concurs. The pressure's not building and she's conscious. She'll want to stay home.'

Home.

Blake.

Kids.

He'd answered all her questions.

His hand was still holding hers and she wasn't letting go. It was helping her ride the pain. She held onto his hand, and it helped.

The waves were receding a bit. A lot? A fog was taking its place—infinitely preferable. She drifted into it, but she still didn't let go of that hand.

'Let yourself sleep,' Blake said, and his voice was right by her ear. She could feel him breathing. She could feel the faint rasp of stubble of his face against hers.

Blake. Here. Good.

Why?

'What...?'

'You hit your head,' he told her. 'Hard. We had to drill a wee hole to ease the pressure.'

'Dr Samford did,' another voice said. A woman. She dared a glimpse and saw the green again as the voice went on. 'He operated on you, down in all that mud and slush. Relieved the pressure before it killed you. How he ever managed it... It doesn't bear thinking about. Everyone's talking about it. Maggie, you're so lucky.'

It was Mary, Maggie thought. With the pain receding it was easier—but not as easy as all that—to think. To figure things out. To realise she knew this voice in green. It was Mary Walford, Theatre Nurse at Corella Base Hospital

Falling. Pete.

Drill a wee hole...

Pressure.

'A...a cranial burr-hole?' Her voice was hardly a whisper.

'A beautiful, successful drill. Ross Myers helped clean it up when we got you here,' Mary said. 'But Blake did the urgent stuff. He's quite some hero. Now sleep, Maggie, love.'

'Blake...'

'I'm going nowhere,' Blake said, in a voice that was so unsteady she hardly recognised it. His hold on her hand didn't ease one bit. 'Sleep as long as you like. I'll be here when you wake up.'

She slept and woke and slept and woke and every time she woke he was with her. He seemed to be drifting in and out of her fog. Holding her. Telling things were okay. His hand was her link to reality. Otherwise she'd float, she thought. Disappear.

Every now and then the pain would rise and she'd need that hand even more. Then there'd be a growl from Blake and movement and people and the fog would descend again.

And his hand kept right on holding her. Stopping her disappearing into the whiteness.

He was her one reality, she thought with the only vestige of reality she had left to her. Blake.

'Sleep,' he kept saying whenever she stirred, whenever things started crowding in. 'There's nothing to worry about. There's nothing to do, my Maggie, except sleep.'

And finally, finally, the fog receded and she woke up. She could hardly explain it. One minute the fog was all-enveloping; the next she was opening her eyes and the fog was gone. The sun was shining on the white coverlet.

Blake was asleep in the chair beside her.

He looked appalling. He looked battle worn, unshaved, gaunt, exhausted. He looked like he should be in this bed instead of her.

His hand still held hers.

She looked down at it, at the lean, long fingers, at the strength, at the link.

She glanced out the window and saw sunshine. Water glistening—the river beyond. No rain.

She turned again to look at that hand, and Blake was wide awake and watching her.

'Good morning, sleepyhead,' he said, and smiled, but his smile was different from any smile she'd ever seen. A warrior after battle. A warrior who'd been too close...

'Sleepyhead yourself,' she whispered. 'You're the one who was sleeping.' She glanced out the window again. 'It's morning.'

'It is.'

'I've been in here all night?'

'You've been in here for two days and three nights,' he said, and waited for that to sink in.

There was a bandage on her head. She put a hand up and touched it. Felt the lack of hair.

'We had to cut it,' he said ruefully. 'I was in a bit of a hurry and I'm not much at hairdressing. When the bandages come off we'll find you a stylist.'

'I'll be punk for a while?'

'Maybe you will,' he agreed. 'Lopsided mohawk. It had to be done. You gave yourself one hell of a bang.'

She lay back on the pillows and thought about it. Blake let her hand go, poured two glasses of water, handed one to her—watched to make sure her shaking hand wasn't about to drop it—and then drank himself. He looked like a man who needed it.

Cranial burr-hole. The words came floating out of the fog. Pressure.

'You operated.'

'I was...lucky,' he said. 'You had a massive haematoma, and I could see you slipping, but Tom was driving his dad's farm ute. It had a toolbox in the back containing a drill, plus a set of lovely, new, clean drill bits. All sizes. Tom had his phone. I rang a neurologist mate in Melbourne. Tom held the phone while I drilled. Thankfully it took the pressure off instantly. Exciting, huh?'

And she heard his voice shake. She heard the lingering terror in it.

She'd seen burr-holes drilled with patients in nice, clean theatre settings, and they were so often too late.

Pressure from bleeding on the brain…

She touched the bandage again and she knew how lucky she'd been.

'Thank you,' she said simply, and he sat again and took her hand and held.

'I never knew how much I needed you,' he said simply. 'Until I thought I was losing you. I've known you for two weeks. I can't possibly need you that much but I do.'

'Blake…' He'd taken her breath away. She lay on the pillows and watched his face, and saw raw, naked need. Pain.

'Blake,' she said again, and reached out, and he moved, gathering her into his arms, gently, tenderly, holding her as she needed to be held. His heart against hers. Washing away the last of the fog. Just holding.

'I need you to marry me, Maggie,' he whispered, and her world stilled.

Marry…

He pulled away at that, and saw her face, and he laughed, a raw, jagged laugh that contained pain as well as humour.

'Um…let's recall that,' he said, and she saw he was striving for normality, for a place that didn't encompass the fear he'd faced. 'It's way too soon.'

'I...I can't...' The fog was wisping in again. All she wanted to do was say yes, sink into this man's arms and never let go, but some vestige of the old Maggie was re-surfacing, ringing warning bells, stopping her from take this amazing, irreversible leap. 'Blake, I can't...think.'

'No,' he said, and he smiled and then he tugged her back to him and he kissed her, a whisper kiss, light, loving on her lips. And then he propelled her back on the pillows. 'Of course you can't. And I can't either, my love. I've hardly slept. You're full of analgesics. We need to sort ourselves out and find some sort of normal-ity and go from there.'

He smiled at her then, and it was a smile that made her heart turn over. It was a smile that had her forget-ting that her head was starting to pound again. It was a smile that made her world shift.

'I'll ring for some more pain relief for you,' he said. 'And then I'll go and wash and sleep. But then I'll come back. But I'll keep coming back, my Maggie. For now and for always, and that's a promise.'

He left. She slept and when she woke up he wasn't there. Mary was, fussing in the background, adjusting drips.

'Hi,' she said, and grinned. 'Welcome back to the real world.'

'Blake?' She couldn't help himself.

'Sent home with a flea in his ear,' she said. 'Ross told him unless he got out of here he'd get Security to eject him. He didn't want two patients and the man's exhausted. He hardly left you for three days.'

'Three days...'

'Oh, he's gorgeous,' Ronnie said happily. 'And his little girl... We brought her in here, you know, while you were so sick, because Ronnie knew he was torn. Ross decided another helicopter trip was worth it to collect her. She's a darling. Half the hospital's in love with her. But, oh, Maggie, Blake's wonderful. What a wonderful solution. You should see him with Pete. Pete's been beside himself, so scared for you, and every time you were deeply asleep Blake'd go to him. We'll wheel him in to see you later, but Blake's reassured him completely.

'Oh, he's lovely… He can be big brother to your tribe—a dad almost—and you can be mum for Ruby. Ross is already talking to him about part-time work here. Apparently he could work here two days, and Sydney three days. It's a happy ever after. The whole valley's happy for you, Maggie. It's a happy ever after for everyone.'

It took her a few more days before she felt anywhere approaching normal. She had more grazes and scrapes than she wanted to think about. She had broken ribs. She was being loaded with antibiotics and care and demands for rest, and she was being told over and over that she was the luckiest woman in the world.

She was.

She lay back on her hospital pillows, she watched the sunbeams on the coverlet, she watched the faces of her scared siblings when they visited—apparently they'd finally managed to set up a barge for river crossings. She listened to Pete's stammering apology, she hugged him, she smiled at Blake, and she watched with love as he played with Ruby on her coverlet.

Then, on the day she was due to leave hospital, she told him she wasn't going to marry him.

* * *

He'd come in by himself. The kids had pleaded to be allowed to help bring her home but that'd mean four kids and a baby. Pete's leg was in a cast so he'd need the entire back seat. It was all or none so he decreed none.

He drove to the hospital using the freshly organised barge, set in place until the bridge could be rebuilt. The worst of the bad weather was gone. The river level was dropping every day, only the mass of debris on the banks showing the maelstrom it had been.

Blake wasn't looking at scenery, however. He knew this would be decision day, and he walked into Maggie's room and he knew the moment he saw her face what her answer would be.

'Too soon?' he asked, trying to keep the tone light. Trying to ignore the lurch in the pit of his gut.

She was dressed, ready to leave with him. She was wearing her faded jeans and a loose, oversized windcheater that was easy to take on and off over her bandaged head.

She was still heavily bandaged. The Corella Valley hairdresser had come in and clipped her lovely curls on the undamaged parts of her scalp back to a boyish, elfin crop.

She looked absurdly young, absurdly vulnerable—and absurdly beautiful. All he wanted to do was gather her into his arms, yet her expression said don't.

'I can't,' she said, and her words were anguished.

'No,' he said. He crossed to the bed where she was sitting and because he couldn't help himself he tilted her chin with his fingers and brushed her lips with his. He wanted—more than anything he'd ever wanted in his life—to gather her into his arms and kiss her as he needed to kiss her, but somehow he held back. Somehow he held to the last vestiges of his self-control.

'I can't marry you,' she whispered.

'That's what I thought you meant.'

'Blake, I'm sorry.'

'Don't be,' he said, still striving for lightness. 'It's your life, Maggie.'

'But it's not my life,' she said, and suddenly she wasn't whispering any more.

He stilled. 'Is that why?' he said slowly. 'Because you're encumbered with the kids, with responsibilities? You know I how much I want to share those.'

'That's just it,' she said bitterly. 'Of course you do.'

She turned and looked out the window. The river was flowing peacefully in the distance. From here they could see the far side of the valley. They could almost see the homestead, filled with kids and dogs and…family.

'It's my dream,' she said.

'Your drink-can dream?'

'Don't laugh.'

'I'm not laughing. I would never laugh at you.'

She turned then and met his gaze straight on. She gazed at him and he didn't falter. He looked back at her, calm and sure, and he tried to put every ounce of love he felt for this woman into that gaze.

'I know you wouldn't,' she said at last. 'I know. But it still is a dream, and if I married you…' She hesitated, touched the bandages on her head as if they hurt—but maybe it was something else that was hurting.

'Blake, these last weeks have been…stunning. For both of us. You've taken responsibility for your sister's baby. You've been immersed in my family up to your ears. You've been hauled out of your life as an independent city surgeon, engaged—all right,' she added hastily as she saw his face—'partnered by a colleague you've been with for years. You've come back to a place that's filled with emotion for you and I've thrown more at you. You've saved my brother's life and you've saved mine.

'That's an awesome amount of emotion to jam into three weeks. Do you think I should ask you to commit for the rest of your life on the strength of it? It's been a crazy, roller-coaster ride, Blake. Now you need to get off the roller-coaster, settle, figure where you want to take things with Ruby and go from there.'

'I need you, Maggie,' he said, surely and steadily. 'Yes, it's only three weeks but when I thought I could lose you...' He broke off and he knew she could hear the power of what he'd gone through.

At the base of a cliff. Watching the swelling...

It still made him feel ill, but it wasn't helping his cause.

'I never knew what love was,' he said simply. 'Until I thought I'd lost you. If love is needing, like needing a part of me...'

'But I'm not needful, Blake,' she said, calmly and steadily. 'I'm grateful—you can't imagine how grateful I am, but I won't marry you because I need you. Even if...even if your need is love. I've fallen for you, hard, but I'm seeing you as a guy who's taken on his baby niece, who helped me save Christopher and Pete, who saved me. And, yes, who needs me. But that's not a basis for a marriage.'

'No, but love is. Surely the two combine. Maggie, I've thought it out. We could organise things... I could work a couple of days in Sydney a week and spend the rest of the time here. We could fill the house with kids. They could come and go as they pleased, back and forth to your mother, back and forth to us. You'd be there whenever they need you. Ruby would have a mother…'

It was the wrong thing to say. He knew it as he saw her expression change. He had this all wrong.

This was not a sure and loving Maggie. This was still a trapped Maggie.

'I would be,' she whispered. 'Ruby's twisting herself around my heart already. But it's not fair.'

'Fair?'

'My heart's already so twisted,' she said. 'From the time I can first remember. "Maggie, push your brother's pram, he's crying. Maggie, your little sister's wet. Maggie, sleep with Liselle, she's having nightmares. Maggie, you need to stay home from school this week, Donny's got measles." And I did it. Every single time, I did it—how could I not? Because I loved them. I love them. And here you are, asking me to love…more.'

'You don't want…'

'Of course I want,' she said, and she tilted her chin and looked at him—really looked at him. 'I'm falling so hard. If you took me into your arms right now…' But she put up her hands as if to ward him off. 'But I don't want you to.

'Really?'

'I don't know,' she said, and she didn't sound sure any more. She sounded…scared. Desolate. 'Blake, I don't know. All I do know is that I'm not game to try. I'd marry you and it'd be gorgeous and the whole valley would be happy for me. The kids would be beside themselves and it'd solve all your problems and I'd end up loving Ruby to bits… And one day I might wake up and think, What did I collect all those tin cans for?'

'We could travel,' he said, slowly, trying to sound confident. Trying to sound like he thought her qualms were minor. 'Together.'

'But I've had…*together*,' she said, and she flinched as she said it. 'I know. That sounds appalling when I say I'm falling in love with you in the same breath, but I've never had anything but together. You've come here for three weeks, you've walked straight into my together and you think it's magic. But you've had, what, thirty-six years of You. I've never had Me and I want it. I want to learn Me.'

She shook her head then, falling silent. He watched her, quiet and still, knowing the time for argument was not now. Knowing that pushing her now would do his cause no good—would even do harm. Knowing he had to let her be.

'Blake, I'm scared,' she whispered. 'I'm terrified I'll wake up in ten years surrounded by more kids and more dogs and more drama, and I'll resent it all and become a bitter old lady who snaps at kids and locks herself in the bathroom and sulks…'

'The bathroom?' he said faintly.

'It's the only place I can ever get away,' she said. 'And even then they bang on the door. "Maggie, hurry up, I need a note for school. Maggie, I need to tell you about my boyfriend. Maggie, if this pimple doesn't go down I'll die." And don't you dare laugh, Blake Samford.'

'I won't laugh. I've told you before, I'd never laugh at you, Maggie.'

'And don't be gorgeous either,' she managed, trying

to glare, only her eyes were filling. She swiped away tears with anger and the desire to gather her in his arms was overwhelming. He didn't. He was proud of himself that he didn't, but it nearly killed him.

'So, what,' he said at last. 'Back to the seven-year plan, huh?'

'I… Yes,' she said. 'It's better than nothing.'

'I'm better than nothing.'

'Yes, you are,' she said, controlling herself again. Taking a deep breath and moving on. 'But you deserve something more than a woman who's scared that marriage might seem a trap.'

'I'd never marry you if you felt like that.'

'Well, then,' she said, and rose and looked down at her packed duffel bag. At her hospital room crowded with flowers from almost everyone in the valley. At him.

'Well, then,' she said again. 'It's time to go home. Time for you to go back to Sydney. Time for me to find another place to live.

'I'm not selling the farm, Maggie.'

'You're not?'

'There's not a thing you can do about that,' he told her. 'I've fallen for the farm as well.'

'You're not…going to live there?'

'No,' he said. 'I wouldn't do that to myself. To live next door to you…'

'You'll take Ruby back to Sydney?'

'Yes.'

'Will you cope?'

'I believe I can,' he said, and managed a grin. 'Without calling on Maggie. But, Maggie…'

'Yes?'

'I'm not moving out of your life. Not entirely. I'm your landlord and I'll need to check the farm out from time to time. As well as that, the kids have done some heart twisting as well. I've promised Pete I'll take him to Sydney and get him some driving lessons as soon as he turns sixteen. I'd like to organise an online tutor for Liselle and her calculus.'

'There's no need—'

'There is a need,' he said softly. 'Just because you can't marry me it doesn't mean I can stop caring.'

'You…understand.'

'Yes, I do,' he said with a heavy heart, and he did. 'I wish I didn't, but I do. I wish… I wish…' He hesitated and then he shrugged. 'I'm not sure what I wish,' he told her, and he lifted her duffel with one hand and took her hand in the other. 'But let's take you home, and let's get on with our lives while I figure it out.'

CHAPTER ELEVEN

CHRISTMAS at the Tildens' was always crazy. Everyone was home, and the tiny house was bursting at the seams.

'Let's have Christmas at Blake's,' Liselle had pleaded. 'It's huge and Blake won't mind.'

He wouldn't mind, Maggie thought. He'd been a constant presence in the kids' lives for six months now and they regarded him more as a benevolent uncle than as Maggie's landlord.

He'd only visited twice, flying visits to install a new farm manager—Harold was too old and Blake didn't want Maggie responsible for his cattle—and to check for himself that Pete's leg was healing as he thought it should.

They'd been fast trips and he hadn't brought Ruby. 'I have a fabulous housekeeper-nanny,' he told Maggie. 'And I've given up the job as Head of Orthopaedics. I'm an Indian rather than a chief now, but it means I spend more time with my little girl.'

He'd brought photographs and he showed them to her with pride, but he made no mention of marriage, no mention that he wasn't coping without her, no mention that she'd made the wrong decision.

She hadn't, she told herself over and over, but the

kids had his number on speed dial, she heard them chatting to him about trivial stuff, and she felt…jealous?

Ridiculous.

But he was a friend. The boys took their troubles to Blake now, and for that she was grateful.

Liselle got first-class honours in her calculus. 'Blake thinks I can be a doctor,' she'd told Maggie, almost bursting with pride. 'He's going to help me.'

Somehow he'd inveigled himself into their lives and she loved him for it.

But not enough?

Not enough to want Christmas at his house. Not enough to think she'd made a mistake.

Now she woke up on Christmas morning and for about the thousandth time since he'd left she thought of him straight away.

She was back at her mother's house. She was sharing a bed with Susie. Liselle was in the bed beside them. Blackie and Tip were under the bed. All her brothers and sisters were home.

She was surrounded, just like always. Any minute now she'd get up and stuff the turkey. Her mother would waft out for present giving and set up candles on the table or make a new cocktail. Her father might drop in later with the pregnant Sashabelle. Expecting gifts. Not giving any.

But things were easing. Donny had finished his apprenticeship and Nickie had graduated and was choosing between three excellent job offers. Two down, six to go.

Six years left?

To what? Kir on the Left Bank of Paris.

It was losing its gloss.

I'm turning sour already, she thought, and decided, Turkey. She tossed back the covers—and paused.

She'd heard a truck approaching—or trucks? They stopped, just outside the house.

As her feet touched the bare wooden floor there was an enormous whine, like the tray on a truck heaving upwards...

And then a crash that had her jumping out of her skin. That had Liselle and Susie sitting bolt upright in bed and the dogs going out of their minds.

Another crash, bigger than the first.

Amazingly Susie was giggling, whooping, heading for the door. And then she looked back as if she'd forgotten something important. She grabbed an envelope from under the pillow.

'Blake said to give you this,' she said importantly. 'But I have to get mine to put on top.' She dived under the bed and hauled out a huge plastic bag filled with... cans. Empty drink cans.

'And me,' Liselle said sleepily. 'Mine are in the wardrobe. Open it, Susie, love.'

Susie obligingly opened the wardrobe—and let loose a cascade of cans.

'They're from the whole of Corella Valley High,' Louise said proudly. 'Six months' collecting.'

The door opened. The rest of her family was crowding in the doorway.

'Here's ours,' they told her, and they were practically buried in cans.

'What...? What...?'

'I've got some, too.' It was her mother, holding two small bags of cans like they were diamonds. 'I had to change drinking bottled tonic to canned tonic, just for you, love. But it was worth it. You're a good girl, Maggie.'

'But it's mostly from Blake. It's Blake's present.' Christopher was practically bouncing with excitement. 'Come and see, come and see, come and see.'

So she went, pushing through a sea of cans, still clutching her unopened envelope.

Peter had the front door wide, and his beam was almost wider. 'How cool is this?' he demanded. 'Blake says these are from the whole of Sydney Central Hospital for six months. And it's every single person in the valley. And Donny's garage and our school and university, and Blake says we have enough for at least six months...'

'Shush,' Susie said, bossy and exasperated. 'She hasn't read the letter.'

She wasn't looking at the letter. She was looking at a mountain. Cans, cans and more cans. The entire yard was buried under drink cans.

'Two shipping containers,' Pete said, awed. 'Two full shipping containers, plus what we've got. You have no idea, Maggie...'

'Blake...' she breathed.

'Read the letter,' Susie demanded, and finally the little girl lost patience with her big sister, ripped it open, stood in front of her and read out loud.

'"Darling Maggie...". Oooer, darling...'

'Cut it out,' Louise snapped. 'Read it like it is.'

Susie glowered and then grinned and read.

'"Darling Maggie. Seven years is too long. Anything could happen in seven years. They could stop serving kir on the Left Bank. The pyramids might erode. I could wear out waiting. So here's an alternative.

We've weighed our cans and we figure they're good for six months' travel. On your own. With what you already have, plus the extras the kids have found since we weighed them, we reckon you can go and see whatever you want in the world. But before you start objecting, you need to listen to the rest of the plan...'

'I don't need to read this,' Susie said. 'I know.'

'Blake's taking six months' leave,' Liselle said. 'It's paternity leave 'cos he's formally adopting Ruby.'

'And he's staying at Corella View,' Pete said. 'And he's going to teach me cool driving stuff.'

'And we can stay here with Mum or we can stay with him if Mum gets sick of us,' Chris added, with a sideways glance at his mother.

'And Ronnie's promised to look after Ruby if Blake starts feeling...house...house...'

'Housebound,' Louise finished for her. 'But us older ones are planning on coming home often as well. You've done so much for us, Maggie.'

'And Blake and Ronnie have organised you time off work,' Pete added.

'And Blake says he can get you a passport really fast. He says you should go to Africa first 'cos it'll be cold in Europe in winter. But he says it's up to you.'

'Blake...' she managed again.

'A million cans,' her mother said. 'All over my front lawn. I'll give him such a talking to when I see him next.'

'Which would be now,' a low voice said, and she whirled and it was Blake. He was standing on the veranda. Watching. Listening.

He was dressed even more casually than the day she'd first seen him. Faded jeans. A checked, open-necked shirt. Boots. He looked like a farmer rather than a city surgeon.

He was holding Ruby.

Cattleman with baby?

He looked so sexy he made her toes curl.

'You're free,' he said, softly, firmly, lovingly. 'Maggie Tilden, your seven-year plan just turned into now. We've all done it. We love you, Maggie, and we're sending you away.'

'But you'll come back?' Susie asked, suddenly anxious. 'Maggie, you won't forget us? You'll come home?'

Blake was smiling at her. Smiling and smiling. Her heart was turning somersaults, backward flips, any gymnastic manoeuvre it could think of. All at once.

She wished she wasn't wearing pyjamas. She wished she wasn't surrounded by family. She wished she wasn't surrounded by thousands of tin cans.

No, she didn't. She wished for none of those things because for now, for this moment, there was only this man, only this moment, this smile.

Blake.

'You did all this,' she managed.

'Six months' scrounging,' he said, and chuckled. 'I owe favours to every janitor in Sydney.'

'The kids…'

'Scrounged like champions. See, we all want to get rid of you. Mostly because we figure…if we set you free, you'll fly home.'

'Like a pigeon.'

'I prefer dove,' he said comfortably. 'A lovely, loving white dove. Liselle, do you think you might take Ruby for a moment? I can't see any mistletoe but I'm sure there's some around here somewhere. I need to kiss your sister goodbye.'

'Goodbye…'

'With no promises,' he said, as he headed along the veranda to where she was standing, barefooted in her pyjamas, tousled with sleep. As he gathered her into his arms and held her. Just held her. Asking for no promises. Placing no expectations on her.

'We're giving you yourself back, Maggie, love,' he told her. 'We're giving you the world in the shape of a mountain of tin cans. And if you can see your way to steering this way at the end of your adventures…'

'Kiss her now,' Donny yelled. 'Go on, mate, get it over with.'

'No pressure,' Blake said, and his dark eyes gleamed down into hers. 'No pressure, Maggie, love, but if you could possibly tilt your chin…'

She did. How could a girl not?

How could a woman not kiss a man who was giving her the world?

Who wasn't asking her to marry him.

Who was setting her free.

She watched giraffes sway majestically across the African savannah. She woke under canvas and in the dawn she heard lions roaring. She had to shoo monkeys from her breakfast. She wrote to Blake about it.

He sent photos back of Ruby and told her how his work was going and talked to her about a new breed of cattle he thought he might introduce to the farm.

She took camel rides around the pyramids. A kid photographed her for money and she emailed the snap home.

Blake sent a snap of himself riding a horse he'd bought. It seemed Liselle was teaching him how to ride.

She watched funeral pyres beside the Ganges and wondered how she could describe the smell, the sights to Blake. She wandered from street stall to street stall and she didn't get sick once. Blake sounded almost irritated. 'Everyone gets sick—what's your stomach made of?'

He sent advice on hygiene and links to sites on intestinal worms. She laughed but he also sent a picture of him at a staff dinner at Corella Hospital and she looked at Mary standing beside him and she thought... she thought...

No. She wouldn't think. She was free.

She walked the Great Wall in China—okay, not all of it but enough to get sore feet—and she gazed at the hidden warriors with awe and gratitude that she could be in this place at this time.

Blake had seen them, too. She wished...

No, she couldn't wish, for who could wish for more than she'd dreamed of?

She drank Guinness in fabulous Irish pubs. She checked out some ancestors and decided she liked being a little bit Irish.

Blake told her about how Mary had been to Ireland last year and researched all her Irish ancestors.

She was interested—sort of. She liked Mary. Mary was a friend.

Why the niggle?

She dived from a caique into the turquoise waters off a Greek isle. She got sunburned, but she didn't tell Blake because he'd lecture her and she liked being free to get sunburned or not. Didn't she?

She wandered the bazaars in Istanbul, Cairo, Morocco. She looked, she tasted, she smelled and she listened. She drank kir on the Left Bank in Paris. She looked and looked and looked and she felt and felt and felt.

And she tried not to wish for more.

Every night she went back to her hotel room or her tent or yurt, or whatever weird and wonderful place she was staying in and she used the fantastic satellite internet Blake had organised for her and she contacted home.

She told the kids what she'd done that day. Sometimes they were interested. Mostly they were more interested in telling her the things that were happening to them.

And almost every night she talked to Blake, who was interested in her. Who asked the right questions. Who got it that she'd been disappointed in kir. Who grinned when she said the Eiffel tower was just too high and she'd taken the lift. Who agreed that seal colonies stank.

Who showed her pictures of a happy, bouncing, healing Ruby with pride, who explained that her legs were almost in line now, and she was sitting up, and teething. Who talked about the valley with love and with pride. Who spoke of the people he was meeting, of Ronnie, who was awesome at helping, and Mary, who was such a friend...

He smiled at her and said goodnight—even when it was morning his time—and he sent her to sleep happy. Or happyish. For the longer she was away, the more she thought. She was living a dream but what if, in following her dream, she was letting another go?

What if she'd made a mistake?

She hadn't. She knew she'd made the right decision. She loved what she was doing and she embraced it with all her heart, but the heart swelled to fit all comers and there was a corner...a Blake corner...

Please, her heart whispered. Please...

And six months later she walked through the customs gates at Sydney airport, feeling jet-lagged, feeling weird, feeling hopeful but almost afraid to hope...

Blake was there.

All by himself.

No kids. No Ruby.

No Mary.

Just Blake.

'My love,' he said as she reached him, and he held out his arms.

She walked right into them. He folded her against his heart, and she stayed there for a very long time.

He'd organised things so Ronnie was with Ruby, so they had the night in Sydney to themselves.

He took her back to his new little bachelor-nursery pad near the hospital and he made her dinner while she spent half an hour under streaming-hot water and washed every part of her. She dressed in jogging pants and a windcheater because she had nothing else clean. Most of her luggage was still in the back of Blake's car, ready to be taken to Corella Valley the next day. She'd kept only her overnight bag. She should have kept something special aside, she thought ruefully. A little black dress?

A sexy negligee?

But she walked out of the bathroom and Blake was stirring something at the stove. He was wearing jeans and an apron. He turned and smiled at her and his smile said it didn't matter one whit what she was wearing. She could be wearing nothing.

She loved this man with all her heart. She'd loved this man around the world and back again—and she'd come home.

'Will you marry me now?' he asked, and her world stood still.

'I think I might just have stuffed that,' he said ruefully as the silence stretched on. 'Patience is not my strong suit. I thought…dinner. Champagne. Something romantic playing in the background. It's just… I look at you and I can't…'

He stopped. He took off his apron. He took the eight steps that separated them and took her hands in his.

'I got it wrong,' he told her. 'I've had months to think about it, almost a year, and I know exactly how I got it wrong. I told you I needed you. Maybe I do; maybe that's part of the equation, but it's not the main thing here. The main thing, the huge, overriding elephant in the room, or more than elephant if I can think of anything bigger, is that I love you, Maggie Tilden. I've loved you since the first moment I saw you. So…can you cope without the violins and roses? Can we look past the need? Can you forget that I ever needed you and can you just love me?'

And how was a woman to answer that?

With an open heart.

'I…I always have,' she whispered. And then, more firmly, because the joy in her heart was settling, fitting into all the edges with a sweetness that made the path ahead seem sure and true and right, 'My love, I always will.'

And they looked at each other, just looked, and something passed between them, so sweet, so strong that Maggie knew a bond was forged right then that would last for ever.

'I'm not asking you to be mother to Ruby,' he said. 'I've organised—'

'Hush,' she told him, and she placed her finger on his lips. 'I'm not asking you to be a brother to my siblings either, but I have a feeling you already are. And Ruby's as much mine as yours. If you're willing to share.'

'Maggie, to ask you to take us on...'

'I don't think it's taking on,' she managed. 'It's loving. It's different.'

'Six months ago...'

'I wasn't where I am now,' she said, steadily, lovingly, because she'd had six months to think this through and every night as she'd talked to Blake she'd become more and more sure of where her heart lay.

'I've been surrounded by love since I was born. Trapped by it, in a sense. What you've done for me, Blake...you've set me free so I can choose love. I've had six wonderful months of being by myself, but I wasn't by myself. I had the kids in the background. I had Ruby. I had Corella Valley. They were my rock, my base, my knowledge that of all the places in the world, there was a place for me. But most of all there was you. My one true thing. My love.'

'Maggie...' He held her, tenderly though, as if she was fragile. As if she might evaporate. As if she might still gather her things and head out that door, back to the world. 'Maggie, are you sure?'

'I've never been more sure,' she whispered.

'I've organised it. I've cut back, hard. I'm a part-time

doctor until Ruby reaches school age. She's my responsibility, Maggie, not yours.'

'I'll be a part-time nurse, too,' she said comfortably.
'If you don't mind sharing.'

'Maggie…'

She pulled back and looked at him—really looked
at him. Needing him to see the whole package. 'I still
need to stay in Corella Valley,' she said.

'Of course you do,' he said. 'Just lucky there's a fabulous homestead and enough work for both of us. I'm getting on brilliantly with the hospital staff—they've called
on me already, and you should see the new bridge!'

'You'd stay there?'

'The Valley needs an orthopaedic surgeon. It also
needs a fabulous district nurse-cum-midwife. How
lucky's that?'

'Lucky?' she whispered. 'Or meant?'

'I guess meant,' he said as he tilted her chin and
gazed into her eyes. 'Maggie, I've loved you to the ends
of the earth and back and I always will, but now will
you come home with me?'

'I… Something's burning on the stove.' How had she
noticed that when all she could feel was him?

'Maggie…'

'Yes, I will,' she said, positively, absolutely, and she
wrapped her arms around this man she loved with all
her heart. Who cared if the apartment burned—this was
more important. 'I may travel again but it'll take ages to
collect enough cans. Double this time because wherever
I go, you go. Plus Ruby. Plus whoever else needs us.'

'That's a lot of can collecting,' he said unsteadily. 'I
wonder if champagne bottles count.'

'I'm sure they do.' The smell was getting stronger.

Maybe she could be practical Maggie for a moment. 'Blake, the dinner...'

'I s'pose,' he said, and sighed dramatically and swept her up into his arms and held her close. Two strides took him to the cooker and the gas was turned off.

'Disaster averted,' he told her. 'But I'm not thinking dinner right now.' He was carrying her towards the bedroom, laughing down at her, loving her with his eyes. 'So, Maggie Tilden, love of my life, woman of my dreams, will you marry me? Will you take me on as well as all the other wonderful loves you hold in your heart?'

'You're the biggest,' she said, and she smiled back at him. She smiled and smiled, at this lovely, sexy, toe-curlingly gorgeous man who promised to be a part of her life for ever. 'You're the biggest and the best, and you're my for-ever love. Of course I'll marry you.'

And then they reached the bedroom and there was nothing else to say.

Two people were one.

They were Maggie and Blake, and they were starting their whole life together.

And in Corella Valley...

'I've got two hundred and three,' Susie announced, looking at her pile of cans with satisfaction.

'I'm up to four hundred and sixty,' Chris crowed. 'And Liselle says her dorm's up to a thousand. How many do you reckon before we can all go?'

'I'm guessing trillions but we can do it. Maggie'll be so happy.'

'Maggie *and* Blake,' Chris corrected her. 'But you're right. Gee, it's going to take a lot of cans for all of us.'

'We've got time,' Susie said in satisfaction. 'If we just keep collecting and collecting we'll be able to do anything we want. Do you reckon they'll mind that we've filled Maggie's bedroom with cans as a home-coming present?'

'Nah,' Chris said. 'They've got loads of bedrooms. I reckon they'll only want one from now on.'

'Really?'

'Yeah,' Chris said with thirteen-year-old wisdom. 'I think Maggie's given up being alone.'

* * * * *

DARE SHE DREAM
OF FOREVER?

BY
LUCY CLARK

First published in Great Britain 2013
by Mills & Boon, an imprint of Harlequin (UK) Limited.
Harlequin (UK) Limited, Eton House, 18-24 Paradise Road,
Richmond, Surrey TW9 1SR

© Anne Clark & Peter Clark 2013

ISBN: 978 0 263 89871 2

Harlequin (UK) policy is to use papers that are natural, renewable and recyclable products and made from wood grown in sustainable forests. The logging and manufacturing process conform to the legal environmental regulations of the country of origin.

Printed and bound in Spain
by Blackprint CPI, Barcelona

Dear Reader

Ebony and Bartholomew had to wait a long time to have their story told, being the last book in our six-part *Goldmark* series, and I thank them dearly for their patience.

It was definitely an interesting story to write—especially given Bartholomew had made appearances as the bachelor brother in the other five books. And because he was the bachelor brother it seemed only right that he should fall in love with a woman who has the whole package—not only beauty and brains. Ebony comes complete with two children and her mother. It was also important, though, to give Bartholomew a deep yearning to become a parent, and gorgeous Timmy fills that need.

Ebony is someone with a deep yearning to be loved again. Moving back to Australia is a way of making a new start for herself and her children, as well as helping her mother. Family is important not only to our characters but to us as well, and throughout the entire *Goldmark* series 'family' has been our main theme.

The epilogue in this book ties up the six-part series, and is a scene I had in my head almost from the beginning. Remembering loved ones in a positive way can only enhance our lives and help us march into the future stronger, wiser and happier.

Warmest regards

Lucy

**These books are also available in eBook format
from www.millsandboon.co.uk**

Dedication:

To our families:

Ruth, Bill, John, Trish, Laura, Allan, Louise, Sheena,
Will, Brandon, Clover, Janelle, Paul, Kerryn, Dave, Eva,
Natalie, Glenda, John, Kath, Josh, Luke, Vikie, Corey,
John, Catherine, Sean, Rosie, Claire, Anthony, Caitlin,
Mitchell, Mark and, of course, Melanie and Austin.

We love you all.

Tim 1:17

CHAPTER ONE

EBONY parked her car in the hospital car park and headed in for her first day at work at Canberra General Hospital. She kept her head high as she walked through the departments, heading towards the office for the director of anaesthetics.

She couldn't believe the nervous knots in her stomach and told herself that while it was understandable, it was also ridiculous. She'd been working as a neuro-surgical anaesthetist in the United Kingdom for many years and the fact that she'd relocated her family back to Australia meant she was doing the same job but in a different location.

'Breathe. Everything will be fine,' she whispered to herself as she pressed the button for the lift. Five floors up was the department of Anaesthetics. She'd had an online interview with Director Vance, been offered and accepted the position as anaesthetist and now all that was left to do was to sign the final papers that would make her a permanent employee of Canberra General hospital.

'You are a professional. You will be calm and in control.' She forced herself to relax and breathe deeply, stepping confidently into the lift when it arrived, and before she knew it, she was walking down the department's long corridor towards the receptionist's desk.

'Hello. I'm Dr Ebony Matthews, the new anaesthetist.'

'Ah, Dr Matthews. Director Vance is expecting you.' She glanced over her shoulder at the director's closed office door, where raised male voices could be heard. 'Er…he shouldn't be long. Anyway, I'm Michelle and I have your new roster here and the department's guidelines and protocols and a map of the hospital.' Michelle gathered the pieces of paper together and placed them into a folder before handing it to Ebony. 'Can I get you a cup of tea or coffee while you wait?' The phone on Michelle's desk began to ring and the male voices behind the director's door rose a decibel higher.

'Get me an anaesthetist who knows what they're doing!' the booming voice growled, and Ebony froze for a moment, hoping the owner of the voice wasn't going to be one of her new colleagues. Perhaps he was an administrator from another department.

Michelle grimaced at the noise and seemed relieved when Ebony declined the offer of refreshments. 'I'll just sit over here and wait until the director's ready.'

Michelle nodded and turned her attention to answering the phone. Ebony sat on the seat, forcing herself to take the papers out of the folder and at least pretend to peruse them, even though she was listening intently to every word being loudly spoken through the director's closed door.

'I don't want to know about a mix-up in the rosters, Robert. I don't care if your best people are off sick. You don't send me an inexperienced anaesthetist again. I'd rather cancel the surgery than risk a patient's life. I'm head of Neurosurgery and in my theatre my rules apply.'

Ebony closed her eyes and sighed. Head of neuro-surgery? That meant the chances of her working along-side the irate man were extremely high given she was a neurosurgically trained anaesthetist.

'I understand completely,' she heard Robert Vance say in a calm and placating manner. 'We have a new anaesthetist starting today who has specialised in neu-rosurgery. She used to work in the UK with Hartley Grant-Smythe.'

Ebony slowly shook her head. The last thing she needed now was to be working with a neurosurgeon with a temper. During the last few months, she'd re-signed from her very secure job, uprooted her children and moved to Australia. What she needed when she came to work was clear direction in a professional en-vironment.

Of course the surgeon Director Vance was talking to would be impressed with the name Hartley Grant-Smythe as Professor Grant-Smythe was the world's leading expert on neurosurgical procedures, having pioneered a lot of the newest techniques in this area. Ebony had co-authored three papers with him over the past few years, as well as writing a few of her own about the complementary anaesthesia administration for these new medical breakthroughs.

'She's worked with Hartley?' The surgeon's tone set-tled somewhat at this news. 'I want her and *only* her for my theatre lists. Understand?'

'I'll adjust the rosters accordingly,' Robert Vance replied, relief clearly evident in his tone at finding an immediate solution to the problem. A moment later the door to the director's office snapped open and Ebony found herself springing to her feet, her eyes wide, the papers slipping from her hands and fluttering to the floor in a haphazard mess. She looked down at the papers. Darn. There was no time to gather them up before the two men saw her. Talk about making a good first impression! This was the pits.

Ebony squared her shoulders and pasted on her most professional and polite smile for the two men coming through the door.

'Ah…' Robert's smile was wide. 'And here she is now.' He held out his hand to her, neatly avoiding the papers she'd dropped as he stepped closer to shake her hand. 'Dr Matthews. Good to finally meet in person.'

Ebony glanced briefly at the director as their hands connected but apart from that she was more interested in watching the surgeon who had just requested she work exclusively alongside him. He was tall, with short dark brown hair and was dressed in a suit, the jacket having already been discarded. He had intense blue eyes that appeared to be studying her with curiosity.

Robert dropped her hand. 'Dr Matthews, I'd like to introduce you to—'

'Matthews?' Bart interjected.

Ebony swallowed over her own shock as she realised exactly who her new colleague was. 'Bart? Bart Goldmark?' She stared at him in stunned disbelief.

'Matthews? Ebony Matthews?'

Her earlier concern seemed to dissipate as she smiled at his confusion. 'Snowy Mountains High School? You were a few years ahead of me—and actually dated my best friend, Alice.'

'Alice.' He whispered the word and for a split second she saw a flash of pain pierce his eyes before he shook his head and gave her a wide smile. 'Ebony Matthews. Wow.' He held out his hand and she instantly slid hers into it, the warmth of his large palm easily encompassing her small one. Heat spread up her arm at the touch but she ignored it. 'How have you been these past twenty-odd years?'

Ebony smiled brightly at his words but took the opportunity to edge her hand out of his, needing to break the stimulating contact. 'Busy. How about you?'

'Same.' He nodded and crossed his arms over his chest, his gaze quickly encompassing her as though he was trying to reconcile his past image of her with the present one. Ebony fiddled with an earring, feeling a touch self-conscious, wondering if he liked what he saw. She instantly chided herself for being ridiculous. Twenty years was a long time. Of course she'd changed. He'd changed, hadn't he?

She tried to look him over surreptitiously and found herself wondering if his shoulders had been that broad in high school. He was still very handsome, the maturing years only adding to his appeal. When she saw his lips start to curve into a smile, she immediately met his gaze and found him watching her watching him.

'You've worked with Hartley?'

'For the past two years.'

Bart's brow furrowed for a moment and he scratched his head. 'Hold on a second. Have you co-authored papers with him? Matthews, E R. That's you, right?'

'You've obviously read them.'

'They were good.' His smile was widening and Ebony's stomach was fluttering with excited agitation. Had Bart been this good looking back at school? She couldn't remember him setting her pulse racing but back then he'd been dating her best friend so naturally she hadn't seen him in any light other than as her best friend's boyfriend.

'Thank you.' She was starting to become aware of

the director and receptionist watching them with curious interest, their eyes flicking back and forth as though at a tennis match. Bart also seemed to realise they were standing in the middle of the department and cleared his throat.

'Right, I'll be expecting you in Theatre with me today. We'll see how well you fit in with the rest of the team and take it from there.'

'Sounds excellent,' Robert Vance interjected gleefully, before Ebony could respond. 'You two know each other and Dr Matthews clearly has the experience you require, Dr Goldmark. I'll just tidy up the red tape of her appointment here at the hospital and send her down to Theatres, ready for your morning list.'

'Make it quick,' he said, not looking at Robert as he spoke but instead continued to watch Ebony. 'My list starts in forty-five minutes.' He stayed where he was for a moment before shaking his head in bemusement. 'Ebony Matthews. What a small world we live in.' With that, he winked at Ebony, then turned and headed out of the department, leaving her feeling stunned and confused. Had he just been flirting with her?

Ebony quickly bent and began gathering up her papers as Director Vance returned to his office, leaving his office door open for her to follow him. She was glad of the brief reprieve from having everyone looking at her, especially as she needed a few moments to process the fact that she'd be working alongside Bartholomew Goldmark.

He'd been so in love with her friend Alice, even to the point where he'd proposed. Although they'd been young, they'd been determined to get married—until Alice's death. Was it odd that Ebony should be working alongside him now, twenty years later? Or should she have expected to run into some familiar people given Snowy Mountains High School was only a two-hour drive from Canberra? Of one thing she was certain, the years had been good to Bart as he was now more devastatingly handsome than he'd been back then. Tall, dark and definitely handsome, with gorgeous blue eyes.

Ebony stood and shuffled the papers into alignment, tapping them on the receptionist's desk.

'Whooee, that man is like sex on legs. Hottest and most eligible bachelor in the hospital,' Michelle chattered as she fanned her face with her hand. 'It's rare for him to raise his voice like that. Must have been really cross and, well, we all expect surgeons to be a little overbearing and arrogant but Dr Goldmark is really very nice and accommodating.' She stopped, then giggled. 'So what was he like back in high school? I'll bet he was just as handsome then as he is now.'

Ebony smiled but didn't reply. Instead, she shoved the papers back into the folder and pointed to Director Vance's open office door. 'I'd better get this meeting with Director Vance over and done with if I'm to be in Theatre in less than forty-five minutes.'

'Oh. Of course. Yes. You wouldn't want to keep Dr Goldmark waiting.' Michelle sighed.

'No, indeed,' Ebony replied, as she smoothed a hand down her charcoal-grey skirt and straightened her cream shirt before she headed into the director's office. She may be about to work alongside Bart Goldmark but she was also a professional—and for some strange reason she was eager for him to see just how good she was.

There was only one patient on Bart's list that morning, for which Ebony was extremely grateful. After she'd finished her quick meeting with Director Vance, she'd rushed to the elective theatre block—only making one brief wrong turn—and had been welcomed warmly by the theatre clerk.

'Ah. Dr Goldmark said to expect you and he told me to have everything organised as he doesn't want to run late.' The theatre clerk leaned forward a little and said in a stage whisper, 'Timmy's the only patient on the list today and Dr Goldmark always tends to be more particular whenever Timmy needs another operation.'

Ebony nodded as though she understood what that was supposed to mean, wanting the clerk just to hurry up. Her need not to disappoint Bart was beginning to increase. 'So…where do I need to go?'

'Oh, right. Sorry.' The theatre clerk picked up a key and held it out to Ebony. 'Here's a key for a locker. Theatre scrubs are located in the change rooms. The code for the female change rooms is three-seven-nine and your theatre today is theatre five. Timmy's case notes are in the anteroom, ready for you to peruse.'

'Excellent. Thank you,' Ebony said as she accepted the key and walked briskly towards the female changing rooms. It didn't take her long to put her bag and papers into the locker before grabbing a pair of scrubs from the trolley.

Once she'd changed into the baggy blue cotton material, a pair of comfortable shoes on her feet, she grabbed both shoe and hair covers on her way out the changing rooms and followed the signs towards theatre five. In the anteroom was a bench with a set of case notes on it and she picked them up, interested to read about her very first patient at Canberra General.

As she perused the notes, she shook her head as deep sadness started to creep over her. Timmy Schneider, a five-year-old boy who had been diagnosed with a benign tumour at the age of two, was having another round of surgery to correct defects with his shunt. As the encapsulated tumour had been pressing on his cerebellum, an increase of cerebrospinal fluid had pooled in the crevice left after the removal of the tumour. This, in turn, had caused pressure problems for Timmy and so a surgical shunt had been inserted to carry the excess fluid circulating around his brain to empty into his stomach.

Five years old and Timmy had already undergone six surgeries. This would be his seventh. Ebony's heart turned over with sympathy for the boy. The poor little darling. What he must have been going through. To have had more surgeries than years he'd been alive... She swallowed and forced herself to shove those types of deep, caring thoughts into a box and to focus on what needed to be done. It was the one part of her job she often struggled with but she also knew that the caring part of her soul was what made her an excellent anaesthetist.

Besides, Bart would no doubt be here soon, wanting to start his list on time, and if she wasn't organised, if she hadn't spoken to the patient and completed her pre-anaesthetic consult so the surgery could begin on time as scheduled, he might just blow another gasket. Little Timmy deserved one hundred and ten per cent from the medical staff looking after him and she didn't want to be the one rocking the boat, especially not for her first case.

Drawing in a deep breath, Ebony pulled on her professionalism as she heard a bed being wheeled in her direction. A moment later, an orderly and a nurse wheeled Timmy's bed into the anteroom. Ebony smiled at them both but it was the tiny boy, lying in the big, stark white bed that had the side rails up to ensure he didn't roll out, who captured her attention. The nurse was smiling, talking softly to him about a children's television show.

'Which train do you like best?' she asked him as Ebony put the notes on a shelf and came closer to Timmy. She knew, due to the change in anaesthetist, that he hadn't received any sort of pre-medication. The child was lying stiffly, looking straight up, not wanting to make eye contact with anyone. He looked…terrified. Ebony swallowed the lump that instantly stuck in her throat.

'Hi, Timmy,' she said, smiling down at him. 'I'm Ebony. I'm the doctor who's going to be giving you some special medicine to make you go to sleep.'

'Anaefatist,' Timmy mumbled, but his scared blue eyes didn't even waver in her direction.

'Yes, that's right. What a smart boy.' Ebony looked at the nurse, then at the clock, then back to Timmy. She wanted more time with him, to get to know him better, to help him through this difficult time, but the list would be starting soon and it was her job to get the ball rolling.

After the surgery, she promised herself. After the surgery, she would go to the ward, spend time with Timmy, find out what he liked, what made him laugh, what his favourite TV show was, all so that the next time they met, she hoped he wouldn't be as petrified as he was right now.

She was also surprised that neither of his parents had come to Theatres with him as with young paediatric cases, it was hospital rule that the parents could go as far as the anteroom in order to help calm their little ones. Perhaps Timmy's parents weren't capable of doing that. Hospitals, especially theatres, could certainly freak out a lot of adults. At any rate, even though the nurse was doing her best to keep him calm, it was clear it wasn't working. Feeling bad for needing to rush Timmy, she proceeded with her job.

'Timmy, we need to set up a drip in your arm. Can I have a look at your arms, please, sweetie?'

'I'm not a sweetie,' he mumbled, but dutifully held out his arms to her.

'Oh, I'm sorry, Timmy. It's what I call my son sometimes.'

'What's his name?'

Ebony glanced at the nurse and noted the surprised look on the other woman's face as they worked together to set up the drip in Timmy's right arm. 'His name is Clifford. Clifford Dean Matthews...although he likes it better when I call him Cliff.'

'My name's Timothy. Timothy Schneider. I don't have a middle name but I just like being called Timmy.'

'I like the name Timmy, too,' Ebony replied.

'How big is Cliff?'

'Cliff's nine years old and he can't wait until he turns ten but that's not until the twenty-ninth of September so he has a few months to go yet. When do you turn six, Timmy?'

'Really soon, on the seventh.'

'Seventh of which month?'

'April, silly.' Timmy hadn't moved his body, keeping still as though he knew this drill all too well, but Ebony was pleased to note that his eyes had lost their bleakness. 'Bart told me my birfday is at Easter so I get to have presents *and* chocolate eggs.'

'That does sound exciting,' Ebony responded, pleased she'd managed to get Timmy to confirm his name and his date of birth. Easter was only in three weeks' time and she certainly hoped Timmy was healthy enough to return home to his family to enjoy the occasion.

'But I don't have lots of friends.' Timmy's tone dropped.

'Neither does Cliff. We only moved to Australia a short time ago.' She continued to work, to get Timmy's IV lines in so he was set up and ready to go. She also administered a pre-med so that when he was wheeled into the operating room, he didn't get upset with all the sterile-looking machines and the big overhead light. 'Hey, perhaps you two could be friends?'

'It's always good to make a new friend,' a deep male voice said from behind Ebony, and at the sound of Bart's voice, Timmy's entire face lit up.

'There you are,' Timmy said, and started to yawn a bit as the medication began to slowly take effect.

'Sorry, buddy. Didn't mean to miss your ride down to Theatre. I was busy getting changed into my funky blue clothes.' He struck a pose like a body builder, showing off the way he looked in the baggy blue cotton trousers and top. Timmy giggled. Ebony tried not to swallow her tongue at the way his muscled arms flexed beneath the material. He was certainly in good shape.

'Hey, I see you've met my friend Ebony.' Bart smiled brightly as he placed his hand on Ebony's shoulder. The surprise touch, especially as she was doing her best to ignore the way his presence made her feel all tingly inside, caused a wave of heat to flood through her. First a handshake and now a simple touch to her shoulder. She was becoming more aware of him. By some miracle, she managed to keep her smile in place as Bart's deep tone washed over her.

'Ebony and I are really old friends. We even went to the same high school!'

Timmy's eyes widened at this news and he looked from his good friend Bart to Ebony. 'Wow.' Ebony noticed the nurse's eyebrows rise as well and she knew that before Timmy's operating session was over, the entire staff of Canberra General would also know this bit of information.

'So now the two of you can be friends as well.'

'Yep, and I'm gonna be friends with Cliff, too.' Although Timmy barely moved as he spoke, his voice was full of tired excitement as his eyelids began to droop. Ebony's heart turned over for the gorgeous little boy that he was and the fact that he'd already had to go through so much in his very short life.

'It's going to be a great birthday this year, buddy,' Bart continued, thankfully dropping his hand from her shoulder.

'Well, if you will all excuse me, I'll go and get organised in Theatre.' Pleased at having a ready-made excuse for getting away from Bart's over-stimulating presence, Ebony high-tailed it through the double doors into the operating room where the surgery would soon take place. Why on earth was she so aware of him? The question kept churning over and over in her mind. Bart was just an old friend. A gorgeous, handsome old friend. It wasn't as though she was out looking for another relationship either. It was all rather strange. Very strange indeed.

Shaking her head and clearing her thoughts, Ebony headed into Theatre, quickly introducing herself to the rest of the staff. It was clear by some of the puzzled frowns she received that they weren't at all sure why there had been a change in anaesthetist. Still, no one seemed to want to delve into the matter, more intent on getting things checked and double-checked so that Timmy's surgery could start on time.

By the time a drowsy Timmy was wheeled through, Ebony was completely focused on what she needed to do. Bart was in the scrub room, no doubt mentally preparing for the procedure, and by the time he was gowned and gloved, his mask and facial shield in place, Timmy was completely anaesthetised and ready for Bart's attention.

He stepped up to the operating table and addressed his team. 'If you haven't yet met Ebony Matthews, she'll be the anaesthetist for this surgery. Having previously worked with Hartley Grant-Smythe, she comes with excellent credentials. However, this is not Hartley's operating room, it's mine and as such—'

Bart turned his head, pinning Ebony beneath his gaze. His blue eyes, which were clearly visible through the face shield, the rest of his face hidden beneath mask and colourful theatre cap, held a firm hint of determination.

'Timmy's operation will serve as her audition to perhaps become a permanent part of this operating team.'

The cheerful, friendly tone that he'd previously employed when they'd been talking to Timmy was gone. This was the man who had been in Robert Vance's office, a man who was determined to give his patients— and especially young Timmy—one hundred per cent of his skills and knowledge, and the only way he could do that successfully was to have a theatre team that wanted the same thing.

Ebony nodded, accepting his words. As a professional, she had the opportunity to show Bart he could trust her, that she was good at her job and that she would succeed in becoming part of his team.

'All right, then.' Bart winked at her again and she immediately wished he hadn't as a flood of tingles burst to life within her body, unsettling her thoughts. 'Let's begin.'

CHAPTER TWO

THE surgery to replace the blocked section of Timmy's shunt went better than expected and after a few hours, with Ebony monitoring him in both Recovery and Intensive Care, he was well enough to be transferred back to the paediatric ward by late afternoon. Ebony stayed with him, ensuring the blinds in the private room were closed and the lights off, knowing that whenever Timmy opened his eyes, it would be far too bright for him.

When Bart walked into the room, Ebony felt him rather than saw him and the frisson of awareness that tingled its way down her spine made her shudder with delight. She glanced over at him once as he came to stand at the foot of Timmy's bed before returning her attention back to Timmy. Both of them remained silent for a few minutes, content just to watch their little patient.

'I went to ICU to look for him and they told me you'd transferred him back here.' Bart's voice was soft but still held a hint of concern. 'Is that a wise idea?'

Ebony raised one eyebrow and fixed him with a stare. 'Check his notes. He's doing remarkably well.'

'I've read his notes.'

'But still needed to see for yourself?'

'Yes.' Bart looked at the boy lying in the big bed,

his head bandaged, his arm bandaged to keep the IV in place in case he accidentally pulled it out. 'He's lucid?'

'Yes. He wouldn't be back in the ward otherwise. He was awake a while ago, asking for you. He'll be glad you're here.'

'He's a special boy.'

At his words, Ebony looked at Bart more closely, re-alising that he wasn't simply worried about Timmy be-cause he was his patient. There was clearly far more to it than that. 'There's a strong connection between the two of you,' she stated, and even though Bart's eyes narrowed at her words, he didn't take his gaze from Timmy's supine form.

'He's my patient.' The words were still soft but the words were clipped and she noticed his jaw clench in annoyance.

'It's more than that,' Ebony remarked, as she shifted around the bed to check Timmy's IV. 'You care for him and he cares for you. He's emotionally attached to you, Bart.'

'Well, there's no one else for him to be attached to,' he growled, and Ebony was surprised at this reaction. 'Of course I care about him. So do most of the staff in the ward and the theatre team and the recovery staff.' He pushed a hand through his hair, causing the ends to stand up a little, making him look delightfully di-shevelled in the darkened room. 'Most of us have been here from when Timmy was first diagnosed. We're *all* emotionally attached to this little boy but that only makes us work harder where his treatment and surger-ies are concerned. All the staff who know him have been affected by his bravery, his acceptance of his situ-ation even when things went from bad to worse.' Bart clenched his jaw tightly.

'What happened?' Ebony asked the question softly, glancing from Timmy and back to Bart, eager to know just how and what made this young patient so different, so special.

'His parents abandoned him.'

'What?' Ebony was a little confused. Surely he didn't mean *abandoned*, as in the physical sense?

'They decided after his second surgery that it was going to be too hard for them to face having a child who required repeated surgeries and might possibly end up with permanent brain damage. They didn't have the time or the money to waste on him.' There was disgust in his tone and she could see his anger simmering beneath the surface.

'I…had…' Ebony's mouth went dry and she shook her head '…*no* idea,' she whispered, looking down again at the small boy who had been so incredibly brave before heading into surgery.

He'd been lying in that big bed, being pushed through the hospital corridors, staring up at the lights on the ceiling, terrified beneath the sheets, and there had been no loving parent beside him to hold his hand or offer comfort. Instead, it had been left up to the staff who had taken him to their hearts to provide as much caring and support as they were able to, but at the end of the day they went home to their own families, their own problems, their own lives, and Timmy was left… where? In foster-care? All Ebony's maternal instincts came flooding to the fore and she reached out a hand to touch the little boy's arm, needing to make contact with him as empathy pumped through her.

'They turned their backs on him,' Bart continued, his deep words falling softly in the quiet room. 'He was almost three and while he was in hospital recovering from his latest surgery, they just upped and left. Moved their belongings out of their house, jumped in their cars and moved interstate.

'The department of child services managed to trace them to Melbourne but only long enough to have them sign over their care of Timmy to the State. The next time they tried to contact the parents, they'd moved on again. No one knows where they are and, quite frankly, I personally don't care.' His upper lip was curved into a snarl of disgust at what Timmy's biological parents had done, and Ebony didn't blame him for feeling that way.

'They gave up any right they had to their son, signed him over to the department, and it was only thanks to my involvement with ACT NOW—uh, that's the Australian Capital Territory's Nocturnal—'

'Outreach Welfare,' she finished for him. 'I know. I've registered to volunteer with them as well.'

'Good. We need more good doctors. Anyway, through being able to call in some favours, I managed to get Timmy placed with a foster-mother who is a retired nurse so she's able to provide the care he needs. For now, at least.'

Ebony noticed Bart slowly relax his clenched fists as he spoke and when he finally met her gaze, she could see the love he felt for this gorgeous boy reflected in his blue eyes. Where he'd previously looked at her with annoyance, anger and disdain, he was now looking at Timmy with pure paternal adoration. It was how her late husband, Dean, had often looked at Maddie and Cliff.

'Thank you for explaining, Bart. It's very clear now why everyone seems so attached to Timmy.'

Bart was silent for a moment or two before asking softly, his voice still gruff but more calm, 'How is his pain level?'

'He's doing extremely well. He's relying on less medication than after his previous surgeries. I'm not sure whether that's because his pain tolerance levels have increased or whether his previous doses were incorrect.'

'I'd go for the latter.' Bart walked around the bed and picked up Timmy's notes from the bedside table, where Ebony had been making clear and concise notes. 'It's why I wanted a different anaesthetist.' He flicked back a few pages then looked at what she'd written. 'Why are your prescriptions so different? That's a big drop in the medication dosage.'

Ebony shrugged. 'I've calculated the dosage from his height and weight measurements taken this morning prior to his surgery. Timmy is much smaller than the average five-year-old, no doubt due to the initial tumour pressing on his cerebellum and obviously inhibiting his developmental pathways. I've also changed the medication from his previous surgeries. I think that's making the biggest difference.'

Bart was still flicking through the notes, then he looked across at Timmy. 'And he's not in any pain?'

'Have a look at his readouts,' she suggested, pointing to the EEG and ECG machines presently monitoring Timmy's status. 'He's coping exceedingly well. He came round in Recovery much faster, was only in ICU for about an hour before he was occasionally opening his eyes and asking for you. It's why I brought him back to the ward. The last time he was completely lucid, he told me he was hungry.'

'That *is* a good sign.'

'Yes. I'd still like to keep a close eye on him for the next hour or two and I'll leave detailed notes for the night-shift nurses because if he's going to have any sort of reaction, it'll be then. These first twenty-four hours are indeed crucial.'

'That's why I'll be staying.'

'Here?' She raised her eyebrows. 'Oh, you mean you'll go to the residential wing and—'

'No. I mean here. As in staying in this room, monitoring Timmy all night long. I've already arranged for a bed to be brought in for me.' He looked again at the boy and once more Ebony was struck by the level of paternal love radiating in Bart's eyes. 'Thank you for taking such good care of him.'

'Does that mean I'm part of the team? That I passed my audition?' She couldn't help the small smile that touched her lips.

'With flying colours. Timmy's recovery is evidence of your obvious expertise.' His words were deep, rich and held the slightest hint of admiration. Ebony couldn't believe it but she actually felt her cheeks start to grow warm beneath his gaze and she quickly turned away, the earlier tingling awareness she'd experienced beginning to expand and spread throughout her entire body.

'Oh. Well. Uh…thanks,' she muttered, astonished to note her voice was a little husky. She quickly cleared her throat, unable to believe how she seemed far too aware of his nearness, the warmth of his body not too far away apparently affecting her ability to form words. Her fingers were busy checking the drip, working on automatic as she did her best to ignore the way Bart's words had made her feel special.

'I give praise where it's due and right now I'm more than happy to have you on the team as *my* anaesthetic practitioner. I'll let Robert know it's official.'

Ebony nodded, deciding it was better not to speak at all for a few moments. The thought of working with

Bart, day in day out as well as probably seeing him at the ACT NOW vans, filled her with both excitement and trepidation, mainly because the last thing she'd expected on meeting up with him again after all these years had been that she'd be attracted to him.

Of course, she'd always known he was good looking, fair and just, but in the past, to her way of thinking, he'd always been Alice's one true love. From the moment he'd met Alice at school, the two of them had only had eyes for each other. They'd been friends for a few years until Alice had been old enough to date but when her parents had realised the seriousness of the relationship and that Bart had proposed marriage to nineteen-year-old Alice and she'd accepted, they'd done their best to separate the two.

That had been so long ago and now both she and Bart were very different people from who they'd been back in high school. The connection was there but the knowledge only provided background colour for the flood of zinging sensations that kept pulsing through her body when he looked at her in such a way and spoke to her with that rich and delightful baritone of his. Still, the point remained that, regardless of these crazy sensations, there was simply no room in her busy life for feelings of this sort.

Pushing aside her silly schoolgirl reaction to her colleague, she focused her thoughts on her patient and after checking the read-outs from the machines monitoring Timmy's vital signs, she noticed a slight, positive change in the information as the little boy tried to shift, his legs and toes moving beneath the covers.

'Bart,' Ebony whispered, and nodded towards the bed. Bart moved closer and together they watched as the little boy opened his eyes. It took him a moment or two to focus then a small, contented smile touched the corners of his lips.

'Bart.' Timmy all but sighed the name, clearly knowing that if Bart was there, looking after him, everything would be all right.

'Hey, buddy. Good to see you smiling again.'

'It's over?'

'It's all done. Everything went really well.' Bart smiled and nodded and when Timmy tried to lift his hand, trying to reach out to them, Bart quickly placed his hand over the boy's little one. 'Rest and relax now.'

'You'll stay?'

'Absolutely.'

'All night?'

'All night, buddy. I'll be here.'

'And Wanda?'

'Wanda will be here soon.'

'And Ebony?'

'I'm here, Timmy.' She smiled down at him. He was so brave for someone so young and her maternal heart swelled with pride, even though she barely knew him. With what Bart had told her about Timmy's past, anyone who knew the story would undoubtedly feel the same way.

'And you stay, too? You and Bart could sleep next to each other,' he stated, closing his eyes, his words beginning to get a little drowsy.

Ebony glanced momentarily at Bart, her eyes widening at the suggestion of staying with him here, in this private room, all night long. 'Er...' She tried to speak but closed her mouth instead and swallowed over the sudden dryness of her throat, ignoring the way Bart seemed to be enjoying her discomfort at the innocent suggestion.

He didn't help matters when he winked at her, clearly enjoying the opportunity to tease her a little. The smile on his lips and the brightness in his eyes reminded her of how he'd been all those years ago as a carefree young adult with his whole future ahead of him.

Ebony cleared her throat, jerking her gaze from Bart's to look at Timmy once again. 'I'll stay for as long as I can and I'll see you again in the morning.'

'Remember Ebony has a son, too,' Bart added.

'Oh, yeah,' came Timmy's relaxed reply, and a moment later he drifted back to sleep.

Ebony quickly turned her attention to the read-outs, needing to busy herself while her heart rate returned to normal due to Bart's casual teasing.

'The EEG shows he's slipped back into a comfortable slumber,' she reported a moment later.

'That's evident by looking at his relaxed little face. He really *is* doing much better this time around. It's great.'

Ebony nodded, then asked, 'I take it Wanda's the foster-mother?'

'Yes. She's a great woman, helping many different kids and women over the years, and while she would have liked to have been here when Timmy came back to the ward, she presently has three single mothers and their children staying with her so her hands are very full.'

'Good heavens, that's a lot. What a lovely woman she must be. There are so many great people working with ACT NOW. They're all so giving and generous with their time because, let's face it, people simply want someone to just sit and listen to what they have to say, to make their voice heard.' She stopped and sighed. 'Sorry. I do tend to get carried away a bit.'

'Don't apologise. It's refreshing.' She could feel Bart watching her closely and wanting to pretend his notice didn't affect her, she crossed to Timmy's case notes and wrote a few more lines. Finally, she turned and found his attention still on her.

'Something wrong?' The indicator on her self-con-sciousness meter was beginning to rise, not to mention the warmth flooding through her.

'No. I was just wondering what had brought you back to Australia. Why you gave up your job working with Hartley.'

'I guess it does seem like a bit of an odd career choice but my father passed away and my mother's all alone.'

'Family.' He nodded as though he understood. 'It's so important.'

'Of course you'd understand, especially with all your brothers. You have four brothers, right?'

'Correct, and one surrogate sister. They're all fine, married with a gaggle of children, enjoying their lives.'

'And you? Not married?'

Bart laughed without humour. 'Me? No.' He turned to look at Timmy and for a moment Ebony had the feel-ing that in some ways he wouldn't mind being married with a gaggle of children of his own. It was clear given his bond with Timmy that he'd make a dedicated father. 'How about you? Married?'

Ebony remained silent for such a long moment that Bart turned to look at her. 'Widowed,' she offered. 'In fact, he mentioned once that he knew you. Dean Bax-ter?'

'Dean? We went to medical school together.' Bart took a few steps towards her. 'I'm sorry to hear of his death.'

'Cancer,' she supplied quietly.

Bart slowly exhaled. 'It's the plague of our century. Everyone knows someone who's either passed away or has had treatment for it. So you uprooted your son and moved back here to Australia to be with your mother. Admirable.'

'I have a daughter, too. Maddie. She's hit her teens and…' Ebony sighed and shook her head.

'Is so full of hormones?' he asked.

'Exactly.' She sighed again. 'When Dean first passed away, I didn't cope at all well. I put up my personal shields to protect my heart from further pain. I threw myself into a routine where I existed either at home or at work, functioning on autopilot.'

'It's how a lot of us get through. We pull the rules and regulations tightly around ourselves, desperate to find some level of control because our worlds have just been ripped apart.'

'Exactly.' She bit her lip and shrugged one shoulder. 'I had no idea how to cope, how to raise two children on my own. Cliff was the same age as Timmy is now, having his fifth birthday a few weeks after Dean's death, and it was the most difficult birthday party to get through.' Ebony looked off into nothingness as though somehow gazing back into her past.

Her words were soft. 'I just kept telling myself that Dean was at work, that he'd been delayed in surgery, that he'd be home later that evening to wish his son a happy birthday.' A tear slid silent down her cheek, her words thick with emotion.

'Maddie had a tantrum, which turned out to be the first of many. She kept yelling at me to stop pretending, that it didn't matter what I did, Cliff's birthday was ruined because her dad was dead.' Ebony opened her eyes and was astonished to find Bart standing near her, holding out a tissue. She accepted it and smiled at him, drawing in a long breath, determined to regain control over her emotions.

'I see the pain in the world and I want to do whatever I can to fix it but…what hope do I have if I can't even fix my own family?' She dabbed at her eyes, then blew her nose. Sighing, she walked to the little basin by the door and washed her hands.

'How old did you say Maddie was?' Bart's deep words, his tone rich with concern, floated over her like a warm, comfortable blanket.

'Thirteen. Filled with hormones and anger and denial. She doesn't talk about her father. She didn't want to move to Australia.' Ebony turned to face him and spread her arms wide, shrugging her shoulders. 'She hates me.'

As the words came out of her mouth, so her desperation and despair began to overflow, one tear then two gathering in her eyes before slipping over her lower eyelids to slide down her cheeks. For the first time in years she was having great difficulty in controlling her emotions and to her complete embarrassment the dam burst. She raised her hands to cover her face, the pain and desolation she'd tried to keep at bay for far too long flooding through her.

'Oh, Eb.'

She barely heard Bart's words but in the next moment she was startled when his arms came around her, drawing her near and holding her close. She had a brief second of wanting to turn tail and run but it didn't last, especially when it was far easier to accept the comfort he was offering. She'd missed having big strong arms around her. She'd missed the support and encouragement, and where she'd long accepted her husband was gone forever, just being *held,* especially by someone she trusted, made all the difference.

Bart knew what loss was like. He knew how painful it could be. Not only had his fiancée died but his parents had both been killed in a freak avalanche when he'd been twenty, leaving him and his brothers orphans. Ebony knew he was only holding her out of friendship, literally offering her a shoulder to cry on so that she could continue to do her job because no surgeon would want to work with an overwrought anaesthetist.

As thoughts of Maddie, of Cliff, of Timmy's situation and that of so many others like him, abandoned and hurt, pulsed from her in the form of anguished tears, Ebony started to feel a level of calm contentment settle into place. Slowly the tears ebbed and she started to breathe more deeply but still he kept his arms around her.

He'd never been able to turn away from a weeping woman and Ebony was no different. Such extensive upheaval and change in a person's life was difficult to cope with and obviously Ebony had been doing whatever was necessary in order to hold her family together. She also had the recent loss of her own father to mourn and was probably helping her mother to cope as well. So much pressure on such small shoulders, and to top it off, she'd started a new job which was a whole new stress in itself.

Bart closed his eyes as he rested his chin gently on Ebony's head, recalling how he'd felt when she'd mentioned Alice's name. Alice. It had taken him years to mourn her and even now he still felt so helpless whenever he thought about the way she'd died. A train crash, overseas. Her parents had only taken her because they'd thought he was a bad influence. They'd wanted to break them up, to separate her from 'that Goldmark boy', telling Alice she was too young to know her own heart and that it was utterly ridiculous to think about getting married at the age of nineteen.

Alice had been very close friends with Ebony and had once told him that she wanted Ebony to be bridesmaid at their wedding. Ebony was a link to Alice and initially he hadn't liked the fact that someone in this hospital, apart from his own family, knew of his past. Now, though, being here with Ebony, seeing her honest pain where her children were concerned and how touched she'd been on hearing Timmy's story, he couldn't imagine her spreading any sort of gossip regarding his past.

It must be soul-destroying to think that her own teenage daughter hated her. He couldn't even imagine how painful that must feel, that a child she'd carried in her womb, nursed at her breast, had cuddled and loved as a toddler, looked at her through disinterested eyes, arms crossed, jaw clenched. No wonder Ebony's calm façade had cracked, no wonder her sobs were so heartfelt. She was a woman who understood personal pain and emotion.

She was breathing more normally now, with only the occasional little sniffle and hiccup. 'I'm sorry,' she mumbled against his chest.

'Don't you dare apologise.' Bart's words were soft yet firm as he gently rubbed her back. 'You and I both know that grief comes in many disguises and right now, along with everything else going on in your life, you're grieving for the innocent child your daughter used to be.'

'Yes. That's it exactly. I knew you'd understand, especially as you had a hand in raising your younger brothers.'

'Teenagers can be horrible,' he agreed, and Ebony lifted her head, expecting Bart to release her from his arms, to step back, to put some much-needed distance between them, but he didn't. Instead, she found herself standing in the circle of his arms, her hands resting against his firm chest, looking up into his incredibly handsome face.

Neither of them moved. Time appeared to stand completely still, except for the increase of her heart rate. She splayed her fingers, telling herself she was getting ready to push herself away from him but knowing she was lying. The feel of him, so close, so strong, so... masculine. Where she'd initially been comforted by his arms, accepting what he was offering, she was now highly aware of just how close they were, of the way his gaze seem to drop to encompass her mouth as though he could think of nothing else but lowering his head so their lips could meet, providing them with the opportunity to explore and taste and tantalise each other.

His scent blended with hers, creating a heady combination of pheromones which neither seemed able to ignore. Swallowing, she licked her dry lips, her heart pounding so wildly against her ribs she thought it might break through. Not since Dean had she felt such overpowering and overwhelming sensations and as she looked into Bart's eyes she realised she honestly had no idea what to do next.

CHAPTER THREE

'Eb...?'

The one syllable from his lips was a whispered question of uncertainty and Ebony unconsciously licked her lips, again.

'Yeah?' she replied, the word hardly audible, her mouth barely moving, her heartbeat feeling as though it was about to stop at any moment.

'What...? Is—?'

The sound of voices outside the closed door of the private room made him stop. Bart's eyes widened as he glanced behind her, their minds seeming to flood back to a level of normalcy as they realised if they didn't move, they'd be caught in what would appear at first glance to be a compromising position. It would only add to the gossip already circulating that the new neurosurgical anaesthetist was an 'old friend' of the hospital's number-one bachelor.

As one, they both stepped back, ending the impromptu embrace, ending the awareness zinging between them, ending the need to question what on earth had just happened. Bart walked to Timmy's bedside and Ebony pulled the over-bed table towards her and made another notation in the case-notes. By the time the door to the room opened, both were completely engrossed in looking professional.

'Wanda,' Bart said, looking towards the door. 'He'll be so glad you're here.'

'Hi, Bart.' Wanda rushed to the other side of Timmy's bed and placed a caring hand on the boy's chest as though to reassure herself he was still alive, still breathing, still all right. 'I received your messages. Thanks for keeping me informed. I came as soon as I could.'

'You managed to get someone to cover for you?'

'Darla came over.'

Bart's smile was natural. 'Good ol' Darla.' He turned to Ebony. 'Er…she's my brother Benedict's wife.'

'Oh.' Ebony nodded politely then smiled at Wanda, proffering her hand. 'Hi. I'm Ebony.'

'She's my new anaesthetist,' Bart added. 'She'll be looking after Timmy from now on and I have to say that his recovery so far has been much improved from the last time, thanks to Ebony's care and treatment.'

'I was surprised he was back in the ward so soon. He's always been in ICU overnight before.' Wanda shook Ebony's hand. 'Thank you.'

Ebony smiled warmly this time, liking the genuineness of the other woman. 'Timmy's a special boy.'

Wanda returned to Timmy's side and brushed the backs of her fingers across the little boy's cheek. 'Yes. Yes, he is.' She paused for a moment, then looked at Bart. 'Will this surgery hold him for a while?'

'I'll watch him closely but I'm hoping it'll be at least another six months, if not twelve, before he requires further intervention.'

Wanda smiled brightly at this news. 'Then we'll be able to get him well and truly settled with another foster—'

'Let's just get through the next few days before we jump any more hurdles,' Bart quickly interrupted, and Ebony was left with the distinct impression there was something else going on that he clearly didn't want her to know about.

'Well,' she said, adding her signature to the case notes before closing them. 'I'd best head home.'

Bart glanced at the clock on the wall, noting it was just after six o'clock in the evening. 'You may even make it home in time to have dinner with your family. That'll be good.'

Ebony held his gaze for a moment, hugging the notes to her chest as though they would provide a means of protection from his hypnotic blue eyes. 'Yes, it will.' She forced herself to look away, blinking one long blink before focusing on Wanda. 'Nice to meet you.'

'Likewise.'

Ebony headed for the door but stopped and turned back to look at Bart once more. 'And…er…thanks.'

'No problem.' He nodded.

'Call me if you need me.' Her eyes widened as she realised how that might have sounded. 'For Timmy, I mean.'

Bart's lips twitched into the smallest smile. 'I knew what you meant,' he said as she quickly opened the door and exited the room. He stared at the closed door for a few seconds, the smile on his face increasing slightly at the way Ebony's eyes had opened, at the way a small tell-tale blush had instantly stained her cheeks and the way she'd fumbled slightly with the doorhandle.

In some ways, it was good to note he hadn't been the only one knocked off balance by their embrace. Where initially he'd only meant to comfort her, he still wasn't sure what exactly had changed when they'd stood there, staring into each other's eyes, because friendship had been the furthest thing from his mind. In other ways, it served as a warning to watch himself, to ensure that he did keep the relationship between himself and his new anaesthetist purely professional.

'So...what was all that about?' Wanda asked, and when he looked at his friend, he saw a wide and interested grin on her face.

Bart shrugged and turned his attention to Timmy's read-outs. 'Ebony has a hormonal thirteen-year-old daughter at home, one who doesn't appear to like her for moving them halfway across the world.'

'Isn't the father just as much to blame?'

Bart glanced at Wanda. 'He passed away.'

'Really?' Wanda didn't offer any of the usual platitudes. Instead, her eyebrows rose with distinct interest. 'So she's single?'

'She's also an old friend...sort of.'

'Uh...more information, please?'

Bart rolled his eyes. 'We went to the same high school. That's all.'

'Uh-uh. That's *not* all and I'm willing to bet there's far more to it than that, but I can see you're putting up walls so I'll let it go.' Wanda grinned brightly. 'For now.'

'Gee, thanks,' he remarked, pleased that the next time he looked at the EEG read-out, it showed that Timmy's brainwave patterns were changing from sleep to awake and when the little boy opened his eyes, Bart smiled at him.

'Hey, there, buddy. Look, Wanda's here.'

While he watched Wanda bend down and kiss Timmy's cheek, talking softly with the boy, Bart's heart once more swelled with fatherly-type love. He realised he'd cared about a lot of people in his life, he'd experienced all sorts of emotions such as sibling love, avuncular love, friendship love, but with Timmy, something new had definitely developed over the past few years and whenever Wanda mentioned that it was time to see if they could place Timmy into a long-term foster-family, one that would provide him with a normal upbringing and shower him with love, Bart had always found a reason to resist.

It wasn't that he didn't want Timmy to find that sort of happiness. God definitely knew, the boy deserved that and much, much more, but in Bart's mind there was no one who could possibly love the boy as much as he did. He spent time with Timmy when he was well, organising his surgical roster and clinic schedule as best he could in order to be a part of the boy's life but knowing all the time he couldn't offer himself as permanent parental material.

While Timmy required medical attention, Bart's hands were tied. If he were to proceed with applying to foster Timmy, it would mean he could no longer operate on the boy. As there was no one else in Australia with the skills Bart possessed—the skills necessary to do such intricate brain surgery—then there was no one else who could operate on Timmy. No. It was far more important at present for Bart to be the little boy's surgeon, to ensure the little boy had every opportunity at an amazing future. And because of this, it also meant there was no room in Bart's life for any other emotional upheaval.

A picture of Ebony came into his mind, safe and secure in his arms, her hands pressed against his chest, her wide green eyes staring up at him with totally unexpected confusion, her plump lips parted and almost begging for his kiss.

He closed his eyes for a second, annoyed with the perfect clarity of his memory.

'Bart? You OK?' Timmy's voice brought him back to his senses and as he opened his eyes and smiled, knowing it was imperative to keep any other surprise emotions Ebony might awaken clearly at bay.

'Yeah, buddy, I'm fine. How about you? Any pain?'

'No.' Timmy yawned. 'Sleepy.' He closed his eyes for a moment. 'Hey. Where's Ebony?'

Bart nodded, pleased Timmy could remember Ebony being there. 'She had to go home, remember?'

'Oh, yeah.' Timmy yawned again. 'I like her.'

'She seems very nice,' Wanda added.

'What about you, Bart? You like her, too?'

And despite the stern rearranging of his thoughts, despite the fact he knew even admitting to himself that there had been a definite moment of intense awareness passing between Ebony and himself, he couldn't deny Timmy's simple question. Did he like Ebony?

'Yeah, buddy. I *like* her.'

Ebony paced around her mother's darkened living room, looking unseeingly at the photographs on the walls. The same ones had been hanging here since her parents had moved from Tumut to Canberra the year after she'd finished high school. The clock on the mantel showed it was almost three o'clock in the morning. She shook her head, wishing she was able to sleep, but her mind was simply way too active and after tossing and turning for the past few hours she'd decided it was best to try making herself a warm drink. Her empty cup sat on the coffee table and she wished the warm milk's calming effect would hurry up and kick in.

When she'd arrived home from the hospital, her

thoughts had still been whirling around, not only about Timmy's operation and recovery but also how she'd somehow ended up crying in Bart's arms, telling him how her daughter hated her!

'Looks like you won the bet. She *is* home in time for dinner,' Ebony had heard Maddie snarl to Cliff when she'd walked in the back door. Ebony had put down her bag, keys and shed her light jacket before heading towards the dining room, where she'd been greeted with the delicious aroma of her mother's Hungarian goulash. Her stomach had grumbled and she'd suddenly realised just how hungry she'd been.

'Mum!' Cliff had jumped up from his chair at the table and rushed to her, arms wide before he'd wrapped them about her in a welcoming hug. She'd hugged him back, thankful for his reaction, especially as she'd looked over his head to see Maddie rolling her eyes.

'You're such a baby, Cliffy,' she'd teased.

Cliff had let go of Ebony and turned to yell at his sister. 'Don't call me Cliffy. I don't like it.'

'It's all right, Cliff. She didn't mean it.' Ebony had glared at Maddie in a way she'd hoped had been strict and authoritarian but Maddie had ignored it.

'Yes, I did. Cliffy, Cliffy, Cliffy,' she'd chanted, and Cliff had lunged at his sister, knocking over his glass of milk in the process, just as Ebony's mother, Adele, had been carrying through the large pot of goulash. Maddie had jumped up from the table, narrowly missing her grandmother, the two children then proceeding to taunt each other. The result was that Ebony had sent Maddie to her room, needing to raise her voice to the teenager as she'd had to most nights since they'd arrived in Australia.

Even as she thought about the whole debacle, pacing

the lounge room at three o'clock in the morning, Ebony shook her head. 'What am I supposed to do?' she asked the darkness. Maddie had stayed in her room, refusing to speak to Ebony but allowing Adele to take a tray of food in to her. Maddie had told her grandmother, in a rather loud voice, just how much she loathed her new school, loathed Australia and loathed her mother most of all.

Even though the teen had declared these sentiments almost every day for the past month, Ebony still wasn't used to hearing those hurtful words coming from the young girl who had laughed and hugged and kissed her in the same way Cliff still did. 'Where has my girl gone?' she whispered, reaching for a tissue and forcing herself to stop obsessing. She knew things would settle down eventually, that Maddie wouldn't stay this horrible, hormonal age for ever, and that she just needed to ride out the storm, but it was much easier said than done.

Ebony stood and started pacing again. She needed to do something to take her mind off the way Maddie made her feel. Her thoughts turned instantly to Bart and the way he'd held her so close, the warmth from his body wrapping itself around her, bringing comfort to her tumultuous life. He'd smelled so good, too. A subtle spice with a hint of solid, earthy sensation. She stopped pacing, closed her eyes and breathed in deeply, her senses able to recall the exact scent.

Her eyes snapped open. 'Too many emotions,' she muttered. She was experiencing too many conflicting emotions. Whenever she felt this way, she turned to work. It would always be there to get her through. At work, she could focus on other people, her patients, caring for them, ensuring everything went smoothly, and now her thoughts turned to her one and only patient—Timmy.

Even at the thought of the little boy, she felt her mind start to settle. From what Bart had told her, Timmy hadn't exactly had the most wonderful life so far but there was always hope on the horizon. She wondered how Timmy was doing and, after glancing at the clock again, she made a quick decision to give the ward a call to check in on him. Retrieving her phone, she called the paediatric ward, pleased when it didn't take long for the ward staff to answer.

'This is Dr Matthews…er, Ebony Matthews,' she clarified as she headed back to the lounge, eager for news of Timmy's condition.

'Yes?' There was a vagueness to the night nurse's tone and Ebony shook her head at the realisation that the woman didn't know her from a bar of soap.

'I'm the attending anaesthetist for Timmy Schneider. I was wondering if I could get an update, please.'

'Uh…' Ebony could hear pieces of paper being swished and shuffled around on the desk and a moment later the nurse replied, 'Just a moment, please.' With that, Ebony's call was transferred to the holding pattern, horrible old bell-ringing music filling her ears. It was good that the nurse was checking who she'd said she was but at this moment all Ebony wanted was some good news. It *had* to be good news otherwise she was positive Bart would have been on the phone long before this, demanding she get her butt back to the hospital, *stat*.

It was much more than a moment later when the call was reconnected but this time, instead of the higher-pitched voice of the ward sister, the deep masculine tones of Bartholomew Goldmark came down the line.

'Ebony?'

'Oh…uh…hi, Bart. Sorry. I didn't mean the
to wake you.'

'I wasn't sleeping.'

'Oh? Is everything all right? Is Timmy OK? Do I
need to come in?' Her words tumbled over each other
and she could have sworn she heard Bart's soft, rich
chuckle float down the line.

'Everything's fine, Eb.'

'Oh? Well…uh…that's good, then. Timmy's really
fine?'

'He's sleeping peacefully.'

'But you're not?'

'Neither are you,' he countered.

Ebony closed her eyes. She'd walked right into that
one.

'So…' He sounded as though he was walking, carrying the portable phone away from the sister's desk.
'Why don't you tell the doctor what's wrong and I'll
give you a prescription?'

'Where are you?' she asked, as his words became
softer.

'I've just come back into Timmy's room. The hospital should really get more comfortable beds for adults
to sleep on. These camping stretchers are horrible. I've
taken to dozing in the big armchair instead. Easier to
really stretch the legs.'

'I guess there's no point in saying you should have
gone home and managed at least a few hours in your
own bed. After all, from the roster I brought home with
me, you're due back in Theatre in six hours' time.'

'As are you,' he pointed out. 'Besides, I wouldn't
have slept at home anyway. I'm far more relaxed just
sitting and watching Timmy. So, now that we've ascer-

tained that Timmy is just fine, let's turn our attention to you. Why can't you sleep?'

Ebony shifted on the lounge, repositioning herself so her legs were tucked beneath her and her head was resting on three cushions. His voice was soothing, calm and downright sexy and as he wasn't here to notice her blushing or the fact that he could fluster her with just one look, she closed her eyes and decided to allow his hypnotic words to relax her. Sighing, she remarked quietly, 'Stuff.'

'Ah. A technical term. Well, it just so happens, I'm an expert at deciphering technical terms.' Ebony smiled at his words but he cleared his throat and continued. 'Stuff, eh? Uh…work stuff? Family stuff?' He paused for a long moment, his tone dipping slightly as he said, '*Other* stuff?'

Was he referring to what had transpired between the two of them after she'd disgraced herself by blubbering all over his shirt? She sort of thought he might be. 'All of the above?' she answered on a slight laugh, which seemed to disappear as quickly as it had come.

'OK, then. Let's deal with each complaint. One at a time and let's begin with work stuff.' He cleared his throat. 'Nervous about tomorrow's surgery?'

'Not particularly.'

'The staff, then? You're nervous about working with a new team. You shouldn't be. You were exceptionally brilliant today but, then, after working with Hartley for a few years I wasn't the least bit surprised by your abilities. Add to all of that the fact that Timmy is progressing marvellously and it means, as far as my professional opinion is concerned, you have no cause to be concerned about work.'

Ebony's smile was soft and dreamy as she pondered

telling him that *he* was the reason she was anxious about work. Working alongside him, day in, day out. Being attracted to him. Knowing his past. Never sure what she could and couldn't say in case he exploded again. Having to look across the operating table into his deep, blue eyes that seemed to cause her insides to tremble and her mind to turn to mush. *That* was the work stuff that was bothering her but there was no way she could admit as much to Bart.

When she didn't add anything to the discussion, he continued. 'Right. That's problem number-one solved. Next topic—for fifty points—is family stuff and, re-member, you can be honest with me. I'm a professional.'

'Professional what?' she teased softly, and heard him chuckle, the deep sound filling her with hope. Perhaps this was exactly what she needed. A different perspec-tive. An outsider's perspective. A man's perspective.

'So…did your daughter give you a hard time when you arrived home?'

'Of course she did. It's Maddie's thing. It's what she does now. She back-chats everything I say with huge helpings of sarcasm. She picks on her brother, teasing him to the point where he gets upset, though I've al-ways heard her apologise to him later. And luckily for her, Cliff is a very forgiving boy.

'Then she'll sneer at my mother but also apologise later. Yet with me she keeps on chipping away at my life, poking hot needles through my heart with her words, yelling at me for ruining her life. She'll stare at me with such venom and hatred in her eyes and then stomp around having a tantrum like she used to when she was two years old, but this time her words pierce deeper and leave large scars that at the moment I don't think will ever heal.'

'Hmm. That *is* interesting. *Very* interesting,' Bart remarked, doing a bad impression of Freud, and yet she found herself giggling. He cleared his throat. 'Sorry. Didn't mean to channel dead psychiatrists. I guess it's of no real help if I just tell you she's an average teenager and she'll grow out of it?'

'Placating words are all well and good, Bart, but I just…I seriously don't know what to do and the longer this goes on, the more concerned I become about her. She's my *daughter*. I love her.'

'Of course you do.' He paused then exhaled slowly. 'You're after practical advice?'

'It can't hurt and you did help raise your brothers.'

'True. I can recall some very hairy times, especially with Hamilton, during his teenage years. Poor big brother Edward got the brunt of it and when he'd had enough, he'd send Hamilton to Canberra to spend time here with me.' He chuckled. 'Thank goodness those days are over.'

'But you can offer me some good advice, I hope?' She opened her eyes and watched the shadows dance on the ceiling, a sliver of light from the street shining in through a gap in the curtains. 'What have you got, Doc?'

'Why not bring her along to the ACT NOW vans one night?'

'What? Are you insane? It's hardly safe for—'

'She'll be fine,' Bart countered immediately. 'My sister-in-law, Darla, holds a young girls' get-together a few times a week. It's not just for kids who are on the street but for kids like Maddie who are just having a hard time adjusting to the life of a typical teen. Darla has a gift for working with teenage girls.'

'She's Benedict's wife?'

'Yes. Darla had a horrible childhood with a drug-addicted mother and all sorts of terrible things happening to her, which is why she's able to help so many women—both young and old. During her time working with ACT NOW, so many women have been able to leave abusive relationships and accept help, changing their lives forever. Now, I'm not saying that Maddie is drug addicted or being abused but she's hurting deep inside and as a result she's punishing you.'

He paused for a moment, obviously waiting for her reaction to this suggestion. 'Go on,' she encouraged.

'Bringing Maddie along to ACT NOW might just open her eyes to the plight of others, to let her see that her own world isn't as bad as she thinks. She has a roof over her head, clothes on her back, food in her stomach and people who love and care about her. Plus, she'll be able to gather a sense of what *you* do when you volunteer, how you help others. At the moment you're just the mother who's made her travel halfway around the world, ripping her from her comfort zone. She doesn't see how brilliant you are or the amazing work you do. It's important she realises that.'

Ebony shook her head. 'It's nice of you to say all those things, Bart, but I'm still not sure. Maddie has her father's stubbornness and I'm sure you can recall just how stubborn Dean could be on occasion.'

'I do and as such I stand by my prescription, Ms Matthews,' he remarked, returning to his psychiatrist's tone. 'Letting Maddie see that there are other kids less fortunate than her may make her start appreciating what she *does* have. I'm happy to come and talk to her if you think it'll make a difference.'

'Really?'

'I take it she was close to Dean?'

'She was a daddy's girl all right and she cried herself to sleep every night for well over six months after his death.' Ebony thought for a moment. 'Perhaps if you came around, met her, formed your own personal opinion and, sure, if you feel comfortable talking to her about Darla and ACT NOW, then be my guest. I'm getting so desperate it's definitely worth a try.'

'OK. I'll drop around on Wednesday evening. You could invite me to dinner. You know, as an old friend of the family.'

Ebony shifted in the chair, sitting up a little higher, her eyes wide open. 'Dinner?' Bart wanted to come over for dinner?

'The evening family ritual where you gather around a large table and partake of a shared meal?' he offered with a slight chuckle.

'Funny. Uh…Wednesday night, that's tomorrow. Um…I guess that should be all right. I'll check with my mother and get back to you.'

He laughed again. 'It really does sound like we're back in high school. Right. That's another bit of "stuff" sorted. Now, on to the last point that is stopping you from getting a good night's sleep.'

'*Other* stuff,' she said, mimicking the way he'd said it before.

'Yes. *Other* stuff.' His smooth baritone washed over her and she had difficulty not sighing out loud at the sound. Didn't he realise how glorious it was just to ease back into the cushions once more, close her eyes and allow his warm tones to wash over her? 'Now, please, correct me if I'm wrong, but I'm presuming this *other* stuff you speak of might refer to that crazy moment we shared after I comforted you?'

Ebony's eyes snapped open and almost every muscle in her body tensed. He was going to talk about it? Admit it? Actually state that there was definitely something strange happening between them, rather than just ignore it?

'Crazy moment?' she squeaked.

'When I looked into your eyes and the entire world seemed to freeze and all I could think about was how much I wanted to kiss you,' he continued, his tone still calm and matter-of-fact, but she could have sworn his voice was thicker, more husky than before. 'Is that the *other* stuff that's keeping you awake, Ebony?'

'Uh…' She swallowed. 'Yeah.'

'Then you felt it, too?'

Ebony was a little astonished at his words, not having expected him to be quite so open and forward. However, she knew she couldn't leave him standing out there on that ledge of honesty all alone, especially when she *had* felt something.

'Yes,' she said after a moment's pause.

'Good.' She heard him let out a relieved sigh. 'That's very good news,' he continued. 'Admitting there's something strange happening between us is the first step to dealing with it.'

'We're going to deal with it?'

'I've learned over the years not to leave anything to chance. I much prefer to talk about the elephant in the room rather than ignoring it. I'm the same in Theatre. If people aren't sure what's happening, I much prefer they ply me with a thousand questions than make a mistake. I'm sure you'd agree that where neurosurgery is concerned, there's no room for error.'

'Uh…yes. Of course.'

'The same can be said of physical attraction.'

He was physically attracted to her? Her mouth went

dry at his words and she wished she hadn't finished her milk drink so quickly. 'So er…' Her voice came out as a squeak and she quickly cleared her throat. 'So how do you suggest we *deal* with this?'

'Hmm.' His response was a thoughtful sound and she could well imagine him sitting in Timmy's small private room, in the comfortable chair opposite the bed where he could keep a close eye on everything, frowning a little as he pondered the problem before them. 'That is the question.'

'Well…what have you done in the past? Surely you've dated other staff members before?'

'A few.'

'Michelle told me you were the hospital's most eligible bachelor,' she offered, and was delighted when he harrumphed at her words. 'You don't like the title?'

'It makes me sound like I'm part of some crazy television dating show and have a new woman on my arm every other month.'

'Don't you? Am I just the next woman in a long line of women, all desperate to tame the hospital's most eligible bachelor?'

'Long line of women? Ha. Not even funny. No, the last woman I dated was actually a solicitor and that was two years ago. Besides, permanent relationships and I don't really go hand in hand.'

Ebony raised her eyebrows at this piece of information. 'You were willing to make your relationship permanent with Alice,' she remarked softly, wondering if he was going to bite her head off for even daring to mention Alice's name.

'That was different,' he replied immediately. 'Alice was different. Alice was…' He stopped.

'Your soul mate,' Ebony provided. She had to work

with him and, attraction or no attraction, she needed to figure out how best to do that. 'That's how I felt about Dean.' She paused. 'Does it bother you to talk about Alice after such a long time?'

'I...' He stopped. 'I'm just not used to talking about her. To anyone.'

'Trying to warn me off? I won't talk about her if you don't want to but, Bart, you're the only other person I know who really knew her. The way she smiled, the way her crazy laughter used to always make everyone else laugh because it was so infectious.' Ebony chuckled. 'The way she'd talk so animatedly, always using her hands and sometimes almost hitting strangers in the face with her wild gesticulating.'

'Hmm,' he murmured, but she thought she detected a hint of humour in the sound.

'It's healthy to talk about it because acknowledging their lives helps us to grow into the new people we're becoming. For you and I, our pasts are linked through Alice and Dean, the people we've loved and lost, but that loss shouldn't define our present or our future.'

'*Our* future?'

Ebony faltered. 'That's not what I meant. I just meant that...not of course *our* as in you and me but in *our* as in that we... I meant...you know...that we're not stagnating with our lives...our *individual* lives...because it would be silly not to move forward and...you know, *live*.'

His warm laughter rang down the line. 'You know, I *do* remember you being this crazy and funny when we were teenagers. Good to see that quality is still there, even if you do get a little tongue-tied at times.'

'Especially when I'm being teased,' she countered.

'Fair point.'

'But it still doesn't tell us what to do about this…'
She swallowed, still a little nervous about discussing
this topic openly.

'Attraction?'

'Yes. I was married for a long time and, well, you're
the first man I've been…'

'Attracted to?' His teasing tone was back again.

'Yes…er…since Dean.'

'I guess I should be flattered.'

'Yes. You should be and stop having so much fun
at my expense.'

'You make me smile, Eb. More so than I've done in
a very long time.'

'I take it that's a good thing?'

'That's a very good thing.'

Both of them were silent for a brief moment before
Ebony remarked, 'You're an amazing surgeon, Bart,
and as we need to continue working together, perhaps
it's going to be best if we…ignore this…'

'Attraction,' he offered again with a chuckle.

'Yes, and, you know, just remain friends.'

'Friends, eh?'

'We were sort of friends years ago. We can reconnect
and do it again and actually, as friends, we're already
way ahead of the curve because we *do* know about each
other's pasts. We can help each other.'

'You mean I can help you with Maddie.'

'Yes, please. I really do think she might respond to
you, especially when she learns you're an old friend
of her father's.' Hope was rising in Ebony's chest, not
only because Bart was willing to assist her with her
daughter but because it would be good to have a man
around, especially one she trusted and held in such high
esteem as Bart.

'Of course.' Again he was silent and Ebony started to feel a sense of calm wash over her. They'd felt an attraction and like the mature adults they were, they'd discussed it, figured out a solution and now they could move on. 'OK, then. Friends it is.'

'Good. I'm so happy we've managed to rectify the matter.' Again there was silence down the line and Ebony found herself yawning.

'You sound as though you're ready to sleep now,' he said obviously hearing her yawn.

'Yes, I think I am. Thanks for sorting out my thoughts, Dr Freud. I'll let you get back to dozing and watching Timmy, and please call me if anything should go wrong. That little boy *is* very special.'

'He most certainly is.'

'Goodnight, Bart.'

'Eb?' she heard him say just before disconnecting the call, his tone soft, deep and intimate.

'Yeah?'

'Do you believe there's more than one soul mate for everyone?'

The calm she'd managed to achieve disappeared in a puff as she closed her eyes, recalling all too well how incredible it had felt to be held firmly in his arms, looking up into his hypnotic blue eyes and the way he'd managed to turn her insides to mush. Dean had been her soul mate for years but Dean was gone. Was she doomed to remain alone for the rest of her life or was she going to be one of those lucky people who was blessed twice in love?

'Yes. Yes, Bart, I do.'

Another brief silence came down the line before he said softly, 'So do I.'

CHAPTER FOUR

On Wednesday night, four days since Bartholomew Goldmark had re-entered her life, Ebony couldn't believe how jittery she felt, knowing he was coming over for dinner. On Tuesday evening she'd been rostered on for her first shift with ACT NOW and had met Bart's sister-in-law, Darla. It had been good to get to know her a little better, especially as, come this Saturday evening, Bart had arranged for Maddie to attend Darla's hot chocolate and chat session.

'What did you think of Darla?' Bart had asked earlier in the afternoon as they'd headed to Timmy's room to review his progress.

'She's lovely. Two women came to the medical van that night and it was amazing to see just how she's able to connect with them.'

'She has a gift and she's using it for good. Benedict definitely picked a winner.' They'd reached Timmy's room but just before they'd entered, Bart had placed a hand on her upper arm and she'd been unable to disguise the small gasp that had escaped her lips, his touch warming her body through and through. When she'd raised her gaze to meet his, she'd been unable to contain the way he affected her. Usually at work she was fine. Able to keep her distance and focus on their patients, especially when they were usually in surgery for long stretches of time, but when he touched her, accidentally or on purpose, she found it nigh impossible to disguise the way the man made her feel.

Bart had looked into her eyes, his own widening imperceptibly as he'd read her reaction. Then he'd dropped his hand, taken a small step back and cleared his throat. 'Uh…I just wanted to check the time. For tonight,' he'd added, his voice soft so only the two of them could hear.

Ebony had nodded, smiled, opened her mouth to speak but nothing had come out. So she'd closed her mouth, swallowed and tried again. 'Six-thirty.'

'The perfect time to eat. All emergencies aside, I'll definitely be there.' Then he'd opened the door to Timmy's room, where Ebony was pleased to find Wanda sitting on the bed next to Timmy, reading him a story. With her thoughts once more focused on the little boy, she was able to get through the consult without a hitch.

Now, though, after rushing home from work early so she could at least shower and change before Bart arrived, Ebony stood in front of her closet dressed in her underwear, with no idea what she was supposed to wear.

'This is ridiculous,' she muttered as she pulled out a shirt she usually wore to work. She was halfway through buttoning it when she realised it was wrong and quickly took it off. 'Perhaps just casual. Perhaps a skirt and a knit top.' She'd just stepping into the skirt when her mother knocked once on the door and came in.

Adele took one look at the discarded clothes littering Ebony's bed and quickly came further into the room. 'Well, I was going to ask you to give me a hand with the lasagne but it looks as though you have enough problems of your own. What's with all the clothes, Ebby?'

'Oh, I don't know!' Ebony threw both hands up in

the air. 'I'm being ridiculous. This is ridiculous, Mum. Why is he coming to dinner? Isn't it bad enough I have to put up with him at work all day long?'

Adele frowned. 'I thought you liked Bart? He was always such a nice boy. I did so like his parents and I'm really pleased he's coming around to dinner so we can reconnect.'

'Reconnecting is overrated,' she muttered as she took the skirt off and tossed it onto the bed. 'I'm being ridiculous,' she growled at her reflection before picking up her old, comfortable jeans and pulling them on.

'Well, perhaps just a little, Ebby, but it's quite obvious this man has you in a tizz and that's not necessarily a bad thing.'

Ebony grabbed a pale pink T-shirt with a unicorn on the front, one she'd bought many years ago with Maddie. Matching mother-daughter T-shirts but unfortunately Maddie had long since outgrown hers. 'It is a bad thing, Mum. He's my work colleague.' She slipped her feet into a pair of flip-flops and tugged a brush through her blonde locks.

'And where else are you supposed to meet men? You work all day, you volunteer with ACT NOW a few nights a week and the rest of the time you spend with the children. It's good that Bart has you all flustered, even if all it ends up meaning is that you remember you're a beautiful woman who has the right to seek future happiness.'

'I don't have time for future happiness right now, Mum. Bart's going to be here any minute and apparently you need help in the kitchen.'

'Just making a salad.' Leaving the mess of clothes all over the bed, the two of them headed down the hallway, past Maddie's room, which had a loud, thumping rock beat vibrating off the walls, towards the kitchen, but no sooner had Ebony taken the tomatoes from the refrigerator than the doorbell rang.

Ebony looked at her mother with wild, scared eyes. 'It's just dinner, Ebony. A family meal. Nothing to be worried about. Now, go answer the door.'

'Yes. Right.' She wiped her hands on a teatowel before heading to the front door, but Cliff had already reached it, his hand on the doorknob, looking expectantly over his shoulder, waiting for her permission to open the door. At her nod of assent he opened the door to reveal Bart standing on the other side of the screen door, holding a bunch of pink and white peonies.

'Hi. I'm Cliff,' her son said, as he opened the door. 'Hey, Grandma,' Cliff yelled. 'He brought some flowers.' Cliff grinned widely and held out his hand for the flowers. Bart glanced from child to woman and back again, before handing the flowers over with a smile.

'Hi, Cliff. I'm Bart.'

'I know. Mum told us. You work with her and you knew my dad. Phew! These flowers stink.' He thrust them at his mother, then ran back down the corridor towards the kitchen, yelling, 'Grandma. Where's a vase?'

'Uh…please, come in,' Ebony said as Bart came inside and gestured to the flowers.

'I thought they might brighten up the dinner table.'

Ebony smiled and glanced at the lovely bouquet in her hands. 'Thank you. They're lovely.'

'So are you, especially in your unicorn T-shirt. I like a woman who's not afraid to make a bold fashion statement.'

Ebony couldn't help but laugh and as she shut the door behind him felt all her previous tension begin to slip away. 'Because I'll bet the fashion world is such a high priority of yours.'

He grinned and winked at her. 'You know it.'

'Don't do that,' she chided.

'Do what?'

'Wink at me. It...does things to me.'

'Things?' he raised an eyebrow.

'You know...' She waved her free hand in the air as though trying to find the words. '*Stuff* things.'

'Ah...*stuff* things. So glad you explained. I confess I was a little confused.' He chuckled again and Ebony rolled her eyes as she led the way through the house towards the kitchen so she could put the flowers in water.

Bart couldn't help but note the family photographs and paintings that decorated the walls. It was a home, one that had been forged in love and reminded him so much of his own family home in Oodnaminaby where his oldest brother Edward now lived with his wife Honeysuckle and their children.

Family was so important and he was glad Ebony was a woman who knew that, bringing her own children to Australia to spend time with their grandmother. It made his resolve to try and help Maddie in any way he could even greater. Of course the young teenager wouldn't understand her mother's motives and if he could help her realise Ebony wasn't the enemy, he'd do it.

In the kitchen he was warmly welcomed by Adele, who he vaguely remembered meeting once or twice at community functions in Oodnaminaby. 'I was on several committees with your mother, Hannah,' she told him as she filled the vase with water. 'She always had a ready smile for people, was always willing to help out, to listen to others.'

Adele watched as Ebony unwrapped the flowers

and put them into the vase before looking at Bart and nodding. 'She would be so proud of you and the work you're doing, not only at the hospital and with ACT NOW but also your gracious offer to help us out with Maddie. We're all quite worried about her.' Adele's tone had dipped a little at the end of her sentence, her gaze drifting over Cliff's head, knowing the young boy was probably listening with great interest to every word the adults were saying.

Bart smiled, his heart tightening a little at Adele's sincerity, forming an instant connection with her. It was always this way when he met people who had known his parents, and in some ways it helped form another important connection, making him still feel very close to the memory of the two people in the world who had loved him most. 'Thank you, and I'm looking forward to meeting Maddie.'

'Really?' Cliff snorted with a hint of disgust. 'She's just a bossy big sister. Nothing special.'

'Now, Cliff,' Ebony warned.

'You're lucky to have a big sister. I have four brothers and a surrogate sister, but she's the same age as me.'

'What's surrogate?' he asked.

'Well,' Bart said patiently, addressing his words directly to Cliff. 'Lorelai is her name, and our mums were best friends. When Lorelai's mum died, *my* mum sort of stepped in and became Lorelai's new mum. So although Lorelai still lived at her house with her dad, she would often be at our house, spending time with my mum, doing girl things, and as she was an only child, she liked hanging out and playing with us boys. Also, she's the same age as me and my twin brother, Peter, and the three of us were all in the same classes at school.

'So when I say she's my surrogate sister, it means

she's not a blood relation, as in we don't have the same parents, but I love her like a sister.' Bart touched his chest. 'In my heart, she *is* my sister.'

Cliff nodded, listening intently to everything Bart had to say, but at the end he rolled his eyes and muttered, 'Sisters are overrated.'

Bart chuckled and Ebony couldn't help smiling, shaking her head at his words. 'Oh, Cliff. Go and tell Maddie it's time to set the table, please.'

'Do I have to?' he grumbled.

'Why don't we go and tell Maddie together?' Bart asked, and Cliff's eyes brightened.

'Yeah. She won't be mean to me if you're there.' With that Cliff raced out the kitchen and, after smiling at both women, Bart followed, knowing full well he'd be the topic of conversation between mother and daughter and not really sure he wanted to know exactly what they were saying.

When he'd seen Ebony standing at the door wearing casual jeans, a pink unicorn T-shirt and her hair all golden and loose around her shoulders, he'd had a difficult time not swallowing his tongue. Didn't the woman have any idea just how desirable she was? She'd been right in suggesting they remain friends but he had to admit that hadn't stopped him thinking about her.

Even this morning she'd been the first thought on his mind when he'd woken and that had bothered him slightly. Usually he woke concerned about Timmy and trying to figure out what he could possibly do to ensure the little boy had the best of both worlds—a family that would love and care for him as well as a neurosurgeon who would provide the best care in the world. Ebony simply wasn't like the other women he'd dated in the past.

She *knew* him and that in itself posed a problem. In the past when he'd dated, he'd always held a part of himself back, not wanting the woman in question to delve too deeply into his past. Ebony had been *part* of his past and hearing her talk about Alice had not only opened the door he'd boarded up long ago, it had made him think.

Had he been wrong to close himself off? To unconsciously sabotage every romantic relationship he'd had because he'd been unable to talk about his loss? Was he actually capable of moving on? Of not feeling as though he was cheating on the memory of that pure love he and Alice had shared? *Had* it been pure love, as he'd always thought, or was he just afraid of admitting it had been an inexperienced love, one he'd clung to in order to help him through difficult and depressing times?

Had Ebony been right the other morning when she'd said they needed to talk about those they'd lost so they didn't lose a part of the new person they were becoming?

As Cliff knocked on his sister's door, the one with loud blaring music coming from it, he returned all thoughts of his own dilemmas to the back of his mind, ready to focus on the present.

'Go away!' Maddie yelled through the door.

'But, Maddie, we have company. Mum's friend from work is here.'

'I don't want to meet *any* friend of Mum's,' Maddie yelled back over the music, which only indicated to Bart that the teenager certainly had a good set of lungs on her.

'We've got to set the table.' Cliff tried again, banging on the door. His persistence paid off when Maddie wrenched open her door to glare and yell at her brother—and came to a shocked standstill when she saw Bart standing next to Cliff.

'Hi. I'm Bart.'

Maddie simply stared up at him and even though her blonde hair was pulled into a side ponytail and her teeth were covered in multi-coloured braces, Bart could see the resemblance to both mother and father. She certainly inherited Ebony's soft skin and blonde hair but her eyes were a deep brown, just like her father's.

'Uh…' Maddie faltered, then quickly spun round and flicked off the music, embarrassment tingeing her cheeks.

'Come on,' Cliff nagged. 'We've got to set the table. Bart has to do it, too.'

'Yep. I'm also on table duty.' He shrugged his shoulders then smiled at her. 'You have exactly the same colour eyes as your dad. He was a good friend of mine back in medical school.'

'You *really* knew my dad?' The words were a soft whisper but her tone was still filled with uncertainty.

'Sure. We used to play football together and cram all night long before exams. We even shared a dorm room for a while.' Bart wrinkled his nose. 'He snored really loud.'

'Did he?' Cliff had forgotten all about the table setting and was also lapping up every word Bart was saying. 'I like football but I don't have anyone to play it with.'

'Perhaps I can come over on the weekend and we can head to the park.'

'Can I come, too?' Maddie asked. 'I like to kick footballs.'

'You do not,' Cliff countered.

'Do so,' Maddie growled at him, then smiled sweetly at Bart.

'Sure you can come.' It was then Bart glanced over his shoulder and caught a glimpse of Ebony a little way down the hall, watching the exchange between him and her children. He didn't miss the overwhelming look in her expressive green eyes either, or the way her lips were pursed as though in an effort to control her emotions. 'Why don't we all go?' he suggested, turning so his comments were also directed to encompass Ebony. 'A picnic in the park on Sunday afternoon?'

Ebony nodded, a watery smile on her lips. 'If Timmy's feeling better, he might like to join us.'

'Excellent idea.' Bart's smile was bright.

'Who's Timmy?' Cliff wanted to know as Bart started walking towards the dining room, the children following him like he was some sort of pied piper. Together the three of them set the table while Bart told them about Timmy and Ebony headed back to the kitchen to finish making the salad.

'He's a genius,' she told her mother softly. 'Two seconds with Maddie and she not only turned off her music but is following him around the place.'

'She was always very close to Dean, darling.'

'Total daddy's girl,' Ebony agreed. 'It should make me feel inadequate that a relative stranger is able to connect to my daughter more easily than I can but honestly, Mum, I'm just glad *something* has worked, that she's talking in a normal voice and not slamming and yelling at everyone.'

'Bart's not a stranger, though,' Adele pointed out. 'He knew Dean and, in the way that I knew his parents and you knew Alice, it bonds us all closer together.' Adele put an arm around Ebony's shoulders. 'When we lose someone we love, someone close to us, it really can make a difference just being around people who also knew them. That way there's no reason to explain anything, to tiptoe around the subject of death. We can all chat and laugh and remember happier times we shared with those we've lost.' Adele kissed her daughter's cheek.

'That's why I'm so grateful you've come to live with me in this big, rambling, empty house. I know it hasn't been easy for you, taking the kids from the only home they'd known, but I want you to know I appreciate it. Having you here has helped me more than I can say.' As she said the last words, her voice broke and within a second Ebony had pulled her mother close to hug her.

'Oh, Mum. We love being with you. We're family and families stick together.'

'My sentiments exactly,' Bart's deep voice said from the doorway, and when Ebony looked over at him it was to find both her children standing by his side, having clearly overheard the last part of the conversation.

Adele, never one to make a scene, pulled away and dabbed at her eyes with a handkerchief before heading to the stove and stirring a simmering pot of delicious-smelling food. 'Enough of all this. Who's ready to eat?'

'Me!' Cliff answered immediately, still unsure why his sister had stopped yelling at him and why his grandmother had been crying. It didn't matter. He was hungry.

'That was a lovely evening,' Bart said to Ebony after he'd thanked Adele and said goodnight to the children. Not only had she walked him to the front door but it appeared she was walking him to his car, parked in her driveway.

'Yes, it was. I can't remember when I've enjoyed dinner so much.' She shoved her hands into the pockets of her jeans and smiled at him. Bart watched her closely, noting her relaxed demeanour and realising she meant every word. 'Having you here certainly calmed Maddie right down.' She grinned at him. 'Are you free for dinner tomorrow night, too? And Friday night? Saturday?'

She was only partly joking, realising she *wanted* him to come around every night, not only to help keep her daughter more civil but so they could talk quietly, getting to know each other better. It was strange how he'd made such a big impact on her life in such a short time. Never had she taken to anyone so readily before. Not even Dean.

Bart chuckled and she seemed to almost breathe in the sound. It made him realise that even though they'd made the decision to ignore the awareness that flared so naturally between them, it was still almost tangible. He also wasn't quite sure whether she was joking about the dinner invitations as the way she was looking at him caused his gut to tighten with longing. She was so incredibly beautiful and he enjoyed spending time with her.

Alarm bells at the back of his mind started to ring, warning him it was time to put the brakes on. Attraction he could deal with but it was the desire to know her better, to delve further into her mind, to spend time with her family that was wrong.

'Seriously,' she added after a moment, fiddling with her earring, a habit he'd noticed she had whenever she was a little nervous, 'I could get used to eating tantrum-free dinners, especially after a long day in Theatre.'

He unlocked his car and opened the driver's-side door, pleased she'd stayed on her front lawn rather than following him out onto the road. Sitting near her at dinner had been bad enough when it had come to controlling his attraction to her, and he'd been glad to have the rest of her family around them at all times. Now, though, it was just the two of them and keeping their distance was important if this friendship thing was going to work between them.

The breeze around them started to pick up and when he glanced at the starry night sky, he noted there wasn't a cloud to be found. 'Go on inside. I don't want you getting cold.'

Ebony chuckled a little. 'This isn't cold, Bart. This is…a nice evening by English standards.'

'Of course. I keep forgetting. How will you be when summer hits?'

'That's not for at least another eight or nine months and hopefully by then we will have all become more acclimatised to the Australian weather, but from what I can remember, Canberra's summers aren't too hot, not compared to other states in Australia.'

'True.' He nodded, thinking he'd better get out of there quickly given they'd resorted to discussing the weather. 'Well, thanks again for a great evening.'

'No. Thank *you*, Bart.' She removed her hands from her pockets and took a few steps closer to his car. 'I don't think you have any idea just how much difference you've made in all our lives.' Her tone was intense, her words sincere and heartfelt, and Bart wanted nothing more than to walk round his car and haul her into his arms, needing to reassure her that things would get better, that he was there to help and support her in any way he could. Instead, he forced himself to stay right where he was, his hand tightening on the open car door.

'Hey, that's what friends are for.'

Ebony nodded. 'Yes. Yes, it is.' She sighed and shoved her hands back into her pockets as though his mention of the words 'friends' had set her mind back on a more even path. She swallowed and nodded. 'If Timmy's awake, tell him I said sweet dreams.'

He angled his head to the side, a small smile touching his lips. 'How did you know I would be heading back to the hospital? Am I that predictable?'

'With the way you care about Timmy? Yes.'

'OK, then. I'll be sure to tell him.' He paused once more, knowing he had to leave but also wanting to prolong the minutes he could spend in her company. 'I'll see you tomorrow.'

'Tomorrow,' she repeated, and watched as he climbed into his car. A moment later he'd buckled up and started the engine, tooting the car's horn as the car pulled away from the kerb. She waved and smiled and stood there until the car had turned at the end of her street. Shoving her hands back into her pockets, Ebony stayed where she was and allowed her shoulders to sag.

Why was it so exhausting to fight the natural instinct to throw herself into his arms? Why did they have to keep their distance? Why couldn't they simply give in to their urges and desires and see where this attraction might take them?

'Hey, Mum!' Cliff called from the front door. 'You stayin' out there all night? It's time for my goodnight cuddle!'

'And that's why,' she said softly to herself. 'On my way,' she called to Cliff as she headed back inside. As she went through her night-time routine she knew that even though she might be able to push thoughts of Bart to the back of her mind for now, once she was alone and lying in bed, relaxing amongst the pillows, they'd return and yet again her dreams would be filled with the two of them together.

'Inevitable?' she whispered into the darkness of her bedroom a few hours later. 'I hope so.'

CHAPTER FIVE

BART unlocked his front door and walked into the dark house. He'd been spending so much time at the hospital lately it was nice to actually come home and sleep in his own bed. Timmy had been asleep when he'd checked on him but had roused when Bart had kissed the boy's forehead.

'Goodnight, Bart,' Timmy had mumbled sleepily as he'd snuggled into the stark, white sheets. 'I love you.'

'Love you, too, buddy. Sweet dreams.'

He didn't bother turning on any lights as he removed his shoes and light jacket, not wanting the blaze of bright light to infiltrate his thoughts. Sinking down into his favourite chair, he closed his eyes for a moment, reflecting on the amazing evening he'd had with Ebony and her family.

All the chattering and listening and nodding and helping to clear the dishes and…'familyness' reminded him of his own brothers. The family meals they'd had together when his parents had been alive had been loud and filled with raucous laughter, his parents often mediating small disputes that had sprung up between the siblings.

All his siblings were now enjoying those same little disputes with their own children, gathering around the table of an evening for some togetherness. He missed that. For so long he'd been more than content to remain a bachelor, living his life on his own terms and doing the work that needed doing.

Now, with his increasing paternal feelings for Timmy and the arrival of Ebony and her family into his life, he was starting to doubt the plans he'd made for his future. The single, dedicated neurosurgeon, married to his work, just didn't seem…enough any more, especially when it was far too easy to picture coming home with Ebony in the evenings, discussing their patients and the latest medical breakthroughs and techniques. They'd be met by loud blaring rock music and a house filled with the voices of children laughing and arguing and just being siblings.

The picture was so clear he sat up straighter in the chair, his eyes snapping open. He whipped his cellphone from his pocket and pressed a pre-set number.

'Hello?' a tired voice answered.

'Pete?'

'Bro'. It's late. Have you forgotten the time difference between Canberra and the snowy mountains?'

Bart grinned at his twin brother's reply. 'There *is* no time difference.'

'My point exactly.' He could hear Peter turning over in bed and mumbling to his wife that 'it's just Bart'. 'What's up?'

'Do you think, if Alice had lived, we'd still be together?'

'Whoa!' Peter's voice was more alert now. 'Where has this sprung from?'

'I've just been…' He stopped. There was no hiding anything from his twin. Although they weren't identical, the two of them had been together since birth and knew each other instinctively. It was best to just blurt everything out. 'Do you remember Alice's friend, Ebony Matthews?'

'Sure. Blonde. Pretty. Intelligent.'

'I'm working with her. She's my anaesthetist.' Bart groaned and closed his eyes, knowing his brother would connect the dots.

'Uh-huh.' Peter waited patiently.

'She's a widow now. Has two kids.'

'Aha…and you're attracted to her.'

'Yup.'

'Attracted to a woman who knows about your past and has kids. This is sounding like a real problem for the man who swore he'd remain a bachelor forever.' Peter chuckled, unable to resist teasing his brother a little.

Bart growled. 'Pete.'

'Sorry. So now you're thinking about the life you might have had with Alice? Whether you were too young to think about marrying back then? Whether it would have lasted. Whether you've left it too late to really move on and have a family of your own?'

'Yeah.'

'And Ebony? How does she feel about you?'

'Uh…well…' He thought back to the long and lingering looks they'd shared, the way she seemed to churn his insides into tight knots. The sensations were intense and immediate and even at work he was able to sense whenever she walked into a room. 'There's an attraction but Eb is definitely the marrying kind.'

'And you're not?' Peter's tone was serious and he left the question hanging. 'I know you've used your relationship with Alice as a yardstick, that you want that bonding of heart as well as the bonding of mind and soul.'

'Maybe it's time to stop comparing and just accept?' Bart asked softly.

Peter chuckled. 'You always were smart, bro'. You got the brains—I got the looks.'

Bart laughed and after sending his love to Peter's family rang off. He sat in the dark for a few minutes before picking up the medical journal lying open on the coffee table. He didn't need to turn on the light to know the opened page contained one of the articles Ebony had co-authored with Hartley. He'd hunted out all the ones she'd written, reading them eagerly, impressed by her intellect.

'A definite bonding of minds,' he murmured into the dark. That didn't bother him as much as the way Ebony also appeared to be breaking down the barriers he'd erected around his heart so many years ago, making him realise that there was a lot of things missing from his life.

'Just accept.' Those were the words his brother had used. Could he just accept the way Ebony made him feel? Accept the way she was infiltrating his life? He wasn't sure.

On Friday, after Cliff had finished school, Ebony picked him up and brought him to the hospital to meet Timmy. As she'd suspected, the two boys hit it off right away. Both of them liked to build with moulded plastic bricks and all too soon they were in the paediatric ward's playroom, constructing a futuristic city and allowing their imaginations full reign.

'They're like two old men, nattering away to each other like that,' Bart said from behind her, and Ebony turned from where she'd been watching the two boys to smile at him.

'You're not wrong.'

Bart returned her smile and Ebony felt her insides relaxing. Why was it that a few seconds in his presence did more for her mood than anything else? What was it about him that so appealed to her? Was it his dark good looks? His hypnotic blue eyes? His perfectly curved mouth, which, she was quite sure, would fit so perfectly over her own?

'A perfect pairing,' he remarked, and for a split second she stared at him, unsure what he was saying. Had she spoken out loud?

'Uh…' She swallowed and cleared her throat, trying to figure out what she was supposed to say, how she was supposed to explain having spoken out loud like that, but when he pointed to the two boys, still engrossed in their imaginary land, she let out a sigh of relief. She hadn't betrayed her thoughts after all.

'Uh…yes,' she remarked, fixing her gaze on the boys knowing she'd have a better chance at concentrating when she *wasn't* fantasising about Bart's mouth on hers. 'It's good to see Cliff making friends. Believe it or not, he tends to be rather shy at school.'

'Timmy's the same. Not into sport because his head injury prohibits him doing things, and he much prefers to read a book or play a game.'

Ebony nodded. 'Which is probably why it was an excellent idea to get the two of them together.'

'Mission accomplished,' he agreed.

'Hey. Bart's here,' Timmy announced, and waved at his hero. Cliff looked up and waved as well, both boys eager to have Bart's attention.

'That's my cue,' Bart murmured, and walked past Ebony into the playroom. She watched as he sat down on the floor next to Timmy and began building a new addition to the imaginary city. Cliff seemed to lap up the attention, which was good news as since his father's death he often had trouble relating to adult males, thinking that if he allowed himself to make friends with them, they'd die, just like his father had.

'Fear of being abandoned by an adult male,' the child psychologist had deduced. 'He'll grow out of it, eventually.' And now, given his positive reaction to Bart, it appeared it was so. She stood there and watched them all for a few more minutes, boys being boys. Having grown up with so many brothers, especially having his twin, Peter, around all his life, Bart clearly knew how to relate easily to the two young boys so that when the ward sister came to say it was time for Timmy to return to his bed, Bart quickly scooped the five-year-old into his arms before any protests could arise and carried him back to his room. He chatted with Cliff the whole time, not leaving him behind and asking him to help out by opening the door to Timmy's room and making sure the bedcovers were pulled back.

Ebony knew the ward sister would have done all that but it was the fact that Bart was including Cliff, making him feel useful, that melted her heart. He really was quite a man and would make a wonderful father.

As soon as the thought entered her mind, she quashed it as best she could. It was bad enough she needed to constantly fight the attraction she felt for him, let alone start seeing him as a father figure for her children.

She *knew* he'd be a good father because, along with Peter and Edward, he'd helped raise his younger two brothers. She *knew* he'd be a good father because even at school he'd been able to see into people's hearts, to say the words they'd needed to hear in order to help them change. She *knew* he'd be a good father because of the way he'd talked to Maddie, the way he included Cliff and the way he loved Timmy.

She closed her eyes, knowing it was already too late. She'd always been a hopeless romantic and could quite easily picture Bart fitting comfortably into the new life she was trying to build here in Australia. The problem was, if she allowed her imagination free rein, she'd start hoping and wishing for those things to come true, and when they didn't she'd end up heartbroken and rejected. Hadn't she been through enough already?

'Self-preservation,' she whispered sternly to herself.

'What, Mum?' Cliff asked, and when she opened her eyes she was stunned to find Cliff and Bart standing in front of her.

'Oh…uh…' She glanced at Bart, hoping he hadn't heard her mutterings, before returning her attention to her son. 'Everything all right?'

'Timmy's had such a smashing idea, Mum,' Cliff burst out, his face beaming brightly in an enormous smile.

'He has?'

'Yup.' Cliff looked up at Bart, who gave him a nod of encouragement. 'Uh…well…tomorrow night here in the ward they're having a film night for all the kids and their families who come here all the time and stuff, and it's one of my favourite movies and, well, yeah, like, Timmy doesn't have any brothers and sisters and I don't have any brothers and Timmy said if we pretend I'm his brother then I can come to the movie.' The words had come out in a big rush. 'What do you think, Mum? Can I go? Please? Please? Please?'

Cliff had his hands clasped tightly together, holding them out towards her as he pleaded. Ebony raised an eyebrow and looked at Bart, who only gave her a lopsided smile.

'Well, I don't think we need to lie and say you're Timmy's brother but I think it'll—'

'But he doesn't *have* a brother, Mum, and Timmy and me could be like Bart and his sister who isn't his sister. You know, like he was telling me the other night.'

'A surrogate?'

'Yup. That's it. Timmy can be my surrogate brother and then we can do loads of things together.' Cliff's eyes were bright with excited delight but there was also a hint of desperation about him, as though he really wasn't sure what his mother was going to decide.

Ebony's heart melted. She raised her eyes briefly to look at Bart and was pleased to find him smiling at this turn of events. 'Cliff, of course you can go to the movie, if it's all right with the ward sister.'

Cliff waved her words away as though it was a done deal. 'Bart said he'd talk to her.'

'No.' Ebony shook her head. 'You want to attend, you need to politely ask ward sister for permission,' she countered, glancing at Bart once again, wondering if he was going to contradict her.

'Your mum's absolutely right.' At Bart's words Ebony saw Cliff's excited expression start to fade. She knew he didn't feel comfortable engaging adults in such a fashion but he had to learn. She was about to tell him that she'd go with him but that he had to do all the talking when Bart winked at him. 'How about if I come with you but you do all the talking, eh?'

At this suggestion, Cliff instantly stood up straighter and squared his shoulders. 'Yeah. OK, then.' He took a few deep breaths. 'I can do this. I *can* do this.'

'Yes, you can.'

While Cliff continued to gather his courage, Ebony looked at Bart with amazement. Not only had he supported her but he was willing to help Cliff out.

'You're amazing,' she whispered. Bart stared at her, his brows lifting when he saw her eyes alive with happiness.

'I am?'

'Yes. Most men want to take over rather than help a young boy build up his own confidence.' She reached out and took his hand, giving it a little squeeze. 'Thank you.'

Bart glanced down at her hand in his, tenderly rubbed his thumb over her knuckles. 'You have such small hands,' he muttered.

Ebony smiled. 'What?'

'Your hands, they're so delicate and soft and yet they've been working hard, all alone, for so long.' He raised his gaze to meet hers. 'I'm happy to help, Eb.'

As she breathed in, she found it difficult to stop her eyelids from fluttering closed as Bart's hypnotic scent wound its way around her, drawing her in, making her want more from him than the friendship they'd agreed on. His sweet words, his tender touch… She could drown in his eyes and yet they'd agreed to just be friends. Were they insane?

'Bart? Bart?' Cliff was tapping Bart's arm, trying to get his attention. Bart dragged his gaze away from Ebony, unable to believe how beautiful she was. With her blonde hair pulled back into a ponytail, her casual clothes instead of the power suits she usually wore to work, she looked far younger than her forty-one years. The more he saw of her, the more he became involved in her life, the more he wanted far more from her than the friendship they'd agreed on.

He excused himself from Ebony and followed Cliff, encouraging the boy as he walked right up to the ward sister and spoke calmly and clearly to her, indicating his desire to attend the screening and spend more time with Timmy. He even remembered his manners and when ward sister readily agreed, the smile on Cliff's face made Bart's heart fill with pride. Ebony had done a marvellous job of raising the boy. Cliff raced off to tell Timmy the good news and it was only when he was gone that Bart realised she was watching him closely.

'Thanks again,' she offered.

'You're more than welcome.' He jerked a thumb over his shoulder. 'Have you got time for a quick cuppa before heading home?'

Ebony checked the clock on the wall then looked into Timmy's room, where the two boys were once again chatting animatedly, even though she could see Timmy was starting to tire. 'A very quick one. Although Timmy's vastly improved since his surgery, the last thing I'd want is for Cliff's enthusiasm to exhaust him too much.' Bart laughed at her words as she followed him into the small tearoom, glad to find it empty. She sank down into one of the chairs and sighed.

'Starting to feel the day?'

'Yes. I find paperwork far more exhausting than actually being in Theatre all day.' He chuckled as he made two cups of tea, leaving hers black before handing it to her. 'Thanks.' She sipped the liquid, careful not to burn her tongue. 'Ah…this is just what I needed.' She took another sip then stopped. 'Wait a second. How did you know I have black tea?'

He shrugged one shoulder. 'The other night at your house you had a cup of black tea after dessert. I pay attention.'

A slow smile crossed her lips and she couldn't help feeling insanely pleased that he'd noticed. He didn't sit down but instead kept his distance by leaning against the bench as he sipped his own drink. During the past week, and especially after his phone conversation with her in the early hours of Tuesday morning, Bart had tried to keep a bit more distance between them. They'd agreed to be friends and yet the long and lingering looks, like the one they'd just shared, seemed to happen more often than not.

Yes, he was attracted to Ebony. Yes, he found her intellectually stimulating and, yes, he was fascinated by her, but she had children and he wasn't looking for a family or for permanence. So why was it he hadn't been able to stop thinking about her?

Sitting in Timmy's room during the week, he'd doze off and have the sweetest little dreams about Ebony. It had been quite startling for him as no woman had really managed to get so beneath his skin so quickly, even Alice, and perhaps it was that admission that had unnerved him the most. Therefore, keeping his physical distance from the alluring woman sitting on the chair looking at him through hooded eyes was paramount.

'So,' he said, needing to break the silence before he did something crazy like close the distance between them and brush his lips tantalisingly across hers, because heaven only knew that was what he *wanted* to do, 'tomorrow night. I'll be staying here at the hospital with Timmy so if you want to drop Cliff off before taking Maddie to ACT NOW then—'

'Oh, gosh. That's *tomorrow* night?' She quickly shook her head. 'I mean I *know* it's tomorrow night, that Saturday plus Saturday equals Saturday but I'm just not ready for the next round of tantrums from Maddie in order to *get* her to ACT NOW in the first place.'

'Things haven't improved?'

'Since Wednesday when you captivated her? They have—a little. She's not slamming her doors any more and the music has been kept at a more acceptable level. Last night at dinner we didn't have a tantrum, which was very nice indeed. So, yes, I guess you could say things have improved. Small steps, though, right?'

'Right.'

'The biggest problem is that she can't stop asking about you.'

'Me?'

'When I came home for dinner last night, the table was set, she'd helped Mum prepare dinner and was very disappointed that you didn't walk in the door with me.'

'Oh.'

'She then proceeded to ply me with questions during dinner. Her favourite topic—you.'

'Oh?'

'Yes.' Ebony took another sip of her tea and nodded.

'Does she have a…crush on me?'

'Not an infatuation, no, not in the sense that she's fallen madly in love with you as some teenagers are likely to do from time to time, but rather she's intent on having you for her father.'

'Father!'

'Apparently, according to their way of thinking, I don't even have to marry you in order to achieve this goal.' She laughed a little at the words, working hard to keep a lightness in her tone in case she scared him away.

'I don't?' Why didn't he sound convincing? Why didn't the course of this conversation bother him?

'No. They've decided they're going to "surrogate" you, I think was the term they used.'

'They?'

'Oh, yes, Cliff is equally as taken with you, even more so now that you've helped him secure his seat at the movie tomorrow night.' She angled her head and looked at him, noting his slight discomfort at her words and yet she was positive she also saw a sense of pride travel down his spine as he stood up straight. 'You have a connection to their father so in their minds they've decided you're the perfect replacement.'

'Replacement dad?'

'Yes.' She took another sip of her tea. 'Just wanted you to know that when I say you've had a big impact on my children, you've had a *big* impact on my children.'

Bart exhaled slowly, as though processing her words, before sipping his tea. He put his cup down on the bench and shoved his hands into his trouser pockets before meeting her gaze once more. 'I'm...honoured they would think me suitable for the position.' It also warmed his heart to know he was accepted by her children. Between Maddie, Cliff and Timmy, he was finding the strong paternal instinct he'd done his best to ignore for the past two decades coming to the fore. 'And...that doesn't bother you? That they're looking to replace Dean?'

'Why would it bother me?' Ebony sat up a little straighter in her chair and stared into her mug for a few seconds before answering. 'Dean isn't here and there's nothing in the world I can do to bring him back.' Her tone was reverent but absolute. 'Isn't this what moving on with your life is all about? Moving forward? Making new connections?' There was hope in her eyes as she spoke.

'Or rediscovering an old one?' he offered, his tone holding a hint of promise.

Ebony breathed out slowly, not at all surprised when the atmosphere in the small room began to change. She tried to look away, tried to break eye contact, but it was becoming more and more impossible to do so. Too many times they'd seemed to be caught in such a bubble as this, knowing the right thing to do was to keep their distance yet all the while wanting to do anything but.

When Bart cleared his throat, Ebony stared down into her cup before finishing off her drink and carrying her cup to the sink. Bart shifted slightly while she rinsed her cup then turned to face him. Friends. She was just friends with Bart. They chatted and they discussed. They helped each other out. That's what the two of them had been doing all week long, focusing on their patients during the long hours in Theatre and chatting amicably at other times. She'd tried her best not to be alone with him, as she was right now, because when other people were around it was much easier to keep her rioting hormones under control. Now, though, as far as control was concerned, she was starting to fail—miserably.

'Our lives intertwined years ago,' she said softly. 'Sometimes past friendships have a tendency to unravel and people go their separate ways. Other friendships remain intertwined for a reason.'

'And you think our friendship is like that?' His voice was deeper than before, softer, more intimate, and a flood of warmth spread through Ebony's body.

'Yes. Don't you?' She left the question hanging in the air for a moment but when he didn't reply, she continued, 'After Dean's death I became a single working mother, trying to deal with my own grief and trying to help my kids and juggle my job and…well, I guess I learned to rely on myself. It seemed easier, rather than burdening others with my problems. I don't tend to ask anyone for help, but with you…' she shook her head slowly '…everything is different. I don't know why.' She shrugged one delicate shoulder. 'It just is.'

Bart watched her closely for a moment and then, as though unable to help himself, as though his hand had a life of its own, he stepped forward, effectively closing the distance between them, and tucked a lock of hair, which had come loose from her ponytail, behind her ear. 'Eb.' He looked down into her eyes and slowly exhaled, the atmosphere between them thickening instantly. 'You don't need to do everything by yourself any more.'

She swallowed over her suddenly dry throat. 'Some habits are hard to break.' Her words were soft as she gazed into his eyes. 'Especially where my children are concerned. They're all I have left.'

He nodded. 'I understand. Family's very important and young Cliff…he sure does look like his father. Maddie, she's just a confused teenage girl who inherited the stubborn temper of her father.'

'You noticed.'

'Dean was my friend, Ebony, and because of that I want to do all I can for his children. We may have lost touch over the years but he was there when I needed him. He managed to help me through a difficult time.'

'When Alice passed away,' she stated, nodding her head, the lock of hair he'd previously secured behind her ear falling loose again.

'Yes.' At the mention of Alice Bart immediately paused, wanting to withdraw from Ebony, to put some distance between them, which he realised was his default setting. As soon as any woman started getting too close, started *knowing* him, he'd withdraw, but with Ebony it was different. She knew his past and she accepted it, just as he knew hers. He *did* want to help her and that sensation wouldn't be denied. They may have connected on an intellectual level but the urgency beating through him, the need to support her, was genuine and heartfelt.

'I want to help you and Maddie and Cliff.' His words were adamant and filled with truth. 'I want to do everything I can not only for my old friend but also for *you*. You're a remarkable woman, Eb. You deserve a world of happiness.'

He reached out to retuck the hair behind her ear, the action slower, more tender than before, his fingers lingering on her cheek causing a wave of delighted anticipation to shiver through her. 'You deserve to be appreciated.' His words were soft, intimate, meaningful. 'You deserve to be cherished.' He cupped her cheek with his hand and brushed his thumb across her lips, causing her to gasp with longing.

'Friends?' The question was a soft whisper.

'Always but...' He exhaled harshly. 'I...I can't stop thinking about you, Eb, and it's starting to drive me crazy!'

'I know what you mean.'

'Do you?' He brushed his thumb once more over her lower lip and she couldn't help the sigh of longing that escaped, her eyelids fluttering closed as she tried hard to regain control over her thoughts, over her emotions, over her desperate need to feel Bart's mouth pressed firmly and gloriously against her own.

She was sure this time, especially as they'd already both acknowledged an underlying attraction, that Bart would follow through on the urgent pull they were both experiencing. This would be the first time a man had kissed her since Dean's death and where she'd thought she'd never be interested in anyone else again, Bart was proving her wrong.

She'd tried dating a few times about two years ago but even going out with another man for dinner or to the cinema had seemed wrong and besides, she hadn't wanted to upset the children so she'd pulled away from any possible romantic entanglements and had thought it would always stay that way...until Bart. Until they'd met up again and she'd been instantly aware of him.

Standing here now, with her face tilted towards his, his breath fanning her face, their scents mingling to form an intoxicating combination of need, desire and want, she was delighted to find that her heart could still beat violently against her chest, that she could feel that thrill of excitement spread around her body like wild-fire, that it was possible to find happiness after so much sorrow in her life.

She could feel him moving ever closer with an agonising slowness that she hated and loved at the same time. This was it. She was about to be kissed by another man...and it was thrilling. With one hand still cupping her cheek, he slid his other hand to her waist, edging her a few millimetres closer, the powerful sense of something extraordinary happening between them only serving to freeze this important moment, burning it into her memory permanently.

And at the first touch of his mouth to hers, a soft, barely perceptible kiss so sweet and tender and deliciously tantalising, Ebony sighed, lifting one hand to rest it lightly on his chest, wanting to feel if his heart-beat was pounding as erratically as her own. When she felt him pull back, just for a moment, she swallowed and opened her eyes, surprised to find her eyelids lazy and heavy with romantic want.

He was looking at her, looking at her mouth, her cheeks, her neck, her eyes and back to her lips, a dazed expression on his face. He didn't say anything but instead swallowed and continued to stare at her. He didn't remove his hand from her waist, or the one cupping her cheek, his thumb moving ever so slightly in the tiniest of circles.

What did he see? she wondered. Did he think what was happening between them was a mistake? She wasn't sure herself but what she *did* know was that where she'd been doing her best to see him only as a friend and colleague, she'd failed dismally, especially when her dreams had been filled with scenarios just like this one.

Bart, holding her close, touching her tenderly, his deep blue eyes bringing to life the dormant emotions she'd thought she'd never feel ever again. The longing in her heart, the need to know whether this thing between them was something worth pursuing had only increased every morning when she'd woken fresh from vivid dreams of the man presently studying her face so intently she was sure he was about to say they'd made a terrible mistake.

'Ebony, you really are incredibly beautiful.'

CHAPTER SIX

'I AM?' The words were spoken with wonder but filled with hope. As they'd already admitted an attraction to each other, she shouldn't have been surprised to hear Bart say such wonderful things but the knowledge that he thought she was beautiful filled her with resounding relief as well as quiet confidence.

When Dean had passed away, she'd often questioned whether or not she'd be able to feel such intense emotions for another man, and whether another man would ever think she was beautiful, and yet here she was not only trying to control the explosion of fireworks deep within her from his tantalising kiss but delighting in the knowledge he thought she was pretty.

'How can there be any doubt in your mind? Your eyes are like the deepest emeralds, shining bright with respect for our colleagues, with compassion and caring for your patients and with love for your family. You're a survivor, Eb. A strong, independent woman who is captivating me.'

She splayed her fingers wider on his chest, momentarily enjoying the feel of his firm torso beneath her fingers as she drank in the wonderful words he was saying. The heat from his body was transmitting itself through her hand before running up her arm, only adding to the fire he'd already lit deep within her.

Ebony gazed up at him, unsure what she was supposed to do or say next because when he spoke to her in such a way, his deep voice resonating throughout every fibre of her being, he turned her mind to complete mush. Instead, she began to slide her hand further up his chest and around his neck, intent on assisting him to lower his head and touch his lips to hers once more. This time, though, she wanted far more than a teasing and tantalising kiss. Her fingers played with the ends of his hair as she eased up slightly onto the balls of her feet, stretching her neck, showing him she was as much affected by all of this as he was.

'Eb,' he breathed, his gaze dipping to encompass her parted lips, ready, willing and waiting for him to taste them. This past week, he realised, had been absolute torture on his senses. Not only had he been worried about Timmy but to add his rising emotions for Ebony into the mix and to say he felt as though he'd been living on a roller-coaster was an understatement.

Their breaths began to mingle the closer they came to eliminating all remaining distance between them. Ebony closed her eyes and began adding pressure to the base of his neck, but as Bart's hand at her waist began to draw her ever nearer, she realised he needed no prompting to give them both what they'd been yearning for.

Another second and it would happen...but within the next instant Ebony found herself rudely propelled from his embrace. She put both hands out towards the sink to steady herself, completely bewildered and unsure what was happening.

She was about to turn and question Bart when she heard it. The sound of one of the nurses talking, her

voice getting closer to the tearoom, and the next instant
the door opened. Ebony quickly picked up Bart's cup
from the bench, emptied the contents down the drain
and began rinsing it out.

'There you are, Bart. Oh, good, Ebony, you're here,
too,' the nurse said. 'Timmy was asking for you…' She
pointed to Bart. 'And Ward Sister wants you…' she
pointed to Ebony '…to confirm the decreased dosages
in Timmy's medication.'

'Right,' Bart said.

'Good,' Ebony added, as she washed her hands and
wiped them on a piece of paper towel. They both turned
to head out of the small room, Bart politely standing
aside to allow her to pass in front of him. 'Thank you,'
she murmured, wondering if her cheeks looked as hot
as they felt. She glanced briefly at Bart as she passed
him, their eyes meeting and holding for a moment, but
the message was clear—that had been a close call. To
be caught kissing in the paediatric ward tearoom would
have given the hospital gossips a mine of information
and right now she was very pleased Bart had heard the
nurse approaching.

'Sorry about that,' he murmured quietly as they
walked down the corridor towards the nurses' station.

'Thank *you* for having such good hearing.' His lips
twitched into a smile at her words before he headed
off to Timmy's room. 'I'll be there in a moment to say
goodnight to Timmy and to collect my son,' she told
him, before giving her full attention to the ward sister.

By the time she entered Timmy's room, Cliff had
his coat on and was already saying goodbye to Timmy,
who was snuggled into the covers, ready to go to sleep.
'Has he eaten?' she asked Bart, who shook his head.

'He's worn out. *Happily* worn out,' he added, smiling down at Cliff. 'Thanks for coming in and playing with Timmy.'

'I can't wait until tomorrow night. That movie is going to be brilliant. Hey, Timmy—' Cliff began, but when he looked at his friend, it was to find him fast asleep. Cliff instantly dropped his voice to a hushed whisper. 'Oh, sorry.'

'I'm looking forward to it, too,' Bart added.

'Would you like to come for an early dinner first?'

At the invitation it was on the tip of Bart's tongue to refuse. She'd already managed to infiltrate his defence systems, which meant he was presently treading new ground. He needed a bit of space from the delectable Ebony and although his heart was urging him to accept, he had to force himself to take things slowly.

'Timmy's doing well,' she continued, looking lovingly at the sleeping boy. 'And there's the possibility it might be good for him to get out of the hospital, even for an hour.'

'Timmy can come to *our* house,' Cliff said with great enthusiasm, but quickly dropped his voice when Ebony put her finger over her lips to remind him to speak quietly. 'For dinner!' he finished.

Bart frowned for a moment, absorbing this new possibility. Ebony made a valid point. It would do Timmy the world of good to get out of the hospital's confining four walls and with the bond he was forming with Cliff, it could only enhance his recovery. Besides, both himself and Ebony would be there to keep an eye on things, ensuring Timmy didn't take a turn for the worse.

'It's a good idea and you're right, it might do him the world of good. Let's see how he's feeling tomorrow, but I'd say it's a tentative yes.'

Cliff quietly punched the air. 'Yes!'

Ebony's smile was happy and bright. 'Excellent. I know my mother would love to meet Timmy. So would Maddie.'

'I don't think Maddie wants another surrogate brother,' Cliff whispered loudly. 'She doesn't even like this one.' He jabbed a finger into his chest.

'Yes, she does, mate,' Bart said, crouching down to Cliff's height. 'Maddie's a bit like your building bricks, a little bit all over the place at the moment but she'll pull herself together real soon.'

'Ohhhh!' The sound was long and filled with understanding as though that particular analogy explained everything to Cliff in a simple and effective way. 'I get it, now.'

'Say goodbye to Bart,' Ebony prompted, expecting Cliff to simply wave at Bart, but instead her son all but launched himself into Bart's arms, giving him a big hug.

'Bye, Bart. See you tomorrow.'

Bart was a little surprised at the action, his gaze glancing up to Ebony's. She was smiling brightly, sighing at the sight.

'I did mention the impact you've had on him,' she said softly.

As he released the boy, he ruffled Cliff's hair. 'I'm looking forward to it.'

Cliff laughed. 'Dad used to do that,' he said, and with a wide, beaming smile Cliff caught his mother's hand in his and proceeded to tug her from the room.

'Never thought I'd be jealous of my son,' she remarked, her gaze blending with Bart's, her meaning clear because right now she would love nothing more than to give him a huge hug goodbye.

'I'll ruffle your hair tomorrow,' he joked, and winked at her.

'Funny,' she returned, trying to ignore the way his wink had ignited another round of fireworks within her.

Cliff chattered all the way home and by the time dinner had been eaten and the children were in bed, Ebony finally allowed herself to think about those incredible and intimate moments she'd shared with Bart.

Every time she recalled the soft, tantalising sensation of having his lips brushing gently across her own, a shiver of secret delight passed through her. She wasn't exactly sure what the kiss had meant or whether it had changed their original decision to ignore the attraction and just remain friends. Ignoring the chemistry that flowed so naturally between them hadn't seemed to have worked this past week so perhaps it was better to investigate exactly where these riotous emotions might take them. She hoped so because she would be delighted to accept more of his tantalising kisses and warm embraces. Another shiver passed through her and she leaned her head back against the chair and closed her eyes, determined to relive every second.

'Bad day?' Adele asked as she came and sat down in the lounge next to her daughter, Ebony's eyes snapping open guiltily. She quickly pushed the emotion away, knowing her mother couldn't possibly know the direction of her thoughts. 'Or is it Maddie that has you closing your eyes, searching for some peace?'

Ebony shook her head. 'Actually, things aren't so bad at the moment so I'm just lapping it up.'

'Before things change again, as they inevitably do,' Adele agreed on a small laugh.

'Especially where teenagers are concerned,' Ebony added.

'Or where handsome neurosurgeons are concerned,' Adele countered, and Ebony turned her stunned gaze full on her mother. 'Well, if I wasn't sure before, I am now.' She pointed to Ebony's face. 'That's your guilty look.'

'What?' She tried to feign nonchalance. 'No, it's not. It's my exhausted after a hectic first week in a new job look.'

'Mmm-hmm,' Adele teased. 'OK. I'll pretend to believe you but remember, darling, I know how to read your expressions just as much as you know how to read Cliff's and Maddie's.'

Ebony sighed, giving up on pretence, and leaned back amongst the comfortable cushions. 'I just…' She shrugged. 'I never thought I'd feel this way again. It's scary and fantastic and powerful and—'

'And how does Bart feel? There was definite tension between the two of you the other night at dinner so I'm presuming he's on board with all of these crazy emotions?'

Ebony frowned. 'I think so. At least, I hope so.'

'I was surprised a man of his stature hadn't been snapped up a while ago.'

'I have a feeling he doesn't want to get too close to anyone in case he loses them.'

'Like Alice?'

Ebony shrugged. 'I think so. They were so in love, so connected. Feelings that intense don't come around every day.'

'But when they do, they shouldn't be ignored.'

'No.'

Adele gave her hand another squeeze. 'You might be just the person to help him move forward, to take that all-important step out of the past and really start to live again. He went through so much grief in such a short period of time, poor man. His parents and Alice.'

Adele frowned and shook her head sadly. 'You need to help him, Ebby.'

Ebony nodded. 'I hope so.' She hoped her mother was right. She wanted her mother to be right but what if she *was* able to help Bart come out of the past, to take a step forward in his life, and he took that step with someone else? She couldn't deny her heart was already involved with his, even if it was just in a small way.

Bart had shown her that she could still *feel*, that her sensuality hadn't died along with Dean, that she was a desirable woman, a beautiful woman. She knew he truly cared about her, but she wasn't sure if that caring stemmed more from a sense of duty to look after his old friend's widow, or if it was solely because of what he felt for *her*. Dean had helped Bart through a tragic time and now, with Bart's strong sense of duty and honour, would he only stay in their lives because he felt there was a debt to be repaid?

Throughout the night she tossed and turned, sleep evading her as a variety of thoughts paraded around her mind, refusing to let it shut down. She was glad when the sun started to peek through the curtains of her room and, kicking off the remaining covers, she quickly showered and dressed.

Busying herself with catching up on her paperwork and helping her mother to clean the house, Ebony managed to hold all thoughts of Bart at bay until five o'clock that evening, when the doorbell rang.

'I'll get it!' Maddie and Cliff chorused, both of them running for the front door.

'I said I'd get it.' Maddie growled at her brother as she elbowed him out the way.

'But Timmy's here,' Cliff protested, shoving her back.

'Enough!' Ebony's curt tone cut through their bickering like a knife. '*I'll* get the door.' She walked towards them and opened the front door, shaking her head as her gaze settled on Bart standing behind Timmy's borrowed wheelchair. 'Hi,' she murmured as she opened the screen door to let them in.

'Hey, your big head bandage is gone, and why are you in a wheelchair?' Cliff asked Timmy, his eyes wide with delight.

Timmy, a small bandage still covering the rear of his head and a bung still taped to his hand to allow the staff easier access for giving him any necessary injections, said matter-of-factly, 'It's the rules of the hospital 'cause I'm still a patient and sometimes I get tired easy and this is way cool.'

'Can I have a go?' Cliff was eyeing the wheelchair eagerly.

'Ahem!' Maddie glared at her brother and when he reluctantly turned his attention from the wheelchair, she planted her hands on her hips and said, 'I haven't been introduced to Timmy.'

'Oh.' Cliff turned back to his inspection of the wheelchair. 'Timmy, this is my sister.' His tone sounded bored. 'Maddie.'

'Hi.' Maddie smiled brightly at the five-year-old. 'Did you want me to push you into the lounge room?'

'Sure,' Timmy said, but then, much to Maddie's chagrin, he shifted over so Cliff could squeeze in next to him. Maddie had no option but to push both boys into the lounge room, leaving Bart and Ebony chuckling in the entry hall.

'I think it's going to be an interesting dinner,' she murmured.

Bart agreed, looking into her upturned smiling face. 'You look lovely.' He waited whilst Ebony shut the door then placed a hand on her elbow and leaned down to press a kiss to her cheek. 'And taste delicious.'

'Oh. Uh…' She swallowed, her body instantly warm from his touch, her knees trembling from his chaste kiss. 'Thank you.' She was dressed in a pair of dark denims, boots, a white long-sleeved cotton top with a pale blue T-shirt on top. As she was heading out to ACT NOW with Maddie later on, it was casual but comfortable and she still looked absolutely gorgeous. Then again, in the past week he'd seen her dressed in professional suits, in scrubs and in T-shirts with unicorns on the front. A smile touched his lips as he remembered the unicorns. Delightful.

'Come on in,' she said. 'I know we're on a tight schedule so we'll be eating pretty much straight away, if that's all right with you.'

'It's fine.' He shoved his hands into his jeans pockets to stop himself from touching her again, from putting both hands onto her shoulders and pressing his mouth to hers in a long and soul-satisfying kiss, rather than the light peck on the cheek he had to content himself with.

He swallowed as he followed her to the kitchen, noticing as they passed the lounge room that Timmy had taken off the jacket and scarf Bart had insisted he wear as it had just been starting to get cool when they'd left the hospital.

'We're having pasta tonight,' Ebony announced, bringing his attention back to her, and as she walked in front of him he couldn't help but watch the sexy swish of her hips. This attraction he felt towards her was really starting to get a little out of hand. Last night, knowing how incredible and tantalising Ebony could taste, his dreams had been far more intense than ever before.

For the first time in…well, since Alice, a woman was

tying him in knots. While he may have dated on and off over the years, he'd never met woman who had filled his thoughts so completely until now. He knew she wasn't the type of woman to involve herself in a casual relationship, especially having been happily married before and also having children who relied on her. If he did want to spend more time with her, to get to know her much better, to see where on earth this mind-blowing attraction might lead them, he had to be prepared to face the consequences. The thought didn't scare him nearly as much as it had done previously.

During the past week he'd started to realise it was possible for him to allow himself to really feel, to really care and perhaps to even see where this powerful force that existed between himself and Ebony might lead. If things had moved this fast after just one week, was he prepared to stay on this out-of-control freight train if it led to marriage?

His lips twitched into an ironic smile and he shook his head. If his brothers could only guess at his thoughts, those of the only Goldmark bachelor left, they'd all be laughing right about now.

CHAPTER SEVEN

THROUGHOUT dinner, Ebony was pleased to see that Maddie didn't have a tantrum and remained calm in front of their guests. She did, however, insist on being seated next to Bart and told him more about her past few weeks of starting at a new school than she'd ever told Ebony. Thanks to Bart, she now knew her daughter had a friend called Amy, that her favourite subjects were science and food technology, and that her home-class teacher had long grey hair down to her waist.

'She could at least colour it,' Maddie stated with a hint of disgust, rolling her eyes.

Timmy and Cliff were like two peas in a pod and Ebony was pleased to see Timmy eat quite a bit of food, given his condition.

'Looks like his appetite is back,' she remarked to Bart after dinner, as they all rugged up ready to brave Canberra's cool autumn evening. 'Did he wake up last night for something to eat?'

Bart nodded. 'The night sister told me he woke at three o'clock this morning and ate a whole sandwich. No reactions. He didn't have much to eat throughout the day but I was impressed with what he ate tonight.'

'Good. Here's hoping he really is turning that next

corner. If so, he could go home midway through next week, don't you think?'

Bart hesitated as he watched Cliff and Maddie working together to help Timmy into his jacket and scarf. Maddie even went to the cupboard to get a blanket to tuck around Timmy in the wheelchair, more than likely to ensure Cliff didn't hitch another ride than for warmth. Still, it was nice to see the children working together and caring for someone other than themselves.

'Bart?'

'Sorry?'

'You were miles away.' She studied him for a moment. 'Is everything all right?'

He watched Timmy for a moment longer, then closed his eyes and shook his head. 'Everything's fine.'

'I disagree.' When she put her hand on his arm, Bart opened his eyes and allowed Ebony to steer him into the doorway of the dining room so they were out of earshot of the children. 'What's going on?'

'It's nothing.'

'It obviously *is* something, Bart. We're friends.' She looked at her hand still resting on his arm and quickly dropped it, lest he should think she was implying something else. There was no doubt there was more coursing between them than just friendship but right now she could see he needed a friend. 'You can talk to me.'

He looked at her, saw sincerity in her eyes and realised she was the only person besides his family he *could* trust. She knew him, she knew his past. She accepted him for who he was and he knew she would always keep his confidences. In one week, seeing how she'd forged ahead with her life since the death of her husband, moving her family across the world to be close to her mother, Bart knew she'd shown him there was hope…hope for a better, more fulfilling life than the one he'd settled for, and because of that, the idea he'd been toying with for quite some time was now going to surface.

'It's about Timmy.'

'So I'm gathering.' She smiled encouragingly, amazed at how nervous he appeared.

'I want to be his father.' The words shot from his mouth before he could stop and think about what he was saying.

Her smile widened, thinking how utterly adorable he looked when he was out of his comfort zone. It was clear those words had been incredibly difficult for him to say and although she'd gathered as much, just by watching Bart and Timmy interact over the course of this past week, of how much Bart honestly cared for this little boy, she didn't want to trivialise this moment by saying the wrong thing. Instead, she decided to stay silent in the hope of prompting him to say more.

'That's wrong, isn't it? I know it's wrong. How can I treat him? How can I be objective in his care if I'm emotionally attached? I know all that and I've fought it so much over the years but I just can't help it. I love this kid like he was my own.'

After the words had been spoken, Bart paused for a moment before exhaling slowly. He looked down the hallway at Timmy, who was laughing as Cliff did a few silly walks. A smile instantly came to Bart's lips and when he returned his gaze to Ebony his smile was bright. 'It feels good to finally say all that out loud.'

'I'm glad.' She nodded and reached over to take his hand in hers, giving it a reassuring squeeze. 'And can I just say that you're *already* a good parent, Bart, even though you probably don't realise it.' At his slight frown she continued, 'For the past few years you've been spending more and more time with Timmy, haven't you? The other day Wanda told me how you're always at her house, either taking him out or helping him through things. You love that little boy and he loves you. It's only natural you want him to be part of your family.'

Bart looked at her for a long moment, the smile slowly sliding from his face. 'I can't do it, though. I can't apply to eventually become his guardian.'

'Why not?'

Bart stared at her with incredulity. 'Because if I adopt Timmy, which I've finally managed to admit is what I really want, then I wouldn't be able to operate on him. I wouldn't be able to be his surgeon. I know what needs to be done.' He stabbed a finger at his own chest. 'I know the burden I carry every time I take the poor little mite back to surgery and how difficult it is to distance myself from my emotions.'

Ebony gave his hand a reassuring squeeze. 'Of course it's getting harder and that won't change, Bart, because you love him. Timmy is in your heart and there's nothing you can do about it. Do you know, that's the one thing I truly admire about you—your heart, once given, is resolute. When you make up your mind to do a particular thing, it gets done. You were raised with strong and wholesome values and now you can pass them on to Timmy.' Her words were filled with a strength and passion he'd never really noticed before.

'Bart, the reason doctors aren't allowed to operate on family members is because of the emotions involved. Now, from what I can see, you're already emotionally involved so why not take the next step? Apply to become his foster-father. Make him a permanent part of your life.'

'Then who will do his surgeries?' Bart let go of her hand and held both of his wide, desperation in his voice and eyes. 'I'm caught between a rock and a hard place, Ebony.' He lowered his arms and shook his head. 'You are right, though. I am already attached. Emotionally attached. I feel like his father and, given I never thought I'd ever have children of my own, it makes Timmy all the more special to me.'

'Submit an application,' she urged softly, letting him know it was all right to take that big step into the un-known. He'd opened up to her. He'd held her in his arms, he'd brushed his lips across hers and now he was opening up his heart to her, telling her his deepest needs and looking to her for support.

'Then I can't operate.' He folded his arms firmly across his chest.

'True. And there's no denying he'll require more surgeries over time. Shunt patients always do, but that might not be for at least the next three to five years. I mean, look at him tonight, how good he's feeling, how happy he is. He's doing so well, which means you have time—time to train another specialist.' She thought for a moment, racking her mind for other possibilities to help. 'Hartley would even come and operate if you asked him.'

'What? Fly out from the UK? Just to do Timmy's surgery?'

'If you asked him.' Her answer was an eyebrow raised in disbelief. 'Hartley thinks the world of you, Bart, far more than you obviously realise.' She placed her other hand on his cheek and smiled, loving the fact that she was allowed to touch him in such a way. 'Just think of the time you and Timmy can spend together. You'll be there to monitor him, to help him adjust to what he can and can't do. Excessive pressure build-up is the enemy of all cerebral shunts but you know the signs and symptoms far better than Wanda or anyone else. You'd be able to get him into hospital before things became worse.'

'You make it sound so straightforward.'

Ebony chuckled. 'Now we both know that isn't true, not where government departments are involved.'

He smiled and was about to say something else when Maddie's impatient voice broke through their intimate discussion.

'Are we going or not?' the teenager demanded, her words travelling through the house. Ebony quickly removed her hand from Bart's and walked into the hallway. Maddie was standing with her hands planted firmly on her hips, glaring at her mother. When she saw Bart also come out of the dining room her brown eyes widened. 'What were you two doing?' she demanded, her gaze flicking between the two adults.

Ebony frowned at her daughter's attitude. 'Talking,' she answered, refusing to allow Maddie to get a rise from her. 'Is Grandma ready?'

'Almost,' Adele remarked, and bustled from her room with her coat, scarf and bag bundled in her arms.

'Good, because I just want to get this thing over and done with,' Maddie huffed, staring at her mother. 'Then I can get back to the more *important* things in my life.'

Ebony sighed sadly, heartily ashamed of her daughter but still completely unsure what to do or say. 'First off, mind your manners.' She was about to say more when Timmy interjected.

'Maddie, why are you angry?' It was Timmy's innocent question that caused everyone to stop. No one moved.

Ebony watched as Maddie turned and looked at Timmy, her eyes widening imperceptibly at the tiny blond boy in the wheelchair. 'I'm not angry. I'm annoyed.'

'Oh.' Timmy shrugged, then thought for a moment before saying confidently, 'I get annoyed, too.' Then he turned and looked at Bart. 'Is annoyed when I cry when I have the needles?'

Bart smiled sadly at him. 'No, buddy. That's just being sad.'

'Oh.' He thought about that for a moment. 'Is annoyed when I don't want my head cut open again?'

Bart picked the boy up off the bed and held him in his arms. 'Yeah, buddy. That's being annoyed.'

Timmy looked at Maddie, pleased he now understood the emotion. 'Yeah, I get annoyed too.'

Throughout the exchange Ebony felt as though she'd been watching a tennis match, looking from Maddie to Timmy and back again, noting the softening in her daughter's eyes as she realised that, compared to Timmy, she really had nothing to be annoyed about.

Maddie opened her mouth to say something then closed it again before turning and stalking towards the door. She opened it and they all went outside, Adele and the boys heading to the hospital with Bart while she and Maddie were destined for the ACT NOW vans.

'See you later, Timmy,' Ebony said, reaching into the car to give both boys a hug and to drop a kiss on their foreheads. What was natural for her to do to Cliff felt perfectly natural to do to Timmy as well. 'Be good for Bart and Grandma Adele and enjoy the movie.'

'Yes, Mum,' Cliff replied.

'Yes, Mum,' Timmy said too, and both boys giggled. She closed the door, a smile on her lips, and turned to see Bart watching her. He'd just finished putting the wheelchair into the boot and now stood there, staring at her. Had he heard Timmy call her 'Mum'? Did that bother him? Unfortunately, she didn't have time to dwell on such thoughts as she had an impatient teen to deal with. She walked towards Bart.

'You have fun, too. Be good. Don't talk too much during the movie,' she said in her mother-knows-best voice, and was rewarded with a smile from Bart.

'You can't help it, can you? You just need to mother everyone.'

She shrugged and, standing on tiptoe, managed to press a kiss to his forehead. Both of them grinned. 'What can I say? I'm a nurturer.' With that, she winked at him before heading towards her own car, where Maddie was all buckled in and huffing impatiently to be getting this 'thing' over and done with.

'I'll try and come by later. See how things went,' Bart called, still smiling at her as he opened the passenger door for Adele.

'OK. See you then,' she called, and before she knew what she was doing, she'd blown him a kiss.

At first Bart wasn't sure he'd seen the action correctly but as he drove back to the hospital he asked Cliff, 'Does your mother usually blow kisses?'

'Yup,' Cliff answered. 'Especially if we're going in different directions. She says it's a way of sending your love to the person you can't be with. I still blow kisses to my dad. Makes me miss him less.'

Bart clenched his jaw, knowing Ebony would have been the one to instigate such an action in order to help a younger Cliff to deal with the grief of losing his father. She really was quite a remarkable woman.

At the hospital, Bart felt a little self-conscious heading towards the paediatric ward with Ebony's mother and son in tow. It really had felt like they were one big family, eating together around the family dinner table, then Mum and Dad heading off in two different directions but planning to meet up later. Was this what domestic bliss was all about? If so, he had to admit, he was starting to like it.

'What's funny?' Timmy whispered loudly as he looked up at Bart.

'The movie,' Bart responded quickly, ruffling the boy's hair and pointing to the screen.

'Oh.' Timmy turned his attention back to the screen, leaning against Bart as comfortably as though Bart were nothing more than a lounge chair. Indeed, by the end of the movie, both Cliff and Timmy were using him like a beanbag and Bart was grateful they felt comfortable with him, especially Cliff.

'Time for me to take Cliff back to his mother and time for you to get some sleep,' Bart announced as Timmy got into bed. The little guy was yawning widely and was adamant that he wasn't tired.

'I want Cliff to stay,' Timmy protested as he lay down, yawning once more. 'I'm not tired,' he remarked, his eyelids beginning to droop.

'Yeah. I want to stay,' Cliff said, climbing into the big armchair and curling up, his own eyes drooping, too. 'We can talk and talk and talk, eh, Timmy?'

'Yeah,' Timmy responded with another yawn.

'I'll stay with them,' Adele said as she entered the room. 'We can all talk about the movie while we close our eyes.' She shifted Cliff off the big armchair before sitting down and pulling her grandson into her arms. The boy snuggled in close to his grandmother.

'Yeah,' he said.

'Yeah,' Timmy added again.

'Go and check on Ebony. She'll be pulling her hair out worrying about Maddie and will no doubt need your calm assurance that everything will be all right.'

'Good idea. Yes. OK. I'll go and check on Eb.'

'Eb?' It was Cliff who spoke, yawning a little. 'I've only ever heard Daddy call her that.'

Bart's gaze snapped to Adele's, only to find the older woman scrutinising him much more closely than she had all evening. 'Oh? Did he? I remember a lot of people calling her that at school. At least, I think they did.' He frowned and crossed to Timmy's side, quickly tucking the boy in and giving him a goodnight kiss. 'Anyway,' he said to Adele, 'if you're fine staying here—'

'Go.' Adele shooed a hand at him, in much the same way Bart could remember his own mother doing. 'Find Ebony. Help her.'

With a nod Bart turned and hurried from the room, amazed at the sensation of the world starting to close in on him. Somehow Ebony Matthews and the rest of her family had managed to infiltrate their way into his heart in an alarmingly short space of time. Perhaps it was the old connection of having grown up in the same district, the fact that Adele had known his parents, the fact that he'd attended the same high school as Ebony, that he'd known her husband and that she'd been Alice's best friend.

He would find Ebony now and he would help her in any way he could, just as he would any other member of his extended family. His parents were gone. Alice was gone. His life was so incredibly different now, from what it had been back then with all his hopes and dreams for a wonderful future.

Ebony had suffered that same sense of helplessness, losing not only her husband but her father as well. She was an incredibly strong woman, a woman who had somehow managed to infiltrate his senses, causing him to kiss her in such a tantalising way.

Was there something developing between them that was not only far more intense but far more permanent than either had ever thought possible? And if in the past only Dean had ever called her Eb, why had she let him call her that?

CHAPTER EIGHT

'Hi, Eb.'

Bart walked up to Ebony, who seemed to be hovering around the ACT NOW food van, absent-mindedly talking to Keith, one of the other volunteers, her gaze fixed on a small picnic table nearby where Darla, Maddie and a few other girls were sitting and chatting, their empty hot-chocolate cups and cake-crumbed paper plates on the table in front of them indicating they'd been there for quite some time.

Ebony instantly spun round to look into his eyes and in that moment he saw the nervous maternal worry reflected in the green depths. Good heavens. Didn't the woman have any idea just how expressive her eyes were and how they appealed to that primal, deep-seated need to put his arms about her and protect her for the rest of her life? He shoved his hands deep into the pockets of his jeans to stop himself from touching her. Friends. He was here as her friend, to offer her support and encouragement.

'Bart.' She sighed his name, her body visibly relaxing. 'I'm so glad you're here.' She turned her attention back to watching the girls but stepped back a little, bringing her body into closer proximity to his.

'How's it going?' Bart forced himself to stop trying

to memorise every move Ebony made and to look at where his sister-in-law was talking and laughing with the teenage girls.

'I don't know. Maddie's arms are still crossed but not as tightly as they were at the beginning. She's even smiled once or twice.'

'It looks as though she's eaten her cake and finished her hot chocolate. That's a good thing, right?' he added with encouragement. Unable to resist the lure of touching her any longer, of letting her know just how much he supported and cared for her—as a friend—he put his hand on her shoulder, giving it a quick squeeze. Before he could drop it back to his side, Ebony placed her hand over his and held his fingers in place.

'I hope so.' She turned to face him again, lifting his hand from her shoulder but not releasing her hold on him. Looking up into his face, she shook her head, holding fast to his hand, almost desperate for the support he was offering. 'She's so lost, Bart. She used to be so happy and carefree when she was younger. If this doesn't work, I…I don't know what to do.' Tears began to gather in her eyes and Bart found himself once more succumbing to the need to hold her close and protect her.

He placed his other hand on her shoulder, seeing how much she loved her daughter, how she'd do anything to help her, how a mother's love—even if it was being rejected—never failed. It only highlighted just how special Ebony was with the way she loved and gave and cared for her children.

'She's such an angry, lost little girl, and I love her so mu—' Ebony's voice broke and she hiccuped.

Bart glanced over to where Darla and the girls were starting to stand, finishing off their session. Keith in the food van had tactfully turned away from them, busying himself. Inside the medical van behind them would be his good friend Jordanne Page, doing her shift with one of the other doctors. He knew they were there, he knew there was movement around them, but when he looked into Ebony's eyes the world around them seemed to fade away, leaving just the two of them.

A woman in distress who was silently asking to lean on him for support, for courage, for strength to get her through this situation.

He swallowed, calling on every ounce of self-control to stop him from hauling her close. 'Of course you're worried. She's your daughter. Of course you love her and want happiness for her. That's a natural maternal reaction and you *are* doing whatever you can to help.'

His words were earnest as he looked at her, her head and shoulders sagging a little as she tried her hardest to hold back her tears. Bart placed a hand beneath her chin and lifted her head so their eyes could meet, his touch gentle and caring. 'You're a good mother, don't ever doubt that—and at least she came along.'

Ebony snorted at that and rolled her eyes in an action that reminded him of Maddie's strong defiance. 'Not after a yelling match when we arrived here. According to her, not only am I now ruining her life, I'm interfering in it.'

'And yet she's stayed over there with Darla and the other girls. Hopefully she's listened. It may just take a while for her to process everything she's heard.' He shifted and put both hands on her shoulders, looking deeply into her eyes, desperate to reassure her. She was such an amazing woman, especially as she'd managed to have such a strong impact on his life in such a personal way in such a short space of time.

He lifted one hand and tenderly brushed a tear from her cheek with his thumb, loving the feel of her smooth, soft skin. The urge to lean down, to brush his lips across hers, to taste her once more was overpowering but he was there to support her, not to plunder her delicious mouth for his own selfish gain. He cupped her cheek and smiled reassuringly, his gaze connected to hers. 'Give it time, Eb.'

'Eb?' Maddie's voice cut through the bubble around them like a scalpel.

Bart instantly dropped his hands back to his sides as Ebony stepped away, turning to face her daughter.

'Maddie! Uh...how did things...er...?'

'Eb?' She glared first at Bart then at her mother, wild fire and hatred shining in her angry eyes. 'Only *Dad* ever called you Eb. That was his special name for you.'

'Maddie, that's not actually tr—'

'You've forgotten him. You've moved us halfway around the world to this horrid place and now you're starting a new life with a new man.'

Bart shoved his hands into his pockets but didn't shy away from Maddie's accusing stare. 'Maddie, listen, it's not—'

'No. You're *not* my dad,' she yelled, tears in her eyes. 'And I thought I was special to you but you only pretended to like me so you could get to *her*.' She stabbed a finger towards Ebony. By now Maddie had managed to completely work herself up into an angry frenzy.

'How could you do this? Do you need to take *everything* away from me? Any time I like something, you take it. I liked our home in England. I liked my friends, my school, my painting class. Then when we get here, you spend all your time at the hospital or here...' She waved a hand at their surroundings, a few of the ACT

NOW people stopping and staring at the scene Maddie was making but she either didn't notice or didn't care. 'And all the time you're with *him*. You loved Dad. He loved you. If you'd died, he would never have even looked at another woman. I wish *you* had died. I wish *Daddy* was still alive.' Hot and angry tears were now running down Maddie's cheeks. 'I hate you. *I hate you!*' With that, she turned and ran down the street.

'Maddie?' Ebony's voice broke as she called after her daughter, pain, fear and mortification filling her senses. She spun and looked at Bart, her eyes wild with uncertainty and indecision. What did she do now? Should she run after Maddie? Should she let her go? Give her space? But she couldn't. This was her daughter!

'Go.' Bart's simple word was enough to propel her into action and within a matter of thirty seconds Ebony took off after Maddie.

'What happened?' Darla asked, coming to stand beside him. Bart shifted feet and raked both hands through his hair.

'I was stupid. I shouldn't have let my feelings for Ebony get the better of me but she was looking up at me with her big green eyes and…well…I just wanted to protect her, but then Maddie said that the only reason I was being nice to her was so I could get in with Ebony and…' Bart stopped and ran his hand through his hair again. 'What a mess.'

'So go and clean it up. Go after them, you nut.' Darla pointed down the street where they could just see Ebony disappearing around a corner in hot pursuit of her daughter.

'Maybe I shouldn't. Maybe they need to yell at each other, to get it out, and it would be better if I wasn't in the way.' He shook his head. 'I never should have… I should have left Ebony alone.'

'Uh…no, you shouldn't. Bart, face facts. I can see it as plain as anything in your eyes. You're falling for Ebony and I know you, brother-in-law. I know what you've been through and I know your heart is not easily touched. The fact that Ebony, especially in such a short space of time, has managed to break down those hard walls you put in place all that time ago is testament that there is something very strong and very real happening between the two of you.

'Your lives have already intertwined. Whatever happens between Maddie and Ebony *is* your business, Bart. That poor girl has such issues with abandonment and the last thing she needs is to think that you're already shutting her out. You're already emotionally involved and in the long run it'll be far better if you're there when they work it out.'

Bart processed Darla's words. Were his feelings for Ebony really that obvious? She was certainly unlike any other woman he'd dated over the years and she'd certainly affected his life in a powerful way. He closed his eyes for a moment and shook his head.

'But—'

'Both of them need you. Don't think, Bart. Just go.' Darla again pointed down the street and this time Bart realised his sister-in-law was right and immediately took off after Ebony and Maddie. He sprinted around the corner then stopped. There was no sign of either of them. Where had they gone? It was starting to get dark and the streetlights were coming on and this area wasn't particularly the safest, especially once the sun went down.

'Ebony? Maddie?' he called as he walked down a

smaller street. He rounded another corner and was about to call out again when he heard Ebony's voice, calling her daughter's name with urgency and fear.

He closed his eyes for a split second. Maddie had managed to get away, which brought a whole new range of scenarios to mind. These streets weren't safe, especially for a young teenage girl. There had been a lot of gang violence in these parts and his gut twisted with the sharp memories of some of the things he'd seen, of what had happened to other young girls about Maddie's age.

The paternal instinct he'd experienced with Timmy began to kick in towards Maddie. She was Ebony's daughter and he cared greatly for Ebony. She was Dean's daughter. A mixed-up and confused girl who had lost her father. He owed it to his old friend to look out for Maddie and he owed it to Ebony to help in any way he could, both physically and emotionally. Darla was right. He was already involved.

When he heard Ebony's voice once more, he sprinted off quickly in that direction and after rounding a few more corners he almost ploughed into Ebony. She screamed once when he appeared so suddenly, covering her mouth with a trembling hand. Then, when she realised who it was, she clasped hold of both his arms. 'I can't find her, Bart. I can't find her!' The tension, the fear and desperation in her tone shot straight to his heart and before her anguish could bubble over completely Bart quickly took her hand securely in his and together they ran down the street.

'Where is she? I need to find her. I need to tell her how sorry I am, how much I love her. I need her, Bart. She's my girl.' Tears and emotion were choking her words, her voice hoarse and dry as they ran, search-

ing. Ebony brushed away the tears so they didn't im-
pair her vision.

'We'll find her.' His words were resolute and filled
with a confidence Ebony didn't feel. When they turned
another corner, they came to a cul-de-sac and Ebony
stopped dead, puffing and panting and absolutely desperate.

'Where *is* she?' Unable to stop herself any longer,
Ebony allowed the tears to flow. 'Maddie!' She yelled
again, but her only answer was barking dogs. The streetlights were all well and truly on now, the sun appear-
ing to have set rather quickly while they'd been running
around. Where was she? Where was her little girl?

'Maybe she's gone back to the van,' Bart suggested,
offering Ebony a clean handkerchief. 'I'll call Darla.'

'I love her so much and I know she's hurting. Doesn't
she think I feel her pain? She's *my daughter*!'

'I know. Shh.' Bart put one arm around Ebony's
shoulders, holding her close as he continued to scan the
area for any sign of Maddie, his other hand holding the
phone to his ear. 'Darla, it's me. Any sign of her?' He
paused, listening to what Darla had to say. 'Right. OK.
No that's not far. We'll try there.' He disconnected the
call and shoved his phone back into his pocket. 'Darla
suggested a few places to look.' Bart once again took
Ebony's hand after she'd blown her nose.

'I don't usually fall apart. Sorry.'

'Don't you dare apologise, Eb, and you fall apart
all you like. I'll be here to help put you back together
again.'

'It's the kids. Any time they're sick I fall apart.
They're my weakness. I can handle anything else life
throws at me, loved ones passing away, busy days at
work, confusion in my life—I can do it all, but if one

of the kids starts running a temperature, I'm a mess.'
She paused and called, 'Maddie!' one more time.

'Mum?'

Ebony stopped dead, her heart thumping wildly
against her ribs. Had she just imagined hearing Maddie's voice? Was she so desperate that now her mind
was playing tricks? 'Did you hear that?' she whispered
to Bart.

'Yes.' He glanced around, his eyes now accustomed
to the dark.

'Maddie? Where are you?'

'Over here.'

Both Bart and Ebony turned to see Maddie coming around a different corner before running straight
towards them. Ebony let go of Bart's hand and ran towards her daughter, arms held wide, relief and happiness filling her to the brim. The instant Maddie was in
her arms, both of them burst into tears.

'I didn't mean it. I'm sorry.'

'I couldn't find you. I was worried.'

They talked over each other, their words blending.
Bart came over and did the most natural thing in the
world. He put his big strong arms around the two of
them, sending up a silent prayer of thanks as he held
them close. He was even happier when both of them
leaned into him, accepting the comfort he was offering. They only stood there for a few minutes, relief
washing over them all, before he said softly, 'Let's head
back to the van.'

'Yes.' Ebony sniffed and wiped at her eyes, all the
while not letting go of Maddie's hand. Thankfully, Maddie didn't seem to want her to let go. 'And call Darla.
Let her know—'

'I'm on it,' he said, pulling his cellphone from his

pocket as the three of them headed off together. He walked a few steps behind Ebony and Maddie who were walking arm in arm, wanting to give them a bit of space but also determined to protect them from any possible threat.

'I'm sorry, Mum,' Maddie said as they walked along, Bart talking softly to Darla on his phone. 'I didn't mean to run off and I didn't know where I was going and by the time I looked around me I didn't know where I was and—'

'Shh.' Ebony stopped her. 'You're safe. That's what counts.'

'It started getting dark and I lost my bearings and I wanted to get back to you, to find you, but I couldn't,' the girl continued, and Ebony realised she needed to talk, needed to get the adrenaline out of her system. 'And when I went round one corner there was a big dog there and…' The words continued to spill forth and Ebony listened, offering comfort and reassurance. They weren't as far away from the van as Ebony had first thought, and realised they'd been weaving in and out of the all the little nooks and crannies nearby, even though it had felt they'd covered a lot of territory.

When they came to the main road where the ACT NOW vans were stationed just off to the side, the brighter streetlights and car headlights shone into their eyes, momentarily blinding them as the beefy sound of the cars passed by. Ebony was about to open her mouth to reply to a question Maddie had just asked when there was a sudden long screech of car tyres. She tensed. Then there was the sound of a sickening thud, an angry yell combined with a scream of terror.

Ebony shielded her eyes from the bright car head-lights with one hand and drew Maddie close with the other. The loud noise had startled them all and although everything was happening very quickly, time seemed to slow down. It had a habit of doing that. When tragedy struck, time seemed to freeze and Ebony knew if you weren't careful, you could lose yourself in that one terrifying moment.

She didn't want that for Maddie. Not when it appeared her daughter had finally found a way to break free from the castle of ice she'd built around herself these past four years. She wanted to protect her daughter against any more pain and hurt, which was why she cradled the teen's head against her chest, wanting to avert Maddie's eyes from what she knew had just happened. Ebony had been a doctor for a long time. She'd worked in Accident and Emergency, she'd seen things that even now could still give her nightmares, and she knew all too well what the sound of a person being struck by a car sounded like.

And just as time seemed to freeze, a thousand thoughts flooding through her mind, it could speed up so fast you felt as though you'd just come through some sort of instantaneous transportation device.

'Ebony.' Bart's words were brisk. 'I'll need you.' He was already running towards where she could now see a body lying on the road. The workers at the ACT NOW van were springing into action, some on their cellphones making calls to emergency services, others coming out to help control traffic so that no one else got hurt. Darla was coming out of the medical van, a first-aid emergency kit in her hands as she raced towards her brother-in-law.

Maddie was struggling against her mother's strong hold and Ebony's heart pounded with pain as she watched her daughter's eyes widen with shock at what lay before her.

'Ebony! I need you,' Bart called again.

'I'll take her,' a voice said near Ebony, and she saw Keith stretching out his hand towards Maddie. 'Come and help me in the food van. We'll need extra hot drinks and…stuff,' he finished, and as though on wooden legs, finding it difficult to turn away from the horrific scene before her, Maddie allowed herself to be led away.

'Thanks, Keith,' Ebony called, wanting to keep holding her daughter but knowing that it was impossible. The person lying on the road needed her help. This was her life. Juggling motherhood and work. Juggling teenage hormones and those of her own increasing emotions for Bart.

As she checked the road, which now had traffic backed up behind the victim, and crossed carefully to where Darla and Bart were pulling on gloves, she hoped Maddie wasn't going to be scarred by this event. Shaking her head, she pushed all extraneous thoughts to the back of her mind and focused on the task ahead. This was her job.

CHAPTER NINE

'CAN you hear me?'

'Hand me the scissors,' Bart said a moment later as Darla hooked a stethoscope into her ears and listened to the breathing of the twenty-something woman who was lying sprawled on the bitumen. Ebony tugged on some gloves and handed Bart the scissors before reaching for the cervical collar Jordanne had had the presence of mind to bring over. Four experienced doctors attending to the young woman only seconds after the initial impact was hopefully a good sign for a positive outcome to this ugly scenario.

The road had now been blocked off and the other ACT NOW volunteers were directing traffic around them. The March evening was cool but none of them felt it as they continued to work to stabilise their patient, everyone calling out different vitals and information as it came to light.

Bart cut away the woman's clothes to reveal extensive gashes and swollen red skin. Ebony checked the woman's eyes, monitoring her breathing and quickly mentally calculating drug dosages. 'Pupils equal and reacting to light but sluggish,' she reported.

'Airway is clear. Breathing shallow.'

'Patient has voided, indicating possibly bladder rupture.'

'Possible pneumothorax. Thoracic fourth and fifth ribs feel fractured, right side more affected than the left,' Jordanne, who was an orthopaedic surgeon, confirmed.

'Carotid pulse is weakening.'

'Is she bleeding at the back of her head?' It was Bart who asked the question and Ebony quickly and carefully felt the woman's skull, thankful the cervical collar was helping to hold her neck firm.

'Large laceration and possible skull fracture.' Ebony held up her hand and realised her glove was covered in blood. There wasn't much light coming from the streetlamps but she could hear someone setting up emergency lights in the distance. Still, she didn't need to know what colour her glove was to know they needed to work faster.

'I'll stabilise and bandage. Ebony get an IV set up, saline and plasma,' Bart ordered. 'She's losing blood fast.'

'Any sign of a medical alert bracelet? Necklace?' Ebony asked, doing a visual check as she shifted position to make room for Bart. 'Any wallet? Purse? Identification of any sort?'

'Can't see one,' Darla responded, and felt in the woman's pockets. 'Nothing here either.'

'Can you hear me?' Ebony called, and checked the woman's airway again. 'Starting to rasp.'

'We may need to intubate,' Bart said.

'I'll go get the IVs and intubation kit.' Ebony stood and pulled off her gloves, balling them inside each other.

'Be careful, Eb,' Bart warned, as she headed towards where the traffic was crawling past on the other side of the road. He lifted his head for a split second and even though the light wasn't perfect, she could have sworn she saw the worry in his eyes. She certainly heard it in his voice. She nodded once, then turned back to fulfil her task.

At the ACT NOW vans she could see Maddie in the food van with Keith, spreading margarine over several pieces of bread. Keith looked across and caught Ebony's gaze, quickly giving her a thumbs up. Ebony breathed a small sigh of relief at knowing her daughter was fine for the moment, and quickly headed into the medical van, reaching for the supplies they would need.

When she returned, after weaving her way through the slowly moving traffic, she pulled on another pair of gloves, relieved to hear the sounds of sirens filling the night air around them. Back at the Jane Doe's side, she set about inserting the IV drip, erecting the portable stand to hold the plasma bag in place. Once that was done, she started on the plasma drip but given a fracture to the right radius and ulna, she shifted to the woman's left leg, having been informed by Jordanne that the left foot appeared to be the better option for the other IV line.

'Pupils still equal and reacting to light but sluggish,' Bart called.

'Breathing rasping. Fractures to right radius and ulna; right tibia and fibula. Both femurs feel intact and T-Four and-Five are confirmed breaks but possibly more. Pelvic instability indicates a fractured sacrum, possibly also acetabular cup and possibly neck of femur dislocation,' Jordanne said.

'Pelvic fracture fits with internal organ damage. Her BP is dropping, indicative of internal bleeding,' Darla added.

'Can you hear me?' Bart called, and was rewarded with the smallest flutter of the woman's eyelashes in return. 'We're here to help you,' he said again. 'Hang in there.' He lifted his head and looked at Ebony. 'Eb? Two hundred micrograms of ketam—'

'I'm on it,' she interposed as she withdrew a vial from the emergency kit and ripped open the sterile wrapping from a syringe. Carefully, she administered the analgesic into the IV and had just finished flushing it through when Darla pulled the stethoscope from her ears.

'Respiration is decreasing.'

'Prepare to bag-mask and resuscitate,' Bart ordered.

A second later Jordanne announced, 'She's stopped.'

'Bag her,' Bart said, and Ebony and Darla worked together to fit the mask securely over the patient's nose and mouth then squeeze the bag so the chest cavity could be seen inflating.

'With the probability of a pneumothorax, there's no possibility of CPR,' Jordanne announced. 'We need to get her on oxygen.'

'Do you want me to intubate here?' Ebony asked, and glanced at Bart. He was checking for a pulse.

'Nothing yet. Give it another minute.'

The sirens were getting ever closer and sounded as though they were busy trying to make their way through the cars that were crawling very slowly past the accident.

Ebony continued to squeeze the bag as she saw Bart recheck the dressing around the patient's head. It was clear he wasn't happy with something and she had a feeling that he'd be wanting to take this woman directly to Theatre the moment they arrived at the hospital. It could turn out to be a very long night.

She'd have to get her mother to come down here to pick up Maddie and take both kids home and put them to bed. She didn't like missing out on night-time routines, especially as in the past it had only given Maddie another reason to be angry with her. Ebony focused her thoughts as the ambulance crews drew the vehicles as close as they possibly could to the victim.

The police had arrived and were now doing a better job than the volunteers at directing the traffic, which, thankfully, had now decreased dramatically. It was one thing she'd liked about Canberra—its ten minutes of 'rush hour' traffic.

'Still no pulse,' Darla announced.

'Intubate.' Bart made the call and Ebony immediately administered succinylcholine to ensure the patient was still during intubation. 'She'll be going directly to Theatre once we arrive and we'll be able to get more concentrated air into her lungs.'

Ebony nodded and while she was intubating the patient with Darla's help, the paramedics came over. Bart and Jordanne began to give them a rundown on what had happened and the patient's injuries.

'Female Jane Doe. Struck by car—hit and run. Multiple trauma. Myocardial infarction, internal injuries—'

'Can I get some oxygen please?' Ebony called.

'Pulse is back.' Darla announced.

'Let's get her transferred and on her way to the hospital,' Bart said, pulling off his gloves and helping the paramedics get things ready. Ebony was still monitoring the patient closely when he returned to her side with the oxygen bottle. 'Here you are.'

'Thanks, Bart.' Ebony continued to do her job, caring for her patient, but when she glanced up at Bart she was again surprised to see a deep frown of concern marring his brow—and it wasn't for their patient, it was for her.

'Go. Take Maddie. Get Cliff and your mother and head home.'

'But you'll need me in Theatre. Mum can take the kids home.'

'Maddie needs you, Ebony, especially after everything that's happened tonight.'

'I know.' Ebony allowed her gaze to momentarily stray to the other side of the road where she could just make out Maddie still in the food van with Keith. 'But this is my job. I'm a doctor and sometimes things don't go quite according to plan. She also needs to realise that.'

'It's your call.'

'Thanks, and I appreciate your support—and you did say that I'd be doing all your patients' anaesthetics from now on, which includes emergencies. Let's stick with the protocols.'

He nodded once, accepting her decision. 'Time to get moving, then.' He took over caring for the patient. 'Go and talk to Maddie. Explain what's going on. Two minutes.'

Ebony stood and headed to the food van. It was only as she headed over that she realised she had blood on her clothes. She sighed. There wasn't much she could do about that right at this moment. She looked up into the food van and into her daughter's worried eyes.

'Mum?'

'I need to go to the hospital, Maddie. Stay here with Keith until Grandma comes to pick you up.'

Maddie stumbled from the van, holding out her arms wide, in need of a motherly hug, but Ebony put her hands on Maddie's shoulders. Pain flashed in the teenager's eyes but this time Ebony quickly addressed the issue.

'I can't hug you, sweetheart. God knows I want to—I *need* to, even if it's just to reassure myself that you're all right—but I have…' She stopped and pointed to her clothes. 'I have blood on me.'

It was then Maddie stopped and really looked at her mother, the colour draining from her face. 'Are you hurt? What happened? Is that…?' Her eyes widened and she covered her mouth with her hand. 'That's that other lady's blood?' The words were barely a whisper.

'Yes. I need to go to the hospital with Bart. The woman needs immediate surgery if we're going to save her life.'

'You can *save* her life?' Maddie made it sound as though it was an impossibility.

'Bart and I are going to use every ounce of our training to try.' She pushed some hair back behind Maddie's ear. 'It's what we do, darling. Every day. I look after the patient, ensuring they stay asleep, monitoring their heart rate, while surgeons like Bart perform miracles.' Her words were soft and her heart was almost bursting with pain and pleasure as she watched the words slowly sink in. Maddie had always known her parents were doctors but Maddie's experience with doctors so far in her thirteen years had only been visits to the GP. Now dawning realisation washed over her face and she swallowed, nodding almost imperceptibly.

'Ebony?' Bart's deep voice cut across the noise and she turned to see him beckoning to her.

'I've got to go. I'll see you at home in the morning.' Ebony bent and kissed her daughter's cheek. 'I love you, Maddie. Don't ever doubt that.' She pulled back and caressed her daughter's face once more. 'Stay with Keith until Grandma gets here. OK?'

'OK, Mum. I'll help out all I can.'

Ebony smiled brightly, her heart melting with pride. 'That's my girl.' With that, Ebony turned and ran towards the ambulance, climbed into the back and disappeared from her daughter's view.

'How is she?' Bart asked as she sat alongside him to care for their patient whose pulse rate was now starting to improve, thanks to the oxygen.

'Maddie?'

Bart nodded.

'I think she's finally realising there's another world outside her own.'

'Good. She should be proud of her mother.'

Ebony smiled. 'You know, I think she might be.'

It was a good five and a half hours before Bart was satisfied he'd managed to settle the swelling around the brain. The scans of Jane Doe's skull had shown a small blood clot beginning to form in the cerebrum and it had taken Bart a little longer to remove it than usual. Prior to Bart heading into surgery to do his part, Ebony had anaesthetised the patient so that the general surgeons could clamp the bladder rupture and also identify the source of the patient's internal bleeding.

By the time she was taken to Recovery, it was the wee small hours of the morning and Ebony was completely exhausted.

'Having *another* coffee?' Bart asked, as he walked into the consultants' tearoom where he found Ebony standing at the urn, pouring boiling water into her cup.

'I was tempted because I still have to drive home but, no, I'm actually having some green tea.' Bart pulled a face and she laughed. 'I guess that means I can't tempt you.'

'I'll stick with black tea, thanks.' He crossed to her side and took a cup down from the cupboard, his arm brushing lightly against her shoulder. Ebony gasped. 'Uh…sorry,' he murmured, as all the repressed emotions he'd thought he'd managed to put in a clearly marked box at the rear of his mind came flooding to the fore.

'It's OK.' She smiled and walked to the lounge, tucking one leg beneath her as she sat down, almost sighing into the comfortable cushions. 'I guess we're usually more careful about accidentally touching and all that but right now, Bart, I'm far too exhausted to make excuses.'

She sipped her tea and smiled at him as she sank down deeper into the lounge, resting her head on the side of a large cushion. They were locked away in a quiet room, the hustle and bustle of the hospital just outside those doors, but for now the peace surrounding them was exactly what she needed.

Bart jiggled a teabag in his cup of hot water as he watched her closely. 'Unguarded? Exhausted? Out of excuses?' He slowly walked towards her and sat at the other end of the lounge and watched her carefully as he sipped his tea. 'You really shouldn't say things like that to a man who's having a devastating time trying to stop thinking about you.'

'I don't want you to stop,' she whispered, the words springing forth from her lips before she knew what was really happening.

'You don't?'

'No. I don't want to fight this any more, Bart.'

'You're tired, Eb. Perhaps it's best if we don't—'

'I never thought I'd *feel* again.' She leaned forward

and put her tea down on the table before snuggling back into the lounge. 'And it's *you* who makes me feel alive, Bart. It's *you* who I think about when I wake up every morning and it's *you* I dream about every night when I go to sleep. I want to feel your arms around me. I want to hear your calm voice soothing away the worries and pressures of my day. I want to spend time with you. I want you to get to know my children.'

She closed her eyes and sighed again before smothering a yawn. 'I just want my life to move forward and I can't help thinking that perhaps it's supposed to move forward…with you.'

With her eyes closed and half-asleep against the big, blue cushion, her hair still tied back from being in Theatre, the cotton scrubs she wore far too big for her, she was exhausted and probably had no idea what she was really saying, but Bart couldn't help but be moved by her words.

She was soft and gorgeous and alluring and as she sighed again he couldn't resist the urge to touch her. He put his cup down on the table next to hers then shifted closer, stretching out his hand to brush his fingers tenderly over her cheek.

'Don't go to sleep, Eb,' he murmured.

'Hmm? Why not?'

'Because it'll make it even more difficult to drive home.'

'Maybe. Or I could just sleep here.'

'You'll get a stiff neck. You're all bent and at a crazy angle.' As he spoke, he slid his hand beneath her neck and urged her up. Like a floppy rag doll, she simply yawned again before snuggling closer into him.

'Mmm. This is where I want to be,' she whispered, and closed her eyes, relaxing against him. Bart swallowed as the scent of her shampoo, sugar and spice and all things nice, filled his senses.

'Is it?' He paused, waiting, but received no answer to his question. Exhaustion had finally caught up with her and although he knew he needed to get her home, he also just wanted to sit here, to let the world turn for a while without either of them having to make a decision about what move to make next. No doubt she hadn't meant everything she'd said and in the morning she might have quite a different opinion to the one she held now.

Ten minutes passed. Fifteen. Still, she dozed against him and, still, he let her. No one else came into the consultants' private tea room and even if they had, there was no way Bart was going to quickly shift Ebony out of his arms just to quell the gossips. He had to admit that he loved the feeling of her in his arms and perhaps she was right. Perhaps their lives were meant to take the same road.

Was it really possible that after so long, after so many long and lonely years, he'd finally found the one woman who had a hope of understanding him? Of not just seeing him as an eligible bachelor or a surgeon or the leader of a team? She saw him as a man…a man she wanted to spend more time with…a man she was attracted to. Could he do this? Could he take this chance?

For years he'd always accepted that he'd missed his one true chance at happiness, that if he'd fought harder for Alice, had had the guts to stand up to her parents and tell them that he intended to marry their daughter, they might not have sent her away on that ridiculous gap year and she might never have been killed.

But she had been killed and his life had ended, thrust into a holding pattern for over two decades until a firecracker named Ebony had re-entered his world and turned it upside down with a flash of her smile and a wiggle of her hips.

Her even breathing started to change and she shifted in his arms, one hand sliding across his chest, her fingers caressing the muscles beneath his hospital scrubs. 'Mmm.'

Was she dreaming? Did she know where she was? He looked down at her and at the same moment she tilted her head to look up at him.

'Bartholomew.' His name was a caress upon her parted lips and as her gaze held his, as her tongue came out to wet her lips in anticipation, he swallowed hard before doing the only thing he could—and that was to lean down and capture her luscious mouth with his own.

CHAPTER TEN

EBONY sighed into him, unsure whether she was still dreaming or whether this was real. It didn't take her senses long to realise this was absolutely nothing like her dreams—the sensations magnified a hundred per cent. With Bart's mouth pressed softly to her own, moving slowly as though he was savouring every second of the touch, Ebony's mind focused on nothing except the way he was making her tremble all over and how she never wanted this moment to end.

His arms around her were so secure, so protective. She twisted round a little, angling her body so she was closer to him, needing to let him know she was right there with him, willing, ready and able to take this next step with him.

He seemed more than content to have her near, his hands linking to ensure she didn't go anywhere. On and on, his slow and gentle lips were creating havoc with her equilibrium and she matched his controlled intensity, gasping a little when he edged back, nipped her lower lip playfully with his teeth, and looked down into her upturned face, his breath fanning her cheek. This was definitely no dream. This was real. It was true. It was…perfect.

'Eb?'

'Shh. Just kiss me and don't ever stop,' she murmured, and leaned into him, this time deciding it was her turn to take the lead. While she loved his soft and tantalising kisses, it was also becoming increasingly difficult to curb the mounting desire that flooded through her every time she was within cooee of him. Now that she had him close and comfortable right beside her, now that he was receptive to her embrace, to her kisses, to coming along with her on this wild and unpredictable ride, she wanted to show him exactly how he made her feel.

It wasn't that she hurried the speed of the embrace, it was more than she increased the power behind her kiss. Slow. She wanted everything to be slow, to savour every moment, to have it burned into her memory to help keep her warm on those cold Canberra nights when he wasn't right beside her.

She slid her tongue seductively over his lower lip, coaxing his mouth to open, to accept her movements as she lifted her hand and plunged her fingers into his hair, effectively holding his head in place. He couldn't believe how powerfully her seduction was affecting him.

He loved it that she was confident enough to take the lead, to let him see exactly how he could affect her, how she wanted him, how her need for him was as desperate as his was for her. They were in this together and the knowledge gave him the power to take that step outside his comfort zone, to allow Ebony to guide him towards a deeper understanding of his heart and hers.

Both of them were at a point in their lives where things were by no means simple. She had her children and her mother to worry about. He had Timmy to consider and yet despite his best-laid plans, he hadn't been able to curb the natural chemistry between himself and

Ebony since the first moment they'd laid eyes on each other. It seemed so long ago, yet it wasn't.

It seemed impossible that his heart could be touched in such a short space of time, yet being with her now, holding her in his arms, accepting the tantalising and highly seductive kisses she was offering seemed the only logical way to proceed. They'd tried to be just friends, caring and supporting each other, but caring and supporting each other had only served to magnify the firm undercurrents that existed between them.

He groaned slowly with delight as she leaned into him, her mouth torturing him in ways he hadn't known a kiss could. Soft. Powerful. Evocative. It was clear she was trying to show him just how much he'd come to mean to her and he tried his best to do the same thing. If things continued the way he most definitely wanted them to progress, to let nature take its course, then he'd end up making sweet love to her right here in the consultants' tearoom at two o'clock in the morning. She was too special for anything like that and deserved better, yet somehow it was becoming increasingly difficult for him to find any inner strength to resist her.

'Ebony.' Her name was a desire-filled caress and, realising he needed to be the strong one here, to gently ease the situation back to a more normal rhythm, he loosened his hold on her and brought his hands up to cup her face. 'Ebony,' he tried again, and this time she eased back. Both of them were breathing erratically as they stared into each other's eyes.

'Bartholomew.'

He pressed another kiss to her lips. 'There's no denying it now,' he whispered, glancing at her mouth and indicating he wanted nothing more than to continue kissing her.

'No. No point.'

'We need to move forward from here.' His breathing was settling to a more normal rhythm as he moved his hands to her shoulders, then slid them back around her, snuggling her closer into his body.

'Forward is good.' She reached out and lovingly ran her fingers through his hair, delighted she now had permission to caress him in such a familiar way.

'We don't fight this attraction.'

'I like the sound of that,' she murmured, her heart singing loudly, delighted he was being so forthright about moving forward—together.

He smiled at her words. 'And we get to know each other better.'

'And that includes spending time with the kids— Timmy as well.'

He nodded. 'I like the sound of that, too.'

Ebony slowly exhaled, allowing the rioting emotions that had been overtaking her senses only moments ago to ebb out of her body, knowing there would be more and more occasions in her future for Bart to hold her and kiss her in such a way. The thought thrilled her to the core but she forced herself to focus on what they were discussing.

'We need to start planning Timmy's birthday party. There's only one week to go and I'm so happy he's able to be discharged. He's such a gorgeous boy.'

Ebony rested her head on Bart's chest, her arms around him, and Bart couldn't believe how right, how perfect if felt just to sit with her like this. He'd never experienced such an overwhelming sense of comfort and calm as he did now. His love for Alice, which had been his constant companion for the past twenty-odd years, now seemed like that of a young man.

What he was feeling for Ebony was the love of a more mature man, one who had been through a lot of emotional upheavals as well as floundering around in a sea of confusion. Ebony had come into his life and within a short time had shown him there was much more living for him to do. Part of that living included herself and her children but a big part of it included owning his paternal feelings for Timmy.

'Eb?'

'Mmm-hmm?' She felt so relaxed, so content.

'I've made a decision…about Timmy.'

Ebony lifted her head and looked at him. 'OK. What have you decided?'

'I'm going to go for it. I'm going to apply to foster him. I'll never know if I don't try, right?' At the bright and encompassing smile that lit her glorious face, lighting up her eyes and filling him with a sense that this was indeed the right course of action to pursue, Bart continued, 'I'm not saying that anything is wrong with him being at Wanda's but—'

'You love him, Bart. He loves you. That much is clearly evident to anyone who sees the two of you together.'

'And you're right about his surgery. It might be several years before he requires further intervention and I have some very promising registrars on my team who have been a part of his care for the past year, and I can train them.'

'Plus there's Hartley as a back-up,' she pointed out.

'Yes.' He breathed in deeply and when he exhaled he felt as though an enormous weight had been lifted from his shoulders. 'This is right.'

'It is. Moving forward—in so many ways.' She leaned up and pressed her mouth to his, the tantalising touch causing another round of fire sparkles to burst to life throughout her body. Good heavens. Was it going to be like this every time they touched? She most certainly hoped so. When she pulled back, she was astonished to find him frowning. 'What's wrong?'

'Well…what's Timmy supposed to do during the day while I'm at work? Who will look after him then? I'm sure Benedict and Darla would be more than happy to help out on occasion but perhaps I should hire a nanny? A live-in housekeeper?' He shook his head and shifted round so he was facing her. 'Ebony? Moving forward with this decision, it changes…' He stopped and shrugged.

'It changes everything,' she finished for him. 'Kids will do that to you but the good times far outweigh any hassle. Just think of seeing Timmy every morning, of having breakfast with him, of getting him ready for school, dropping him off. Of the way he'll put his arms around you and kiss your cheek and say how much he loves you—because he does, Bart. That kid loves you with all his heart. As far as he's concerned, you *are* his father and he's probably seen you in that role for quite a few years now.'

Bart nodded, liking the picture she painted. 'But what about after school? I'm usually in Theatre. You know the drill.'

'You do whatever any other working parent has to do. You use out-of-school care or, as you've mentioned, hire a nanny. Alternatively, he could…' She stopped, her mind thinking things through at a great rate of knots. 'He could go home from school with my kids and stay at my house until we're done in Theatre.'

'But your mother?'

'Wouldn't mind in the slightest. She loves being a

grandmother, of being there for her grandchildren. It's given her a new lease on life, which she's needed to help her get over my father's death. She's even started going to art classes at the local neighbourhood centre during the day while the kids are at school and she told me the other day she's also planning to volunteer again with ACT NOW, but of course we'll check with her.'

Ebony reached out and ran her fingers through his hair again before she pressed a kiss to his lips. 'It's all good, Bart, and as we've said, we're going to do this. We're going to date. We're going to become involved in each other's lives. Get to know the kids better.'

'The kids.' He frowned and shook his head, wondering if they weren't actually moving a tad too fast. 'Words I never thought I'd—' He stopped as fear and trepidation started to take a grip around his heart.

What on earth was he thinking? Sure, he wanted Ebony. There was no doubt about that. Sure, he wanted Timmy to be in his life. There was no doubt there either, but to actually follow through on his wants was something Bart hadn't done before.

Denying his heart, accepting that he would remain a bachelor forever had been a difficult pill to swallow at first, but he'd done it. His one true love had been taken from him and so, he'd thrown himself into work, firm in the belief that his heart had been too damaged ever to be touched again.

Now, though, when he looked at Ebony he couldn't believe how incredible it was to have her in his arms, to have her mouth pressed firmly against his, drawing him in with her slow and powerful seduction. There was hope and excitement in her eyes and it was infectious the way those same emotions began entering his own life.

He liked the way she brushed tender hands through his hair and caressed his cheek. The way she leaned forward and brushed another one of those mind-numbing kisses across his lips, of the way she had such an enormous desire to be there for others, to support them and help them in any way she could. She was a remarkable woman.

He eased up out of the comfortable lounge, unable to resist kissing her delicious mouth as he moved, excited and nervous and a little concerned at all the changes taking place in his life, but right now he needed to focus on getting them out of the tearoom and back to their respective houses.

'Sleep,' he murmured near her ear, his breath fanning her neck, causing goose-bumps to pepper her skin. She smiled at him.

'You do have a point. I guess we should go and check on our patient and get ready to head home. Sleep is good.'

'Especially for those of us who didn't have twenty winks.'

She giggled and had the grace to look a little coy as she uncurled her cramped and tired limbs, allowing Bart to pull her to her feet. 'Oh. Yes. Sorry about falling asleep.'

'It's fine. It's been an emotionally draining time for you.'

'Ain't that the truth,' she remarked, stretching her arms above her head, hoping to bring a bit of relief to a few of her tired muscles. Dragging in a deep breath, she filled her lungs completely, lowering her arms a little and carefully tipping her neck from side to side to work out any kinks.

When she returned her gaze to Bart's, it was to find

him staring at her with deep appreciation. His eyes dipped momentarily to her waist and as she glanced down, she realised that her scrub top had ridden up when she'd stretched but had not come down when she'd lowered her arms, baring her midriff.

'Oops.' She quickly pulled the top down, warmth flooding through her at the smouldering look in his eyes.

'Don't rush on my account.' He slid his arms around her waist and drew her close for another quick kiss.

'Mmm. Part of me doesn't want to leave this room,' she confessed. 'The other part of me, the sensible part, knows it's essential.' She shook her head. 'I hate my sensible side some days.'

Bart chuckled, murmuring his agreement. 'Let's go and check on Jane, then I'll walk you to your car.'

'I'd like to stop in and see Timmy, if that's all right.' At his quizzically raised eyebrow, she continued. 'Every night, before I go to bed, I always go into my kids' rooms and check that they're both breathing. I think it stems from checking on them when they were babies and it's just a routine I've got into. Now I can't lie down and go to sleep unless I know they are both alive and well in their beds.' She spread her arms wide. 'It's a mum thing, I guess.'

'It's a nice thing. Sure, we can check on Timmy and *then* I'll walk you safely to your car.'

'Chivalry?'

He chuckled. 'Something like that.'

They tipped out their forgotten drinks and rinsed the cups before heading to Recovery, where they reviewed Jane Doe's status and Ebony wrote up notes for the necessary medications. At this stage their patient was stable in an induced coma, which would hopefully allow her body to heal enough. She'd be moved to the intensive care unit soon, where the next few days would be critical. Ebony knew it was only the fact the woman had received immediate expert attention that she had any hope at all of making it through.

Once they were finished in Recovery, they headed to the paediatric unit, where they both stood over Timmy's bed, watching him sleep. 'So peaceful,' she murmured, watching Bart as he placed his hand on the child's head, his love so evident.

'If you want to stay with him longer, I can get one of the security guards to walk—'

'I want to walk you to your car, Eb. I need to know you're safe.' There was a protectiveness to his words that told her not to bother arguing.

'OK, then. Let's head home to bed.' With that she walked out of Timmy's room and even though Bart knew she didn't mean that the two of them should head home to one house and to one bed where he would lie next to her and hold her throughout the night, he couldn't deny the appeal of such a idea.

Ebony couldn't believe how happy she was. Everything seemed to be settling down—work, family life and, of course, her new relationship with Bart. They decided to keep it low key as far as the hospital went.

'To give us both time to adjust to these new emotions before other people start giggling and gossiping about us behind our backs every time we walk past,' Bart had rationalised, and Ebony had agreed. Of course, at work, they were both consummate professionals, working hard to provide their patients with the best outcomes possible.

Their Jane Doe patient, who had been identified as

Clara Hawthorne, finally regained consciousness after five days in an induced coma. She was now in an orthopaedic ward under Jordanne's care, recuperating.

Timmy had been discharged into Wanda's care but only for a short time while the paperwork for a temporary residential carer was rushed through for Bart. 'It's only because I've been working with the system for such a long time that I was able to get such preferential treatment,' he told Ebony as they sat around a small outdoor table in the back garden.

They'd had a busy day celebrating Timmy's birthday. 'It's been so long since this house has been filled with the happy sounds of children playing games, popping balloons and eating cake,' Adele had said once the last party guest had left. Together with Cliff and Maddie as well as the other children who lived at Wanda's, they'd enjoyed a typical six-year-old's birthday party, but the part Timmy was most looking forward to was having a sleepover here, staying in Cliff's room.

Now Cliff and Maddie were trying to teach Timmy how to play basketball. Maddie was refereeing, awarding far more penalties to Cliff than to Timmy. Although it was now April and the morning weather was definitely turning more towards winter, the midday sun was bright and quite pleasant, matching Ebony's mood.

'He's younger than you,' Maddie was whispering animatedly between her teeth, directing her comments towards her brother while Timmy concentrated on bouncing the ball. 'We need to help him and, besides, he doesn't know what the rules are so just cut him some slack.'

'It's nice to see her thinking of others instead of just herself,' Ebony said softly.

'Is she still going to Darla's group?'

'Yes, and helping Keith in the food van, but only for about an hour two days a week. She generally helps him to make soup and pairs napkins with bowls.'

'Great. It's a definite start.'

'Yes. Now she says she wants to be a social worker, really wanting to help people.'

Bart smiled. 'And she'll do it. She seems the type of girl who can do anything if she puts her mind to it.' He turned and looked at Ebony. 'Like her mother.'

Ebony chuckled. 'Is that an insult or a compliment?'

'Why would it be an insult?'

'You're implying I'm stubborn.'

'Am I?' He feigned ignorance and she laughed, shaking her head at him and waggling her finger.

'You're in a cheeky mood today.'

He shrugged his shoulders and leaned over to take her hand in his. 'I can't remember the last time I felt so at peace. Timmy's progressing very well, although I think he's really going to sleep well tonight after such an exciting day.'

'So will I,' she said.

'I've spoken to my registrar about taking over Timmy's care and he's delighted to do it, determined to work hard and listen to instruction.'

'Excellent news. What else is making you happy?' she fished, turning in her seat so she was facing him, giving her undivided attention to him.

'Spending time with Cliff and Maddie too and enjoying Adele's delicious cooking for dinner every night this week.'

'Uh-huh. And?' she fished.

'Working out a routine between Wanda and your mother so Timmy gets to spend more time with Maddie and Cliff.'

'Well, Timmy is their surrogate brother,' Ebony pointed out, all three children having informed the adults of the official change.

'True. Very true.' He nodded, then shrugged. 'And that's about it, I think.'

'Nothing else to add?'

'I don't think I've forgotten anything.'

'Nothing else is making you happy?' she asked with a mock growl and was rewarded with a bright smile.

'Well…now that you come to mention it…' Bart teased as he leaned forward, bringing his face right up close near hers.

'Yes?' she whispered.

'There is the fact that I can't seem to get enough of your delectable mouth.'

'Mmm.' The next moment he pressed his lips to hers in a kiss that, even now, even after being able to kiss him whenever she wanted all week long, still managed to set her on fire.

'Ugh, gross,' Cliff moaned. 'They're at it again.'

Ebony laughed and they pulled back, looking over to where the three children were watching them. She winked at her son.

'Kissing is gross,' he continued.

'Yeah,' Timmy chimed in, not really sure what he was agreeing to but not wanting to be left out of any conversation.

Bart chuckled. 'You might change your tune when you're older, boys.' He turned to smile at Ebony.

'Isn't being a parent fun?' she said, unable to believe she could be this happy. Bart made her happy. Bart and the children and her mother and all of them together made her cup of happiness run over. 'You're going to have a great time adapting when you get custody of Timmy.'

'Um…' Bart eased back in his chair, his brow furrowing. 'About that…'

'What?' Ebony tried to ignore the instant wave of worry that washed over her. Her eyes were wide, the children's laughter fading into the background as she looked deeply into Bart's blue eyes, noticing they were filled with concern mixed with a hefty dose of pain. 'What is it?' she asked when he remained silent.

'I did some checking,' he eventually replied, his tone dropping to barely a whisper so the children didn't overhear their conversation.

'And?' Her palms were starting to perspire, her nerves strung taut. What on earth had happened and why hadn't he mentioned it sooner?

'I can't apply for custody, temporary or otherwise.'

'But you work for ACT NOW, you're a trained surgeon. You, better than anyone else in this world, know what's best for Timmy, especially given his condition.'

'*I* know that and *you* know that but Child Services won't even entertain granting custody as I'm a bachelor.'

'What?' She breathed the word, her eyes wide in shock. 'That's double standards. Single women are granted custody of children all the time.'

'I know and, yes, it is double standards. You'd have no problem applying for custody and yet I get turned down even before the process begins.' He shrugged his shoulders, trying for nonchalance, but Ebony could see this information had clearly gutted him. 'But that's the way it is.'

'Oh, Bart.' She reached for his hand, pleased when he didn't pull away. 'There has to be another way. You and Timmy belong together.'

He shook his head and placed her hand back in her lap before standing. 'Apparently not.' With that, he turned and stalked briskly into the house. Ebony glanced across at the children, pleased to see them all still happily playing.

A moment later she stood and followed Bart inside, walking through the house until she found him standing at the front window, staring out into nothingness. 'Bart, let's talk about this.'

'No.'

'Why not?'

He turned to face her, spreading his arms wide. 'Because that's it, Ebony. Game over. I can still be Timmy's surgeon, training my registrar so he can assist me with any future surgeries. I can see him at Wanda's and arrange for Timmy to have sleep-overs at my house. I can spend as much time with him as my schedule allows and that's enough.' He dropped his arms back to his sides, swallowing over the lump in his throat. 'It has to be because that's all I have.'

'Oh, Bart.' She went to him, putting her arms around him but he made no effort to hug her back. Ebony eased back, her mind working quickly, wanting to do whatever she could in order to fix this problem for him, to see both him and Timmy happy and together—father and son—just as it should be.

'I need to start distancing myself from him.'

'What? Why?'

'Because eventually he *will* be fostered by a family and that family may not want me in his life.'

'Another family?' she murmured, her mind starting to buzz as several different thoughts flashed before her eyes. 'Hang on. Maybe there *is* something we can do.'

'There's nothing.'

Ebony's mind was whirring with possibilities and before she'd had time to fully process them herself she stated, 'What if we…got married?' She smiled at him, eagerness in her eyes, her heart pounding wildly against her chest.

'What?' He stared at her as though she'd just grown an extra head.

'You said earlier that it would be easier for me to apply for custody of Timmy, so what if I do that? What if *we* do that? Together.' Her words were adamant and he realised she was completely serious. '*We* could be the *family* that fosters Timmy.' She spread her arms wide as though she'd just performed a magic trick.

'Ebony? We can't get married.'

'Why not? It works on several levels. My children need a father, Timmy needs a mum and dad and, well… we're already attracted to each other. The children get along together, they all adore you, we have this big rambling house and a resident grandmother to help us look after them all. It's perfect.' And the fact that I'm hopelessly in love with you, she added silently, but knew if she mentioned love, Bart might think she was trying to force him into emotions he didn't have.

'Marry?' Bart felt his chest begin to constrict. He'd always known Ebony was the marrying kind and he'd been working hard to accept that, but to have her blurt something like this out—seemingly from nowhere—was unsettling him. For years he'd always thought he'd missed his one opportunity to marry, to settle down and have a family. Alice had died and he'd locked his heart up…until Ebony had burst into his life, filling it with colour and laughter and a vibrancy he hadn't known was missing.

Now she was suggesting a marriage of convenience?

Why? Was it just for Timmy and her children or was it because she missed being married? Missed being in a long-term, permanent relationship? She'd already admitted that Dean had been the love of her life. As she hadn't bothered to mention love in her proposal, did that mean she saw him as second best? As some sort of consolation prize?

Bart shook his head. 'Are you even listening to yourself?' he growled impatiently, turning away from her, his tone similar to the one she'd heard him use on her first day at Canberra General. 'A marriage of convenience is a ridiculous idea.'

Ebony tried to ignore the sharp stabbing pain in her heart. She'd hoped he'd like the idea, especially with the way she felt about him. Secretly, she'd been hoping he'd declare his undying love for her and then they could embrace and everything would be perfect.

That didn't happen.

'Why?' she asked, trying to ignore the lump in her throat.

He whirled around to face her. 'Because we don't—' He stopped, seeing the tears gathering in her eyes. He'd been about to say because they didn't love each other but right now, at this very moment, he wasn't absolutely sure that was the truth. In fact, he wasn't one hundred per cent sure of anything.

'Marriages should be based on respect and trust and…' He stopped again and swallowed, realising he *did* respect Ebony and he *did* trust her. They'd connected on an intellectual level, he'd known that for some time now, but what about his heart and soul? He definitely cared for her—deeply—but was it enough to grab her hand and race down the aisle?

Ebony had just proposed to him for no other reason

than it made sense given their individual situations. It was wrong and although he had his parents' marriage, as well as those of his siblings, being held before him as shining examples of a love-filled life together, there was no way he could bring himself to even consider accepting Ebony's proposition.

He shook his head and fished his car keys from his pocket. 'I need to get some air.' With that, he headed for the front door, jerking it open before he strode purposefully towards his car.

'Bart? What are you doing?'

'Injecting some distance.'

'Bart, wait,' she implored, following him out, fearing for his safety if he persisted in driving in this condition. 'Let's go back inside and talk about this.'

'There's nothing more to talk about, Ebony.' He unlocked the car and opened the driver's door.

'Bart? *Please?*' She had no idea where he was going or what he was going to do, and the helplessness that gripped her heart was overpowering her ability to think clearly enough to say something to snap him out of it.

'I'm not your child, Ebony. I'm not here for you to control and I certainly don't need you to solve all my problems.'

She watched as he climbed into his car, hoping he'd stop, but instead he started the engine and with a small squeal of tyres he drove away. Bart was gone.

CHAPTER ELEVEN

OVER the next few days Ebony pulled her professionalism into place and did her job perfectly. She spoke to Bart only when it was necessary and always with regard to a patient. She tried not to let her gaze linger on his gorgeous features, remembering how he'd held her close, how he'd kissed her lips, how he'd often looked at her as though she really was vitally important to his life. She was determined to hide her heartbreak from him and the rest of the world. She was glad she hadn't confessed her true feelings for him because it was clear he didn't reciprocate them.

After he'd stormed out of her house and driven off, Ebony had gone back inside and done what had needed to be done. Where she'd felt like crying, like going after him, like contacting Child Services and telling them they were making an enormous mistake with their stupid double standards, she'd pulled herself together, pasted on a smile and headed back into the garden where the three children had still been playing.

'Where's Bart?' It had been Cliff who had asked the question, the three of them having abandoned trying to play basketball, instead sitting in the sandpit moulding and sculpting.

'He had…an emergency,' was all Ebony had been

able to say. Then she'd shepherded the children inside, telling them that it was starting to get too cold for any of them to be outside and had agreed to let them watch a movie.

When her mother had surfaced and asked after Bart, Ebony had simply answered the same way. 'Emergency.' That night, once all the children had been tucked up safely in bed, Timmy, still super-excited to be having a sleep-over—and in a bunk bed—Ebony had tried to call Bart, hoping he was all right. She'd already tried to call him several times and had left messages. She'd called the hospital, hoping someone would tell her they'd seen him, but no one had.

Where was he? Was he OK? Had he had an accident? Panic and worry had gripped her heart, the pain in her chest starting to choke her, and slowly the tears had started to slide down her cheeks. Once the floodgates had opened, they had poured out, her heart breaking for the man she'd fallen in love with, the man who'd turned his back on her. Perhaps she was better off without him? Even as the thought had entered her mind, she'd rejected it. Bart didn't love her, didn't need her, didn't want her, and she had to accept that.

Finally, though, he'd returned one of her text messages, letting her know he was OK. No doubt he'd only done that so she'd stop bothering him but she also hoped he understood just how much he meant to her, how much she truly cared.

In the days following Timmy's birthday sleep-over, Ebony still felt bone weary, mentally fatigued and broken hearted. Bart rejected her attempts to get him to talk, telling her straight out that it was over. He was intent on shutting her and everybody else out, everyone except Timmy.

Thankfully, he was still going round to Wanda's house to see the six-year-old but on the two occasions where Timmy had come to her place in the afternoon to see the other children, the little boy hadn't seemed as happy as usual.

'What's wrong?' Ebony had asked him as she'd driven him back to Wanda's house.

'I miss seeing Bart lots. When I go into the hospital, I see him lots and lots. At Wanda's I don't see him as much.'

'That's because he has to go to the hospital to help other people,' she'd offered as a way of explaining, although she couldn't help but remember Bart's comment about starting to distance himself from the young boy.

'Yeah.' Timmy had sighed and hadn't said anything else, but she'd been able to tell her answer hadn't satisfied him much.

Bart continued to be the brisk neurosurgeon, the professional colleague, but Ebony had to admit that when he looked right through her as though she meant nothing to him, that the times they'd shared were well and truly over, she couldn't help but feel gutted. Several times she had to hide in the female change rooms until she could pull herself together, patching up her breaking heart. It wasn't until one long day, after six hours in Theatre, he'd snapped at one of the more experienced theatre nurses for something rather trivial that Ebony realised he wasn't coping either.

The realisation melted her heart and that evening, as she snuggled with both her children on the lounge and watched a family television show, she started to think about Bart, about how she could help him. She was a nurturer and when the people she loved were hurting, she wanted to help in any way she could. Bart was im-

portant to her, even if he didn't feel the same way. She
would always love him. He was handsome and funny
and highly intelligent. He'd touched her heart, her soul
and her mind, and nothing would ever change that.

Ebony continued to think things through as she
laughed with her children and kissed them goodnight.

'Mum?' Maddie asked as Ebony headed out of the
bedroom.

'Yes, sweetie?'

'Are you and Bart…fighting?'

Ebony's eyes widened at that. 'Fighting?' She forced
a smile and was about to deny it but then she looked
at Maddie's big eyes, concerned eyes, and realised she
owed her daughter more than platitudes. She walked
back to Maddie's bed and sat on the edge. 'We're not
fighting.' Ebony caressed her daughter's cheek. 'He just
needs some space to sort a few things out.'

'Do you love him?'

'Yes.' The answer was simple and straightforward.

'Does he love you?'

Ebony sighed and then slowly shrugged her shoulders. 'I don't know, sweetie.'

'I miss Dad but…' Maddie stopped and took her
mother's hand in hers. 'I know we can never get Dad
back and that he would want us to keep on going, to
keep on being our best and finding lots to laugh about,
and if Bart makes you laugh and makes you happy and
makes me and Cliff and Grandma and Timmy happy,
then we should try to be together, right?'

'Right.' The word was a whisper, Ebony's throat
choked over with emotion to hear her daughter speaking
in such a grown-up way. The child was gone. Just like
that. In one split second and with such insight her Mad-

die had taken that leap over the chasm so many teenagers fell into and had landed firmly in the adult world.

'I miss Daddy. I loved my daddy.' Tears came into Maddie's eyes and Ebony tried hard to control her own, to be strong and brave for her daughter, but knew she was failing miserably.

'I loved him, too.'

'But our hearts are big. We can give so many people love, can't we, Mum?'

'Yes.' Ebony sniffed and reached for a tissue, wiping away Maddie's tears.

'Like Timmy. He's lost so much, hasn't he? His parents didn't even want him.'

'That's right, darling.'

'You've *always* loved me, Mum. Even when I was so horrid to you.' Maddie's lip quivered again and she sniffed. 'I'm sorry, Mummy. I'm so sorry.'

'Oh, baby.' Ebony gathered Maddie close to her and held her tightly as the girl sobbed into her shoulder. The pain. The tears. The realisation that life wasn't fair. All of it seemed to wash out of them both and when the sobs finally began to ease, they both wiped their eyes and blew their noses.

'We'll get through this,' Ebony promised her daughter.

'Bart's hurting, too, Mum. I saw the way he was looking at you last week and it was the same way Cliff looks at a chocolate bar—with total love. He loves you, Mum, and you love him, and we should all have another chance to be happy. Right?'

Ebony smiled and shrugged. 'If only it were that easy.'

'Why isn't it easy? Just go over to his place, tell him you love him and then he'll tell you he loves you and then you can kiss and be all mushy and then get married.' Maddie smiled and nodded.

Ebony kept her smile in place as she kissed her daughter's cheek, not wanting to explain all the complexities of the adult world just yet. 'Good idea.'

'So you'll go see him now?'

'I…I'll think—'

'Go, Mum. Just go. Don't think any more. I know as soon as he knows you love him that it'll all be perfect.'

Ebony stood and smiled, dabbing at her eyes with a tissue. 'Yes, Miss Bossy.'

'Hey, I get it from you.'

Ebony nodded. 'Yes, you do.'

Maddie yawned and closed her eyes, ready now to relax and go to sleep, all her pent-up anxieties and tension having been released with a good healing cry. 'Goodnight, Mum.'

'Sleep sweet, my darling. I love you.'

'Love you, too, Mum,' Maddie mumbled, already drifting off to slumber land.

Ebony walked out into the brightly lit hallway, blinking a few times to adjust her vision.

'Everything all right?' Adele asked when Ebony headed into the kitchen for a soothing cup of tea.

'Sure.'

'Maddie's a wise girl.'

'You heard?'

Adele shrugged. 'I was on my way in to say goodnight and, well, I didn't mean to eavesdrop.' Ebony filled the kettle and sat down on a stool, feeling wrung out and exhausted. 'So are you going over to Bart's?' Adele pointed to the clock. 'It's not too late. Only half past nine.'

'I doubt he'd want to see me, Mum.'

'Why? What happened?' But before Ebony could reply, Adele held up her hands. 'On second thoughts, it's none of my business. The fact of the matter is that you love him and he loves you and life is far too short for the two of you not to work it out.'

'I don't know if tonight's the right night to drop over.'

'Why not? You're already so connected with Bart in so many different ways, the past, the present…what about trying to find a future, eh?'

'And what if that step into the future is one…he doesn't want to share…you know…with me?'

'Don't be daft. The man's crazy about you. Anyone who's seen the two of you together would come to the same conclusion.'

Ebony shook her head, unable to believe it. First Maddie and now her mother, both believing Bart loved her. Well, if he did, he had a funny way of showing it.

'Go to him, Ebby.' Adele reached over and placed her hand on her daughter's. 'He needs you.'

Ebony closed her eyes for a moment, accepting that even if Bart didn't want to spend the rest of his life with her, then at least, given the fact that she was head over heels in love with him, she should tell him. She owed him that much. If he rejected her love, at least she'd be able to start picking up the pieces of her life yet again and moving on. She was strong, she was stubborn… and she was scared of a life without him.

Bart looked down at the words of the book he was trying to read, determined to concentrate, but a whole three seconds later a vision of Ebony swam before his eyes, looking at him with hope in her eyes, asking him to marry her. Her emerald green eyes had been bright with hope and he'd crushed it.

'You're an idiot,' he grumbled into the dark and quiet room. Ebony had helped him to live again, had shown him it wasn't too late to really connect with a person, to hope for a better life, a better future. Finally, after far too long, he'd been able to let go of the picture-perfect life he'd always thought he would have had with Alice. The past was the past. Ebony had taught him that. What mattered now was the present and the future.

What sort of future *did* he want to have? His gaze drifted down the corridor to where Timmy was sleeping soundly in the spare bedroom. Wanda had called him earlier in the night, concerned about Timmy, saying he was starting to go off his food, but when Bart had rushed around to check on the boy he'd found Timmy with his bag packed, sitting on his bed, dressed in pyjamas, declaring to Bart that he was coming for a sleepover.

'Wanda said I could go if you said yes,' he'd told Bart, clinging to his hand, and it had been then, as Bart had looked into the little boy's eyes, that he'd realised it didn't matter what Child Services decreed, he loved this boy. Nothing would ever change that and he'd been wrong to try and distance himself from that love.

So he'd gathered up Timmy and his bag, thanked Wanda and brought the boy back to his place for a sleep-over. They'd had dinner together, played some games and watched some TV before Bart had checked Timmy's teeth and read him a story before tucking him in for the night.

Timmy had shown no sign of a poor appetite, or a temperature, or any other signs or symptoms that might indicate the shunt wasn't working properly. What had happened was that a smart little six-year-old boy had taken matters into his own hands in order to get through to Bart.

He closed his eyes and shook his head. What a fool he'd been, thinking he could lock up his heart as he'd done all those years ago when Alice had died. He'd been hurt and he'd reacted badly. Not only to Timmy but more importantly to Ebony. Fortunately, it appeared Timmy was more than happy to forgive and forget but what about Ebony?

Would she listen to him? Give him the opportunity to grovel and apologise? He knew in his heart that he'd already fallen in love with her but admitting it was a powerful and scary step to take, especially after the appalling way he'd behaved.

At work, he'd found himself wanting to ask her about Maddie, about Cliff or whether Adele had managed to finish her still-life drawing before her class. He was interested not only in Ebony but in the rest of her family...the family she'd offered him, and he'd rejected.

A knock at the door made him open his eyes and sit up a little straighter in the chair. Who would be calling round at this time of night? Putting down the book, he stalked to the door and opened it abruptly.

'Oh! Don't *do* that, Bart.' There stood Ebony. On his doorstep. Late at night. Telling him off! 'Opening the door that quickly! You startled me.'

He drank in the sight of her, his gaze flitting over her, unable to believe she was actually there. 'What are you doing here?'

'Can I come in? Please?'

'Huh? Oh, yes. Of course. Please.' He instantly stepped back and held the door open for her. She came inside, noticing that the lounge room was dark except for one small reading lamp over in the corner near a large wing-backed armchair.

'To what do I owe the pleasure of this visit?' He switched on an overhead light.

'Leave it off, please,' she said quickly. 'If you don't mind.'

'OK.' He turned the light off again then headed over to the armchair, indicating the lounge for her to have a seat. She walked into the room, looking around, taking in alphabet flashcards that were still in a mess on the coffee table.

'Is Timmy here? Or have you just been practising your alphabet by yourself?'

Bart allowed a small smile to touch his lips. At least she didn't appear too angry with him. 'He's come for a sleep-over.'

'That's great.'

'Yes.' Bart drummed his fingers on the arm of the chair, trying to remain calm, to be cool, yet all he could wonder was what on earth had brought Ebony to his place at this hour of the night. 'Is everyone all right? Your mother? The children?'

'They're fine.'

'The hospital? Everything all right with the—?'

'Everything's fine, Bart.' She sat on the edge of the lounge, her coat still on, fiddling with her car keys and silently berating herself for being talked into coming. There was no way this man wanted to open up to her. If he'd wanted to do that, he would have done so by now, but instead he'd chosen to keep his own counsel and she was almost positive he wouldn't want to sit here and chat politely about anything, let alone how much she loved him and wanted him in her life. She stood.

'I shouldn't have come. Sorry.' She'd taken but three

steps towards the door when she felt Bart's hand on her arm.

'Don't go, Eb.' Slowly she turned to face him, looking into his hypnotising blue eyes that never failed to make her heart beat faster. 'Let me take your coat.'

She hesitated for one second before shrugging out of her coat and handing it to him.

'Please, sit down.' He led her back to the lounge, his hand warm and tender on her arm, and this time they both sat down facing each other. He rested one arm down the back of the lounge and gave her his undivided attention. 'So…to what do I owe the pleasure of your company?'

'Um…' How was she supposed to tell him she'd come to confess her love? That she wanted to have a life with him and that the silly proposal of the marriage of convenience had been her way of trying to tell him how much she cared?

'Well…uh…' She took a deep breath and decided the best way to proceed was to explain her earlier actions. 'About my…proposal. I don't want you—'

'I handled the whole situation badly,' he interjected. 'I'm sorry, Ebony. You were just trying to do what you thought was right, especially for Timmy, and I can't thank you enough for the idea.'

'The idea?' Good heavens the man was thick. 'Bart, I love Timmy. My children and my mother love Timmy and if Child Services are going to employ double standards then I'm willing to use them. I want you to know that, after discussing it with my mother, we're still going to go ahead and apply to be his foster-family.' She clasped her hands together, her words tumbling over each other. 'The idea of another family fostering Timmy, of all of us not being able to see him or to be a part of his life, was more than any of us could bear. Plus, under this arrangement, it would also mean you could have as much access to him as you want.' She breathed out, pleased she'd managed to say all that without her voice wavering.

Bart sat there, completely stunned, looking at the woman before him as though she were an angel. His own personal blonde-haired, green-eyed, gorgeous angel.

'I love Timmy…and…' She paused, her heart pounding wildly against her chest. 'And…I love, you, too. I only suggested the marriage of convenience because I thought that was what you might want.'

'What I might…?' He blinked one long blink before smiling brightly at her. 'Ebony, why would you think I'd want a marriage of convenience?'

'Because you gave your heart to Alice all those years ago. I didn't want to force your emotions, to tell you how much I loved you and for you not to be able to say it back.' She shrugged one shoulder. 'It backfired because you still walked out.'

'I was an idiot.'

'No argument here.' But he still hadn't said anything about returning her feelings. Ebony clenched her hands together again, unsure what to do or say next. She'd told him what she'd come here to say, so she guessed now it was time to take her leave. 'Well…I'd best be going.'

'Why?'

'What?' She frowned at him. 'What do you mean, *why*?'

'I mean don't leave just yet.' He shifted forward a little on the lounge, his gaze dropping to her mouth, her perfect mouth that could evoke such a powerful need and desperate longing within him.

She was here. Sitting in front of him. Waiting. She was a woman who had loved and lost and yet had had the courage to continue with her life, moving forward, helping others, nurturing and loving those around her... and now she'd confessed to loving him.

'I need you to stay.'

'Why?'

He moved closer still, his arm down the back of the lounge now dropping around her shoulders. The woman beside him was so generous and loving and giving and kind. 'I've been an absolute fool, Eb. Alice is gone. My life has moved on. Of course I've known that for such a very long time but I never thought I'd ever be able to open my heart again, to lay myself—the real me—bare before someone new, someone who didn't understand, but you *do*. You understand me perfectly.' He placed his free hand over hers.

Ebony looked down at his hand holding hers, his gentle caress showing her he really cared. Then, before she could stop herself, she raised his hand to her lips, wanting him to know that she was still his, in every way, shape and form. That her heart belonged with his, that their lives belonged together.

He let go of her hand and cupped her face in his hands, bringing his mouth down to meet hers without hesitation, both of them sighing into the kiss. It felt so right to be together, so right to entwine their lives around each other's, to look forward to the future.

'I love you, Eb,' Bart whispered against her mouth.

'What?' She breathed the word, unsure she'd heard him correctly. His kisses said he loved her but the words, oh, the words were music to her heart.

'I love you, Ebony Matthews. I should have told you sooner but I was...confused.'

'And I guess my silly proposal didn't help.'

'It wasn't silly, it was brave. I was just too wrapped up in my own little world to realise that a woman like you wouldn't suggest such a radical course of action if she didn't truly love all the people involved.' He brushed another kiss across her lips. 'You're strong and beautiful and remarkable and I could go on for ages here.'

'I don't mind.' She giggled and kissed him again. 'You can tell me every day.'

'I intend to.' He stopped and took her hands in his again, gazing deeply into her eyes as he slid from the lounge, going down on bended knee.

'Bart?' Her eyes widened. 'Are you sure?'

'How could I not be? I was a fool before but not any more. Finally, I have perfect clarity and that's because I love you, Eb. You're my second chance and I'm yours. Heart, mind and soul.' He raised her hands to his lips and kissed them.

'You once said you believed a person could have more than one soul mate and you were right. I want to be with you forever. I want to be with you and Timmy and Cliff and Maddie and Adele. We *are* a family. One mother, one father, three kids and a grandmother. All of us have loved and lost but look what we've found.'

'We've found each other,' she replied, and leaned forward, kissing him.

'Marry me, Ebony. Please?'

'Oh, Bart,' she sighed, and after pressing another kiss to his lips she tugged him back up onto the lounge beside her. 'Of course I will. I need you in my life because you make me so happy. You make my children so happy, and not only that but you've introduced us all to Timmy, and we all love him, too. We'll work through things, talking and helping and raising those three amazing children. Moving forward. Loving each other more and more every day.'

Before she could say anything else he kissed her again and the two of them were silent for some time, more than happy to be absorbed in each other's arms, their hearts entwined forever.

'Do you mind?' she asked a while later as she snuggled against him.

'Mind what?'

'Not being a bachelor any more? Having an instant family?'

His smile was bright as he looked into her eyes. 'I love it.'

EPILOGUE

THE small church in Charlotte's Pass was packed. People were squashed up together on the long wooden pews, others were standing at the back and around the sides, with some of the smaller children sitting cross-legged on the floor at the front.

'And now,' the minister said, 'Edward Goldmark, head of the Goldmark family, would like to come forward and say a few words.'

Edward nodded at the minister then turned to look at Honeysuckle, the woman who had brought so much love back into his life all those years ago. She leaned over and kissed him, smiling her encouragement. 'I love you, Eddie,' she whispered.

It was exactly what he needed to hear as he made his way through the crowded church to the front. Large vases of bright flowers were positioned on either side of the altar and as he pulled a piece of paper from his inside jacket pocket and placed it on the pulpit, he breathed in their fresh scent, instantly reminded of the garden his mother had planted all those years ago. Where in the past memories of his parents had brought him only grief, he could now think of them with comforting peace.

Edward cleared his throat and looked at the sea of

people before him. 'Twenty-five years ago today, there was an avalanche here, in Charlotte's Pass. Forty-five of our loved ones died. Over the past few weeks I've spoken with the families who were directly affected by this tragedy and although all of them were happy for me to be their choice of speaker here today, I'd like to take this opportunity to say that I know your pain, I feel your grief, but I also share with you the peace that only the passing of time can bring.'

He looked down at his notes, astonished when his vision began to blur. He'd been positive he'd be able to get through this without breaking down. He'd read the words printed on the page over and over again, trying to commit them to memory in case something like this happened.

What he hadn't counted on was the piercing pain in his heart or the way it temporarily robbed him of his voice. After a moment of trying to focus on his deep breathing, he looked up and saw his wife coming towards him. His Honey. She came to stand beside him and did nothing more than place her hand firmly in his own, sharing her strength with him.

'In the entryway of this church is an inspiring mosaic memorial to those we lost that fateful day. A mosaic of sunbeams shining down on the village of Charlotte's Pass, with forty-five white doves flying upwards towards the sun, each dove containing the name of a loved one.

'Alma Rogers was a school teacher. Karl and Alison Schtumpkey and their two teenagers were here on holidays.' As he continued to read through the list a few people from the different families came out to the front and joined hands, supporting each other. 'And, lastly, Hannah and Cameron Goldmark, doctors in this district.'

He looked down at the list for a moment, needing another moment to compose himself. Honey handed him a tissue and he thankfully dabbed at his eyes. When he looked up again it was to see his four brothers, Peter, Bartholomew, Benedict and Hamilton, and his surrogate sister Lorelai making their way to the front. He waited for them and they gathered around him.

'This day—the anniversary of their passing—has always been a difficult day for me, unable to believe another year has come and gone without them. But then I look around at what my life has become during these past twenty-five years, of how my brothers and sister have grown, have found their own lives and their soul mates.'

More people came to the front and among them were Peter's wife Annabelle, Lorelai's husband Woody, Hamilton's wife Ruby, Benedict's wife Darla and Bart's wife Ebony. Although Bart had been the last of them to get married, only three years ago, he'd inherited three children and a mother-in-law, and all of them were here today, now a permanent part of the large Goldmark family.

'Family is important,' Edward continued, his gaze settling on his cousin Viola Goldmark, who was next to her son Brandon and his wife Clover. They were all standing together, their arms linked, Clover holding a toddler in her arms. 'And families keep on growing, keep on expanding, keep on living. We're *living*. We're carrying the legacy our loved ones have left behind. We're sad they're not around to see the day-to-day changes in our lives but we hold them forever in our hearts, telling our children about them, sharing stories and binding even closer to those who have helped and supported us through all these years.'

Edward looked at Lorelai's father, BJ, the man who had stood firmly beside him after the tragedy while Edward had done his best to raise his younger brothers. BJ was now surrounded by a plethora of grandchildren of all ages, holding his hand, sitting on his knee and showering him with love.

Some of Edward's nieces and nephews came up and joined their parents, Timmy, Bart's youngest son, who was now nine years old, was dutifully picked up by his father.

'Family is important. Family is necessary. Family is love and today, here in this chapel to commemorate those we lost so very long ago, *we* are family. Those who were taken from our lives would be so proud of who we've become.'

'Yeah!' Timmy yelled loudly, and started clapping his hands. 'Family!'

Everyone in the church stared at the little boy for a moment then, as though a fresh wave of love swept through the place, they all joined in. Clapping and cheering. Celebrating not only the lives of those they'd lost but celebrating the family surrounding them and the bright, glorious future still to come.

* * * * *

A sneaky peek at next month...

Medical Romance™

CAPTIVATING MEDICAL DRAMA—WITH HEART

My wish list for next month's titles...

In stores from 1st February 2013:

❏ The Brooding Doc's Redemption – Kate Hardy

& An Inescapable Temptation – Scarlet Wilson

❏ Revealing The Real Dr Robinson – Dianne Drake

& The Rebel and Miss Jones – Annie Claydon

❏ The Son that Changed his Life – Jennifer Taylor

& Swallowbrook's Wedding of the Year – Abigail Gordon

Available at WHSmith, Tesco, Asda, Eason, Amazon and Apple

Just can't wait?

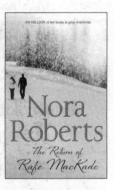